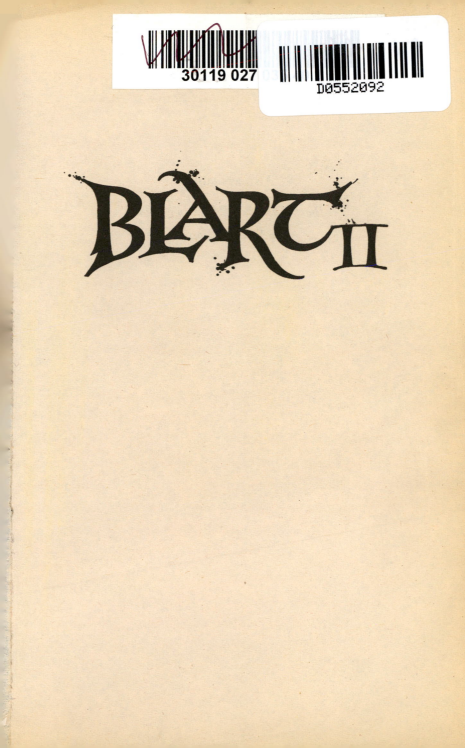

BLART II

Also available

*Blart: The Boy Who Didn't Want
to Save the World*

Chapter 1

Blart was master of all he surveyed.

On condition he didn't look very far. Or very wide. But if he concentrated on staring straight in front of him and bent his head downwards, then he was still just about master of all he surveyed – one field, one pig shed, one small barn and two pigs.

'Here, Venerable. Here, Bede.'

The pigs looked up at him. They saw a gawky looking fifteen-year-old boy whose mouth was hanging open. His face was smeared with dirt, his jumper was torn and his trousers had muddy knees. Fortunately none of this interested the pigs. What interested them were the apples he held out towards them. They snuffled over and began to eat. Blart listened appreciatively to the munching. *However bad things are,* he thought, *the sight of a pig eating an apple raises your spirits.*

Because otherwise things were very bad.

After saving the world from the evil Zoltab and his foul minions, Blart's real dream had come true. With the reward money given to him by King Philidor the Happy, monarch of Elysium, Blart had purchased a large farmhouse, two orchards, three barns and ninety-eight pigs, and all the fields he could see from where he stood (without bending down).

But only a year later, the two apples that the pigs were now munching were the last that he possessed, and as he no longer owned either of the two orchards, he had no way of feeding the pigs once those were gone. And from the noises the pigs were making they were very close to being gone indeed. Faced with the prospect of the loss of his livestock, Blart acted as countless farmers (but not many fifteen-year-old boys) had done before him down the ages – he leant against a fence, stuck a bit of straw in his mouth and wondered where it had all gone wrong.

And then he remembered where it had all gone wrong – Milkdale.

Chapter 2

Milkdale was a friendly village. Ducks quacked by the pond, children ran hither and thither, shouting and laughing, their mothers brought chairs outside their houses and gossiped amiably about which family in the village had the biggest lice infestation, whose husband was a good-for-nothing drunkard and who should be clapped in the stocks and pelted with rotten fruit. But unlike some villages where the gossip was malicious and muttered slyly behind people's backs, here in Milkdale it was done cheerily in the open – the woman whose husband was a good-for-nothing drunkard changed each week so nobody felt picked on, and the children constantly passed their lice around so nobody was infested long enough to become the village scapegoat. Indeed it was precisely this reputation for friendliness that had appealed to Capablanca the Wizard when he had strongly recommended to Blart that this was the place to buy his pig farm. Capablanca thought that it would take Blart at least a year to offend all the local people.

Blart's year was up. Even so, as Blart walked down the main street he was surprised to find that there was nobody his own age to tell about his heroic exploits. He wondered what had happened to the boys and girls of the village recently. They never seemed to be around when he appeared. Still, not one to be put off by this setback, Blart walked on to the one place in Milkdale where he knew you could always find people to tell about your heroic exploits – the local inn. Many youths would have been daunted at the prospect of entering such a place at Blart's age, but Blart was not like other youths. He pushed open the door of The Happy Hangman and stomped in. But even here the threat of yet another retelling by Blart of the story of how he saved the world had caused most of the customers to swallow their ale in uncomfortably large gulps and rush out of the back door when they saw him coming. The inn was empty except for a thin old man with unkempt whiskers, hunched over a half-filled tankard. For in every inn there is at least one man who so likes his ale that there is nothing that can shift him from the bar.

Or possibly it was just that he'd never met Blart.

Blart was about to rectify the situation. He pulled up a bar stool and sat down.

'I'm a hero,' he announced. 'I've saved the world. You owe everything to me.'

'I haven't got much,' pointed out the man.

'You can thank me for it,' Blart told him.

The man didn't answer. Instead he sank his face grudgingly into his beer, muttering about youngsters being seen and not heard.

Martin the landlord emerged from the cellar. 'Where have all my customers gone?' he demanded. 'It was heaving before I nipped down to change the mead.'

'Maybe it's him,' suggested the old man.

As Martin's gaze fell upon Blart, a new customer – a tall thin man with sleek black hair, slicked into a neat ponytail – entered the bar and looked around.

'Blart, my friend. How pleasant it is to see you.'

Chapter 3

Uther Slywort was rumoured to be the richest man in the shire. He was certainly the most unscrupulous. And he was the only person in Milkdale whom Blart could consider a friend. He listened to Blart's stories and he had recently taught him how to play cards.

A secret smile seemed to hover at the end of Uther's thin lips as he peeled fine leather gloves from his fingers. 'Fancy a quick hand of Muggins?' he said when he was sitting down with his flagon of mead in front of him.

Muggins was the card game Uther had taught Blart. It was, Uther had explained, a regional card game, unknown in other parts of the world. Indeed it was so regional that it was only played in Milkdale. And in Milkdale it was only ever played by Uther Slywort and Blart.

'I don't want to play Muggins,' replied Blart.

Although he knew Uther was just being friendly, there were times when Blart wished that Uther had never troubled himself to teach Blart to play Muggins. Because once Blart had learnt the rules and had some early success at the game, Uther Slywort had suggested that they bet on the outcome of each hand. Luck, it seemed, turned cruelly against Blart as soon as wagers were introduced.

'Nothing ventured, nothing gained,' persisted Uther. 'I can feel your luck is changing.'

'No.'

'We don't need to play for stakes,' said Uther mildly. 'We can just play for amusement.'

He reached into a deep pocket and pulled out a pack of cards. He shuffled them quickly, cut them, and then dealt. One card appeared under Blart's nose.

'I've got the eight of clubs,' said Uther, turning over his card. 'What's yours?'

Blart stared at his card.

Muggins is a very simple card game. The dealer deals one card to the other player and one to himself. Both players turn over their cards. If the cards are different (for example, a nine and an eight, or a three and a queen) then the non-dealer wins. If, however, they are a pair (for example, two nines or two queens) then the dealer wins. Even Blart had grasped (after a little while) that as the non-dealer the odds of winning the game were drastically in his favour, for the chances of the cards not being a pair were far greater than the chances that they would be. Once he had understood this he became determined to play Muggins for money with Uther.

But to Blart's horror, as soon as he had begun to play

Muggins for money the cards didn't seem to stop falling as pairs. Pairs of tens, kings, threes, fives – Uther himself professed to be amazed at the number of pairs that were turning up. Never had he known such a run of bad luck for the non-dealer, he informed Blart sympathetically. Every pair that had turned up lost Blart money until he had no more money. Then Uther suggested that they used Blart's pigs and fields to represent money. Blart had refused. He had lost his money, but he could never gamble with his pigs, he told Uther.

But there was a little voice in Blart's head that kept whispering to him that he'd just been unlucky.

The next evening he had gone to The Happy Hangman and bet his pigs and his fields.

And he had lost.

Indeed he might well have lost absolutely everything if Martin the landlord hadn't said he was closing the inn for the night and thrown them both out.

That had been a month ago.

Uther sat back in his seat and waited.

What harm could it do, Blart wondered to himself, *to turn over this one little card?* After all it wasn't like they were even betting on this card. So it would be just to see what it was.

Uther Slywort continued to neither move a muscle nor twitch a nerve.

Blart turned over the card.

The three of spades.

'You would have won,' observed Uther.

Quick as a fox, he gathered up the cards and began to shuffle. Blart watched the blur of Uther's hands as the cards whizzed through them. He fanned them out on the table, gathered them in, shuffled them vigorously, cut them into two piles, riffled them together and dealt one card to each of them once more.

'Should we play for stakes?' Uther asked.

'No,' replied Blart. 'I'm not playing. Well, not really.'

'Just as you like,' agreed Uther amiably. 'You're in charge. Sometimes it's nice just to play a friendly game.'

'Yes,' said Blart.

Uther turned over his card.

'The four of spades.'

Blart fingered his own and then stopped. Wasn't there something wrong with doing this? he asked himself. But it was just a friendly game. It didn't make any difference what he turned over. Nothing would change.

He flipped the card.

'The nine of hearts,' observed Uther. 'You must be hitting a lucky streak.'

Uther gathered, shuffled and dealt again. Immediately he turned over the seven of clubs. Blart turned over the queen of diamonds.

'Three in a row,' Uther commented. And then almost as an afterthought he added, 'You could have won ten pigs, a field and an orchard by now.'

Blart didn't say anything.

'I'm so grateful we haven't been playing for stakes,' Uther continued jovially. 'Still, I've finished my drink and I must be off.'

He banged his tankard down cheerily on the table.

'One more game,' said Blart.

'I've got things to do,' explained Uther, standing up.

'One more game,' insisted Blart.

'I'd love too oblige you, Blart, but –'

'For stakes.'

'It's not to do with whether it's for stakes or not,' explained Uther. 'It's just that I haven't got the time really. What stakes were you thinking of?'

'Everything.'

'That would be two pigs, one shed, a barn and a field, wouldn't it? I only ask out of academic interest because, as I say, I haven't actually got the time.'

Blart confirmed that two pigs, one shed, a barn and a field would indeed be the stakes.

'What can I say, Blart? Uther Slywort can never let a friend down. You want to play, then I will play.'

This grand gesture of friendship so overwhelmed Uther that he had to wipe a tear from his eye as he sat down.

Once the tear was gone, he whipped out the cards from his pocket, shuffled them once more and dealt one each to himself and Blart.

As soon as it was in front of him Blart turned the card over. A king.

'Any card but another king and you win,' commented Uther. 'And with the lucky streak you're on I can't believe that ... oh ...'

Uther laid his card face upwards.

Another king.

Blart stared at it in disbelief. Then he covered his face with his hands. Then he peeked through his fingers to give the card one more chance not to be a king. It remained a king. A king that spelt Blart's ruin.

'Oh dear,' said Uther, reaching into a pocket inside his coat and swiftly pulling out a piece of parchment he seemed to have prepared earlier. 'I can hardly believe it myself. Still, rules are rules and we have to play by them even if neither of us wants to. So if you would just make your mark here, then I'll own the remainder of your farm and we can move on.'

He pushed the piece of parchment under Blart's stunned and disbelieving nose. Blart was too shocked to resist. He placed his dirty finger on the parchment and made his mark.

Uther grabbed the parchment, rolled it up and replaced it in the depths of his great coat, briefly revealing a luxurious lining and many hidden pockets. Blart placed his head on the table and began to moan.

'Now I've got nothing.'

'Blart,' said Uther, 'I am a good and generous man. I feel terrible about the tricks the fickle fortune of fate has played on you. I will give you a chance to win it all back.'

'How?'

'One final game of Muggins,' answered Uther. 'No pair and you get everything back. One pair and I win …' Uther paused. 'Oh, there's a problem. There have got to be stakes on both sides. What could I win if you haven't got anything?'

The hopeful flush on Blart's face became a rash of concern. What if he couldn't make the bet?

'I know,' said Uther. 'Why don't you bet yourself?'

'Myself?' repeated Blart doubtfully.

'That's right,' confirmed Uther. 'It isn't as though you've got anything to lose. You have no family and no means of support. As soon as you finish that drink Martin will throw you out of his inn and you will be left to starve on the open road.'

'But I'm a hero,' countered Blart. 'I saved the world.'

'Heroism butters very few parsnips in the real world,' Uther informed him. 'How I wish it could be different, but we live in hard and cruel times.'

Blart thought about what Uther had said. It was true, he concluded, that he had nothing to lose and everything to gain. And yet he hesitated. Even a boy as uninformed about personal freedom and liberty as Blart still found himself hesitating before risking it on a hand of cards.

But then he remembered his farmhouse, his barns and his orchards. And above all he remembered his pigs. In his mind's eye he saw them snorting and wallowing in their own muck. The beauty of this vision overwhelmed his doubts.

'Let's play,' he said.

Quick as an eel, Uther was back in his seat, dealing a card for Blart and himself.

Blart, his hand shaking like a salt cellar in the grip of a hungry knight who had been served a badly seasoned stew, turned his card over.

An ace!

Uther now revealed his own card.

Another ace!

'No,' cried Blart dejectedly, as the vision of his pigs snorting and wallowing in mud slowly dissolved in his mind.

Another parchment was placed before Blart.

'Your mark, please,' demanded Uther.

And Blart had lost his freedom for ever.

Chapter 4

'Most impressive,' said Uther. 'And to think you've only two hours' more digging.' He stood at a distance lest Blart's spade threw up soil that might mark his overcoat.

Rain poured down on Blart. He had not dug like this since he was unexpectedly put to work in the Great Tunnel of Despair by Zoltab's evil minions a year ago. He hadn't liked it then and he didn't like it now. The side to Uther's character he had revealed since Blart had placed his mark on the parchment was not to Blart's taste at all. There had been no more pleasant chats or sympathetic expressions. Instead there had been fourteen-hour days and an unceasing hard physical grind. All in all, slavery wasn't working out anywhere near as well as Blart had hoped.

'I'd like to resign,' said Blart.

'You can't resign from slavery,' said Uther. 'It's a job for life. Now I'm going inside for a cup of tea. Two hours will fly by in the wink of an eye.'

And with these depressing words he retired to the farm-house. As the door opened, Blart caught a brief tantalising glimpse of the bright orange fire dancing in the kitchen grate. With a weary sigh he raised his spade to continue digging. But he was exhausted and simply lifting it drained the last of his strength. He felt his legs buckle and he slumped face forward in the mud.

'Blart!'

Blart didn't care how much Uther shouted. He couldn't dig any more. He buried his face deeper in the mud.

'I don't know what you're doing in the mud but I would appreciate an answer.'

Blart was confused. The voice was familiar but it was not Uther's.

'Your manners still leave a great deal to be desired.'

Blart raised his face from the mud.

'Capablanca!'

The bearded face of the old wizard was peering down at him.

'Have you come to rescue me?' asked Blart.

'Not exactly,' answered the wizard.

'What are you here for, then?'

'I've brought some bad news,' said Capablanca awk-wardly. 'We are wanted men.'

Blart was not used to being wanted, and in his present muddy state he was touched.

'Who wants me?' he asked.

'Us,' corrected Capablanca. 'The Duke wants us, and all his knights and soldiers too. But not in a good way. They want us dead or alive. Or both.'

Chapter 5

'Both?' said Blart, missing the greater significance of Capablanca's news once more. 'You can't be dead and alive.'

'No,' hissed Capablanca with exasperation. 'But you could be dead and I could be alive. Or the other way round.'

Capablanca had not seen Blart for a whole year and was already beginning to feel that it was nowhere near long enough.

'Blart!' Capablanca spoke firmly. 'Even now the Duke's soldiers are heading towards Milkdale. We must flee at once.'

The farmhouse door opened and Uther Slywort appeared in the doorway.

'What's all that noise?'

'Who's that?' Capablanca asked Blart.

'He's my owner.'

'Your owner?' echoed Capablanca.

'I lost myself at cards,' explained Blart.

'Who's that on my property?'

'I am Capablanca,' answered Capablanca. 'The second greatest sorcerer alive today.'

'Second greatest?' said Blart. 'Last time I saw you, you were the greatest.'

'It's only a temporary blip,' said Capablanca testily, 'and there's no time to discuss it now. We must leave immediately.'

'He's going nowhere,' interjected Uther. 'Who else is going to dig this mud?'

'That is not my concern,' answered Capablanca. 'I am here to take Blart with me to save the world.'

'Again?!' said Blart. One could empathise with his surprise.

'There's no time to explain now,' said Capablanca. 'The Duke's soldiers are on their way with orders to capture us dead or alive.'

'The Duke?' queried Uther. 'No doubt he has offered some reward for information leading to your capture.'

'He has,' confirmed Capablanca.

'Is it a large reward?' inquired Uther casually.

'I have little interest in money,' replied Capablanca. 'Would a thousand gold pieces be considered substantial?'

Uther's sly smile suggested that it might.

'And where are the Duke's soldiers now?'

'They will probably already have reached Milkdale village,' answered Capablanca, 'which is why Blart and I must flee immediately.'

'What a coincidence,' remarked Uther. 'I was just about

to go into Milkdale to buy some, er … milk.'

And Uther made to pass. Capablanca blocked his way.

'Perhaps you should read this proclamation first,' the wizard suggested and he pulled a slightly soggy parchment from his cowl, which he proceeded to unroll.

'*Hear ye, hear ye, hear ye,*' began Capablanca. '*I, the Duke of Northwestmoreland, do offer a reward of one thousand gold pieces for the capture of Blart and Capablanca, dead or alive.*'

'I know all that,' said Uther, trying to pass.

'*Or any of their associates,*' read Capablanca. And then he paused significantly.

'You appear to have paused significantly?' said Uther.

'Because you are Blart's owner,' answered Capablanca. 'Which makes you his associate. If you go to Milkdale the Duke's men will capture you dead or alive.'

'Let me see that!' Uther snatched the proclamation from Capablanca's hand and read it for himself.

The rain continued to pour down on the three figures in the farmyard and the dusk of Capablanca's arrival had now thickened into night.

'But this is terrible,' Uther said after reading the proclamation twice more. 'This means that I'm wanted dead or alive too.'

'Exactly,' said Capablanca. 'Your only hope is to throw in your lot with us and flee immediately.'

But even as he spoke the sound of hooves pounding in the distance told him that they had waited too long already.

The Duke's soldiers had reached Milkdale, interrogated Martin at The Happy Hangman, found out Blart's whereabouts and were now only minutes away from arriving at the farm and capturing them all, dead or alive.

Or both.

Chapter 6

'Run!' shouted Blart.

The sound of galloping hooves grew louder.

'If we run we will be hunted down and caught,' snapped Capablanca. 'They have horses, we do not. Our only hope is to hide.'

The cries of the Duke's men urging their mounts on reached the farmyard.

'Where can we hide?' he demanded of Uther.

Uther had only recently won the farm from Blart and had not explored its nooks and crannies. He looked blank. In desperation, Capablanca turned to Blart. Blart realised that they were both depending on him.

'Pigs!' he announced defiantly.

'Pigs?' queried Capablanca and Uther in unison.

'Hide among the pigs,' said Blart.

It might work. The Duke's men were at the gate. There was no time to do anything else. Blart and Uther hurried off towards the pig shed, with Capablanca hobbling behind on his aged legs.

And not a moment too soon. For only seconds after they disappeared from the farmyard, a cohort of the Duke's men galloped in, dismounted and pulled out their swords. They had the options of dead or alive, but from their grim demeanours and the cold steel in their hands it was obvious that they were leaning heavily towards the former.

The three fugitives' sudden appearance in the pig shed had startled the unfortunate creatures, who proceeded to run around and bump into each other.

'They're all moving around,' protested Uther. 'If we hide behind them and the Duke's men come in to search for us, the pigs will move out of the way and we'll be caught.'

Blart realised that there might be a flaw in his plan. But he was not going to admit it.

'Maybe the Duke's men will think we're pigs too.'

'What?' Uther shook his head. 'We're all humans. They're all pigs. Why wouldn't they notice that?'

'We could oink,' Blart said.

Uther stared at him in disbelief.

Blart was about to stare back but he was distracted by a better idea.

'When Capablanca first came to see me last year he turned the kitchen table into a pig. He can turn us all into pigs too and then the Duke's men wouldn't be able to find us. Can you turn us into pigs?'

Still panting after attempting to run, Capablanca struggled to get his breath before answering.

'Only for a short time,' he answered finally. 'And I can only turn you two into pigs. I must remain a wizard in order to keep the spell working.'

'So Blart's plan won't work,' observed Uther. 'They'll capture you and then you won't be able to keep the spell working and we'll turn back to humans and be captured ourselves.'

Blart was not known for coming up with good ideas. But having got so close he was unwilling to give up on this one so easily.

'We could sit on him.'

'What?' Now it was Capablanca's turn to sound unsure.

'We could sit on you,' repeated Blart. 'Two pigs can easily sit on a person and cover him up.'

There were voices outside the barn.

'We've got to try it,' whispered Capablanca. 'Just try not to squash me.'

Suddenly the wizard was very still and moments later piercing blue light flashed from his eyes towards Blart and Uther.

There were two more pigs in the shed.

The door squeaked as it opened. Two of the Duke's men poked their heads round the door.

'I definitely thought I heard voices, Bob,' said one.

'I thought I heard them too, Much,' said another.

They opened the shed door wider and entered warily. Each held a lantern in one hand and a sword in the other.

'It's only pigs in here, Bob,' observed Much.

'But I'm sure I heard voices,' persisted Bob.

'Pigs can't talk, Bob,' asserted Much confidently.

'Not normally,' agreed Bob. 'But these might be strange pigs.'

Much took two bold strides further into the shed and held his lantern high. The pigs moved away from him.

'They look like normal pigs to me, Bob,' said Much. 'Come and look at them for yourself.'

Reluctantly, Bob followed Much into the shed.

'See?' said Much, whose life philosophy embraced the traditional virtue of believing what he could see with his own eyes.

'All right, they look normal,' conceded Bob, 'but that doesn't mean they are normal.'

Unlike Much's philosophy, Bob's was built on the assumption that things were almost certainly worse than they looked.

'Why not?' persisted Much

'I've heard what the captain says,' answered Bob. 'He says that this lad Blart and this evil sorcerer Capablanca are in league with the Dark Lord Zoltab. They couldn't put it on the proclamation because it would scare the common people too much. But let me tell you, if Zoltab's involved then talking pigs could be the least of our problems. He's the most evil thing there's ever been.'

'Oh,' said Much, taking a step back. The mention of Zoltab's name had a sobering effect on all who heard it.

'So,' said Bob, 'let's get this search done as fast as we can and get back to the others.'

The soldiers, holding their lanterns high and keeping close together, stepped into the middle of the shed. The pigs shuffled away. Somehow the pigs seemed to know that sharpened steel, be it swords or carving knives, was best avoided.

Except for two.

'This is strange,' said Bob. 'These pigs aren't moving.'

'Perhaps they're sitting on their eggs,' suggested Much.

The observant reader will notice that Much was not a country boy.

'Eggs!' repeated Bob derisively. 'Pigs don't have eggs. They have piglets. Hens have eggs. Now let's get these pigs moved and get the shed searched. Hie. Move, pigs. Move!'

The two pigs remained exactly where they were.

'I've never known such stubborn pigs,' commented Bob.

'I'm going to shift these pigs if it's the last thing I do. I am not going to be defied by creatures that spend their lives covered in mud.'

'Actually, they don't appear to have much mud on them,' observed Much.

They both looked closer. Compared to the other pigs in the barn, indeed compared to any other pigs anywhere, these pigs were suspiciously clean.

'What are you two idle layabouts doing?'

Much and Bob jumped to attention. Behind them stood the captain of their cohort, a small man with a big voice.

'We were searching the shed, sir,' said Much.

'But some of the pigs are being uncooperative,' explained Bob.

'Uncooperative pigs?' fulminated the officer. 'I'll give you uncooperative pigs.'

He pulled out his sword, strode straight across the shed and jabbed it into the leg of the first pig he encountered. The pig oinked in pain and stood up to reveal a slightly squashed wizard.

'Aha!' said the captain.

'Aha!' said Capablanca. In his surprise he lost his concentration and the spell was broken. To the amazement of the soldiers, the two clean pigs who had been sitting on him were suddenly Blart and Uther.

'You stabbed me for nothing!' said Blart ruefully, indicating a flesh wound on his arm.

The captain fixed Blart with a steely glare.

'I am searching for an ugly stupid boy and you fit the description exactly,' he said. 'I charge you with being a foul cur and an enemy of the state.'

'A what?' asked Blart.

'And I charge you,' the captain continued, pointing his sword at Capablanca and Uther, 'with being associates of a foul cur and an enemy of the state.'

'I was just passing,' protested Uther desperately.

'I am ordered to take you dead or alive. Do you surrender?'

'No,' said Capablanca defiantly.

'Don't we?' asked Blart.

'I might,' considered Uther.

The captain looked a little frustrated. 'If one of you refuses, then all of you refuse.'

'I refuse,' said Capablanca.

'Then dead it is,' said the captain. 'Which is always my preferred method. Men! Charge!'

Swords at the ready, the three Duke's men lunged forward. Before them stood one old man and two former pigs. They were doomed.

Chapter 7

When I say they were doomed, I refer not to Capablanca, Uther and Blart but to the three Duke's men. For though they were strong and well-armed and trained to act as a team in combat, they were still doomed to defeat. For their opponents had one thing in their armoury that the Duke's men could not compete with.

Magic.

Actually two things.

Magic and pigs.

A brief beam of blue light flashed from Capablanca's eyes and suddenly the pigs began to advance. Little did the soldiers realise that Capablanca had cast a spell on the pigs (animals being much more susceptible to magic than humans) that ensured they were not seeing Duke's men at all. They were seeing the tastiest swill they had ever set their eyes upon and were intent on eating it.

'Oi,' said Much. 'What are those pigs doing?'

'Ignore the pigs,' said the captain. 'Keep your mind on

the criminals.'

'They're still coming,' said Bob.

'You are soldiers,' the captain reminded them sternly. 'Your job is to do the Duke's bidding and capture his enemies.'

The pigs began to run towards the soldiers. The soldiers charged towards the Duke's enemies. The pigs had never seen moving swill before but they were prepared to chase anything that looked so tasty. Just before the three soldiers could get near enough to thrust their rapiers deep into the hearts of Blart, Capablanca and Uther, they were overrun by a slavering pack of pigs, who weren't going to let their supper escape that easily.

'Aaargh,' the Duke's men cried as their weapons fell from their hands and they were trampled to the floor.

'Grab their swords,' instructed Capablanca. The blue light flashed from his eyes again and the pigs, who had been about to tuck into three hearty portions of swill, stopped. Their swill had suddenly become three soldiers. The pigs looked at their ex-swill for a while in disappointment and then wandered off.

Blart, Capablanca and Uther stood over the soldiers with their swords pointed menacingly at the soldiers' chests.

'You would kill us,' said Uther, holding his sword to the captain's neck.

'No,' said Capablanca, placing a hand on Uther's arm. 'The Duke's men were acting in good faith. They believed that we were in league with Zoltab.'

The wizard's words reminded Blart of something he had wondered about earlier.

'Why do they think we are in league with Zoltab? We were the people who defeated him.'

Capablanca was silent.

'Yes,' added Uther. 'Blart used to bore the whole of Milkdale telling them how he defeated Zoltab. Why do they think we're on his side?'

'We have no time for these discussions,' snapped Capablanca, looking unusually sheepish. 'Soon the other soldiers will notice these three have vanished and come looking for us.'

'What should we do?' asked Blart.

'There are three of us and three of them,' answered Capablanca. 'We will put on their uniforms and ride off with the troop. They will never know that anything is wrong. Then we will slip away during the night.'

'You won't get away with it,' interjected the captain.

'Silence!' ordered Uther.

'Take off their clothes then tie them up and gag them,' said Capablanca.

'I warn you,' said the captain, 'that stealing the clothes of a Duke's soldier is a very serious offence. You will be punished.'

'We're already wanted dead or alive,' Uther pointed out, then, turning to the wizard, he added, 'and perhaps while we're tying and gagging these men and then changing into their uniforms you could tell us why.'

'You make it sound like it's my fault,' said Capablanca testily. 'You shouldn't leap to conclusions.'

'Even if they're right?' asked Blart.

Capablanca pretended not to hear.

'Anyway, wizard,' said Uther. 'I want to know why I'm wanted dead or alive and I want to know now.'

'I suppose you were going to find out sooner or later,' Capablanca grumbled. After a long, dramatic pause, he began. 'Following ten arduous years of research in the great and ancient Cavernous Library of Ping, I discovered a prophecy …'

'I've heard this before,' said Blart, yawning. 'And it wasn't very interesting then.'

Capablanca ignored Blart. Experience had taught him that it was the best thing to do.

'The prophecy,' the wizard continued, 'stated that Zoltab would escape from the Great Tunnel of Despair and take possession of his vast black palace called the Terrorsium, from which he would then conquer the world. The only person who could prevent him was a hero who would be the first-born son of the first-born son of the first-born son, going back through eternal generations to the beginning of time. I realised that there was little time to save the world, so I immediately left my books and rushed off in search of the hero, and after much research I found Blart.'

'Blart!' interjected Uther.

'He got it wrong,' explained Blart.

'It was more a case of not being perfectly correct,' snapped Capablanca. 'I was meant to find Blart's elder brother, but Zoltab's Ministers had spirited him away. And so it came to pass that Zoltab escaped and took possession of the Terrorsium and was only a day away from beginning his conquest of the world. But a small band of questors, led by myself, took Zoltab's power away, captured him and took him from his palace.'

'I was the biggest hero,' pointed out Blart. 'Without me Zoltab would have triumphed.'

Capablanca looked irked at this further interruption to his narrative.

'That may be technically true,' he conceded. 'But it was largely accidental heroics.'

'It was still heroics,' said Blart. 'And you said if I was a hero people would sing ballads about me and I've never heard anybody sing a ballad about me, so I think you've got me to be a hero under false pretences.'

A cunning look came into Capablanca's eyes.

'Blart is right,' he admitted. 'He was the hero who was responsible for getting Zoltab out of the Terrorsium.'

'See,' said Blart to Uther.

'Unfortunately,' continued Capablanca, 'this action is why we are all wanted dead or alive.'

'What?' protested Blart. 'You just said I was a hero.

People can't want heroes dead or alive.'

'I'm afraid,' said Capablanca. 'That I must formally withdraw your heroic status as you are responsible for saving Zoltab.'

Chapter 8

'Saving him!' parroted Blart in shock.

'Saving him,' confirmed Capablanca. 'It turns out that the Terrorsium was built in a rush on very shaky foundations and that only a few minutes after we saved him it was going to collapse, killing all Zoltab's Ministers and minions and entombing the immortal Zoltab for eternity.'

'I only did what you told me,' said Blart. His proud boasts of a few moments ago were swiftly forgotten.

Capablanca gave Blart a contemptuous look.

'Unfortunately this was also foretold,' he continued. 'Zoltab's return was doomed before it had even occurred.'

'But our quest?' said Blart.

'Sadly our quest was a waste of time,' confirmed Capablanca.

Blart was shocked into silence. Not because he wasn't used to wasting his time but because he wasn't used to wasting his time that energetically.

'When was it discovered that Zoltab's return was

doomed?' asked Uther.

Capablanca looked annoyed.

'It was discovered only recently by a young upstart wizard called Teichmann in his researches in the Cavernous Library of Ping,' Capablanca answered bitterly. 'For this discovery he has been credited with the title of Greatest Sorcerer in the World. A title that is rightfully mine.'

Capablanca had gone very red in the face during this last speech.

'Does it bother you?' asked Blart, who was never that quick on the uptake.

'Bother me?!' shouted Capablanca. 'Of course it bothers me. A young whippersnapper takes my title – a mere lad of ninety, who doesn't know a spell from an incantation. And what is worse he was not even a wizard from birth but was a late starter after being a friar for a number of years. But that title will be mine again. Mark my words.'

'How did he discover that Zoltab's return was already doomed,' asked Uther, 'when you, the Greatest Sorcerer in the World, could not find out during ten years' research?'

'That's what really annoys me,' said Capablanca, who was now entirely caught up in his own indignation. 'There was another book in the library which was on loan while I was doing my research and which I knew nothing about. It was returned the day after I set out to search for Blart. It makes reference to a later prophecy about Zoltab's return, which states nobody should worry about it because the Terrorsium will collapse on him and entomb him for eternity.'

'Why does that annoy you?' asked Uther.

'The book was overdue,' answered Capablanca. 'This whole misunderstanding is the fault of the librarian.'

Blart grasped the significance of what the wizard had just said.

'You mean that if you'd just waited one more day then you would have discovered that I didn't have to go on the quest.'

Capablanca looked uncomfortable.

'You have to understand that as soon as I read the prophecy I realised that there was very little time. I had to act. I had to try and find you straight away and save the world.'

'Not even one more day?' said Uther incredulously.

'Hindsight is a wonderful thing,' snapped Capablanca. 'Anyway, what is important is that Teichmann, in his desire for glory, revealed what he had discovered, and in some quarters what he has revealed has been misinterpreted.'

'How?' asked Blart.

'The fact that we plucked Zoltab from the Terrorsium moments before it collapsed and took him away has been seen by some people as evidence that we rescued him.'

'How many people think that?'

'Everybody who's heard the story.'

'But,' said Blart, 'you took Zoltab away and put him in a dungeon. All you need to do is to tell the Duke or whoever where Zoltab is and they go and see for themselves that we're not on his side.'

'If only it were that simple,' said Capablanca.

'It sounds simple to me,' said Uther. 'And if Blart can work it out then it must be simple.'

'It would be if I knew where Zoltab was,' explained Capablanca exasperatedly.

'You mean you lost him?' said Blart. 'How could you lose him after all that time we spent finding him?'

'I didn't lose him.'

'Then why don't you know where he is?'

'Because I forgot.'

'You forgot?' shrieked Blart. 'After you went on and on about how important it was to catch Zoltab, then you forgot about him?'

'I forgot deliberately,' explained Capablanca.

'That makes it much better,' said Uther sarcastically.

'All I know,' continued Capablanca, 'is that I put Zoltab somewhere incredibly safe. But I feared that Zoltab's Ministers and minions would come searching for him, and that one day they might capture me and torture me. I feared that if their tortures grew too foul and painful I might reveal Zoltab's whereabouts, so I cast the Great Spell of Fog on the part of my brain that knew of Zoltab's location, which means I no longer know where he is. It was a very brave thing to do.'

'Sounds a very stupid thing to do to me,' observed Blart.

'Can't you undo the spell?' asked Uther.

'The Great Spell of Fog is one of the few irreversible

spells,' answered Capablanca glumly. 'It has covered that part of my brain for ever. And it also means I have terrible difficulty remembering where I put my spectacles.'

Neither Blart nor Uther mustered any sympathy at this new revelation. They were too dumbfounded by the dire circumstances into which they had been thrust.

'What are we going to do?'

A lifetime spent regarding himself as the wisest and cleverest man in the world had left Capablanca physically incapable of saying the words *I don't know*. So instead he replied, 'We must escape from the Duke's men and quickly find Princess Lois and Beowulf the Warrior. As they were your fellow questors they too are wanted dead or alive, but they do not know this yet and so could easily be taken unawares.'

'I'm not too worried about them,' said Blart. Neither of them had been very nice to him, one commenting frequently on the drawbacks of his appearance and the other regularly threatening to make it even worse by cleaving him in two.

'You should be worried,' said Capablanca. 'For if they do not know where we imprisoned Zoltab then we will be unable to prove our innocence and will be hunted for the rest of our lives.'

By now they had completed their tasks. Bound and gagged and dressed only in their shabby undergarments the Duke's men sat shivering in a corner of the barn. Blart, Capablanca and Uther stood in front of them, finely clad in the Duke's livery. The captain was the smallest of the three so Blart had worn his uniform while Capablanca and Uther were dressed as common soldiers. Capablanca wrapped their old clothes in a bundle to take with them.

'We must now try to slip past the Duke's men,' he said. 'Keep your wits about you at all times and be prepared to react to unforeseen situations.'

'Like what?' said Blart, who didn't really appreciate the idea that unforeseen situations could not be reliably predicted.

'Like somebody noticing we're not really the Duke's men,' suggested Uther. 'They will spot Blart in a second. His face is nothing like the captain's. The captain has a moustache and a lean tanned look about him, whereas Blart's complexion is blotchy and pasty.'

'I have sensitive skin,' said Blart defensively.

'Obviously we will wear the visors on our helmets down,' Capablanca told them. 'Drop your visors and let us go.'

They dropped their visors and walked over to the shed door, wondering what lay beyond.

'Try not to talk,' Uther said to Blart. 'But if you must, remember to speak in a low manly voice and not that nasty high-pitched nasal whine you normally speak in.'

'We must go now!' instructed Capablanca, defying his aged stoop and forcing himself to stand up straight and tall. 'I'm surprised we haven't been discovered yet. Our luck can't hold much longer.'

Without further ado the three newly recruited Duke's men opened the shed door and prepared to face the farmyard.

Chapter 9

Any hope that Blart, Capablanca and Uther could pass unnoticed was dashed as they approached the yard. The whole cohort had mounted their horses and was waiting for them.

One soldier detached and approached. *He knows, he knows*, Blart thought. *Perhaps I should confess and blame Capablanca and Uther and then I will be spared and my comrades will be killed.*

'Sir!' The soldier came to a stop in front of Blart. 'I am glad you have returned.'

Blart couldn't believe it. The solider was convinced.

'The men await your orders, sir.'

This was unexpected. Blart had often been given orders and had regularly refused orders but he had never been asked for orders. He was stunned into silence.

'Is there anything wrong, sir?' said the soldier.

At a loss for words Blart shook his head vigorously. Unfortunately he had not secured the chinstrap on his helmet properly and it tipped alarmingly to one side. He only just managed to grab it before it fell. This did not give an impression of military competence and for the first time the soldier looked a little doubtful.

'Are you sure there isn't anything wrong, sir?' he asked.

'No.'

Blart finally managed to squeeze a word out of his nervous mouth. Unfortunately he had forgotten Uther's advice of only a moment ago and the word came out in his high nasal whine.

'What was that, sir?' said the soldier.

The soldier's expression was moving rapidly towards suspicion.

'Why is your visor down, may I ask?'

Blart didn't know what to say. But fortunately he was in front of a man who did. Uther's authoritative tones rang out behind him.

'What impertinence!' said Uther. 'Why is your visor up is what the captain wants to know. The captain has ordered us to put our visors down so that we are ready for battle at all times. He is doubtless refusing to address you because you are unprepared for battle and are therefore dishonouring the traditions of the Duke's men.'

'But we're miles from anywhere and there are no enemies in sight,' protested the puzzled soldier. 'And the captain never said we had to have our visors down before.'

'Do you reject the orders of your own captain?' Uther's

voice reached new levels of cold anger.

Uther's haughty confidence overwhelmed the soldier.

'I'm sorry, sir,' he said to Blart, 'it's just —'

'Silence!' commanded Uther. 'The captain does not wish to hear your grovelling apology. He wishes you to return to the cohort and pass on his order.'

Happy to escape with no actual punishment bar a severe telling-off, the soldier immediately backed away.

'Yes, sir. Thank you, sir. Very good, sir.'

The news that the captain wanted visors down spread swiftly among the cohort and the clanging sound of armour rang around the farmyard as they were urgently shut.

'The captain says that we must pursue the traitors,' Uther announced. 'There are signs that they made their escape not long before we arrived. Let us light our torches and ride through the night for the Duke.'

The soldiers cheered Uther's speech. They lit their torches and prepared to ride like a hurricane.

'Lead your men in the pursuit,' hissed Uther to Blart. 'They are ready to follow you anywhere.'

The soldiers looked to Blart. With no other option he kicked the side of his horse, who began to trot.

'What are you doing?' hissed Uther, catching him up. 'We're supposed to be rapidly pursuing traitors, not taking the Sunday air in the royal park.'

'Trotting is all I can do,' answered Blart.

'You must gallop,' insisted Uther. 'The men expect it.'

Capablanca rode up to join them.

'The men think something's wrong,' hissed Capablanca. 'They're muttering among themselves.'

The cohort trotted into a dark forest.

'At least try a canter,' said Uther.

Hearing the mutterings of the men grow louder, Blart reluctantly spurred his horse on to a canter. All the riders behind him felt the surge in pace. This was what pursuing the enemy was all about, they thought, and they let loose a war-like cheer.

The cheer unnerved Blart, who fell off his horse.

The mutterings in the cohort grew into open doubts.

'He fell off his horse.'

'I ain't following a man who can't ride.'

Soon the doubts would swell to barefaced mutiny. Someone with a quick wit needed to step in and save the situation by convincing the soldiers that everything was all right.

'I've hurt my arm,' said Blart.

'Comrades,' urged Uther in desperation. 'We are under attack. The captain has been hit by an arrow that has thrown him from his horse. We must all quickly dismount and fan out to search for his attacker.'

No soldier dismounted. Though it was dark by now the light of the torches meant that the men were very dubious of any attack.

'I saw no arrow,' shouted an anonymous voice from the

back of the cohort. His words were supported with grunts of agreement, none of which could be traced because the men had all lowered their visors. Things were looking ominous.

'I saw no arrow either,' said another voice.

'Nor me.'

Any moment now one would find the courage to disobey the order and all would be lost.

'Of course you saw no arrow,' shouted Capablanca suddenly. 'Why would you see one? The captain was felled by an invisible arrow.'

This was perhaps not the most convincing explanation. Luckily it was the Dark Ages, when people believed that you could see if someone was a witch by throwing them into a pond and that if someone pulled a sword out of a stone then they were entitled to be king.

The threat of invisible arrows had an immediate effect on the soldiers. They tumbled off their horses and crouched low, scanning the surrounding trees for these imaginary missiles.

'Aaargh,' cried a soldier, collapsing on the ground. 'I've been hit by an invisible arrow.'

This was a surprise.

Two soldiers rushed over to their fallen comrade, who was writhing about on the floor.

'I'm hit in the leg,' cried the soldier.

Now fully convinced that invisible arrows were raining down upon them, the soldiers scattered into the surrounding trees.

'We must take our chance,' urged Capablanca. 'Climb on to the back of my horse, Blart, and we will flee before they realise what has happened.'

'I don't think I can get up,' protested Blart. 'The invisible arrow has hurt me too much.'

Capablanca sighed. 'There's no such thing as an invisible arrow,' he said. 'I made it up.'

'But what about him?' Blart gestured towards the lame soldier.

'I think it might have been a touch of cramp, sir,' admitted the shame-faced soldier.

'Quickly,' urged Uther. 'Before they realise what's happened and come back.'

Blart gingerly rose to his feet. Capablanca grabbed him and pulled him on to the back of his own horse.

'Let's go.'

The wizard and Uther spurred their horses and galloped deep into the forest. The soldiers watched them go in disbelief.

Soldiers are not complex thinkers. Without orders they tend to become confused. Seeing their superior officer disappear into the forest meant only one thing for the soldiers. They would have to catch him or think for themselves. The fear of the challenge of independent thought overcame the soldiers' fear of invisible arrows and they swiftly emerged from the undergrowth, mounted their horses and gave chase.

Chapter 10

Through the forest thundered Capablanca, Blart and Uther. Behind them drummed the hooves of the soldiers' horses.

'We must go faster,' said Capablanca, bravely ignoring the juddering pain that was shooting through his body as the horse galloped and Blart clung on.

'Throw the boy off the back of your horse,' suggested Uther. 'He is nothing but useless ballast.'

Blart wasn't sure what useless ballast was but he was confident that it wasn't nice.

'We need him,' replied Capablanca.

'We need to live more,' insisted Uther. 'He's slowing you down. Soon they'll be able to see us.'

And it was true. The pursuing soldiers all had one horse each. Meanwhile Blart and Capablanca had only one horse between them due to Blart's poor riding skills. Their horse would tire first.

'All we need to do is get to the edge of the wood,'

said Capablanca breathlessly. 'There the Duke of Northwestmoreland's lands come to an end and we enter the lands of the Earl of Nethershire. They won't follow us there.'

Though they could not understand it this news seemed to spur on the horses, who surged forward towards the edge of the wood.

Behind them the noise of the chasers grew louder. But the forest boundary was within reach and Blart, Capablanca and Uther flashed across into the lands of the Earl of Nethershire.

It was almost a furlong before they could bring their horses to a halt. They wheeled round to see the Duke's men emerge from the wood and reach the border of his lands. They waited for them to stop.

The Duke's men didn't.

'Oh,' said Capablanca.

'Another great plan,' observed Blart.

'They're trespassing,' said Capablanca indignantly.

'They're trespassing towards us,' pointed out Uther.

They urged their horses on again. Ahead of them was the Churn, a river that slithered its way through the plains of Nethershire. With no bridge in sight, their only hope was that their horses would leap across or, the river being too wide, swim it. The horses, however, both decided that it would be far easier not to attempt to cross the fast-flowing river at all, and so came to an abrupt stop that sent Capablanca, Blart and Uther flying over their heads and crashing down the riverbank.

The Duke's men, seeing what had happened, slowed their horses cautiously to a trot.

'Any ideas?' asked Uther sarcastically, picking himself up.

Capablanca shook his head.

Knowing they had their prey cornered, the Duke's soldiers advanced steadily.

'Do you know you're trespassing?' Capablanca shouted to them. 'This arrest will be declared invalid in any court of law.'

'If you're who we think you are,' shouted back one soldier, 'we're not going to arrest you. We're going to kill you. Now pull up your visors.'

There were no options left. Capablanca and Uther put up their visors and prepared to fight to the death like men.

Blart, on the other hand, was backing into the tall reeds that grew beside the river.

'Just as we suspected,' shouted the soldier. 'You are not members of our cohort. You are associates of Blart, the friend of Zoltab. And you must die.'

Blart felt a clunk. He had walked into something in the reeds.

His hand felt an oar.

'Now, when you say associate,' Blart heard Uther begin in his best argumentative style, 'could you define just exactly what you mean by it because –'

'There's a boat here,' shouted Blart.

Uther stopped talking and started running. Capablanca followed. They plunged through the reeds towards Blart.

'After them!'

The soldiers jumped off their horses and charged.

Blart, who was rather shocked by the turn of events, was the only person to remain still.

'Push it out,' shouted Capablanca, hobbling as fast as he could.

Belatedly Blart too leapt into fantastic action. His nervous shaking hands untied the boat from its moorings and pushed it out. The strong current tugged at the little craft and all Blart's strength was needed to stop it being pulled away.

Uther and Capablanca splashed past him and collapsed into the boat.

Uther leant over the stern.

'If you could let go,' he said. 'You are preventing our escape.'

'I'm stuck in the mud,' explained Blart. 'Pull me in.'

'Another time,' said Uther, loosening Blart's fingers.

Blart heard the murderous cries of the soldiers behind him and felt the surge of the water as it prepared to pull the boat away from him for ever.

But just before the river could grab the boat and the soldiers could grab Blart, a bony arm shot out and hauled him over the side.

The boat was spinning away. Behind them the soldiers hollered in anger.

Chapter 11

The recent rain had swollen the river and it was flowing fast. By morning it had taken the questors far from the wrath of the Duke and his men. At first they had tried to steer the boat, but it soon became apparent that the boat was in the grip of the river, for better or worse, and so, leaving it to the will of the water, they each gradually drifted to sleep, as the boat floated further and further into the unknown.

Blart was the first to wake. He looked up at a bright blue sky. He listened to the gurgle and slap of the river.

Capablanca stirred, waking up from a dream in which he was turning the final page in an ancient book in the Cavernous Library of Ping which would have revealed a spell which, when cast, would once and for all confer upon him the title of Greatest Sorcerer Ever. It was a dream he had a lot.

'Where are we?' demanded Uther grumpily. He had been halfway through a dream in which he had owned the biggest farm in the world and everyone was his slave and had to work for no money. It had been the best dream he'd had for ages.

Capablanca looked down at the river, which was now calm and serene. It gave no hint as to their whereabouts. He looked out at the empty grassy plains that surrounded them. They gave no clue. He looked up at the sky to see if the position of the sun could aid him. It couldn't. It looked as though Capablanca was going to have to answer with his least favourite phrase – three little words that made him feel physically ill to say.

But before he could open his mouth, Blart shouted, 'There's a sign!' He was right. A roughly hewn sign stood in the centre of the river.

The wizard, by squinting his eyes, managed to pick out the words.

'I can now answer your question about our location with complete confidence,' he told Uther smugly. 'We are approaching the Rapids of Hell, which lead to the Devil's Falls.'

'Rapids?' said Uther.

'Falls?' said Blart.

Capablanca looked pensive.

Already the tranquil river had begun to run faster. Ripples had become waves. Drift had become current.

'Perhaps it won't be so bad,' said Capablanca.

'What do the words Hell and Devil conjure up in your mind?' demanded Uther.

'Perhaps we are passing through a land which is steeped in the traditions of irony,' countered Capablanca.

'How ironic does that roar sound?' recountered Uther.

The three questors listened. In the distance there was an unambiguous unironic roar of water.

Bang!

They were all thrown forward in the boat as it bumped violently into a rock.

Crash!

The boat hit another rock and spun round.

Bang! Crash!

As they entered the rapids, the boat picked up speed. Water spilled over the sides.

'I've read about this in the Cavernous Library of Ping,' shouted Capablanca.

'All he does is read,' observed Blart. 'When he's not doing that he's messing my life up and keeping me away from my pigs.'

'My pigs,' corrected Uther.

'In a situation like this,' continued Capablanca, determined to put his learning to good use, 'according to *Being Shipwrecked Made Easy* we should lash ourselves to the mast.'

The boat lurched alarmingly to one side as it was smashed against another rock and more water flooded in.

'This boat hasn't got a mast,' Blart pointed out.

A further wave buffeted the boat and sent him flying backwards into Uther. The roar of the approaching waterfall grew louder.

'Hold on to whatever you can,' shouted Capablanca.

Blart grasped Capablanca firmly.

'Not me,' cried Capablanca, kicking him off. 'Hold on to the boat.'

Shocked into an unusual state of obedience by the ever-growing roar, Blart entwined himself around the seat.

And just in time too. The roar grew louder, the boat got faster and the crashes grew ever more violent. The three questors closed their eyes as the boat raced towards the thundering Devil's Falls and plummeted over.

Chapter 12

'Glug,' gurgled Blart.

He was in the middle of a deep, calm, blue pool. Above him was the angry white cascade of the Devil's Falls. He took a brief moment to be amazed that the deep, blue pool and the angry white cascade were the same thing – water.

Then he remembered he couldn't swim. Immediately he remembered, he began to sink.

His eyes darted around the pool in the hope of seeing something he could grab hold of and float on.

There was nothing.

The water covered his head and he fought for breath.

Then, suddenly, he felt a tug from behind.

He was being pulled – pulled hard and fast through the pool. And then up. Up towards the surface, banging against rocks on the way. And then he was being scraped over more rocks as he got closer to the sides of the pool. By now he could have climbed up himself but the force kept pulling him relentlessly. He was buffeted, banged, jarred and scratched and then, suddenly, he was out of the water on dry land. He opened his eyes.

Uther and Capablanca looked down at him.

'Trust you to be nearly drowned,' said Capablanca, 'while the rest of us had the good sense to stay in the boat.'

'He's still alive,' said Uther, shaking himself dry. 'That means you owe me double the fee for saving him.'

'You didn't need to drag him over the rocks like that,' said Capablanca critically. 'His clothes have been torn to pieces. He'll have to have new ones or he'll catch a chill that could become a fever and then kill him.'

'I'm c-c-cold,' shivered Blart.

'Follow me,' said the wizard.

Cold and shivering, Blart followed Capablanca and Uther. They left the pool behind them and fought their way through briars and nettles until, bleeding and exhausted, they came upon a rough path. They followed the rough path until it became a smooth path which seemed to be well used. Capablanca stopped and looked about him.

'I have been doing some calculations,' he began smugly, 'and I have concluded after studying various astrological, geographical and geological features —'

'What?' said Blart, taking a break from shivering for a moment.

'The land and the sky,' explained Uther.

Capablanca affected not to hear.

'I have concluded,' he continued, 'that overnight the river swept us right through the lands of the Earl of Grindstone and has now deposited us in the lands of the Prince of Murkstan.'

'Murkstan?' repeated Uther.

'With an M,' said Capablanca.

'Oh,' said Uther.

'Is there a problem?' asked Capablanca.

'Possibly.' Uther looked shifty. 'It's just that they are not very advanced in their business practices,' he grumbled. 'Suffice it to say I must warn you that if I am discovered in Murkstan I am liable to immediate arrest. I must be incognito.'

'Wh-wh-what?' said Blart, shivering again.

'Nobody must know I'm here,' explained Uther.

'Indeed?' said Capablanca distractedly.

'There!' said Uther. 'A cottage.'

As they drew closer they saw that it had a well-tended garden, smoke coming out of the chimney and bright flowers in boxes on the window sills. It was the kind of cottage that gave cottages a good name.

'Wait here,' Capablanca said to Blart. 'I will see if I can borrow some clothes for you from the good inhabitants of this cottage.'

'H-h-how do you know they're good?' asked Blart. 'They might be horrible.'

'One should always expect the best of people,' said

Capablanca.

'W-w-why can't I come in?' asked Blart. 'I am cold and there's a fire.'

'We cannot allow the good people of the cottage to be suddenly shocked by the sight of you in shredded trousers.'

'I will wait outside too,' said Uther.

'Why?' said Blart, who was not fond of Uther's company since he'd tricked Blart into slavery.

'Because there's the slight possibility that I sold these people some of my Marvellous Miracle Seeds when I was passing through the area in days gone by.'

'Marvellous Miracle Seeds?' said Blart. 'They sound great. What do they do?'

'It turned out that it would be a miracle if they did anything,' said Uther. 'I was let down by my supplier.'

Capablanca and Blart stared hard at Uther, who maintained an air of studied innocence.

Shaking his head, Capablanca walked over to the cottage and knocked on the door.

Half an hour later, Capablanca emerged from the house with a large package and a big smile. He had not looked so well since the quest began.

'You look happy,' said Blart suspiciously.

'I have had a pleasant conversation and a piece of cake and a glass of cordial with the woman of the house and her six pretty daughters,' answered Capablanca. 'Why wouldn't I be happy?'

Capablanca tossed the package he had brought over to Blart.

'They very generously gave me some clothes for you.'

Blart eagerly tore open the package. But on seeing the contents his face fell.

'It's a dress,' he said.

'It's a woollen dress,' said Capablanca, whose poorly hidden smile was becoming an unsuppressed chortle. 'A woollen dress that will keep you warm.'

'But it's a dress.'

'There was a woman and her six daughters,' said Capablanca in exasperation. 'What did you expect? A suit of armour?'

Blart threw the dress on to the ground and lapsed into a sulk. A cold sulk.

'Put it on!' ordered Capablanca. 'The woman in the house told me that a cohort of the Prince's soldiers passed through here a day ago, asking questions about allies of Zoltab. It is obviously not just the Duke's men who are pursuing us now and we cannot hope to elude them for long. We must press on to find Beowulf the Warrior and Princess Lois in the hope that they can lead us to Zoltab's prison, so we can prove our innocence and save our lives.'

'Do you promise that as soon as we can we will get me some boys' clothes?' Blart demanded of Capablanca.

Capablanca nodded.

'And you promise not to laugh.'

Capablanca nodded.

'And you promise to turn Uther into a toad if he laughs.'

Capablanca nodded.

With a sigh and a particularly violent shiver Blart bent down to remove his trousers.

'There!' said Capablanca. 'I bet you're warmer now.'

Blart stood before them in a bright red dress.

'It brings out the colour in your eyes,' observed Uther without laughing.

'Shut up,' said Blart.

'But we should really must do something about your posture if —'

'Shut up,' said Blart again.

'Uther,' warned Capablanca.

Strictly speaking Uther was correct. For Blart stood with his arms hanging loosely at his sides, his knees slightly bent and his head drooped forward. It was obvious he had never been to finishing school.

'Let us go,' said Capablanca.

'Where?' asked Uther.

'We must head for Illyria with all speed to find the Princess and hope to pick up news of Beowulf's whereabouts on the way,' said Capablanca. 'We must keep moving if we are not to be caught.'

The urgency in Capablanca's tone galvanised the others and they immediately set off. Their vigorous walking generated heat and Blart swiftly felt the advantages of the woollen dress. He stopped shivering and began to feel like himself again. Just to make sure he really was himself he did some grumbling to Capablanca as they walked about how unfair it all was and how much he'd rather be with his pigs. It felt good.

They followed the road over a hill and into another unattractive valley. By now, night was upon them and they needed to find somewhere to stop. Luckily, nestled in the valley was a village. As they got closer a sign announced they were entering Screeb. In keeping with the surrounding countryside it was not the most prepossessing village. Instead of pretty cottages, there were functional houses. Instead of gardens or pretty flowers, there were a lot of sheds. Instead of a green or a pond in the centre of the village, there was a set of stocks.

At the outskirts of the village Blart insisted they stop.

'I can't go into the village,' he said to Capablanca. 'People will laugh at me.'

'We'll get you a change of clothes as soon as possible,' Capablanca reassured him.

'I'm not going to be laughed at,' insisted Blart. 'I hate being laughed at.'

'They will only laugh at you if they think you're a boy,' said Capablanca. 'If they think you're a girl they will simply admire your dress.'

Blart was dismayed. He felt the solution to his problem was to return him to being a convincing boy, not to make him an ever more convincing girl.

'Simply bury your head in the side of my cowl and people won't see your face,' said Capablanca. 'Anybody watching you pass will think you are my very shy granddaughter. Then we will take a room in the local tavern and I will go out to procure your clothes and you will emerge as a strapping youth with nobody any the wiser.'

Capablanca was stretching the truth to snapping point. There was no way Blart was going to emerge as a strapping youth whatever clothes they found for him.

'Come on, Blart,' urged Capablanca. 'We must go on. Remember that we are wanted dead or alive. Who knows what is behind us?'

'I'll tell you what, Blart,' added Uther. 'If you do this then I'll give you back one of your pigs.'

'Really?' said Blart. His resolve, previously insurmountable, was suddenly weaker.

'Yes,' said Uther.

'All right, then.'

Blart took a deep breath and buried his face into the wizard's cowl.

And so they walked into the village. Little did they know that in Screeb shyness in maidens was prized above all other virtues. A girl in a red dress with her head buried into what they assumed was her grandfather's cowl to hide her modesty was a bright beacon to any young buck in the village. The local young men appraised her with wanton eyes as she passed along the village street. The mystery conjured up by the maiden's modesty played havoc with their emotions. Eventually one particularly bold young man hailed the wizard.

'Sir,' he said, 'my name is Kmoch. Is that your granddaughter with you?'

Capablanca grunted his assent.

'Tell me now, would she be wanting a tour of the village?'

Capablanca grunted his disapproval.

'I have five cows of my own and I stand to inherit a whole herd when my father dies,' the young man informed him. 'And between you and me he's not looking too well.'

'Your cows do not interest me, stranger,' said Capablanca gruffly, continuing to walk towards the tavern. 'And nor does the well-being of your father.'

The haughty tone of Capablanca's dismissal merely heightened Kmoch's desire to know the name of his granddaughter. *Surely*, he reasoned, *this maid must be rare indeed if I am not worthy to know her name*. Like many young men, emboldened by his imagination and watched by his peer group, he spoke rashly.

'What if I were to offer her my own name?'

Capablanca stopped and stared at Kmoch.

'You want to marry my granddaughter?'

Kmoch nodded. Blart buried himself even deeper in the wizard's cowl.

'Even though you've never seen her face or heard her speak?'

Kmoch nodded again. 'She is obviously a shy and modest maiden. I would be the envy of all here if she were to take my hand.'

'I don't want to get married,' squeaked Blart and in his desperation to get his message across his voice rose even higher.

'I think my granddaughter has made herself clear,' said Capablanca firmly. 'And now, if you don't mind, we are going to seek out rooms in the local tavern.'

And with that Capablanca ushered his granddaughter away from the suitor.

'I shall not give up,' Kmoch shouted after them. 'I shall pursue your fair granddaughter with renewed ardour, and I am confident of success!'

Chapter 13

'We would like a room for the night,' Capablanca told the landlady of The Rabid Dog when she finally emerged from the cellar. 'I see from a sign outside that your rooms are only one crown, which is very reasonable.'

'A room?' said the landlady, looking as though such a request was most unexpected. 'Why?'

'To stay in overnight,' explained Capablanca.

'Will you be wanting a bed in it?' said the landlady.

'Of course.'

'You should have said,' the landlady told him.

'Surely beds are standard?' said Capablanca.

'Not in this tavern,' she replied.

'Well, we would like a bed,' confirmed Capablanca. 'In fact, we would like three beds.'

'I think we can manage that,' agreed the landlady. 'Now, will you be wanting a door?'

'A door?' Capablanca was even more staggered. 'Are you telling me your rooms don't have doors?'

'Some do, some don't,' said the landlady enigmatically.

'Well, we would like one that does,' Capablanca informed her. 'How can a person sleep soundly without a door to close behind them to give them privacy?'

'You want to sleep?' the landlady exclaimed. 'You really are fussy customers.'

'Didn't I say I wanted to sleep?' demanded Capablanca.

'No,' said the landlady. 'You said you wanted to stay in it overnight.'

'We want to sleep,' confirmed Capablanca.

'So that means you'll want sheets and a pillow and a blanket. All these extras are going to cost you.'

'The room does come with four walls, a ceiling, a floor and a window?' said Capablanca.

'Of course it does.' The landlady looked hurt. 'Eleven crowns. Payment in advance, please.' Grimly, Capablanca reached into his purse and counted out eleven crowns.

Grumpily, the landlady showed them up to their room.

She could not depart soon enough for Blart, who was finally able to pull his face out of the repulsive folds of Capablanca's cowl. He rushed to the window and breathed in deeply.

'We have a problem,' said Capablanca. 'I only have one crown remaining. Do either of you have any money?'

'Uther won all mine at Muggins,' said Blart from the window.

'But unfortunately,' added Uther swiftly. 'I had no notice

that we were about to leave when we did and so was unable to gather any of my fortune. I am as penniless as Blart.'

Capablanca shook his head.

'This is no good,' he said. 'We are on the run and we have no money. We will be even more vulnerable to capture. Still, I must use my last crown to buy Blart some new trousers and a shirt. And then we must trust to fortune.'

And so saying Capablanca left the room to search the village for bargain trousers.

Blart and Uther were left alone together.

'Fancy a game of Muggins?' said Uther.

Blart shook his head in a statement of absolute and final refusal.

'Go on,' said Uther.

'I shall never play Muggins again,' said Blart.

Five minutes later, Blart was sitting on the bed, looking at a pair of nines. He had lost the pig that he had so recently gained.

'Bad luck,' said Uther mildly.

Blart said nothing. He simply stomped back over to the window. Having spent so long inside the folds of Capablanca's cowl he now had a much greater respect for fresh air. As soon as Blart poked his head out of the window he was greeted by an excited cry.

He looked down. Below him was Kmoch. And he was carrying a lute.

'What light from yonder window breaks?' shouted Kmoch.

72

Uther pulled Blart back into the room. He was well aware that any less than a fleeting glance at Blart would reveal that he was no fair maiden.

Unfortunately, the sudden disappearance of Blart from the window merely confirmed to Kmoch that his love was as shy and modest as he had hoped.

'My love,' shouted Kmoch with a preparatory strum of his lute. 'I have written you a ballad and I have come to serenade you.'

Blart was horrified. Kmoch was out of tune. But it didn't stop him. He twanged his lute again and began:

'My lady in red
Her name is unsaid
She's gone up to bed
And I wish I were dead
Without my lady in red.'

Blart put his fingers in his ears to drown out the sound. Five minutes later he pulled them out again. Kmoch was still singing. A few minutes later he had moved on to an instrumental solo, before embarking upon a finale of loud strums on the lute, accompanied by whoops. A final shuddering chord brought the song to an end.

'What was that?' said Capablanca, coming through the door, holding a pair of trousers and a shirt.

But nobody answered him. Blart had eyes only for the

clothes — he dashed up to the wizard and snatched them.

'Manners,' said Capablanca.

Blart tore off his red dress, threw on his new clothes and within seconds he looked like himself again. Only Blart considered this to be an improvement.

'I'll be going out for a few moments,' said Uther.

'I thought you were travelling incognito,' said Capablanca.

'So I hoped,' said Uther. 'But we are in dire need of money and I suspect that I am the only one amongst us who has the acumen to make it.'

'How do you propose to do that?' said Capablanca.

'Do I ask you how you cast spells?' replied Uther. 'Leave me to my own devices.'

'Don't attract any attention to us,' said Capablanca sternly.

Uther laughed hollowly in response.

'Attract attention?' he said. 'We've got a youth outside the window, making more noise with his lute than ten tom cats in a sack because Blart has driven him mad with desire, and you ask me not to draw attention to us.'

Without further ado, Uther opened the door they had paid extra for and went out into the town, where night was already falling.

'That door squeaks,' observed Blart.

Uther did not return for many hours. Capablanca and Blart had no money and no food, and time passed slowly.

Blart occasionally broke the silence to whine at Capablanca that everything bad that had ever happened in Blart's life was Capablanca's fault. Capablanca occasionally broke the silence to threaten to turn Blart into a toad. Eventually, bored by each other and by themselves, they grumpily went to bed. Both of them were sleeping deeply when Uther slipped into the room later in the evening, As he retired to his bed there was the chink of gold coins in his pocket.

Chapter 14

Blart was dreaming he was running in the orchard with his pigs. All was right with the world.

Then there was a huge crash and the door was smashed to smithereens.

He shot up in his bed.

A hulking figure brandishing a sword stood in the doorway.

All was obviously no longer right with the world.

'Where is the damsel in distress?' demanded a deep voice.

'There's no damsel in here,' said Uther.

'I refer,' said the deep voice that belonged to the hulking figure, 'to the damsel sold into marriage against her will. I have come to rescue her.'

'Uther,' said Capablanca. 'What have you done?'

'It was a fair deal,' insisted Uther. 'We spat on our hands and shook on it.'

'Be silent,' said the deep-voiced hulking figure. 'Hand over the damsel in distress. This is your last chance.'

'There is no damsel,' protested Uther. 'You've been mis-informed.'

'Don't lie to me,' said the hulking figure. 'I know that someone in this room sold a shy damsel to Kmoch and his father earlier this evening and I am here to rescue her.'

'It wasn't me,' said Blart, who regarded self-preservation as the most important thing. 'It was him.'

The hulking figure approached Uther's bed.

'Let's not be hasty,' placated Uther. 'I'm sure this is a misunderstanding.'

The hulking figure raised its sword.

Blart thought it was a pity that the room was so dark because he wouldn't be able to see Uther cut to pieces.

'I shall cleave you in two,' pronounced the hulking figure.

There was something familiar to Blart about that phrase. In fact there was something familiar about the voice. In fact ...

'What's going on in here?'

The landlady was standing at the door, holding a lantern.

'What have you done to my door? When I rent out a door I don't expect my guests to turn it into firewood overnight.'

She stepped into the room.

'Why is nobody listening to me?'

The landlady was right. Nobody was listening to her. Instead they were staring at the hulking silhouette, coloured in by the landlady's light to reveal the big, bronzed, burly, bearded figure of Beowulf the Warrior (known to his acquaintances as Beo) – the man who had travelled with Blart and Capablanca and Princess Lois of Illyria when they had journeyed to the Terrorsium and defeated Zoltab, the Dark Lord.

'What's the matter with everybody?' demanded the landlady.

Capablanca was the first to regain his composure.

'Beowulf!'

'Capablanca!'

Beowulf turned to Blart

'Thingy.'

'Do you all know each other?' asked Uther, who had never met Beowulf the Warrior before. While the others were all wide-eyed and slack-jawed with disbelief, Uther was wide-eyed and slack-jawed because he thought he was about to be cleaved in two.

'Yes,' said Capablanca. 'We know each other.'

'If it's not too much trouble,' said Uther evenly, 'perhaps you could ask your friend to lower his sword.'

'Nobody said we were friends,' pointed out Blart.

'Acquaintance, then,' said Uther in exasperation.

'I don't care whether he's a friend or an acquaintance,' interrupted the landlady. 'He is a non-resident and he shouldn't be in a resident's bedroom after nine-thirty at night. Especially if he smashed the door down to get in.'

'Beowulf, I'm sure it would help us all if you were to lower your sword,' agreed Capablanca.

But Beo stood firm.

'I cannot do so until the damsel is freed from distress and the foul cur who besmirched her honour lies dead.'

'Nobody besmirches anybody's honour in my inn,' said the landlady. 'It's in the rules. Just under the bit about evacuation procedure in case of fire.'

'You can put up your sword,' Uther reassured Beo, 'because there is no damsel in distress. In fact, there's no damsel at all.'

'You've murdered her,' accused Beo, taking a firmer grip on his sword.

'Murdered her!' shrieked the landlady. 'That's even more against the rules than honour-besmirching. I'm not putting up with this. I want you all out right now. Come on.'

Finally the landlady had managed to grab their attention.

'Woman,' said Capablanca, 'let me inform you that we are good people who are at risk of being the victims in a terrible miscarriage of justice. I appeal to you to overlook these minor infringements and allow us to stay.'

'Door-smashing, honour-besmirching and murder are not minor infringements,' insisted the landlady. 'I want you out.'

'I appeal to your human spirit,' pleaded the wizard desperately.

'I'm adamant,' said the landlady firmly. 'Nothing will change my mind.'

'How about some gold?' said Uther, reaching under his pillow.

The landlady turned on him.

'How dare you suggest you can buy your way out of this! Rules are rules and –'

'Three crowns,' offered Uther.

'Seven,' said the landlady.

'Five and you leave the lantern behind when you go.'

'Done.'

The landlady grabbed the gold and swept out of the room.

'Everybody has their price,' observed Uther wryly.

'Excuse me,' said Beo, who felt that he had rather lost control of the situation. 'But what about this damsel in distress?'

'There isn't a damsel,' repeated Blart, Capablanca and Uther.

'If there isn't a damsel,' said Beo, dramatically pulling out a shabby parchment that he had hidden beneath his livery, 'then explain this.'

Capablanca squinted at it.

'*I, Uther the Uncle,*' Capablanca began – Uther looked uncomfortable – '*do sell my niece, Blartarina the Shy, to Kmoch for the purpose of marriage, with or without her consent and regardless of the distress caused. Price: five gold crowns. Handling fee: half a crown. No refunds under any circumstances.*'

Everybody in the room looked at Uther.

'You misunderstand,' Uther insisted. 'We needed the money and I simply sold Kmoch his dream. Tonight he will be happy thinking about his future wife. Only later will he discover that his bride never existed. And then he will simply return to being miserable, but he will cherish for ever the memory of his one night of happiness.'

Uther looked at the others. They didn't look impressed by his solution.

'And I shall leave the dress behind as a souvenir.'

Denied his damsel in distress, Beowulf stood deflated.

'So, Beo,' began Capablanca with a forced cheerfulness, 'what have you been up to since our quest came to an end?'

Beo sighed.

'Capablanca, I've had terrible trouble,' he said. 'At the end of our last quest wasn't I made a knight of Zoltab? But when I came back nobody would accept that I was a proper knight. Twas some technicality about Zoltab being a terrible force for evil unable to create a force for good. So it turned out that I had not achieved my dream and still remained a mere warrior. I have spent the past year wandering from place to place, trying to do deeds of chivalry in order to attract the attention of a king or queen who would bestow on me the title I crave.'

Capablanca nodded sympathetically.

'I've had special trouble with damsels,' lamented Beowulf. 'There is not a damsel in distress to be found. Every damsel I meet seems to be happy. They've never had it so good.'

Capablanca nodded sympathetically again.

'And what is worse,' bemoaned Beo, 'I have a terrible pain in my arm whenever I lift my great sword. A doctor told me that I have "warrior's elbow", caused by excessive brutality, and that if I do not rest it then I will lose my ability to cleave my enemies in two. Even threatening your friend with death has caused me much anguish.'

Beo looked very sorry for himself. The wizard was at a loss how to proceed. Fortunately Blart was on hand to help.

'You're wanted dead or alive,' he told the warrior.

'What?' said Beo, grasping his sword firmly once more and then grimacing with pain.

'And it's all the wizard's fault,' added Blart. 'He got all the research wrong and now everybody thinks we're Zoltab's friends and wants to kill us.'

'Is this true?' demanded Beo.

'There is some truth to what he says,' agreed Capablanca ruefully and he swiftly explained to Beo what had recently occurred. Blart noticed that Capablanca rushed through the part where it emerged that the wizard had made a large mistake in his research which entirely invalidated the previous quest, and instead focused heavily on the fact that they were all wanted men, tracked by soldiers who had orders to take them dead or alive and who had expressed a preference for dead.

'What?' repeated Beo. 'Even me?'

'You are a known associate of Blart and myself,' confirmed Capablanca.

'Blart!' Beo was outraged. 'You mean I'm wanted dead or alive because of my association with that vile boy?'

He turned to face Blart, his sword gripped menacingly.

'If I was to cleave him in two then nobody could say I was his associate.'

'I'm afraid they could,' said Capablanca, 'and they would.'

'Couldn't we try it anyway to see if it works?' requested Beo.

'No,' said Capablanca firmly. 'How many times must I tell you that unnecessary violence and killing attract unwanted attention. We must avoid it.'

Beo reluctantly accepted Capablanca's authority.

'How will we save ourselves from being killed?' he asked.

'Aha,' said Capablanca. 'I will answer you. First we will find Princess Lois and alert her to the terrible danger she faces. Then we will try to locate Zoltab's eternal prison, thus demonstrating to the Duke that we are not Zoltab's allies but his enemies, proving our innocence and saving all of our lives. The proclamation can be lifted and we can all live happily ever after.'

'I don't want to live happily ever after,' said Blart. 'It sounds boring.'

Chapter 15

As dawn was breaking Blart, Capablanca, Uther and Beo rode out of the little town of Screeb. Behind them they left a broken-hearted youth, who was never to see his modest lady in red again. He would waste his life writing mournful ballads about lost love and eventually die of despair. There's not much of a story there, so we'll leave him to it.

'Beo,' asked Capablanca as the town of Screeb disappeared behind them. 'There is something very important which I must ask you. Can you remember where I said I was going to imprison Zoltab after our previous quest came to an end?'

'I cannot,' replied Beo. 'You said I could never be told because I would blab Zoltab's whereabouts to the first person who bought me three flagons of ale to drink. I was most offended. It normally takes me at least five flagons before I start to tell people my secrets.'

'It is as I feared,' said Capablanca. 'I do not know where

Zoltab is because of the Great Irreversible Spell of Fog and you do not know and Blart does not know. We must therefore head with all speed to the land of Illyria and seek out Princess Lois. She is the only questor we have not asked, and if she doesn't know, we will probably all die horribly. Perhaps because my gifts include wisdom and foresight I gave her some clue as to Zoltab's whereabouts that I could then decipher. Let us make haste. Onward!'

Capablanca, with Blart sitting behind him, spurred on his horse. Uther and Beo followed. Over hill they went, through valley, through dale, fording streams and rivers, across luscious green fields and through woods. All morning they rode with no pause. The sun blazed above them to signify that it was approaching noon.

'Could we have a rest?' said Blart. 'Bits of me are hurting.'

'No,' said Capablanca, though the wizard's weary body craved one. 'Soon our pursuers will pick up our trail and come after us. We must head for Illyria with all speed.'

Over hills and through valleys they continued. They forded more streams. They left luscious green fields behind them and galloped over blasted heaths. Blart's bottom winced in pain with each movement of the horse. All afternoon they rode without stopping. Then, as the sun sank into the west to signify the end of the day, Capablanca called a halt. Blart clambered off and collapsed face down in the grass. He was convinced he would never be able to sit comfortably again.

'We can stop for the night and give the horses some rest,'

said Capablanca. 'But we will camp outdoors, away from towns and villages. Word spreads faster than any horse can gallop and the story of the disappearing damsel and the smashing up of the hotel may well have drawn the attention of those who are aware that there is a price on our heads.'

For the next hour they worked in silence. Beo disappeared to kill something for their dinner, Uther fetched firewood and built a fire, Capablanca tried to construct a basic shelter and Blart followed a gurgling sound until he found a little stream into which he lowered his sore bottom.

Finally, later that evening, as they sat round the fire, gnawing the last meat from the bones of the two rabbits, the silence was broken.

'We need aliases,' said Uther.

'Are they books with maps in?' said Blart.

Uther shook his head.

'They are false identities,' he explained. 'If they are convincing they can help a wanted man escape detection.'

'Do you speak from experience, merchant?' asked Beo.

'I own there are some places where it has been convenient for me to be known by a name other than that with which I was born,' said Uther evenly. 'If only to avoid misunderstanding.'

'Misunderstanding?' grunted Beo disapprovingly. 'A man should never hide his name. He should announce it proudly and any who have an argument with him should be prepared to feel the thrust of his sword in their guts.'

'A noble sentiment,' agreed Uther with a hint of sarcasm, 'but what if you are a wanted man with a price on his head, who is vastly outnumbered?'

'Then you die,' said Beo simply. 'But you die with your own name on your lips. You die with your pride and your honour intact. Tungsten the Dwarf taught me that.'

'Would you rather not live with your pride and honour dented?' queried Uther.

'Nonsense.' Beo gave Uther a look of disdain. 'A life without pride and honour is no life at all.'

'You could still keeps pigs,' pointed out Blart. 'They don't care about things like pride and honour. They care more about apples and swill.'

'Apples and swill,' repeated Beo with contempt. He turned to Capablanca, who had so far remained silent during the conversation. 'Wizard, will you not explain that it is better to die like a man than to live like a worm?'

Capablanca furrowed his brow. He thought Uther's idea was a good one but hated to admit it.

'Perhaps Uther is right,' he conceded reluctantly. 'Though deception is generally wrong, in this case we must make an exception. We must all pick an alias. What are they to be?'

Beo shook his head to show his disagreement with the wizard's decision.

'I've thought of mine,' said Blart eagerly. 'I shall be Blob the Pig Boy.'

'Nobody will ever see through that, will they?' said Uther sarcastically.

'I know,' Blart said proudly.

Realising that sarcasm was not going to work, Uther was forced to resort to a long and tortured explanation. Finally, he convinced Blart that merely altering the final three letters of his name was unlikely to prevent his being unmasked.

'What shall I be, then?' said Blart sulkily. 'How about a pig and goat boy? That's really different.'

Uther ignored him.

'When you are concocting an alias for a number of people,' he explained, 'it is important to be consistent. If Blart says he's a pig boy and Capablanca says he's an astrologer and Beo claims to be a tax collector then people will think that's a strange group of people to be travelling together and they will wonder. And the last thing that you want after you have created an alias is people wondering.'

'What do you think we should be?' asked Capablanca, who had been on the receiving end of Blart's stupidity more often than most and felt a twang of sympathy.

'A troupe of travelling players,' said Uther.

'You mean actors,' said Beo in disgust.

'The very same,' answered Uther. 'For travelling players are often made up of an unusual combination of men. If asked, Capablanca will be the leader of the company, who plays the narrator. Beo will be the hero's best friend. I will be the hero. And Blart will be the heroine.'

'Why can't I be the hero?' demanded Beo.

'In all the plays ever written,' said Uther, 'the hero always has a fat, funny best friend. It's one of the rules of drama. It was invented by the Greeks. You're the only fat one, so you have to play it.'

'It's all muscle really,' said Beo, but he did not protest further. Drama, he assumed, must be like chivalry, with strange rules that had to be obeyed.

'What's a heroine?' said Blart.

'The beautiful girl who wins the hero's heart,' answered Uther.

Blart grasped the implications of this.

'No, no, no, no, no!' he said, shaking his head vigorously. 'I'm never wearing a dress again.'

'You wouldn't have to,' Uther reassured him. 'We will never give a performance. We will claim that we are on our way to our next engagement and have no time to stop and perform. It is customary for the youngest boy to play the female parts for he has yet to grow hair on his face. A bearded lady would fatally undermine the audience's ability to suspend their disbelief. Do we all have our aliases and our story clear in our heads?' asked Uther.

His three companions nodded grudgingly.

Chapter 16

They travelled for five days across the Prince of Murkstan's lands, keeping away from well-travelled roads and bypassing towns for fear of encountering soldiers who might be searching for them. But despite their caution, occasionally they would meet people who would ask them questions as to their names and their business. Uther's answer that they were a group of travelling players seemed to satisfy everyone. Sometimes people would ask if they were performing nearby so that they could come and watch them. Uther explained that sadly they did not have the time as they were rushing to Illyria to perform in front of King Philidor the Happy and his Queen and their daughter, Princess Lois. The people they met accepted this, for they understood that to perform in front of a king was a great honour for a troupe of players and they wished them luck.

And so, after five days of arduous travel, the companions finally came within sight of the friendliest kingdom in the entire world, Illyria. But before they could enter the kingdom they had to negotiate the Prince's border crossing. As they approached, two fierce-looking guards emerged from a sentry post.

'Stop in the name of the Prince.'

Obediently Blart, Capablanca, Uther and Beo stopped.

The two guards approached them. One pointed his halberd at them while the other aimed his lance. The effect was far from friendly.

'State your business in the name of the Prince and be quick about it,' ordered the guard with the halberd.

'We are nought but a humble troupe of players,' said Uther. 'We are travelling to Elysium in Illyria to perform at the command of King Philidor.'

'Have you got anything to declare?' demanded the guard with the lance.

'Nothing but our love of drama,' answered Uther.

'Why is the fat one carrying such a big sword?'

Beo bristled at this gratuitous insult but Capablanca placed a stern arm on his shoulder to calm him down.

'Tis but a prop,' said Uther. 'A puny thing made from the flimsiest metal. It would shatter into a thousand pieces were it ever to be used in real combat.'

'It looks very thick and powerful to me,' observed the guard with the lance.

'Theatre is all about illusion,' explained Uther. 'What seems to be thick and strong is often weak and flimsy.'

'Hmm,' said the guard with the halberd.

The guards pushed past Uther and approached Blart, Capablanca and Beo. They walked around them slowly.

'What part do you play?' said the guard with the lance to Blart.

'He plays the heroine,' said Uther.

'He can answer for himself,' said the guard.

'I play the heroine,' repeated Blart.

'I pity the hero,' observed the guard with the halberd.

The guard with the lance laughed at the cruel taunt.

'We are on the lookout for a group of desperate men, boy,' continued the guard. 'They have defied an order to surrender and stolen the uniforms of soldiers. We have been ordered to take them dead or alive. Have you seen them?'

'What do they look like?' asked Blart.

'They look desperate,' snapped the guard. 'They are probably armed to the teeth and have the strength of ten men.'

'I don't think I've seen them,' said Blart.

The guard stared hard at Blart. Blart held his breath. The guard turned to his comrade and they moved a small distance away, where they could talk without being heard.

'They know something,' hissed Blart to Capablanca. 'Let's make a run for the border.'

'Stay calm,' whispered back Capablanca. 'They don't know anything. Any moment now they will let us through. If we do nothing we will attract no attention.'

'Do as the wizard said, you little oaf,' ordered Beo quietly, 'or –'

'I'll cleave you in two?' suggested Blart.

Beo's brow darkened at Blart's impudence.

The guards returned from their brief discussion.

'You can pass through the border,' the guard with the halberd informed them.

'Thank you, sir,' said Uther.

'Not so fast,' said the guard with the lance. 'You can go through the border after you have paid the tax.'

'Tax?' It was now the turn of Uther's brow to darken, for he was a merchant and hated any form of tax. 'I did not know that there was a border tax in these lands.'

'It's recently been introduced,' said the guard with the lance.

'With very little publicity,' added the guard with the halberd.

'It's a stealth tax,' explained the guard with the lance.

'I see.'

Now Uther understood. What the guards really meant was they wanted a bribe. Uther much preferred bribes to taxes. You could haggle with bribes.

'What is the price of this "tax"?' he asked.

'One sword,' answered the guard with the lance.

'From a fat man,' added the guard with the halberd.

'No one takes my sword,' bristled Beo angrily.

'How about a dagger?' said Uther, beginning the process of haggling to distract the guards from Beo's outrage.

'A sword,' said the guard.

'Two daggers and a lump of lard.'

Idly, Blart wondered why Uther seemed to carry such a large amount of lard on his person.

'A sword,' repeated the guard. 'Now hand it over, fat man.'

The guards approached Beo. Beo stared menacingly back at the guards.

'Give it here,' said the guard with the halberd.

Beo obeyed. First he offered his sword to the guard with the lance. Unfortunately, he did this point first with a rather over-enthusiastic thrust and it went straight through the guard's heart. Having been unsuccessful in this attempt to hand over his weapon, Beo withdrew his sword and offered it to the guard with the halberd. Beo offered it with a slashing motion that, regrettably, severed the guard's head from the rest of his body.

Both guards lay on the ground, bloody and dead.

'Ow! My elbow!' cried Beo, dropping his sword in pain. 'I forgot my ailment in my anger.'

'I thought the idea was not to attract attention,' said Capablanca with a marked lack of sympathy.

'They won't tell anybody anything,' claimed Beo, nursing his sore arm.

'Dead bodies attract attention,' pointed out Capablanca. And as he spoke, above them, high in the sky, two black dots began circling.

'We could bury them,' suggested Beo.

'Guards vanishing attract attention.'

'Look, wizard,' said Beo. 'I don't think that you're seeing this from my point of view. I'm a warrior.'

'You're a fool,' hissed Capablanca. 'All this time we had travelled undetected and now, just as we're approaching the Illyrian border, you start killing people. Now, come on! We must seek sanctuary in Illyria before the bodies are discovered.'

And so leaving the bodies to the vultures they pushed on past the border of the Prince's land. Two hundred paces later they found themselves at the Illyrian border.

'Welcome,' said the border guard, lifting the barrier.

'Hello,' said Capablanca.

'Now, are any of you smuggling in contraband?' asked the guard.

'Of course not,' said Capablanca.

'Of course you aren't,' said the border guard. 'Live and let live is what I say. Would you like some fruit?'

'That's very kind of you,' said Capablanca, taking a pear.

'Thank you,' said Beo, taking an apple.

'I'd forgotten how much I hated this place,' said Blart, spurning an orange.

For the next two days they travelled across Illyria. As on their previous visit all the people they encountered greeted them with warm smiles and gifts of fruit. Uther had never visited Illyria before and was affronted by the generosity of its people.

'But if nobody sells anything,' he questioned, 'how does anybody make a profit? How does the economy remain lean and dynamic? How can a businessman like myself make an honest crown?'

'Or a dishonest one,' said Beo, who felt that trade was unchivalrous.

'Where's the margin in giving?' demanded Uther. 'Where's the incentive to get up in the morning and get ahead of the others?'

'They have different incentives to get them up in the morning,' said Capablanca.

'Like what?' demanded Uther.

'Like living in peace, friendship and harmony,' explained Capablanca. 'And working selflessly for the benefit of each other and the general good of society.'

Uther shook his head violently.

'That can't work,' he insisted.

'It's been working for hundreds of years,' said Capablanca. 'King Philidor the Happy is the thirty-eighth monarch to sit on the Illyrian throne. They have all presided over a benevolent society. Truly Illyria is a beacon of hope to the world.'

'It's subversive. It should be made illegal,' expostulated a furious Uther.

'Especially the fruit,' said Blart, agreeing with Uther. 'The fruit really gets on my nerves.'

Chapter 17

'May I present Capablanca the Wizard, Beo the Warrior, Uther the Merchant and Blart the …'

The servant turned round to Blart.

'What are you?' he asked him.

'I am a pig boy,' said Blart.

It must be said in Blart's defence that whereas many people would be ashamed of their humble origins in the presence of royalty, Blart positively revelled in his.

'And Blart the Pig Boy.'

With a fanfare of trumpets they were ushered into the glorious golden throne room, at the end of which sat the King and Queen of Illyria. The four companions marched across the marbled floor, their footsteps echoing around them, until they stood right in front of the King and Queen. They bowed low.

'Welcome friends of Illyria,' said the King. 'We are delighted to see you returning to our kingdom.'

'Would you like some fruit?' suggested the Queen,

indicating a bowl of apples, pears, oranges and other fruits.

'No fruit,' said Blart.

'He has a stomach ailment, Your Majesty,' improvised Capablanca hastily. 'But the rest of us would love some fruit.'

Capablanca, Beo and Uther each somewhat reluctantly selected a piece of fruit.

'Now what brings you to Illyria?' said the King.

'Well –' began Capablanca.

He was interrupted by a mighty crash as the throne room door was hurled open. Blart, Capablanca, Uther and Beo turned round to see five foot two of red-headed boiling fury stomp into the room.

They stood face to face with the only grumpy damsel in Illyria … Princess Lois.

'I don't want to get married to any of them,' she announced to the assembled company. 'Not now. Not ever.'

'Hello, dear,' said the Queen.

'Never, never, never!' shouted Princess Lois. 'I don't want to get married and that's final.'

'But you are our only child,' protested the King. 'You must ensure that the royal line of the Philidors continues and that the kingdom of Illyria continues to be ruled wisely.'

'I'm not getting married and I'm not having children and I don't care about the kingdom of Illyria,' the Princess informed the King.

'Hear, hear,' muttered Uther, who as we know was fundamentally opposed to the kingdom of Illyria.

Princess Lois focused her piercing brown eyes upon him.

'Who asked you?' she demanded.

'Er … nobody.'

'Exactly,' said Princess Lois. 'So keep your miserable opinions to yourself.'

'Look who's come to visit us, my dear,' said the King. 'It is Capablanca, Beo and Blart, whom you travelled with on your quest.'

Princess Lois seemed to notice her former comrades for the first time.

'Isn't that nice?' added the Queen.

'I'm not marrying any of them either,' announced Princess Lois.

'That wasn't quite …' began the King.

But it was too late. Princess Lois turned round and marched out of the throne room, slamming the door behind her.

'She's a damsel in distress,' Blart pointed out to Beo. 'Why don't you go and help her?'

Beo seemed to grow a little paler.

'Dinner is served,' said a servant in an appropriately sonorous voice, and much to Beo's obvious relief.

Chapter 18

Dinner was served in the vast state dining room. As the King and Queen explained to Capablanca, it wasn't so much that they liked eating in such palatial grandeur, but that it meant a lot to the servants. The dining room was adorned with carvings of every fruit known to man and was dominated by a great oak dining table.

'That last quest just doesn't appear to have done the trick for Princess Lois,' said the King, putting a piece of succulent melon into his mouth.

'Not that we're blaming you, Capablanca,' said the Queen, swallowing a juicy segment of grapefruit.

The King and Queen both looked at Capablanca with the air of people who really were blaming him, but who were much too nice to say so. Evidently, Princess Lois had not returned from their last quest noticeably wiser, more considerate or with a greater love for her country and her people.

'Oh,' said Capablanca, who, if truth were told, had never been too bothered about Princess Lois's moral development, being rather more concerned with saving the world from an evil despot. Most people would have agreed with his priorities but most people were not Princess Lois's parents and didn't have to live with her door-slamming tantrums.

'We really need her to get married,' explained the King. 'At the moment the Illyrian succession hangs by a thread.'

'Perhaps she hasn't fallen in love,' said Capablanca awkwardly.

'But we have provided her with suitors from every corner of Illyria,' said the Queen, 'and she has rejected all that she has met so far.'

'Mmm,' said Capablanca, who was very uneasy with this talk of emotions.

'Could you marry her against her will?' suggested Beo from the opposite end of the table. 'Then she'd be a damsel in distress and I could rescue her.'

'If you were prepared to marry her against her will,' added Uther, 'I would be able to find you many a baron who would pay a pretty price to marry into royalty.'

The King and Queen reeled back in horror.

'Marry her against her will!' expostulated the King.

'They do it everywhere else with princesses,' pointed out Beo.

'Sell her?!' The Queen was aghast.

'My commission would be very reasonable,' said Uther.

'No!' said the King firmly. 'I could never do that.'

'Our daughter will only marry the man she chooses,'

agreed the Queen.

'If people marry only the people they want to marry then nobody would marry at all,' protested Uther. 'Marriage is naught but a business transaction with flowery dresses.'

'Marriage is a meeting of souls,' insisted the Queen.

Uther groaned.

Fortunately his rudeness was overlooked, because at that very moment the King's steward entered the dining room with a large staff that he banged repeatedly on the marble floor until there was silence.

'I do think he could just cough,' said the Queen quietly to her husband.

'Sssh,' said the King. 'We don't want to upset him.'

'Your Majesties, honoured guests and pig boys,' announced the steward. 'An emissary from the Prince of Murkstan has arrived. He wishes to see you.'

'Could it possibly wait until after dinner?' asked the King. 'I am engaged at the moment in trying to secure the future of the Philidor line.'

The steward shook his head.

'The emissary insisted he should be seen immediately.'

Normal kings do not get bossed about by mere emissaries. But King Philidor was far more accommodating than a normal king.

'Well, if he says it's important then I'm sure it is,' said the King. 'Bring him in.'

'No, Your Majesty,' said Capablanca urgently. 'I am afraid

that we left Murkstan after a little misunderstanding involving some border guards. Perhaps it would be better if you were to see the emissary alone.'

'Nonsense,' said the King, dismissing Capablanca's suggestion with an airy wave. 'If there was some little misunderstanding then we can clear it up as well as hear the emissary's message. All are friends around the King of Illyria's table. Bring him in. We will sort out these misunderstandings over a raspberry compote.'

The steward banged his staff extremely loudly three times on the great dining-room floor.

'I'm coming round to your view about the coughing, my dear,' winced the King.

'Lord Bling, Emissary for the Prince of Murkstan,' announced the steward.

In strode Lord Bling. He wore a gold coat and gold breeches and a gold chain around his neck.

'Greetings, Lord Bling,' said the King.

'The Prince is well, I trust,' said the Queen.

Lord Bling shook his head.

'The Prince is angry, ma'am,' he replied firmly. 'Angry and distressed. There has been foul play in the Principality.'

'Oh dear,' said the King.

'Two of his finest border guards have been murdered.'

'No,' said the Queen in horror.

'Murdered,' repeated Lord Bling, raising his finger to emphasise the word. 'And the Prince demands justice.'

'Quite,' said the King. 'Well, you may tell the Prince that I will obviously support his call for justice, though I would always advise that justice is tempered with understanding and a plan for rehabilitation.'

Lord Bling shook his head again.

'These murderers cannot be rehabilitated, for they face a sentence of death.'

'Death is a bar to rehabilitation,' conceded the King.

'For these murders are not their only crimes,' said the emissary. 'For in the lands of the Duke of Northwestmoreland they did attack a cohort of soldiers and humiliate the captain, and they were also party to the sinister disappearance of a modest and shy girl in a red dress. Everywhere they go they leave innocent victims in their wake.'

'They do seem to be ruffians,' agreed the King.

'But there is worse,' said Lord Bling dramatically.

'Worse!' said the Queen. 'Surely there can be no worse.'

'There is, ma'am,' insisted Lord Bling. 'For they are also believed to be in league with Zoltab the Dark Lord. Such is the swathe of terror that they have carved through society that my master, the Prince, along with the Earl and the Duke, have put aside their previous disagreements and come together to form a Grand Alliance which is determined to rid the world of these evil scoundrels before they can release Zoltab's evil on the world and shroud it in everlasting darkness.'

Lord Bling paused for effect.

'Most admirable,' said the King. 'It is good when old adversaries such as the Prince, the Earl and the Duke are prepared to set aside past grudges and move on with a shared purpose. But tell me, why do you come to me with this news?'

'Because they were last reported to have headed into the lands of Illyria,' answered Lord Bling, 'and the Prince, the Earl and the Duke urge you to join them in their Grand Alliance and find these evil-doers.'

'An Illyrian is always ready to help his neighbours,' said King Philidor. 'It is one of our proudest traditions. Tell me the names of those you seek and I will see what we can do to help.'

'Their names,' proclaimed Lord Bling, unrolling a piece of parchment that he pulled out of his gold coat, 'are Capablanca the Sorcerer, Beowulf the Warrior, Uther the Merchant and Blart the Goat Boy.'

There was a prolonged embarrassed silence. Blart broke it.

'I'm a pig boy,' he said, disgruntled.

Lord Bling started in amazement at these words. Then he looked round the dining table and slowly realised that all four of the scoundrels he sought were in that very room.

'What is the meaning of this?' he demanded. 'How can it be that you, King Philidor, can welcome these criminals and offer them hospitality? I demand that you hand them over to me at once so they can be executed.'

The King looked at the Queen, who looked back

helplessly. As good Illyrians they prided themselves on their friendship, hospitality and obliging nature towards their visitors, always going that extra furlong to ensure a guest's wants were seen too. However, when one guest asked for one's other guests to be handed over so they could be put to death it posed something of a social dilemma.

'These cannot be the men you seek,' protested the King. 'I know they are enemies of Zoltab.'

'Then why did they save him?' demanded the emissary.

'But they captured him,' maintained the King.

'Who told you that?' demanded Lord Bling.

'They did,' said the King.

'Aha!' said Lord Bling, feeling sure that he had spotted a flaw in the King's argument. 'They could have been lying. The enemies of Zoltab are famous for it.'

'That is true,' conceded the King.

'But our daughter, Princess Lois, travelled with them,' maintained the Queen. 'And she told us that they captured Zoltab too. So there must be some mistake.'

Lord Bling's gold bracelets rattled in horror at this news.

'Your daughter is involved with these scoundrels?'

'They are not scoundrels,' protested the King.

Lord Bling shook his head.

'Your Majesty, I can hear no more of these protestations. I am empowered by the Prince, the Duke and the Earl, henceforth to be known as The Grand Alliance of the Prince, the Duke and the Earl – though the Grand Alliance is a permissible shortening when time is pressing – to demand that you hand over these miscreants along with your daughter, whom I now know to be involved.'

'I could not betray my own daughter,' said the King.

'Or our dinner guests,' added the Queen.

Lord Bling drew himself up to his full height.

'Then I am empowered by the Grand Alliance to inform you that if you do not change your mind in a week there will be war. I bid you goodnight.'

And so saying Lord Bling turned on his heel and departed from the dining room.

'It's at times like this that you think maybe it was a mistake not to have an army,' remarked the King.

Chapter 19

'What do I do?' said the King the next morning as he sat in the throne room. Also present were Capablanca, Beo, Uther and Blart.

'You must call this Council of War to order,' explained Capablanca.

'Couldn't we use a different term?' begged the King. 'War seems such a violent expression.'

'War is violent,' interjected Beo. 'There will be corpses piled high, eyes gouged out, limbs lopped off and bleeding stumps everywhere.'

'Oh dear,' said the King.

'The plains of Illyria will echo with cries of pain, shrieks of agony, wails of despair and the tormented keening of widows.'

Beo's description of the horrors of war was tinged with a distasteful hint of relish.

'Thank you, Beo,' said Capablanca. 'Your description is more than adequate.'

'But I haven't done the piteous whimpering of the orphans yet,' said Beo.

'Leave it to our imagination,' said Capablanca firmly.

The King was ashen-faced.

'I cannot allow this to happen to my people,' he said. 'I cannot be the first King of Illyria to allow war to despoil our beautiful land. Tell me what I can do.'

'You must fight,' said Beo.

'You must pay them off,' said Uther.

'You must use cunning,' said Capablanca.

'You must run away with your pigs and leave everybody else to get killed,' said Blart. 'It's what I'd do.'

'The men of Illyria cannot fight,' said the King. 'They have never been trained. Were they to see the Grand Alliance's army rampaging towards them they would simply obey Illyrian tradition and offer them fruit.'

'Armed only with fruit,' Uther agreed, 'they would be ripe for the slaughter.'

'But we cannot pay them off either,' said the King. 'The Illyrian economy does not use money, so we have nothing to pay them with.'

'I knew you'd regret not having money sooner or later,' said Uther with unnecessary glee, considering the circumstances.

The King put his head in his hands.

'There must be something I can do.'

'You could wait,' said Capablanca.

The King looked up hopefully.

'Wait?' he said. 'I can do that.'

'This is what I advise,' said Capablanca. 'Send a messenger to the Grand Alliance, informing them that for an Illyrian to hand over his guests to a military force is a serious breach of etiquette. You will need to take the full week to reach a decision.'

'Right,' said the King. 'And when the week is gone do I hand you over?'

'No,' said Beo, Uther and Blart together.

'I only wished to know the plan,' said the King, a little taken aback.

'In a week,' said Capablanca, 'there will be no need to hand us over, for we will have proved our innocence.'

'How?' asked everybody.

'We will have discovered where Zoltab is imprisoned and demonstrated that we were not his allies but his enemies, and therefore the Grand Alliance's charges will be dropped and Illyria will be freed from the fear of invasion.'

'What about the border guards I killed?' said Beo.

'And the uniforms we stole?' said Uther.

'Once we can show that Zoltab is imprisoned we will be heroes again,' Capablanca reassured them. 'And when you're a hero everybody is prepared to overlook the odd detail.'

Capablanca sat back smugly. The Council of War ruminated for a moment on his proposal. The more they thought about it, the more it seemed possible it would work.

Except …

'We don't know where Zoltab is,' exclaimed Blart.

Capablanca's smug expression disappeared.

'Always focusing on the negative, aren't you?' he snapped angrily.

'But the boy has a point,' said Beo. 'We have no clue where you imprisoned Zoltab and there is the whole world to search. What are the odds that we will find him?'

The Council of War each tried to do a mental calculation whereby they divided the entire world by seven days.

'It is hopeless,' said the King.

'Do not say that,' urged Capablanca. 'There is always hope. Events have moved so fast that we have yet to ask Princess Lois whether she has any knowledge of the whereabouts of Zoltab's prison. We must find her quickly. She may be able to send us in the right direction. What do you think, Your Majesty? Will you send the message to the Grand Alliance? Will you give us a week to save not only the kingdom of Illyria but also our own lives?'

The Council of War waited for the King's decision.

'This is a decision which may result in many deaths,' answered the King gravely, 'and I cannot take it lightly. I will consider it over a piece of fruit.'

The King selected an apple from a nearby fruit bowl and began to munch and think. Blart, Capablanca, Beo and Uther watched and waited. The King became somewhat self-conscious about eating with so many people staring at him and turned away.

Finally, King Philidor swallowed his last bite of apple and discarded the core.

'Steward!' he shouted.

The King's steward, who had been waiting at the door, entered the throne room.

'Your Majesty?'

'Send a message to the Grand Alliance,' commanded the King. 'Tell them that I will hand over those they seek in a week.'

The search for Zoltab was on once more.

Chapter 20

It was agreed that Capablanca and Blart were the two people best placed to explain the situation to Princess Lois.

They found her sitting on a terrace outside the palace, where she was amusing herself by spinning a large key on her finger.

'Go away,' she said when she saw them approaching.

Capablanca shook his head.

'We cannot go, Princess, for we need your help most urgently. The future of us all is at stake.'

Princess Lois yawned.

'Listen,' said Capablanca and as briefly as possible he explained the dire situation that they faced. 'I must ask you to think back deeply into your memory and tell me whether you have any clue as to where I might have imprisoned Zoltab.'

Princess Lois considered Capablanca's request.

'I'll help you if you help me.'

'What do you want me to do?' he asked.

'I don't want to get married,' said Princess Lois.

The wizard, who had feared some difficult assignment, was delighted by the surprising ease of the task the Princess had given him.

'You don't have to,' he responded with alacrity. 'The King and Queen are adamant that you will only marry when you freely give your consent.'

'I haven't finished yet,' continued the Princess. 'Not only do I not want to get married, I do not wish to be repeatedly courted. I have had to put up with a pathetic stream of soppy boys all telling me how pretty my eyes are and how sweet my smile is and how fair my face is —'

'But your face isn't fair,' interrupted Blart. 'You've got freckles.'

'I know I've got freckles, weasel-features,' said the Princess. 'I happen to like them. But the blubbering fools whom my parents want me to marry think that a girl is only happy when her face is as white and boring as a piece of paper, so they lie to me.'

'I think it's called a compliment,' corrected Capablanca.

'I hate it. If you can get rid of all these suitors then I will help you, and until you do I won't.'

With that the Princess turned her back and continued to twirl the large key on her finger.

Capablanca sighed.

'I'll see what I can do.'

The wizard shuffled into the palace, shaking his head.

Blart and Princess Lois looked at each other.

'Let me tell you some interesting things about pigs,' began Blart.

Fifty-three interesting things about pigs later, the wizard returned. He had spoken to the King and Queen and found a way of bringing the wooing to an end forthwith. The Queen accompanied him to explain this new development to the current contender for her hand. She was surprised not to see him in attendance.

'Princess Lois,' she demanded. 'Pray tell me, where is Anatoly the Handsome?'

'I don't know,' shrugged the Princess.

'Why isn't he here taking advantage of the romantic setting to liken your complexion to the roses that bloom all around?'

The Princess shrugged again.

'This is most unusual,' said the Queen. 'I am always loath to criticise anyone but the young man assured me that he would spend all morning courting you and now he's not … Lois, what are you doing with that key?'

'Oh, the key,' said the Princess, who seemed to notice it for the first time. 'Nothing.'

For those who have never visited Illyria it may be appropriate at this juncture to explain why seeing a key in the possession of the Princess had so piqued the interest of the Queen. It was because the Illyrians, as well as being the happiest and the most generous, are also the most trusting people in the world and they do not have locks on any of their doors. The one exception to this is the great diamond-encrusted tower that stands in the centre of the city of Elysium. Because this tower contained the map that revealed the whereabouts of the Great Tunnel of Despair where Zoltab had originally been imprisoned, it had been granted a door with a key. The only key in Illyria. Which for some reason the Princess now held in her hand.

'Lois,' said the Queen. 'Is it possible that you have some-how managed to trick Anatoly the Handsome into entering the Great Tower of Elysium and then locked him in?'

'It's possible,' conceded the Princess nonchalantly.

'Please hand over the key,' said the Queen. 'Why, if it were to get about that a visitor to Illyria was locked up in a tower the shame would be unendurable.'

'I could endure it,' said the Princess.

'So could I,' said Blart.

'Nobody asked you, stoat-face,' said the Princess.

The Queen took the opportunity provided by Blart's distraction to deftly slip the large key off the Princess's finger. She immediately disappeared to liberate Princess Lois's unfortunate suitor.

'Princess,' said Capablanca urgently as soon as the Queen was out of earshot. 'I have spoken to your father, the King, and he has agreed that wooing is cancelled forthwith. Now, did I give you any clue of where I imprisoned Zoltab? Any clue at all?'

The Princess thought hard.

'No,' she said.

'Zounds,' cursed Capablanca. 'You were our last hope, the last of the original questors who captured Zoltab. If you do not know then our chances of finding him are nil and we are all doomed.'

'She isn't the last questor,' said Blart.

'Of course she's the last questor,' said Capablanca. 'Unless you mean Tungsten the Dwarf, who died in the Terrorsium a year ago and is therefore no use at all. Not that we don't miss him, obviously,' he added lamely.

The Princess stood up.

'Where are you going?' asked Capablanca.

'I cannot help you,' said the Princess. 'And now I don't have any suitors to follow me round, I'm going out.'

'Ah,' said Capablanca awkwardly. 'Perhaps I should tell you that the wooing was cancelled because I informed the King and Queen that you are the only person who knows the location of Zoltab's prison and if you do not accompany us then we will be unable to find him and prove ourselves innocent of the charge of being Zoltab's allies and save the country of Illyria in the process.'

'But I don't know where Zoltab is,' said the Princess.

'If you were to admit that,' said the wizard, 'then the wooing would start once more. The only way for you to remain unwooed is to accompany us on our quest.'

'But I can't help,' said the Princess.

'Neither can I,' said Blart, 'but I've got to go.'

'You must come, Princess,' urged Capablanca. 'Fate and Destiny seem determined to reunite all of us and we must assume that they are doing so for a reason. And if you don't come you'll soon be being wooed again.'

Princess Lois stood for a moment weighing up her options.

'I suppose I'll come, then,' she said finally.

'Good,' said Capablanca.

Blart took the opportunity to say, 'It wasn't Tungsten I was talking about when I said the Princess was the last questor. I was going to say …'

At that moment Anatoly the Handsome appeared on the terrace. He was tall and he was dark. He had soulful eyes and a sensitive mouth. He had a fine brow on top of which sat a fine head of elegantly tousled hair. He had a noble bearing and an attitude of relaxed confidence.

'My beautiful Princess,' began Anatoly plaintively, 'some cruel force has recently separated us and each second we have spent apart has seemed like a minute, each minute has seemed like an hour …'

The Princess raised her eyes in suffering.

'But what is worse,' continued Anatoly, 'I hear that you no longer wish to receive my suit. This can be no more than natural modesty, which must for decorum's sake pretend to rebuff my ardour.'

'I'm not pretending,' the Princess assured him.

'But,' continued Anatoly, 'is it not sweeter to taste a pear which has dangled for a while tantalisingly out of reach than to pick one which lies on the ground available to all?'

The Princess's brown eyes gleamed with fury.

'You'd better not be comparing me to fruit,' she warned.

Oblivious to the warning signs, Anatoly rushed forward and knelt at her feet.

'But I must compare thee to fruit,' he protested, 'for you are sweet and smooth and full of nature's bounty. And if it would not make you blush let me say that like the juiciest of fruit you are ripe for the picking.'

Princess Lois stared down at Anatoly.

'It won't make me blush,' she told him. 'But it might make me hit you.'

'A hit from your ruby red lips is all I desire,' said Anatoly, closing his eyes and puckering his own mouth in expectation.

A moment later Anatoly lay flat on his back and his nose, that was neither too big nor too small, too wide nor too thin, was pouring with blood.

'Lois!'

The King and Queen appeared on the terrace just as their daughter was admiring her handiwork.

'Assaulting your suitor is against all Illyrian tradition,' the King told her.

'She's merely playing hard to get,' said Anatoly the Handsome as he applied a handkerchief to his bleeding nose.

'She's playing it well,' said Blart.

Fearing a prolonged argument, Capablanca butted in. 'As

soon as the Princess departs on our quest these unIllyrian displays will cease.'

'But I'll miss her,' said Anatoly the Handsome, dropping a blood-sodden handkerchief on to the terrace.

'Absence makes the heart grow fonder,' counselled the Queen.

'Has anyone a spare handkerchief?' asked the bleeding suitor. 'Mine is full of blood and all I have to staunch my wounds is this piece of parchment that I picked up in the tower.'

From his pocket Anatoly pulled a piece of parchment and made to wipe his nose with it.

'Stop!' ordered Capablanca.

'But I'm bleeding,' protested Anatoly.

'Any parchment that was found in the Great Tower of Elysium must have enormous significance,' Capablanca told him. 'Hand it to me immediately.'

Anatoly handed over the parchment.

'Aha!' said Capablanca. 'Just as I thought. There is writing upon it.'

'What does it say?' asked the King.

'It is written in an ancient language,' explained Capablanca with a rueful shake of his head, 'which only the most educated and intelligent people in the world would be able to understand.'

'So you don't know what it says?' asked the Queen.

'It so happens I can read it,' he said reproachfully. 'But

you must wait a moment whilst I decipher it.'

Everybody dutifully waited a moment.

'I have it!' exclaimed Capablanca, and slowly he began to read:

> *'There will come a time when friends are enemies and enemies*
> *are friends*
> *When Zoltab, twice imprisoned, may once more be freed*
> *To destroy the world or be defeated*
> *By the hand of the husband of his betrothed.'*

Capablanca looked up.

'What does it mean?' asked the King.

'Not all of it is clear even to a great prophecy reader like myself,' said Capablanca. ' "*The husband of his betrothed*", for example, is a most unusual phrase. It would suggest that Zoltab can only defeat himself.'

'That means he doesn't understand,' translated Blart, jabbing a thumb at the wizard.

Capablanca gave Blart yet another in a long series of threatening looks, none of which had any effect on him.

'But what is clear is that it is foretold that Zoltab will be freed again,' explained Capablanca with much concern in his voice. 'Last time he was freed he was determined to destroy the world. We prevented that on our last quest. But if he were to escape again then things would undoubtedly be worse.'

'Worse?' repeated the King and Queen.

'Undoubtedly,' said Capablanca. 'This time he'd be angry.'

The terrace was reduced to a fearful silence as they all wondered how terrible the return of Zoltab would be.

Anatoly the Handsome had never heard of Zoltab, so he broke the fearful silence first.

'Princess,' he said, wiping away the last of the blood from his nose. 'Now I have been fortunate enough to have received your fist may I one day hope to gain your hand?'

'The only thing you'll gain from my hand is a slap,' snapped the Princess.

The Queen put her hands over her ears.

The King sighed and muttered that a challenging journey might be just what the Princess's baffling attitude was in need of.

Early next morning, before the dawn had broken, the Princess rode out of Illyria alongside Blart, Capablanca, Uther and Beo. All the questors were reunited. Or were they? Had not Blart said that there was a questor missing? But what did Blart know? He was nothing but a pig boy. Surely he could not be right and Capablanca wrong?

Chapter 21

The sun rose as they crossed the north-eastern border of Illyria. The questors felt the rays of the distant golden orb pierce their cold bones and give them a sense of new purpose and hope.

Then it started raining.

They reached a crossroads. Capablanca held up his hand.

'Look carefully around you,' he said. 'For we must surely have passed this set of crossroads on our way back to Illyria from the dread land of the Terrorsium. Concentrate hard. Any brief flash of memory may set us on the right road to Zoltab's prison.'

The questors concentrated hard. They got wetter.

'I remember,' said Beo at last.

'What?' said Capablanca.

'This was where we split up,' agreed Princess Lois.

''Twas here that you bade us leave you to the task of disposing of Zoltab,' Beo began. 'You told me to escort the Princess and that horrible boy to the court of King Philidor without killing him on the way. Then you said I was to tell the King all that had happened whilst you would deliver Zoltab to the place where he would be eternally imprisoned.'

'Did I say where I was going?' demanded Capablanca.

Beo shook his head.

'Did any of you see which direction I took?'

'You told us not to,' said Princess Lois. 'You warned us that any clue could help the minions of Zoltab when they came to search for him. You waited until we had set off for Illyria before you departed.'

'Didn't one of you take a sneaky peak behind you to see which way I went?' asked Capablanca desperately.

'I did,' said Blart.

'Excellent,' said Capablanca, grasping Blart's shoulder with unusual warmth. 'So which direction did I go?'

'I've forgotten.'

'What?' said Capablanca and his fingers dug into Blart's shoulder.

'Ow!' said Blart, twisting his body free. 'It's not my fault. I can't remember what happens every time I don't do what people say. There isn't enough room in my head.'

'Perhaps I could make more room in your head,' suggested Beo, gripping the base of his sword in a most threatening way, 'by cleaving it in two.'

'You've got Warrior's Elbow,' Blart reminded him. 'You can't cleave anything.'

'I have it no more,' answered Beo. 'The rest in Illyria has

cured the pain and I am now ready to cleave all those who offend me.'

'Oh,' said Blart.

Beo eyed him threateningly.

'He's going to kill you, Blart,' Princess Lois explained cheerfully, just in case Blart hadn't noticed.

'He can't,' protested Blart.

'I think he can,' said Princess Lois. 'He's had lots of practice killing other people.'

'But I'm just a boy,' wailed Blart. 'And I'm defenceless.'

'Just the way I like 'em,' said Beo gruffly.

'But I can help on the quest.'

'I don't think you can.'

'I have seen no evidence,' agreed Uther.

'I know that there's one questor who isn't here and who might remember where Zoltab is imprisoned,' protested Blart.

'You are a fool, boy,' Beo told him. 'All the surviving members of our quest are here. And they can all watch you die.'

'Pig the Horse isn't,' said Blart quickly.

Capablanca looked up suddenly.

'What did you say?'

'More of his nonsense,' Beo assured the wizard.

'Repeat it,' demanded Capablanca.

'I said Pig the Horse isn't here.'

Capablanca, so recently slumped in an attitude of defeat,

was now on his feet.

'The boy has something,' he said. 'Pig the Horse must have carried Zoltab and me to his new prison. He will know where it is.'

'Do we know where this horse is?' asked Uther.

'No,' said the Princess. 'But even if we did he couldn't help. Pig the Horse can fly but he can't talk.'

'He could guide us though,' mused Capablanca.

'But we don't know where he is,' Princess Lois reminded him.

'We may be able to find him,' said Capablanca. 'The Great Spell of Fog that I cast upon my own memory only blanks out what I did with Zoltab. My memory is unaffected from the moment when I returned to the Cavernous Library of Ping and was received by a special committee of wizards.'

'What happened then?' asked Princess Lois.

Capablanca puffed out his chest with pride.

'All the wizards present, even those who had previously been my enemies, were forced to admit that I had saved the world.'

'I thought I saved the world,' said Blart.

'I thought we were in this mess because it turns out nobody had saved the world,' remarked Uther.

Capablanca looked peeved at having his glorious memories clouded by inconvenient facts.

'At the time,' he insisted, 'everybody thought I had saved the world and the wizards declared three days of feasting to celebrate my achievement and announced that I would have a commemorative chair placed in the Cavernous Library of Ping, which would be made to measure by the finest furniture makers to ensure it was shaped precisely to fit the contours of my buttocks, so I never again would suffer discomfort during my research.'

'You had a chair named after you,' said Blart scornfully.

'It was my finest hour,' remembered Capablanca wistfully. 'Just as it was my lowest moment when, after the discovery of my slight misunderstanding in the case of Zoltab's prophecy, the wizards on the Oversight Committee had the chair chopped into firewood and burnt. But I promise you that one day those furniture makers will once again have to take precise measurements of my buttocks and build an even grander chair.'

'When I asked what happened,' said the Princess, who had heard far more about the wizard's buttocks in the last couple of minutes than she ever wanted to, 'I meant what happened to Pig the Horse.'

'What?' said Capablanca. 'Ah yes. Pig the Horse. He too was honoured by the committee. With a special pain-free spell they branded a sign on his forehead which was to tell all wizards that he was never to be captured again, and then he was given his freedom.'

'A chair for you and a mark on his forehead for Pig the Horse,' said Blart. 'You wizards are pretty mean when it comes to rewards.'

127

'It is not the value of the reward that matters,' explained Capablanca. 'It is the significance of those who award it in the eyes of the world. A whole kingdom given to you by a fool is less valuable than a medal given by a genius.'

'There are those who would disagree with your understanding of economics,' observed Uther. 'But tell me, what was the mark the wizards branded on to Pig's forehead?'

'It was unmistakable,' Capablanca told him. 'It was a flash of red lightning. No other horse in the world would have it.'

'Why do you want to know?' said Blart, noticing that Uther, who was usually a confident man, seemed to be a fidgeting a little nervously.

'I may be able to help you find this horse,' said Uther. 'But if I am to help then I want your word that nobody will harm me for my part in what I am about to tell you.'

The questors looked hard at Uther.

'You have our word,' said Capablanca suspiciously.

'You must understand that I was merely an agent in this matter,' said Uther warily.

'Get on with it, merchant,' urged Beo menacingly.

'Just less than a year ago I came across an old acquaintance of mine in a seedy tavern in Murkstan. By profession he was a horse trader and he told me that he had recently acquired, from a source he refused to divulge, the most interesting piece of horseflesh it had ever been his fortune to discover – a flying horse.'

Simultaneously the questors had a sharp intake of breath.

'He told me that he had a problem,' continued Uther. 'For though the horse was unique he could not think of how to sell it in order to get the best price.'

'Surely a rich man would have paid a vast quantity of gold for a flying horse,' said Beo.

'That is where you are wrong, warrior,' said Uther. 'My acquaintance had approached certain rich lords and barons and offered to sell them the horse, but he had been rebuffed. Nobody wished to take the risk of riding a horse that could at any moment take off and then fly higher and higher into the sky until its rider was roasted alive by the rays of the sun.

'So I asked to see the horse,' Uther continued, 'and my acquaintance agreed. He led me through a warren of tiny streets and alleys before we came to a rough stable. Inside was tethered this great horse. My acquaintance threw open the stable door and flashed a lantern on the noble steed. Immediately I saw the red lightning fork flashing on its forehead —'

'It was Pig.'

'Immediately I saw Pig,' said Uther, 'I knew where there would be a market for him.'

'Where?' asked Blart.

'The circus.'

'The circus,' shouted Princess Lois in outrage. 'How dare you?'

'I agree,' said Capablanca. 'That our former comrade,

125

who rescued us from the Terrorsium, should have to suffer such indignities is outrageous.'

'His dishonour should be avenged,' said Beo, raising his sword again.

'Now, now, now,' said Uther quickly. 'Remember that each of you has given me your word that you will not hurt me. I did not know that this Pig was your friend.'

'Tell us what happened next,' the wizard ordered Uther.

'It was a simple enough transaction for a skilled deal-maker such as myself,' said Uther immodestly. 'Outside the town there was a circus. I suggested to the owner he come and see something that would make his circus the envy of all others. He came, he saw Pig – the red flash of lightning on the horse's head particularly impressed him.'

'How terrible,' remarked Capablanca, 'that a mark of honour from wizards should be seen as nothing more than a tawdry temptation to a showman.'

'And then,' said Uther, 'after a little persuasion, Pig flew.'

'When you say "persuasion" you mean that you whipped him,' snapped Princess Lois and there were tears of anger in her eyes.

'Whatever was needed to smooth the wheels of business was done,' replied Uther calmly.

'You will pay for each of those cruel strokes one day,' the Princess told him bitterly.

'But I don't understand,' said Blart. 'Why didn't Pig just fly away?'

'It was really quite ingenious,' began Uther and then, remembering who his audience consisted of, he stopped and began again.

'It was really quite cruel,' he said. 'I'm shocked by the depravity of these circus folk.'

'Get on with it,' growled Beo.

'The shameful practice,' said Uther, 'consisted of tying Pig the Horse down at all times.'

'But then he couldn't fly,' said Blart. 'I wouldn't pay to see a horse that couldn't fly. You can just go to a field to see that.'

'There was enough slack in the rope,' explained Uther, 'for Pig to fly to the height of the big top. He would then circle over the audiences' heads, ridden by Sheba the Fearless, a daredevil bareback rider, who would guide him around hoops of fire that she would jump through. So you see, Pig could use his flying skills to entertain the crowd while at the same time never ever being able to use his skills to escape.'

'Poor Pig,' lamented Princess Lois.

'What was the name of the circus?' asked Capablanca.

'The Beserker Circus.'

'The Beserker Circus?' said Princess Lois. 'They passed through Illyria only last week. They were heading north-east to the land of Cumbrianstar.'

'What are we waiting for?' said Capablanca. 'Let us ride north-east and rescue our comrade.'

Chapter 22

'ROLL UP! ROLL UP! Tonight and tomorrow night in Gibb's Field will be your only chance to witness the most spectacular, the most extraordinary piece of entertainment ever seen in this or any other part of the world. Bring your wives. Bring your children. Bring your neighbours to the Beserker Circus.'

The big fat man banged his drum.

'We have jugglers.'

Bang.

'We have clowns.'

Bang.

'We have acrobats.'

Bang.

'And topping the bill is the one and only Diablo the Flying Horse.'

Bang. Bang. Bang.

With whoops and cheers the circus parade moved on down the main street of the town of Hookteryard. Children ran behind the parade, screaming with excitement. Their parents waved and cheered. The townsfolk stared out of windows at all the colour and bustle.

The questors watched the parade disappear down the narrow road. They had ridden hard for a day and a half to catch up with the circus.

'It's the wrong horse,' said Blart as the tail end of the parade vanished.

'What do you mean the wrong horse?' said Capablanca.

'Their horse is called Diablo. Our horse was called Pig. We've found the wrong horse.'

'Or they've changed his name, stoat-face,' said Princess Lois.

After asking directions Capablanca set off purposefully towards Gibb's Field. Within a quarter of an hour, the questors found themselves on the outskirts of Hookteryard, looking out over Gibb's Field at a big tent that was obviously used for the circus. Near the tent there were carts and tables and various circus folk chatting and shouting, but there was no sign of Pig the Horse.

'We must ask someone,' said Uther.

'Who?' said Capablanca.

'I will find someone but it would be better if we did not all go into the field at once. Such a large group of people may attract attention.'

Capablanca was torn. Uther's argument made sense and if anybody was going to be able to find out the location of

Pig the Horse it would be him with his wheedling ways. But Uther couldn't be trusted alone with Pig.

'You must take the Princess with you,' he told Uther.

'She will just start shouting at everybody,' said Uther, 'and I won't be able to discover anything. Let me take Blart instead.'

Capablanca looked doubtful.

'He is so gormless,' explained Uther. 'Nobody would suspect him for a moment of being up to no good.'

'That is true,' agreed Capablanca reluctantly.

Uther opened the gate and led Blart into the muddy field and towards the big tent. Nobody seemed to notice them.

'Mind the guy ropes,' said Uther.

They were now very close to the tent. One flap was suddenly thrown back and a cheerful fat woman with a very red face came out to them.

''Allo,' she said in a strange accent. 'What do you want?'

'Greetings,' said Uther, inclining his head respectfully. 'My nephew here is desperate to see the circus.'

'The show is not until this evening. Come back then. Your nephew will have a great time.'

'Excuse me,' persisted Uther, 'but is it true you have a flying horse?'

'Of course it's true,' said the fat lady. 'Do you think we are liars?'

'Of course not,' said Uther. 'But my nephew was so excited when he heard there was a flying horse. Would it be possible just to take a quick peak at the horse before we go? Just for my nephew, you understand.'

The woman began shaking her head, but Uther produced a gold coin and the shaking head began to nod.

'You can try,' said the lady, pocketing the coin. 'Simply go through the gate into Gibb's Pasture. But I don't rate your nephew's chances of getting a glimpse.'

'Why?' asked Uther.

'You'll see.'

'Come on, Blart,' said Uther. 'We must go to Gibb's Pasture.'

Blart followed Uther. They passed through the circus folk in Gibb's Field until they reached a gate that led into Gibb's Pasture. Once through the gate they appeared to be on their own. There was a tent at the far end of the field.

'They must keep Pig the Horse in there,' said Uther and he immediately started towards it. Blart reluctantly followed.

They reached the tent. Uther took a careful look to the left and a careful look to the right. Nobody.

'We must be quick,' said Uther. 'Tell me straight away if this is Pig the Horse.'

The merchant whipped back the flap of the tent. Blart looked in. There, tethered by a thick rope to a metal stake hammered firmly into the ground, was the huge black horse that had carried Blart and his fellow questors to glory a year ago. All that was different about him was the red slash of lightning branded on to his forehead.

'That's Pig,' said Blart.

'Are you sure?'

Blart nodded.

Pig whinnied and tugged at his rope in obvious distress. This was a horse that was not meant to be tethered.

Chapter 23

'Vat are you doing?'

Blart and Uther turned round. Behind them stood six huge men sporting six huge moustaches. Each wore only the briefest pair of pants and so the full power of their muscled bronzed limbs and torsos was visible for all to see.

'Vat are you doing?' repeated the man with the biggest moustache. 'Tell me now or I vill tear off your limbs and feed zem to ze lions and ze tigers.'

Blart gulped. They reminded him of Beo, but with fewer clothes.

'Hello,' said Uther. 'My nephew just wanted to catch a glimpse of the flying horse and so —'

'Nobody sees ze flying horse,' said Big Moustache. 'By order of Mr Beserker. You are brekking Mr Beserker's rules. I and my bruzzers should tear off your limbs and feed zem to ze lions and ze tigers.'

'Your brothers?' said Uther.

'My bruzzers,' said Big Moustache. 'We are ze Chigorin

137

Bruzzers, famous in our country as ze strongest strong men in ze world. We can tear off ze limbs of a grown man and –'

'Pleased to meet you,' said Uther, closing the flap of the tent and beginning to back away. 'I'll be looking forward to your act this evening.'

'You should not be here,' said Big Moustache. 'Mr Beserker tell us to guard zis horse. He tell us to guard zis horse like it is our own muzzer.'

The Chigorin Brothers each wiped a tear from their eye at the mention of their mother.

'Mr Beserker tell us zat people vill come to try and steal zis horse. He tell us zat when people come to try and steal his horse zat we should tear off ze limbs and –'

'Well, we were just going,' said Uther, continuing to back away from the Chigorin Brothers. 'We're very sorry for the inconvenience. As I say, my nephew just wanted a quick peek but obviously if that's not allowed then we'll be on our way. A simple misunderstanding. We don't want to take up any more of your valuable time.'

Uther and Blart continued to edge backwards.

'Stop!' ordered Big Moustache.

Uther and Blart stopped.

'I go and get Mr Beserker. He tell me that if zere is anybody coming near ze horse then he vants to see zem and if he don't like vot he sees zen zere will be ze tearing of ze limbs.'

'Surely there's no need for …' began Uther but he was

silenced by the huge palm of Big Moustache.

'Vait!' he ordered. 'I am going to get Mr Beserker. My bruzzers vill vatch you.'

Big Moustache stomped off towards Gibb's Field. His five remaining brothers made a circle around Blart and Uther. Each folded his arms and watched intently. It was most unnerving.

'Those are very impressive moustaches,' said Uther.

The brothers stared harder.

'Their eyes really bulge, don't they?' observed Blart.

Blart and Uther lapsed into silence. However determined a person is to have a friendly conversation with somebody, it is impossible if the other person won't try.

Presently Big Moustache returned with an angry-looking purple-faced man, who stomped across Gibb's Pasture. In his right hand he carried a whip. In his left hand he carried another whip. He was obviously a man who liked to hit things.

As he approached, the Chigorin Brothers' circle parted to allow him to get as close as possible to Uther and Blart.

'My name is Beserker,' he announced. 'This is my circus. This is my land and in that tent is my flying horse. What are you doing here?'

'My simple nephew wanted to catch a glimpse of your wonderful flying horse,' said Uther.

'Wanted to steal it more like,' snapped Beserker. 'Who sent you?

'Nobody,' insisted Uther. 'We're just interested in having

a look. It would mean a lot to my nephew.'

'A likely story,' said Beserker. 'Will you be saying the same when I've whipped you to within an inch of your lives and the Chigorin Brothers have torn off your limbs?'

'We probably wouldn't be saying much by then,' agreed Uther. 'We'd probably just be screaming.'

'And a good thing too!' yelled Beserker. 'Horse thieves should be screaming. All the time.'

'But we're not thieves,' insisted Uther.

'How do I know?' demanded Beserker. 'Prove you're innocent or I'll flay the hides off both of you.'

'Just look at my nephew,' indicated Uther. 'He's too stupid and useless to steal the most important horse in the history of circus.'

Beserker looked at Blart, who managed with no effort whatsoever to appear hopelessly stupid. For the first time a flicker of doubt ran across Beserker's brow and the colour in his face lightened slightly.

'He does look stupid and useless,' conceded Beserker.

He thought for a moment.

'But you don't look stupid and useless. You look sly and wily.'

'Appearances can be deceptive.'

'Maybe you should let me go and just tear his limbs off,' suggested Blart, who felt that the time was right to broker a compromise.

'No,' Beserker shook his head. 'I'm either tearing the

limbs off both of you or none at all.'

'May I strongly recommend you go for the second alternative,' said Uther. 'My nephew Blart is a great lover of the circus and is eager to see yours this evening, but I cannot imagine that even his devotion can withstand the forcible removal of his arms and legs.'

'Hmm,' said Beserker. 'I must think.'

Beserker thought. The Chigorin Brothers stared. Blart scratched himself.

'I am in a good mood. You may go,' announced Beserker. 'And anyway, the lions and tigers have already been fed today.'

Blart and Uther needed no further encouragement. They rushed through Gibb's Pasture, through the gate and over Gibb's Field as fast as their unremoved legs could carry them.

Chapter 24

'No' said Blart. 'No, no, no, no, no.'

'It's our only hope,' said Capablanca.

'Then we'll be hopeless,' said Blart. 'I don't mind being hopeless. Everybody has been telling me that I'm hopeless all my life and it's never done me any harm.'

'This is not a matter of you being hopeless,' said Capablanca. 'This is a matter of the whole quest being hopeless, which is a much more important matter. Now, for the last time, will you do it?'

'No,' said Blart firmly.

Blart and Capablanca turned away from each other and a sullen silence descended over the group.

Blart and Uther had returned to the other questors and informed them of the good news – that they had found Pig the Horse – and the bad news – that Pig the Horse was guarded by six strong brothers sporting bushy moustaches, who would tear the limbs off anybody who attempted to steal the horse. Capablanca had then thought long and hard and had come up with a plan that was designed to help free Pig the Horse. The plan was for Blart to run away to the circus. Capablanca explained it like this:

'Beserker has already met Blart and he has been convinced that he is a huge fan of the circus. Blart and Uther will go and see the show tonight. Afterwards Blart will pretend to give his uncle the slip and will go and find Beserker and ask if he can run away with the circus. Children are always running away with circuses – it's how they get most of their members. Blart will work very hard so that everyone in the circus likes him. Then, when everyone in the circus is asleep, Blart will sneak into the tent where Pig is being held and untie him. He will climb on Pig's back, charge out of the tent and fly him to a place where we will all be waiting. Immediately we will jump on his back and fly off to find Zoltab's prison.'

Capablanca had stopped and sat back with a satisfied smile on his face after giving all the details of this masterly plan. Blart had set his face into its most stubborn mask of rejection and said, 'No, no, no, no, no.' Which was where we came in.

'If you don't do it,' Beo threatened Blart, 'I'll cleave you in two.'

'If I do it,' Blart retorted, 'then I'll have all my limbs torn off and thrown to the lions.'

'Does it have to be Blart that goes?' asked Uther.

'Of course it does,' answered Capablanca. 'He is a young

boy, and it is only the young who run away with circuses. Adults recognise that it is far more fun to just watch circuses and then go home and put their feet up in their nice warm houses.'

'I'm young,' said Princess Lois. 'I could do it.'

'Nonsense,' said a shocked Capablanca. 'You are a princess and what is more you are a woman. I could not put royal blood in danger.'

'Forget about me being a princess. Pig is a great horse and I want to rescue him. I will do it whether it's part of your plan or not, so you might as well let me.'

'I forbid it,' insisted Beo. 'For a warrior to stand idly by while a damsel who is undistressed becomes distressed is the most heinously unchivalrous act.'

'And yet I fear it is the only solution,' said Capablanca. 'for if Blart will not do it then what choice do we have?'

'You should do it,' Beo shouted at Capablanca, 'rather than risk a wee red girl.'

'I'm not wee,' said Princess Lois angrily.

'You are a great sorcerer. Surely you could cast a spell which would allow us to sneak past these strong men and free Pig.'

The warrior's argument was powerful. All of the questors stared at Capablanca and their faces asked the same question. Why shouldn't the great wizard be able to rescue Pig?

Instead Capablanca looked most uncomfortable. He began fidgeting with his cowl.

'I was wondering when you'd notice,' he muttered.

'Notice what?' said Blart, who hadn't noticed anything.

'The thing is,' the wizard went on sheepishly, 'and it really is most embarrassing – but I am forced to confess that at the moment I am under investigation by the wizards' committee at the Cavernous Library of Ping as a result of my alleged misunderstanding of ancient scrolls and prophecies, and whilst under suspension I have had my magic powers taken away. I can no longer cast any spells whatsoever.'

'But,' interrupted Uther, 'when we were fleeing from the Duke's men you turned Blart and me into pigs. That was magic. If you could do it then, why can't you do it now?'

Capablanca looked forlorn.

'That was my emergency magic,' he explained. 'When a wizard is suspended he is allowed one emergency burst of magic while the investigation is being undertaken. This allows him to get out of a life-threatening situation. After he uses it he is then supposed to return to the wizard's committee to be issued with one more emergency burst but there was no time to do so. Therefore I stand before you as a spell-free wizard.'

The questors looked at Capablanca. Without Capablanca's magic how could they hope to succeed?

'Is that an end to the quest, then?' asked Blart. 'Can I go home?'

Capablanca nodded.

'Of course you'd probably be killed long before you got

home because you are seen as an ally of Zoltab.'

'Oh,' said Blart, who had forgotten that. 'Maybe I won't go home straight away, then, but don't anybody forget that I can.'

'And don't you forget that there's nobody to stop me cleaving you in two,' said Beo, gripping the handle of his sword.

Blart was beginning to realise that the loss of Capablanca's magic powers might not be such a good thing.

'Indeed,' continued the warrior menacingly, 'if you don't agree to go and join the circus right now I might do just that.'

'But …' began Blart.

'Right now,' insisted Beo and the grip on his sword became firmer.

'I'll do it,' said Blart.

Beo's grip relaxed.

'I'm still doing it too,' said Princess Lois. 'He's bound to make a mess of it if I'm not there to help.'

'It is good of you to care for Blart,' observed Capablanca. 'It is what a quest is all about – the forming of alliances and friendships between those who would not normally work side by side.'

'I don't care about stoat-features,' snapped back the Princess. 'I care about Pig the Horse. Blart's too stupid to save him without me.'

And so it was agreed that Blart and Princess Lois should both run away and join the circus.

Chapter 25

The clowns bowed, the jugglers bowed, the acrobats bowed, the fire eater bowed and, after a sneaky crack of the whip from the ringmaster, even Pig the Horse flapped his wings and bowed. The performance was over.

'Clap and cheer as wildly as you can,' hissed Uther, who was sitting in between Blart and Princess Lois. 'You must look as if you've had the most fantastic time.'

The circus performers took one final bow and they danced out of the big tent. The audience stopped clapping and began chattering excitedly and filing out into Gibb's Field.

'Now is the time for you to slip away from me,' whispered Uther. 'Good luck.' And then out loud he said, 'Come along, children, we must hurry back to town. Uncle Uther is thirsty.'

Uther led the way. Blart and Princess Lois followed, but in the mass of people crushed in the aisle and pushing for the exit they seemed to lose contact with Uther.

Uther left the tent in the middle of the crowd. Blart and Princess Lois turned round and together forced themselves against the flow of the crowd back into the tent.

'Don't do anything stupid and mess this up, stoat-features,' whispered Princess Lois.

'Show's over, boys and girls.'

Blart and Princess Lois turned round and found themselves face to face with a clown — a clown whose baggy trousers were saggy and threadbare and whose make-up was no longer quite so bright and cheerful as it had been during his recent performance.

'We know,' said Princess Lois.

'Clear off, then,' said the clown.

'We want to see Mr Beserker,' said Princess Lois.

'I want to see a big bag of gold with my name on,' answered the clown. 'We don't always get what we want.'

'Mr Beserker will want to see us,' insisted Princess Lois with a confidence she didn't really feel.

'Are you going to give him any money?'

They shook their heads.

'Then I doubt very much that he'll want to see you,' said the clown. 'Beserker cares only for money.'

'Please be so good as to tell Mr Beserker we wish to see him.'

'I'm warning you,' said the clown. 'He won't like being disturbed by children.'

'Thank you for your concern,' said Princess Lois imperiously. 'Now if you would be good enough to fetch him.'

There were times when having been brought up as a member of a royal family certainly helped.

The clown grumbled a bit but he soon left the tent to do the Princess's bidding.

'I didn't say anything,' pointed out Blart. 'So don't get distressed.'

'I will be distressed until we can free Pig from this terrible place,' answered the Princess. 'The only way you can stop me being distressed is to make that happen.'

'You don't look distressed,' maintained Blart. 'You look angry. You're supposed to be looking happy because you want to run away with the circus.'

'I'll look happy when I have to,' said the Princess.

Beserker strode into the tent with his whip in his hand. The time to look happy had obviously arrived.

Blart smiled. Princess Lois smiled.

Beserker didn't smile. Instead he stared with intense anger at Blart.

'You again,' he thundered.

Blart nodded and tried hard to keep smiling.

'Haven't you wasted enough of my time today?' demanded Beserker. 'What do you want? And be quick about it.'

Beserker cracked the whip on the ground.

'My cousin and I would like to join the circus,' said Blart.

'What?' demanded Beserker.

'We'd like to join the circus, please,' said Princess Lois.

'We had the most fantastic time tonight watching the performance and so we'd like to join.'

'I'm full,' answered Beserker. 'I don't need anyone else. So be gone.'

'We wouldn't want any wages or anything,' said Princess Lois.

'Wages!' Beserker's face darkened at the mention of the words. 'What is the world coming to when children are learning words like wages? When I first joined the circus I counted myself lucky to be able to work until I dropped and eat the scraps left over from the fire-eater's dinner.'

'We'd only eat scraps and leftovers,' said Blart.

Beserker's face lightened.

'Now we're talking sense,' he said. 'So tell me what can you do.'

Blart and Princess Lois were silent.

'Come on,' said Beserker, cracking his whip once more. 'What skills have you got?'

'I could be an acrobat,' said the Princess suddenly.

'Show me,' ordered Beserker.

The Princess walked into the centre of the ring. She did a handstand. Then she did a cartwheel. Then she did ten cartwheels one after the other going right across the ring. She finished with a spring and a bow.

'Not bad,' conceded Beserker. 'Of course you'll need training. But with that red hair you'd certainly stand out. I might just be persuaded to give you a trial. What about you?

What can you do?'

Beserker stared hard at Blart. Blart asked himself the same question. What could he do? Not much, he told himself.

'I'm a good pig boy,' Blart announced.

Even this claim was dubious considering that the last time Blart was in charge of a group of pigs he had lost them playing cards. However, even being a good pig boy did not look like the kind of claim that was going to impress Beserker if the dark colour his face became was any indication.

'Pig boy?' he repeated angrily. 'What would I need a pig boy for? Do boys and girls like to see pigs doing tricks? Do boys and girls like to see them wave their muddy snouts in the air?'

'Yes,' suggested Blart. It was the wrong answer.

'No, they do not,' roared Beserker with a double crack of his whip. 'The pig is the most useless of all animals to the circus owner. It isn't cute and it doesn't do tricks.'

'I think they're cute,' protested Blart.

'Don't tell me what is cute and what isn't,' ordered Beserker. 'I've been in the circus business for twenty years and let me assure you pigs aren't box office. Now, can you do anything else?'

Blart couldn't. He shook his head.

'Then I can't take you,' Beserker said. 'But I can still take Ginger.'

Princess Lois bristled. Never before had anybody had the temerity to call her Ginger.

'I'm afraid that's impossible,' she said. 'It's either both of us or neither of us. We're very close cousins. I'm sure you understand.'

Beserker was taken aback.

'You're giving me an ultimatum?' he demanded.

Princess Lois nodded.

'Don't give him anything,' said Blart.

'I ... I ... I ...' blustered Beserker. 'I should send you both away with a good kick, but ...' It was obvious Beserker had been very impressed with the Princess's acrobatics and was weighing them against Blart's uselessness. 'I suppose your skills looking after pigs would be transferable to other animals,' he said grudgingly to Blart. Blart nodded. 'Well, maybe we could take you both on a trial basis.'

'Hurrah!' said Princess Lois.

'But it will be hard work and ...' Beserker suddenly remembered something. 'What about your uncle? He seemed very caring when he was trying to get you a glimpse of Diablo.'

'Pig,' corrected Blart before he could stop himself.

'Stop talking about pigs,' ordered Beserker. 'I want to know about your uncle. The last thing I want is relatives coming after me because they think I've stolen their nephew and niece.'

'He is a very caring uncle,' agreed Princess Lois.

'Then I don't want you,' said Beserker.

'When he's sober,' continued Princess Lois. 'However, when he's drunk he forgets all about us. And after the show he was due to go and meet his best friend, Stowshus, in a nearby tavern. He was so eager to get there that he left us behind. Normally when he meets up with Stowshus they drink for two days and two nights and then sleep for a day.'

'Ah,' said Beserker. 'That puts a different perspective on things. Drunken uncles do not usually turn up demanding we give their children back. Welcome to the circus.'

Blart and Princess Lois smiled.

'Now get to work,' ordered Beserker. 'I want to see this big tent cleared up entirely before you go to bed. What are you staring at? Get working.'

Beserker stalked out of the big tent. Blart and Princess Lois reluctantly began to clear up the big tent, picking up all the litter that the night's audience had just left.

Some time later Beserker returned and told them that the tent was nowhere near clean enough and if they didn't do it better he would feed them to the lions and the tigers. Blart and Princess Lois cleaned up even more thoroughly. Beserker returned. He maintained that they had still done an appalling job and that if he weren't so soft-hearted this would have meant a beating, but as it was their first day he would be lenient. Instead he showed them to their sleeping quarters. He took them outside the tent and indicated a brightly painted caravan.

'That's where you sleep,' he told them.

Princess Lois and Blart, who were exhausted from the day's activity, began to mount the three stairs to the caravan.

'Where do you think you're going?' demanded Beserker.

'You said that this was where we sleep,' replied a confused Princess Lois.

'You sleep underneath,' Beserker told them. 'When you start making me some money is when we start thinking about allowing you to sleep indoors.'

With heavy hearts Blart and Princess Lois lay down under the caravan. The grass was damp and the night was chilly. The glamour of the circus was non-existent.

Chapter 26

The crack of Beserker's whip alerted them to the arrival of a new morning.

'Get up! Get up!' he demanded. 'Where do you think you are? Do I keep you here to lie down doing nothing all morning? I do not. Get up! Get up!'

They crawled out from under the caravan. The sun was only just rising and the air was still cold. After a night in the open both Blart and the Princess felt chilled and stiff.

'You, Ginger,' Beserker indicated Princess Lois, 'get to the big top. The acrobats will be there in a moment to begin your lessons. Well, what are you waiting for? Get along with you.'

Princess Lois swallowed her anger and stomped over towards the big top.

'Now you, Useless.'

'Blart,' said Blart.

'Useless,' Beserker assured him. 'Today you're on animal feeding and mucking out. Follow me.'

Beserker led Blart off towards the animal enclosures.

They reached the cages. Standing by them, looking bored, was a fearsome-looking man with a shaven head and a bushy moustache. Moustaches seemed to be big in the circus.

'This is Legendary Lok the Lion Tamer,' Beserker told Blart.

'Hello,' said Blart.

Lok ignored him.

'This is Useless,' Beserker told Lok. 'He's volunteered to do all the nastiest jobs in the circus. Make sure he gets them.'

With that Beserker turned and marched away.

'Pick up that bucket of oats and follow me,' said Lok.

The first animals to be fed were the horses. That is, all the horses but Pig, who was kept separately because of his great value. Blart didn't find this very difficult. Soon they were outside the horse enclosure.

'Pick up that pail of apples and follow me,' said Lok.

The second animals to be fed were the elephants. The poor beasts were chained to the backs of their cages by their feet. At first Blart was terrified by their enormous size but once he realised that they were unable to come and stand on him he found his confidence and was able to feed them their apples. Soon he was outside the elephants' cage.

'Pick up that bucket of raw meat and follow me,' said Lok.

Most people would have realised that any animal that ate

raw meat was probably going to be the most nerve-wracking to feed. And that any animal that regarded raw meat as breakfast would also regard Blart as possible breakfast. Which is why Blart came to a dead stop outside the big cats' cage. The lions and tigers prowled menacingly behind the bars.

'What are you waiting for?' demanded Lok.

The lions and tigers growled. They could smell their breakfast and they were hungry.

Blart remained rooted to the spot.

'Get that cage door open and feed them,' ordered Lok. 'I haven't got all day.'

'You want me to go in there?' said Blart. His voice cracked as he spoke.

'Yes, and be quick about it,' Lok answered.

'Couldn't I just throw the food through the bars?' suggested Blart. This seemed a much more reasonable approach.

'And I suppose they will all share nicely, will they?' said Lok sarcastically.

'I don't care,' answered Blart honestly.

'Well, I do,' said Lok. 'I'm a lion tamer and if I'm going to earn a living then I don't want my lions and tigers tearing each other to bits in a fight over food. Those claws can cause serious damage, you know.'

'I'd guessed,' Blart told him.

'So what your job is,' explained Lok, 'is to make sure that they each get a hunk of raw meat. One hunk per big cat, see?'

'But how do I get them to only take one hunk each?' said

Blart. 'What if one of them wants two?'

'Do I have to explain everything?' said Lok. 'There are four corners in the cage. There are four big cats – two lions and two tigers. You send each big cat to a corner then you stand in the middle and throw each one of them one hunk of raw meat. Then you stay there to see fair play and just before they finish eating you leave with the empty bucket. Nothing to it. Just make sure you leave before they've finished eating.'

'Why?' said Blart.

'Questions, questions, questions,' said Lok. 'The last boy didn't ask this many questions.'

'Where's he now?' asked Blart.

Lok shook his head.

'He got casual with his throwing action. He was in there one day and he threw the hunk of meat too far.'

'And so you sacked him?'

'He wasn't exactly sacked,' said Lok.

Blart looked at him suspiciously.

'Look,' said Lok. 'I don't want to have to tell Mr Beserker that you wouldn't do your job. He tends to get very short tempered when he hears people aren't working and that whip can be quite nasty. Now get in there.'

He hoisted Blart over his shoulder and carried him up the steps to the cage door.

'Eeek,' said Blart. 'Put me down.'

Lok placed Blart right in front of the door to the cage. The smell of the raw meat grew ever stronger in the nostrils of the big cats, who growled even more ferociously as they prowled just behind the gate.

'In you go,' said Lok and his hand reached over Blart's shoulder and turned the handle of the door.

'No!' screeched Blart. 'Nooooooo!'

Chapter 27

Lok was laughing so much he fell off the steps.

'You should have seen your face,' he said.

But Blart could only see Lok's face. It was a face he would have liked very much to punch.

'Gets the new boys every time it does,' Lok told him. 'You don't really think I'd let you go in there alone with those big cats, do you?'

Blart had already seen enough of the circus to think it was completely possible.

Lok reached down. Behind the steps that led up to the cage door was a large stick.

'Now watch and learn,' instructed Lok, opening the door and grabbing the bucket of raw meat.

The growling became snarling.

'Aaaaah!' shouted Lok, thrusting his stick forward. 'Back, you brutes. Aaaahhh! Aaaaahh!'

One lion reeled back. An angry tiger tried to cuff the stick away with his mighty paw.

'Aaaah!' shouted Lok. 'Back, I say. Back.'

To Blart's surprise the big cats eventually retreated to the far side of the cage, where they continued to growl menacingly.

'Quiet,' shouted Lok. 'Now get to your corners.'

The lions and tigers each padded over to their individual corner.

'You see,' Lok called to Blart, 'all this growling is just for show. They know what they've got to do to get their breakfast and they're happy enough to do it.'

Happy seemed an exaggeration to Blart.

Lok tossed hunks of raw meat to each of the big cats. They tore ferociously into them the moment they landed at their paws.

'Nothing to it,' said Lok. 'Look confident and remember to get out before they've finished.'

Lok backed out of the cage.

'Just remember everything I showed you this afternoon.'

'Why?' Blart wanted to know.

'There's a matinee performance,' Lok told him and confronted by Blart's blank face explained, 'that's one in the afternoon. The lions have to be fed just before they go on stage.'

'Why?' said Blart again.

'Because when I put my head in a lion's mouth I want to be absolutely sure that's it's not at all hungry,' said Lok. 'So make sure they all get a big juicy hunk of meat.'

'You can check that,' Blart told him.

'I won't be here,' said Lok. 'I'll be getting changed and putting my make-up on.'

'But I can't go in there on my own,' protested Blart.

'Course you can,' Lok assured him. 'You've just had my masterclass. Point the stick, shout "Aaaaah" and look confident. There's nothing to it.'

Blart scanned Lok's face for any hint that he was joking again. There was no hint. Blart was going to have to go alone into the big cats' cage.

Chapter 20

'We have to get out of here,' Blart told Princess Lois.

'We can't go without Pig the Horse,' replied the Princess.

They were sitting in Gibb's Field, eating the dried bread and bowl of thin soup that Beserker's Circus gave out to its most junior members for lunch.

'You don't understand,' said Blart. 'I'm going to have to go into a cage with lions and tigers this afternoon. On my own. They'll eat me.'

'Stop thinking about yourself,' Princess Lois told him brusquely. 'Pig the Horse is in danger.'

'I'm in danger,' said Blart.

'Stop being so selfish and let me speak, you ugly slug,' hissed Princess Lois.

For someone with such a love of animals, Princess Lois did seem to use them rather a lot when it came to terms of abuse. Still, the abuse worked, for Blart lapsed into silence.

'During a break in my acrobatic rehearsals –'

'You get breaks?' interrupted Blart indignantly. 'I don't get breaks and I have to –'

'Shut up. I am trying to tell you something very important. The acrobats weren't very pleased when Beserker told them I was to join their troupe and during a break I found out why.'

'You're horrible?' suggested Blart.

'They thought I had gone to the toilet,' said Princess Lois, ignoring Blart's intervention, 'but I thought there was something suspicious about them, so I crept back into the tent and crawled underneath the seats until I was close enough to overhear their conversation, and do you know what I heard them saying?'

'No.'

'They were discussing Pig the Horse. They're planning to steal him too, because,' said the Princess, dropping her voice to a whisper, 'the acrobats are all minions of Zoltab.'

Blart dropped his bread into his soup.

'Minions of Zoltab!' he repeated.

'Keep your voice down,' hissed Princess Lois.

'But weren't they all killed when the Terrorsium collapsed at the end of our last quest?' asked Blart.

'No,' said Princess Lois. 'Many minions of Zoltab were elsewhere on that day, preparing for his conquest of the world. From what I overheard it seems they are searching for any of the questors who took Zoltab from them. They know because Zoltab is immortal he must be somewhere and they are determined to find him.'

Blart looked over to the other side of the field, where a troupe of eight performers were eating their lunch.

'They do look shifty and dangerous,' he told Princess Lois. 'Just like minions of Zoltab.'

'You're looking at the jugglers,' Princess Lois pointed out. 'The acrobats are over there.'

Princess Lois indicated a trestle table at the far side of the field, where a group of ten people sat huddled together, eating and muttering to themselves. Blart studied them.

'They look shifty and dangerous too,' he observed. 'But Pig wouldn't help Zoltab's minions.'

'Of course he wouldn't,' agreed Princess Lois. 'But they don't know that, and what foul tortures might they subject him too because of his role in helping us escape with Zoltab!'

'Meal time is over, you no good layabouts,' bellowed Beserker, appearing from the big top. 'Get back to work. We have a matinee performance in an hour and I don't pay you to sit around in fields.'

'What are we to do?' whispered Princess Lois anxiously. 'We must get to Pig before the minions of Zoltab do.'

'I don't know,' said Blart irritably. 'I don't do the plans. That's normally Capablanca's job.'

'You two!' Beserker stormed over towards them. 'How dare you still be sitting down when everyone else has returned to work?'

Beserker aimed a powerful kick at Blart.

'Ow!' said Blart appropriately.

'Get back to work, Useless,' ordered Beserker, 'or I'll get the fire eater to roast you alive.'

As threats go, it was good one. Blart got up hurriedly and rushed back to work. But it meant that he left without agreeing a plan. The questors didn't have one while the minions of Zoltab did. And if the minions were to put their plan into action first, then Pig the Horse could be lost for good, and the questors would never be able to prove their innocence and would be wanted dead or alive for ever.

Chapter 29

'Here, kitty, kitty. Here, kitty, kitty.'

'*Grrrrrrrrr!*'

'Nice kitty, kitty.'

'*Grrrrrrrrrrrrrrrrrrrrr!*'

'Get those cats fed,' shouted Beserker. 'They'll be in front of an audience in ten minutes and I want them stuffed full of meat.'

Blart nodded obediently, picked up Lok's stick in one hand and the huge bucket of raw meat in the other, and walked purposefully up the steps to the cage. Beserker disappeared into the big top. Blart stopped.

'*Grrrrrrrrrrrrrrrrrrrrrrrrrrrrrrrrrrrrrrr!*' growled the lions and tigers.

'Are you purring?' asked Blart.

'*Grrrrr! Grrrrr! Grrrrr! Grrrr! ARRRaaggghh!*'

The big cats confirmed in no uncertain terms that they most certainly weren't purring.

Blart gulped.

Behind him he could hear the music. It was the first half of the show and the acrobats were on. Blart could hear the audience laughing and applauding. He closed his eyes and wished he were among the audience, watching the performance and not here, trying to summon up the nerve to walk into the lion's den.

'Useless!'

Beserker was back.

'I told you to get those cats fed. If you aren't in that cage by the time I get over there then I'm throwing you in without any meat, and you know what that means.'

He began to march over towards the cage. Blart was paralysed with fear. Beserker's face was darker with anger than it had ever been before.

'I knew it,' he shouted. 'I go to all the trouble of letting you join the circus and what do I get? Laziness. You will not do an honest day's work for an honest day's pay.'

'You're not paying me,' Blart reminded him desperately.

'Don't you try to renegotiate your wages with me,' said Beserker, reaching the bottom of the steps. 'Now get in that cage.'

Blart looked at Beserker. Then he looked at the big cats. Beserker was definitely angrier than the cats but he lacked their vicious teeth. Anger – Big Teeth. Blart wanted to face neither.

So he compromised.

He opened the gate of the cage and threw in the raw

meat. He whirled round to find Beserker just a step below him. Desperately, he tipped the bucket's remaining meat and blood over Beserker, who toppled down the steps. Blart jumped down and crawled under the cage to hide.

'How dare you?' bellowed Beserker. 'You'll regret this, Useless. I'll set the strong man on you, I'll set the fire eater on you, I'll set …'

He was distracted from his threats by the discovery that something was about to set on him. A lion was coming down the steps from the unbolted cage.

'Back!' ordered Berserker. 'Help me!'

But his cries for help were lost amid a great cheer from inside the big top. The big cat, unused to freedom, advanced tentatively down the steps.

'Get back,' shouted Beserker. But he was no lion tamer and the big cat showed no sign of obeying. He picked himself up and ran towards the big top.

'The lions are out! The lions are out!' he bellowed, running down the tunnel, covered in blood and giblets.

Blart heard loud screams from inside the big top and watched as people began to stream out in every direction.

Meanwhile the recently escaped lion heard the growls of satisfaction from the other big cats as they tore into the meat Blart had thrown in. The sound and smell tempted him back and he padded up the steps back into the cage. Blart, seizing his chance, crawled out, ran up the steps and bolted the gate behind him.

Which meant that in reality the panicking crowd had nothing to panic about. But panicking crowds are notoriously difficult to get to stop once they've started. The fear of the lions was everywhere. People banged into each other, knocked each other over and trampled on each other.

Blart was watching the chaos when he felt a thump in his back and turned round to see Princess Lois standing behind him.

'What was that for?'

'I was trying to attract your attention,' explained Princess Lois.

'You could have just said hello,' said Blart.

'It's not as much fun,' said Princess Lois. 'Now come on. This might be our chance to get to Pig the Horse while he is unguarded by the Chigorin Brothers.'

In the fevered atmosphere it did not prove too difficult for Princess Lois and Blart to slip unnoticed across Gibb's Field and open the gate that led into Gibb's Pasture. At the far end of Gibb's Pasture was the tent that was home to Pig the Horse. They ran towards it as quickly as they could. Princess Lois pulled back the flap of the tent. There was Pig the Horse. Twice the size of a normal horse and many more times as majestic – he could carry up to five people on his wide strong back. It was a terrible crime to keep such a beast tethered when he should be flying or galloping freely across the plains of Nevod that were his home.

Princess Lois approached Pig.

'Pig,' said the Princess with a tenderness in her voice that was markedly absent in her dealings with humans. 'How could we let these terrible things happen to you?'

The great horse seemed to remember her, for he neighed appreciatively and lowered his head so that he could be stroked.

She turned her attention to Blart. 'Get to work on the knots that so cruelly tie Pig down. We must hurry.'

Blart rushed over to the end of the rope. The knot seemed fearfully complicated.

'There is another rope holding Pig. I'll undo that one,' said the Princess.

Blart began to untie his knot. The thickness of the rope made the task cumbersome but gradually it began to loosen. Pig neighed his appreciation. Loop after loop was undone, each one faster than the last.

'Mine is free,' cried Princess Lois triumphantly.

'There's no need to show off,' countered Blart. 'I only have one loop to go and I bet my knot was tighter than yours.'

Blart reached down to the last loop. As he did so the tent flapped open. Standing in the doorway was Gordo, head of the acrobats, dressed in a tight-fitting blue tunic. Behind him was the rest of his lithe and wiry troupe.

Ten minions of Zoltab.

'What is going on here?' demanded Gordo. 'Ginger, why are you not with the rest of the troupe?'

Princess Lois thought fast. But surprisingly Blart thought faster.

'I was ordered by Mr Beserker to untie Pig the Horse and take him somewhere safe until they could capture the lions and tigers,' explained Blart, his hands pulling frantically at the last knot. 'He told me to take someone along to help me and as Ginger is my cousin I picked her.'

By now the rest of the troupe of acrobats had bounded into the tent. Knowing that they were, in reality, minions of Zoltab made Blart very nervous and his hands began to shake. The final loop of the knot still refused to give.

'Did you say Pig the Horse?' asked Gordo.

Blart froze.

'Don't know,' he said pathetically.

'I think you did,' said Gordo.

'He's always saying stupid things,' said Princess Lois. 'Just ignore him.'

The acrobats muttered among themselves. Blart tugged desperately at the rope. The last loop began to come loose.

'We think you did say Pig,' said Gordo, 'which is very interesting because we have been looking all over for a flying horse called Pig. But we thought this one was called Diablo.'

'Really?' said Princess Lois. 'What a coincidence.'

With a final tug Blart undid the last loop and Pig the Horse was free. Or at least he would be once he was outside the tent. Unfortunately, between Blart, Princess Lois, Pig the

Horse and the outside of the tent were ten angry minions of Zoltab.

'If you know this horse is called Pig,' said Gordo, 'then you must also know about the terrible injustice he was part of when our Master was cruelly kidnapped.'

Princess Lois and Blart feigned innocence.

'Could it be,' said Gordo, 'that we are face to face with Blart the evil goat boy and Lois the evil Princess?'

Blart could take being called evil but to be called a goat boy was more than he could bear.

'I'm a pig boy,' he announced defiantly.

'Then prepare to die, pig boy,' said Gordo. 'For we shall avenge our Master by killing those who took him from us, and then we will fly to his rescue on the back of the horse.'

Things looked grim. They were outnumbered ten to three, which is an unhelpfully complex ratio – so suffice it to say, they were going to lose.

Except that suddenly there was a hubbub outside. A minion of Zoltab stuck his head out of the tent.

'Beserker and the Chigorin Brothers are coming,' he cried.

'Get the horse,' ordered Gordo.

Two minions of Zoltab pushed Princess Lois to the floor whilst another leapt in the air, spun round artistically and kicked Blart in the face.

'Ow!' said Blart, collapsing in a heap.

Gordo grabbed Pig's reins and began to pull. The great

horse resisted with all his might. Two other acrobats joined Gordo and together they pulled even harder. The reins were connected to the cruel bit in Pig the Horse's mouth. With each vicious tug the bit cut into Pig. Without it, he would have held out whether twenty or even thirty acrobats were pulling. But with it he was forced to follow them out of the tent. The remaining acrobats rushed after him.

'Get up!' shouted Princess Lois.

'He kicked me right in the mouth,' said Blart.

'Forget about your mouth,' said Princess Lois, who had seen the cruel bit doing its evil work. 'Think of Pig's mouth. We must rescue him.'

Princess Lois rushed from the tent. Blart followed, wondering why his suffering was always seen to be less important than anybody or indeed anything else's.

Once outside the tent he was met by an amazing sight.

Ten minions of Zoltab were on Pig the Horse's back. Though Pig was indeed a massive horse even he did not have a wide enough back for ten. However, the minions of Zoltab were also acrobats. Four of them sat on Pig's back. Three balanced on the shoulders of those four. Two balanced on the shoulders of those three. And one balanced on the shoulders of those two.

It was a terrible sight. A pyramid of minions charging across the field on the back of Pig the Horse. But there was an even worse sight. Beserker and the Chigorin Brothers, their large moustaches billowing in the breeze as they ran, were heading across the field towards them.

'What have you done to my horse?' yelled Beserker. 'If that horse isn't back in that tent soon then the big cats will be eating your limbs for their dinner.'

Pig the Horse reached maximum speed as he thundered across Gibb's Pasture. From beneath his belly there suddenly emerged his mighty wings. They flapped once. They flapped twice. Pig took off. The minions of Zoltab were lifted into the air. Their leader, Gordo, looked down at Blart and Princess Lois and they could see the sneering laugh on his face. The minions had beaten the questors to the last link to Zoltab's prison. The questors would never be able to clear their names. The minions would free Zoltab and he would once again attempt to lay waste to the world. And the Chigorin Brothers would tear off Blart's arms and legs and feed them to the big cats.

Things looked grim.

Chapter 30

Pig the Horse rose higher. Beserker and the Chigorin Brothers got nearer.

'I think we might be in trouble,' observed Blart.

'Don't be so pathetic,' said Princess Lois with the confidence of royalty. 'Beserker and his walking moustaches would not dare harm us.'

Blart looked at the furious faces of Beserker and the Chigorin Brothers with the lack of confidence of pig boys. He was certain they would dare. He wondered when Princess Lois would remember that she wasn't royalty here but just a normal person with normal limbs that could be torn off and fed to the big cats just like everybody else. Blart took a moment to say goodbye to each of his arms and legs. They were ugly but he was still going to miss them.

Suddenly Beserker stopped running towards Blart and Princess Lois. Behind him the Chigorin Brothers stopped too — their moustaches drooped. They all looked upwards. Above them was a sight to behold.

Pig the Horse was doing loop the loops.

It was magnificent.

Unless you were a minion — for every time Pig looped upside down they were forced to desperately cling on. The four minions actually sitting on Pig had the best grip. The one minion on the top had the worst.

Pig looped. The one minion at the top lost his grip and tumbled to the earth with a fearsome cry.

Pig looped again. The next two minions plummeted towards the ground.

Pig looped a third time. A further three minions of Zoltab hurtled down from the sky.

Only four minions remained.

'Why didn't you do loop the loops for me?' demanded Beserker, waving his fist at Pig far above him in the sky. 'I could have charged more for tickets!'

Pig looped once more. The minions held on. Pig twisted. He shook. He kicked out.

One by one the remaining minions could hold on no longer. They shot through the air and landed with sickening crashes in Gibb's field.

'Try and steal my horse, would you? I bet you would have taken him to Crazy Mike's,' shouted Beserker. 'I will feed you to the lions and tigers.'

The lions and tigers were going to need hearty appetites because they were most certainly going to be well fed that evening.

Pig the Horse flew back towards the field and prepared to land.

'Look at this,' boasted Beserker to some members of the ex-audience who had found their way into the pasture. He pointed towards the horse. 'This answers those do-gooders who say that animals aren't happy in the circus. This beast could have been freed and he is coming back of his own free will. He loves it here, I tell you.'

Pig the Horse landed. His gallop became a canter, his canter became a trot and his trot came to a stop right next to the Princess and Blart.

Pig bent his great legs so that they could climb on easily.

It dawned on Beserker that Pig was not quite so fond of the circus as he had suggested.

'Stop them,' he ordered the Chigorin Brothers.

Blart and Princess Lois mounted. The Chigorin Brothers sprinted, their moustaches streaming out behind them. Pig the Horse stood up and began to move. Faster and faster he charged. The Chigorin Brothers were left behind in a cloud of dust that doubtless meant they would all have to wash their moustaches later.

Pig the Horse's hooves drummed louder as he approached the edge of the pasture. Nearer came the hedge that marked its end, faster went Pig, and suddenly they were free of the ground and rising high into the air, propelled upwards by the majestic swooping of Pig's magnificent wings.

'Well done, Pig,' said Princess Lois. 'You have saved us.'

Far below the tiny figure of Beserker looked upwards, shaking his fist at Blart and Lois. His anger, that had once been terrifying, was now reduced to nothing more than pathetic comedy – his purple face growing ever darker as Blart made rude gestures towards him from above. Meanwhile the Chigorin Brothers were rounding up the acrobats.

Princess Lois leant over Pig's neck and pulled the cruel bit from his mouth. Along with the reins it was dropped to the ground far below. Pig gave a neigh of pleasure to see it go. There would be those who would wonder how a horse could be directed without reins, yet the matter was simplicity itself. Just by putting gentle pressure on one side of Pig's head or the other, the Princess was able to guide him towards the other side of town, where, in a small copse, the other questors awaited them.

Pig landed gently and smoothly.

'Well done,' said Capablanca as he and Uther and Beo rushed up to them.

Princess Lois wasted no time in telling the other questors the terrible news.

'Zoltab's minions were at the circus,' she announced.

'Minions of Zoltab?' repeated Capablanca in shock.

Princess Lois told them how the acrobats had tried unsuccessfully to steal Pig with the intention of using him to rescue Zoltab.

'I fought them off,' claimed Blart. 'There were ten of them and only one of me.'

'One of you is one too many,' commented Beo darkly.

'This is very bad,' said Capablanca, reflecting on the news that the minions of Zoltab were nearby. 'They have obviously recovered far more quickly from the defeat at the Terrorsium than I would have thought possible. Their influence will have spread like plague through the land.'

'I don't think we need to worry about the minions of Zoltab,' said Uther. 'We must worry about finding Zoltab himself.'

'Exactly,' said Capablanca. 'Before the minions find him.'

'That's what I meant, of course,' said Uther.

'Let us go,' said the wizard.

The five questors climbed on to Pig. In the front sat Capablanca, then Princess Lois, then Blart, then Uther and finally Beo. No ordinary horse would have been able to carry five riders, especially when one of them had a body that was as fond of pies and ale as Beowulf the Warrior's. But of course Pig was no ordinary beast. He was twice the size of a normal horse and powerful muscles rippled through his flesh from his shoulder to his fetlock.

Yet even to such a strong beast as Pig the Horse the burden of five riders was heavy. But not only did Pig have strength he also had spirit, and once they were on his back he summoned all his energy and began to canter and then gallop out of the copse where they had met and through the wood. Trees sped backwards past the charging horse and they had to hunch low to avoid being hit by branches. But the great horse never once faltered as he thundered through the trees and then suddenly shot out of the wood, his riders blinking in the sudden sunlight. Almost immediately Pig's wings unfurled and he rose into the sky, leaving the ground behind them. Uther was the only questor who had never previously flown on Pig the Horse and the experience overcame even his normally cynical demeanour.

'This is fantastic,' he shouted as they rose ever higher. 'This is tremendous. This is … oh.'

Uther clasped his hand to his stomach. That part of his body seemed less convinced that the flight was fantastic and tremendous and more of the opinion that it was disorientating and upsetting.

'Ugh,' said Blart, watching the contents of Uther's stomach plummet to the earth and, just for once, he spoke for all his comrades.

Chapter 31

'Is there no way we can get him to understand?' asked Princess Lois, pulling irritably at a loose thread on her red dress.

'The horse must surely be more intelligent than Blart,' maintained Beo the Warrior. 'And he can understand.'

'It is so frustrating,' explained an exasperated Capablanca. 'If I could use a spell then I could explain what we want him to do.'

The questors were sitting by a stream. Pig was nearby drinking from it. They had spent the past few hours trying desperately to communicate to Pig that they wanted him to take them to the place where Capablanca had imprisoned Zoltab. They had flown back to the crossroads where Pig and Capablanca had separated from the other questors – Pig showed no signs of recognising the place. They had reconstructed the way that they had all dismounted and waved Capablanca off before turning their backs so as not to see which way he took. This, too, had failed to have any significant effect on Pig.

'Is it possible that you cast the Great Spell of Fog on the horse as well?' asked Beo.

'I am sure I would not have done,' said Capablanca. 'If we could only establish some form of rudimentary communication with Pig, he would take us to Zoltab's prison,' said Capablanca.

The questors all looked at Pig the Horse, who, after his exertions of earlier in the day, was still drinking heavily from the stream.

'Perhaps I could help,' said Uther.

'You can talk to horses?' asked Beo.

Uther shook his head.

'I am no more than a humble merchant and business-man,' he said, 'but I have travelled widely and I have heard men speak –'

'And women,' interjected Princess Lois.

'I do not listen to women,' answered Uther loftily. 'In my experience they do not have heads for business.'

Princess Lois fixed Uther with a glare that suggested she disagreed.

'I have heard men speak,' continued Uther, 'of a strange old crone who can shout at horses and understand their replies.'

'Can she shout to pigs too?' asked Blart eagerly.

'Where is this woman that you speak of?' asked Capablanca.

'I have heard it said,' answered Uther, 'that she dwells in the enchanted Forest of Arcadium.'

'There is no time to lose,' said Capablanca. 'Flying on Pig we may be able to reach the forest by tomorrow morning. Not only does the destiny of Illyria lie in our hands, there is also the threat that Zoltab's minions will manage to interfere with our plans.'

'They will surely have given up after being outwitted at the circus,' said Uther confidently.

'You are wrong,' said Capablanca. 'They will never give up.'

Uther looked as though he were about to disagree with Capablanca but then changed his mind. 'Let us get going, then,' he said instead.

As soon as they had all mounted, the great horse once more accelerated and rose into the sky. Already the daylight was beginning to fade and after Capablanca had directed Pig to fly to the east the sun set rapidly behind them. The blue sky grew orange and then red as the sun disappeared, and then the red became purple, and finally the purple turned to black. The stars and the moon were the only lights they could see, but Capablanca had studied the stars when he was a younger wizard and their presence was enough for him to navigate by.

Slowly lulled by the easy beating of Pig's wings and fatigued by a day spent being heroic, Blart's head became heavier and heavier and before long he was asleep. All the other questors except Capablanca were soon sleeping too, each leaning forward and resting their heads on the comrade in front of them.

Up front the wizard kept a lonely vigil. There was a weariness in his body that he had never known before and he secretly feared that he would not live to see the end of the quest. He was worried about the news of Zoltab's minions, anxious that the kingdom of Illyria might be doomed, nervous about the unknown dangers which might lurk in the enchanted forest of Arcadia, and absolutely terrified that he might never regain his magic powers or have a commemorative chair carved for him or wipe the superior smirks off the faces of all the wizards who were delighted by his downfall.

Chapter 32

All through the night the great horse flew. At last, far in the distance, the first weak rays of light streaked the sky. The questors woke up cold and stiff. They stretched and yawned and shivered and muttered to themselves. Blart, his fingers cold and white, found a pair of gloves in the pocket of his trousers, and put them on. He hugged himself for warmth and thought of how happy he would be at home by a fire, with pig snuffling noises outside his kitchen window.

And indeed all the questors' minds were drifting off to visions of home. Princess Lois remembered her bedroom with its 'No Fruit Beyond This Point' sign on the door, Beo thought fondly of his happy days as a debt collector and Capablanca remembered his commemorative chair in the Cavernous Library of Ping. But as the sun rose higher and its warmth penetrated their bones they shook off their visions of sleep and thought more of the challenge that lay ahead of them.

'There it is,' said Uther. 'The Forest of Arcadia!'

They looked down. Below them, stretching as far as the eye could see, was a vast unbroken canopy of green. It disappeared over the horizon.

'You'll never find one person in there,' said Blart.

Capablanca nudged Pig the Horse's head to encourage him to circle, hoping that he could spy some gap in the canopy where they could land. But despite all the questors looking as hard as they could no gap appeared.

'We will have to land on the edge,' said Capablanca and he guided them down to a stream. Pig immediately trotted over to the stream for a drink and the questors followed the horse's lead.

'I'm hungry,' announced Blart once he had drunk enough.

'We have no food,' said Capablanca regretfully.

'I've got some lard,' Uther interjected. 'You can each have a bite but it will cost you five crowns a mouthful.'

'Five crowns!' said Capablanca. 'That is an outrageous sum to charge.'

'Market forces,' said Uther with feigned regret.

'What do you mean "market forces"?' demanded Beo.

'We're miles from a market so I can force you to pay what I like,' explained Uther shamelessly.

'But we are comrades,' said Capablanca. 'We will share all the perils and all the triumphs. Surely we can share the lard?'

'No, no, no,' answered Uther forcibly. 'Once you start sharing things you've no idea where it might lead.'

'Mutual assistance and generosity?' suggested Capablanca.

Uther winced.

'As you're my comrades I'll accept an IOU, though obviously the price will have to rise to six crowns.'

'Why?' growled Beo.

'Administration costs,' explained Uther.

'It's not an IOU that you should be getting,' grumbled Beo. 'It's an I kill U. That's what you deserve.'

Uther's comrades looked at him with disgust. Then they heard the angry rumblings of their stomachs. A bit of lard was not the most tempting meal any of them had been offered but there were no other items on the menu. Reluctantly, each agreed to give Uther an IOU. Uther withdrew a lump of lard from his jacket and held it out for them to take one bite each. Capablanca swallowed his mouthful with an effort. Beo had to strain to keep his down. Princess Lois realised that there was something worse to eat than fruit in the world. Blart quite liked his portion and asked for seconds.

'Now with our bellies full and our thirst slaked we will sally forth,' said Capablanca once he had assured himself he was not going to be sick.

'Do we leave Pig here?' asked Blart.

'Of course not,' snapped Capablanca with a little of his old vigour. 'He's got to come with us, so the horse shouter can talk to him.'

'I knew that,' insisted Blart, who had forgotten.

'Go to the stream,' commanded Capablanca, 'and pick up as many pebbles as you can. We will drop them behind us when we are inside the forest and they will set a path to lead us out.'

'Why can't someone else do it?' said Blart sulkily.

'We are all going to collect and carry them,' answered Capablanca, 'for we may have to go deep into the forest and we will need many pebbles to provide us with a long enough path.'

'Oh,' said Blart, deflated.

Chapter 33

The questors collected small pebbles from the stream.

'Now we are ready,' said Capablanca when their pockets were full.

Princess Lois went and fetched Pig and they set off into the forest. So closely entwined were the trees that they were forced to move in single file. Beo led the way, his sword drawn in case of ambush. Behind him was Capablanca. Behind Capablanca was Princess Lois, leading Pig the Horse. Behind the horse was Blart, keeping himself a safe distance from Beo. And finally, bringing up the rear, there was Uther, who dropped a pebble every ten paces to create their path to safety.

The forest was dark and eerie and the branches grew closely together. Often Beo had to hack a way through with his sword and it took all of Princess Lois's coaxing, soothing and reassuring to convince Pig to come. Brittle twigs snapped under their feet and above them the trees creaked ominously. Strange creatures scuttled across the forest floor while above them there were the occasional sounds of birds.

But their calls were not the cheerful chatter of early morning in the fields, rather they were caws and hoots of warning. The questors sensed that the forest was aware of their intrusion and resented it.

Beo decided to sign a song to make them feel better. To lighten the mood he chose the rousing battle anthem, 'Killing Is Lots of Fun'.

'*Well, I woke up a-feeling bad*
And down in the dumps was I
My heart it was both low and sad
I thought that I might cry.

But I remembered these wise words
To rouse you when you're glum
Raise your swords in the air, my boys
Cause killing is lots of fun.

To slash, to stab, to gash, to maim
To hit with sword or mace
All these things are guaranteed
To put a smile on your face.

So when you are in despair
And prone to many a sigh
Lift your spirits and find good cheer
By killing a passer-by.'

Nobody joined in and Beowulf's singing tailed off. Even his deep strong voice sounded weak in the oppressive forest and once more the croak and shriek of strange birds were the only sounds that accompanied them.

But gradually as they fought and hacked their way through the forest the going became easier. The trees were now bigger but they were more widely spaced and so their branches no longer entwined to create a bewildering lattice that Beo was forced to hack through. And though they had still not found a path they were at least able to often walk two or three abreast rather than in single file.

And then as they passed a particularly large oak tree they came upon their first forest dweller.

'Hello,' said a voice.

Each of the questors jumped. Apart from Pig the Horse.

'Who goes there?' said Beowulf, wheeling round.

'Who wants to know?' said the voice.

'I, Beowulf the Warrior, want to know. And it will be the worse for you if you do not answer me.'

'To see, you must look up.'

Looking up, the questors saw thick branches and green leaves.

'I'm looking up,' shouted Beo. 'I can't see anything.'

'Look harder.'

Blart, who had the best eyesight, saw it first.

'There!'

'Where?'

Blart pointed. The other questors followed his finger. Princess Lois saw it next. She made a little squeak of surprise.

Sitting high in the tree was a tiny figure dressed in a mottled suit, with a pair of brown boots dangling over a branch. The tiny figure had a brown face, dry and wrinkled like a walnut.

'Aha,' said Capablanca, finally spotting what everyone else had been looking at for a while. Then he added with an air of great intelligence, 'I thought they were extinct, but that appears to be a tree imp.'

'Sorel the Tree Imp to be precise,' said the tree imp.

'I did not know that tree imps were still in existence,' said Capablanca. 'There has not been a reported sighting for many years. It was believed in the Cavernous Library of Ping that the forest goblins had hunted you into extinction.'

The imp's already wrinkled face creased further in annoyance.

'I know nothing of your library,' said Sorel angrily. 'And although I have searched for years I still believe I may find a mate and the chatter of tree imps will once again echo through the canopy. All I need is a mate and our whole species can be revived.'

'I wish you luck in your quest, Sorel,' said Capablanca to calm the tree imp's anger. 'But now I would ask for your help.'

'My help?' repeated Sorel, who was obviously not so easily mollified. 'You threaten to kill me, you tell me I am extinct and now you want my help?'

Capablanca coughed.

'I agree we didn't get off to the best start,' the wizard acknowledged, 'but we are on an important quest, a quest that may save the world, and to help us we need to find someone who can talk to our great horse Pig. We have heard tell that in this forest there is a person, a gifted horse shouter who can communicate with our horse. You are a tree imp –'

'I know,' said Sorel.

Capablanca was so used to explaining things to Blart that he sometimes made things just a little too simple for everybody else.

'– you know this forest well,' continued the wizard, deciding that it was diplomatic not to mention that the tree imp knew the forest particularly well because it had spent years forlornly scouring it for a mate. 'If anyone could tell us if this horse shouter really exists and where she might be found, then it is you.'

'She exists,' said Sorel, 'and she is called Agnes.'

'This is going to be easier than I thought,' muttered Capablanca.

'And where could we find her?' asked the wizard politely.

'I'm not telling you,' said Sorel. 'Until …'

And he stopped. Impishly.

'Until … ?' repeated Capablanca.

'Until you provide me with a mate,' said Sorel.

Capablanca's polite smile stretched into a taut grimace.

'How can we find you a mate?' he said. 'Tree imps are incredibly rare. You have searched the forest for many years without success. We have less than a week to complete our quest – to prevent Zoltab's return, to save the kingdom of Illyria and to clear our names so that we are no longer wanted dead or alive.'

'It's going to be a busy week,' agreed Sorel.

'We simply don't have the time,' protested Capablanca. 'I must implore you to direct us to Agnes the Horse Shouter.'

'We'll keep our eyes peeled on our quest,' said Princess Lois. 'If we come across a tree imp we'll tell her all about you.'

'What a pity,' said Sorel. 'This is the largest forest in the world. It could take you years to find Agnes whereas I could take you to her in a flash. Years and years and years.'

Capablanca shook his head hopelessly. Yet again the questors appeared defeated. Without Pig the Horse's knowledge, they couldn't find Zoltab. Without Agnes the Horse Shouter they couldn't get Pig the Horse to understand. Without a helpful tree imp they couldn't find Agnes the Horse Shouter. Without another tree imp …

'What's that?' Blart pointed excitedly into the nearby foliage. 'Look!'

Surprised by the unusual energy in Blart's voice, all the questors looked.

'It's a tree imp,' proclaimed Blart.

The questors' hearts leapt. How strange it was that just as the quest seemed doomed new hope was found again. It was as if it was destined to succeed.

'It's a leaf,' said Princess Lois.

All the questors looked closer at the area of foliage Blart was pointing to. His supposed tree imp was indeed a leaf.

'It's shaped like a tree imp,' maintained Blart.

The questors were so deflated that none could find the energy to disagree. It was completely hopeless. It was as if their quest was doomed to fail.

'I think I might be able to help,' said Uther quietly.

'How can you help, merchant?' demanded Beo suspiciously.

'Speak softer, warrior,' cautioned Uther, 'for there are those who might not respond well to what I am about to say.'

'You say you can help,' prompted Capablanca softly.

'I am only telling you this because it is our only hope,' admitted Uther, 'but a couple of years ago I did briefly have some limited dealings in exotic pets.'

'Exotic pets!' said Princess Lois indignantly.

'Amongst the nobility,' explained Uther, 'there is a trade in rare and exotic pets.'

'An illegal trade,' hissed Princess Lois.

'It is certainly on the borders of legality,' acknowledged Uther, 'but then that is where the most creative business is often done.'

Princess Lois glowered.

'I was in the fortunate position,' continued Uther, 'to be able to act as a bridge between the traders in these pets and the wealthy lords and barons who desire them. One day I met a trader, who informed me that he had for sale one of the rarest creatures in the world and asked if I would find him a suitable buyer. The owner of this creature would be the envy of all other collectors for it had never been owned before. The creature he showed me was, of course, a tree imp. Her name was Marjoram.'

'Who did you sell her to?' demanded Capablanca. The other questors, even Princess Lois, craned their necks towards the merchant to allow them to hear.

'There was only one choice,' answered Uther. 'Only one man who would pay what it took to obtain such a creature.'

'Who?' said Blart.

'Baron Kilbride,' said Uther and gulped.

There was a silence. It was not a happy silence.

'What's the matter?' said Blart.

'Baron Kilbride burns wizards,' said Capablanca.

'Baron Kilbride tortures warriors,' said Beowulf.

'Baron Kilbride slaughters merchants,' said Uther.

'Baron Kilbride wants to marry me,' said Princess Lois.

There was another unhappy silence.

'Does he keep pigs?' asked Blart.

Chapter 34

They had no other option. The week was ebbing fast and soon the armies massing on the Illyrian border would pour through it and lay waste to the many orchards.

'We will find you a mate and deliver her to this very tree,' said Capablanca.

'I knew you'd see sense,' said Sorel sourly.

And with that, the questors turned their eyes to the path of pebbles which led back to the edge of the forest. From there Baron Kilbride's fortress lay half a day's flight to the south. Somehow sensing the urgency of the mission Pig's wings beat harder and faster and they flew through the air at great speed.

'If Baron Kilbride wants to marry you, Princess,' asked Beo as they flew, 'then will he not make you his wife by force.'

'He doesn't know what I look like,' said Princess Lois. 'He just heard that my parents were looking for suitors and dispatched a messenger with a proposal of marriage. He does that all the time.'

'Why?' asked Blart.

'He's been married four times already,' explained Princess Lois, 'and each of his wives has met a violent and untimely death, normally involving the removal of their head. He is finding it difficult attracting a fifth.'

'What about you, merchant?' asked Beo. 'As you sold him the pet are you not worried that he will recognise you and wonder why you have returned?'

'He does not know me either,' answered Uther. 'I knew of his reputation and I was sure that were I to walk into the granite fort with a tree imp and offer it for sale then Kilbride would have simply killed me and taken the imp.'

'How did you sell it, then?' asked Beo.

'I used intermediaries,' explained Uther. 'I sent my cousins Igor and Ivor to negotiate terms. Of course, at first Kilbride thought they had the imp hidden somewhere and he threatened and blustered and tortured –'

'Tortured?' interrupted Blart. Torture was one of those activities that Blart felt you should be flying away from rather than flying towards.

'It is sometimes necessary for one's employees to endure a little mild torture in order to oil the wheels of business,' explained Uther. 'They have to earn their bonus.'

The other questors looked at him in horror.

'Eventually,' continued Uther, 'Kilbride was convinced that they didn't know where the imp was, so he agreed to pay

Ivor while keeping Igor hostage. Ivor rode out to a place where I met him. He handed over the money and I gave Igor a box containing the imp, which he took back to Kilbride.'

'Didn't you think of the imp?' asked Princess Lois angrily.

'Of course I thought of her,' said Uther. 'She was the key to me making money. I made sure she was well fed and supplied with water.'

'I meant, didn't you think of the suffering that a wild imp would suffer being stuck in captivity?'

'There's no room for sentiment in business,' insisted Uther.

'What happened?' said Blart.

'That was it,' said Uther. 'Except that, as I predicted, Kilbride was so enraged at having to pay for something that the next time Igor and Ivor were seen they were floating face down in his moat.'

'He murdered your cousins? You must want vengeance,' declared Beo.

'That's one way to look at it,' agreed Uther. 'But then again, what businessman doesn't like to see his labour costs reduced?'

'If Baron Kilbride attacks wizards and warriors and everybody,' said Blart, deep in thought, 'then how are we going to get into the fort to rescue the tree imp?'

'Aha,' said Capablanca. But this time he said nothing else. In his hurry to rush off and liberate the tree imp from Baron

Kilbride he had not given any thought to how he might achieve it. And knowing the Iron Baron's reputation they might all soon be floating face down in the moat.

'I think I might be able to help with that one,' said Uther smoothly.

Uther was really beginning to get on Capablanca's nerves.

'There is one thing that is close to Baron Kilbride's heart,' Uther continued.

'Would that a dagger were close to his heart,' muttered the Princess.

'He is a great lover of the theatre,' revealed Uther. 'But unfortunately he has great difficulty attracting players to appear in his fort. So we will simply knock at his gatehouse, announce we are a troupe of travelling players and we will be warmly welcomed into his fortress.'

'Why does he have difficulty attracting players?' asked Blart.

'He can easily be disappointed,' explained Uther. 'And if the play is not to his liking or the actors are poor then he is robust in his criticism.'

'I can take a bad review,' said Beo.

'His bad reviews tend to involve boiling the actors in oil,' said Uther.

Blart did not like the sound of that.

'Stop this horse,' he said. 'I want to get off. I'd rather risk being wanted dead or alive by people who don't know where I am than boiled in oil by someone who does.'

'Blart, Blart, Blart,' said Uther. 'Do you think I would be going if I thought that I was to be boiled in oil?'

'I don't know, do I?' said Blart sulkily. 'You might like it.'

'I won't find out because it won't happen,' Uther assured him.

'People are always telling me things won't happen when I go on quests,' said Blart. 'And then they always do.'

'Perhaps you haven't been on very well organised quests before,' said Uther.

Capablanca bristled. 'We're getting off the point,' he said irritably.

'I want to get off the horse,' said Blart. 'And go home.'

'Listen,' insisted Uther. 'What we will do is this. By the time we arrive at Kilbride's granite fortress it will be late. Far too late for any theatrical performance. Therefore we will be allowed in with the promise that we will perform the next day. The Baron will be pleased to hear of a rare opportunity to see some players and we will be given food and probably invited to sleep by the great fire in the servants' quarters. But though we will lay our heads down we will not sleep. Instead we will wait until very late and then we will find the tree imp and make our escape.'

'I don't like your plan,' said Beo.

'What is wrong with it?' said Uther.

'There are no dead bodies. If you attack a baron's castle you have to leave a trail of corpses behind you, lying in pools of blood.'

'Why?' asked Uther, who was puzzled.

'It shows that you've been,' explained Beo. 'Then it becomes a deed that people talk about. Perhaps even write a ballad about. Then you become famous, and famous people sometimes get turned into knights.'

'People will not write a ballad about freeing a tree imp,' maintained Uther.

'You never know,' said Beo. 'They write ballads about the strangest things. Why I heard this ballad recently about killing a mouse.'

And before they could stop him Beo launched into song:

'I took my axe
To kill a mouse
Sing Hey! for glory and me
I missed the mouse
And smashed my house
And had no scones for my tea.

I took my lance
To kill a rat
A good man am I and no sinner
I missed the rat
And hit my cat
It really spoiled my dinner.

I took my sword
To kill a squirrel
No limp do I have, nor hunch
I missed the pest
And tore my vest
Sweat dripped on to my lunch.

There is a moral
To this song
A brave man am I with much zeal!
A clash with vermin
Is determined
To cast a pall on a meal.'

'So you see,' said Beo when he'd finished, 'they could easily write a song about killing a tree imp. But only if they know that it's been stolen. If we don't leave at least one bloody corpse behind us then the Baron might think he'd lost it.'

'Trust me,' Uther assured the warrior. 'I know how much he paid for it. He will know he hasn't lost it.'

'I think there's something wrong with your plan,' said Blart, who had finally crammed all of its details into his head.

For once Capablanca was pleased to hear Blart object. He hoped that his objection to the merchant's plan would be a good one.

'What is wrong with it, pig boy?' asked Uther.

'You said that when we lay down our heads we would not sleep.'

'I did.'

'But when I lay down my head I always sleep,' said Blart. 'Sometimes I fall asleep even before I lay my head down. That usually makes me fall over.'

Capablanca sighed. It was always a mistake to rely on Blart.

'That is your objection?' said Uther.

'Yes,' said Blart.

'When the time comes to steal the tree imp we will simply shake you to wake you up,' said Uther.

Blart thought about this for a moment.

'That would work,' he agreed.

Uther smiled.

'And now if there are no more objections to the plan I have outlined we can negotiate my fee.'

'Your fee?' Capablanca was outraged. 'On a quest we do this for honour.'

'We are a fellowship,' agreed Beo. 'All for one and one for all.'

'Yes, yes,' said Uther impatiently. 'You do it for whatever you want. I want money. Or rather I want the opportunity to make money. It won't cost you anything.'

'What do you mean?' said Capablanca.

'Simply this,' said Uther. 'When we return to the Forest of Arcadia with our tree imp we would be most foolish to free the imp until Sorel has shown us to the dwelling place of

Agnes the Horse Shouter, in case the imps rush off and do not keep the promise.'

'I agree,' said Capablanca.

'Yet,' continued Uther, 'when we have been guided to Agnes we no longer need the services of Sorel. Therefore, instead of releasing the tree imp that we have captured we could instead use it to lure and trap Sorel. We would then have two tree imps.'

'I fail to see why this would help,' said Capablanca.

'That is because, unlike a businessman such as myself, you are not seeing things in the long term,' explained Uther. 'After the quest is over I would then, using an intermediary for the purposes of self-protection, sell the two tree imps back to the Baron. One tree imp was worth a great deal. Two tree imps with the possibility of baby tree imps would be worth a fortune.'

'Never!' shouted Princess Lois. 'I am not betraying the tree imps so that you can make money.'

'It would be to break our word,' pointed out Capablanca.

Blart had missed the ethical issues that his fellow questors raised. However, he had foreseen a different problem.

'What if the Baron had got a better pet in the meantime?' said Blart. 'Like a pig.'

'I have given you a plan,' insisted Uther. 'You must give me the imps.'

'No,' said Princess Lois. 'We refuse.'

'Then you can't have the plan,' said Uther.

'What's to stop us?' asked Beo menacingly.

'My copyright,' answered Uther sharply. 'I own the plan and if I say you can't use it then you can't use it. I await an offer.'

'What about the offer not to push you off the horse and watch you tumble to your death?' said Beo, who was still determined to get a bloody corpse into the quest if it killed him. 'Then you wouldn't have the copyright because you wouldn't be here.'

Beo edged closer to the merchant. Uther looked down. The ground below looked a long way off but very solid if you got there too fast. Uther decided to be flexible.

'You can have that plan as a free sample,' he said. 'A loss leader. An early season promotion to foster customer good-will. Perhaps you'll pay for further plans in the future.'

'Look,' shouted Princess Lois.

They looked. In front of them rose the immense granite fortress of Baron Kilbride. Even in the gathering gloom of approaching night, the fortress silenced all the questors as it had silenced many who had seen it before. From above they could see it was square and its eight black towers shot viciously into the sky. The moat was deep and wide and the only entrance was across a bridge that led to a heavily fortified gatehouse.

'A man who builds a fortress like that is sending out a message,' said Capablanca.

'What message would that be?' asked Uther.

'Don't steal my tree imp,' suggested Blart.

The other questors decided that this was not the message that the fortress was sending.

'We must land and walk the rest of the way to the fortress,' said Capablanca. 'As we know, a flying horse attracts attention.'

'And we should not be too hasty,' said Uther. 'Remember that we don't want to get there until late so that the Baron cannot ask us to perform until tomorrow.'

'And we must stick to our story at all times,' said Capablanca. 'If the Baron discovers our true identities we will be killed. If he discovers our true purpose things will be worse.'

As Pig the Horse flew down towards an isolated field to land, Blart dwelt on the prospect of something worse than death. Luckily his brain wasn't advanced enough to come up with something, so he was not as scared as he should have been.

Chapter 35

It was the blackest night that Blart could remember as the questors walked apprehensively towards the gatehouse of Baron Kilbride's fortress. There were no twinkling stars above them and the moon was shaded by cloud.

Beo thundered his great fist against the iron door. High up in the door a grille was pulled back and a dark face poked out.

'Who dares strike the door of the fortress of the Iron Baron?' demanded a guard.

'We are simple players,' said Uther. 'We seek a night's lodging.'

'How will you pay?'

'With a performance,' replied Uther. 'We will pay with our art.'

'Your heart more likely,' said the guard with a guffaw, 'if your performance is not good.'

'We have travelled far and wide,' said Uther. 'Tomorrow we will provide a spectacular show.'

'Spectacular, eh?' said the guard. 'My master will be pleased to hear that, for he finds a rare enjoyment in watching players. That is if the players be good.'

'We are the best,' insisted Uther with complete confidence.

Hearing Uther, Blart almost believed himself to be a talented player.

'I will tell my master's steward that you are the best,' the guard said. 'Therefore be it on your own heads, or lack of them, if that is not the case.'

'We have nothing to fear,' Uther assured him.

'I hope it will be so,' said the guard. 'For I am tired of watching the gatehouse and perhaps if I can come to my master's favourable attention then I may be allowed to ride out with the rest of his soldiers and do some pillaging. My sword is itching for blood.'

Above the questors the grille closed and a moment later the great iron gate swung open. Before them lay a sobering sight. In the vast courtyard of the fortress were many fires that burned a fierce orange in the black night. Around each fire, warming themselves, eating hunks of meat and drinking from flagons of mead, were many of Baron Kilbride's soldiers.

'They have just returned from a raid on the lands of Lord Easy,' explained the guard. 'They plundered much treasure and brought back many prisoners for ransom. The celebrations will continue long into the night.'

But now was not the time for the questors to quail. Uther led them in. Blart brought up the rear, leading Pig the Horse.

'That is a huge beast,' the guard observed.

'He is almost lame,' interjected Princess Lois, who didn't want anybody paying too much attention to Pig.

'Tell the boy to take it to the stables,' commanded the guard. 'He can then join us in the servants' kitchen.'

'Where are the stables?' asked Blart.

The guard hit him in the face. Blart fell over in a mixture of pain and astonishment.

'Where are the stables, *sir*,' the guard corrected him. 'Good manners cost nothing.'

Unfortunately for Blart nice words and fancy phrases were not his strong point. Instead he trudged off in the direction the guard was pointing, mumbling to himself about life's unfairness.

'That boy will find himself with many a fist in his face if he does not learn to respect others,' observed the guard.

'Aye,' agreed Beo, who was only disappointed that the fist in Blart's face had not been his own.

Meanwhile Blart had reached the stables. He had found them simply by following the scent of dung. Blart's nose was particularly sensitive to dung. It was a skill he was most proud of. Once there, he spied a boy even younger and even weedier than himself feeding a horse a bag of oats. Blart's heart leapt. Throughout this quest he had been forced to deal with people who were bigger or scarier than him. Now, finally,

Blart had found someone he didn't need to respect or look up to.

'Oi,' he shouted at the boy.

The boy looked up. He looked suitably nervous.

'What's your name, boy?' said Blart.

'Stodge the Lad, sir,' replied the boy apprehensively.

Blart had never been called sir before. He thought it rather became him.

'Get over here, Stodge the Lad, and see to my horse.'

Stodge rushed over, grasped Pig's reins and led him to the drinking trough.

'He is a mighty fine horse,' commented Stodge deferentially. 'I'll get him some oats when he's finished drinking.'

There was a silence. Blart should really have headed off to the servants' kitchen, but there he would find himself back at the bottom of the social hierarchy. Here in the stables there was somebody who was looking up to him. Blart felt the temptation to linger.

'Is there anything else, sir?' said Stodge.

'I am seeing to things,' answered Blart vaguely. 'Do you have any pigs around here?'

'Pigs?' Stodge's face lit up at the word. 'I wish we did but sadly there are none.'

'That is a shame,' said Blart gruffly. 'It is my habit, Stodge, in quiet moments when I am not seeing to things to pat a pig.'

'They are noble creatures,' nodded Stodge. 'I would

much prefer to work with pigs than horses, but what can I do? My master, the Baron, refuses to keep them.'

Blart studied Stodge with a new-found respect. He had never come across anyone before with a fondness for pigs. However, he wanted to be sure that the boy's devotion to pigs was serious.

'To be a pig boy is a very important position,' he cautioned Stodge. 'You must be dedicated to it.'

'I know,' said Stodge. 'But I believe I could do it. When I was young, before the Baron's men murdered my family and kidnapped me, we used to have a pig and I was in charge of its swill. I made sure that our pig always had swill. I can still hear his oink.'

There was a look of pride in Stodge's eyes as he spoke of his duties. A look that touched Blart's heart. For were not he and Stodge similar? Both orphans. Both great admirers of the pig. Blart, it seemed, had found a friend.

'Would you mind, Stodge,' said Blart with a politeness that he only normally produced when threatened with violence, 'if I sat down and we chatted about pigs?'

'It would be an honour, sir,' said Stodge the Lad and he indicated a bale of hay where Blart could sit. The light of friendship was in Blart's eyes as he sat.

'Where have you been, stoat-features?'

Blart wheeled round. At the stable door stood Princess Lois.

'I have been talking to –' began Blart.

'Nobody wants to talk to you and nobody wants to listen to you,' snapped Princess Lois, cutting him short. 'You have to come with me right away.'

Blart was not going to be ordered about in front of his new friend.

'I will come when I want,' he told the Princess dismissively. 'Stodge and I were going to talk of pigs and swill.'

'If you don't come with me right now then you'll be chopped into pieces and thrown into the moat,' Princess Lois told him.

'You couldn't do that,' said Blart.

'No, you couldn't,' agreed Stodge, standing shoulder to shoulder with his new friend.

'No, I couldn't,' agreed Princess Lois, 'but Baron Kilbride could. And he will. He's demanded we put on a show right away. And if you don't come with me then we'll be one player short and that player will be in a great deal of trouble.'

'But,' Blart's mouth had fallen open. 'We aren't —'

'Quite ready,' said Princess Lois, realising that in his surprise Blart had been about to reveal that they were not real players. 'Now come on.'

She turned and stalked off. Blart had no option but to follow her. He allowed himself one last glance at Stodge. What could have been a beautiful friendship had never even got started.

Chapter 36

Princess Lois walked at such a ferocious pace that Blart found it very difficult to keep up with her. She led him across the courtyard, ignoring the lewd remarks passed in her direction by Baron Kilbride's soldiers, and into the strongly fortified keep. The guards there seemed to recognise her, for she marched straight past them, up the cold stone stairs harshly lit by burning lanterns, and through the kitchen, which was filled with the powerful smell of roasted ox. Blart felt a sudden emptiness in the pit of his stomach, but the Princess did not stop there. Instead she strode up another smaller set of stairs that were not so well lit. At the stop of the stairs was a curtain. Princess Lois pulled it back to reveal the questors' dressing room.

'Where've you been?' demanded Beo, looking up grumpily.

'He was talking swill,' said Princess Lois.

Beo looked at Blart in disgust.

'Could someone remind me why we need him?'

'Our play needs a hero,' said Uther.

'He doesn't look like a hero,' said Princess Lois.

'Maybe not at the moment,' said Uther. 'But after applying some make-up he will be far more convincing.'

'What kind of make-up?' demanded Blart suspiciously.

'Lard-based make-up,' said Uther. 'I have some samples with me.'

'Why do all your products have lard in them?' asked Blart.

'Lard is a versatile substance with multiple uses,' explained Uther. 'You can cook with it, grease with it, make yourself up with it and it serves as a tasty snack in between meals.'

'Cease this discussion of lard,' ordered Capablanca irritably from the corner in which he was sitting. 'You can cake Blart in as much lard as you like but that isn't going to help us get out of this mess you've got us into.'

'What mess?' asked Uther calmly.

'What mess?' demanded Capablanca indignantly. 'We are in the middle of a fortress, surrounded by hostile drunken soldiers. We are about to attempt to entertain a ruthless Baron with a play in the knowledge that if our performance is not to his liking he will have us all killed. The unfortunate problem is that none of us are trained actors and we do not have a play to perform. Therefore, within a minute of entering the feasting we will be recognised as imposters and condemned to death – I call that a mess.'

'I don't understand,' said Blart, who didn't.

'There has been a slight hiccup in my plan,' admitted Uther.

'Slight,' said Capablanca sarcastically.

'The Baron is staying up late to celebrate with some of his officers,' continued Uther, 'and the initial entertainment did not go down well. Apparently the Baron was not fond of mime. Therefore his steward came down to the kitchen while you were dawdling in the stables and told us that we would have to perform this evening – I did try to explain to the steward that we had not had any rehearsal time but he refused to listen.'

'And yet you are always saying that you can persuade anyone to do anything,' said Capablanca.

'The steward was to be thrown into the moat with his legs and arms tied together if he did not provide a satisfactory replacement for the mime troupe,' protested Uther. 'There is a limit to even my powers of persuasion.'

'What happened to the mime troupe?' asked Princess Lois.

'They were taken to the dungeons to be tortured,' answered Uther.

'They're not miming any more,' said Beo grimly.

Blart had been concentrating very hard and he had understood almost everything that had been said. He therefore produced what in his view was the only appropriate response. He panicked.

'What are we going to do?' he shouted.

'Control yourself, Blart,' said Capablanca sternly.

'Stop whining, weasel-features,' said Princess Lois.

'I'm too young to die,' protested Blart.

'You aren't going to die,' said Uther reassuringly. Well, it would have been reassuring were it not for the fact that Blart and everyone else knew that Uther was a practised liar. 'You are simply going to have to act.'

'I'm too young to act,' wailed Blart, who was now panicking properly and therefore did not feel the obligation to make sense any more.

Princess Lois slapped Blart sharply in the face.

'Ow!' said Blart and stopped panicking abruptly.

'I'll hit you again if you don't shut up,' said Princess Lois. 'None of us will ever survive this night if we don't work together.'

'The Princess is right,' observed Uther. 'The Baron wants a play – we will give him one.'

'But I've never seen a play,' said Blart. 'I wouldn't know what to do.'

'It's easy,' Uther assured him. 'All plays are basically the same. Boy meets girl. They fall in love. Girl's father hates boy, says they cannot marry, tries to marry her to someone else. There's a fight. Everybody dies.'

'Is that all?' said Blart.

Uther nodded.

'But we still don't have a script,' pointed out Capablanca,

'and any moment now we will be called into the Baron's feasting room and expected to perform.'

'What we will do is this,' said Uther. 'I will narrate the story. Whenever I say that you should say something then you say it.'

'Won't that be boring?' said Blart.

'You won't say exactly the same thing,' said Uther. 'If, for example, I say "The girl's father was very angry and forbade her to marry the boy," you will shout, "This is an outrage. You cannot marry him. I forbid it." Just say whatever I suggest you say a bit differently and say it with as much feeling as possible. We might just get away with it.'

Capablanca foresaw a problem with Uther's suggestion that they improvise their lines. The problem was Blart. However, before he could raise his objection Uther began giving out parts.

'Blart you will be the hero, Blob. Princess Lois will be the heroine, Aurora. Capablanca will be her father, Craggle, and Beo will be Grasper, the rich merchant he insists she marry.'

Beo exploded.

'Why must I play a merchant? I should be the hero. It is the only chivalrous part.'

'You cannot play the hero,' answered Uther. 'Princess Lois must play the heroine and she must be wooed by someone about her own age, like Blart. It's a rule.'

'But …' Beo began to protest.

Baron Kilbride's steward stuck his head into the room,

silencing the questors immediately.

'This is your five-minute call,' said the steward. He looked more closely at the questors. 'Why are you not in your costumes?'

'It's in modern dress,' explained Uther. 'We are an experimental theatre troupe and we reject the illusions and deceptions of other players. We prefer raw naked emotion.'

'You'll get raw naked emotion if the Baron doesn't enjoy it,' the steward assured them.

Chapter 37

Five minutes later Blart stood behind an arras in the Baron's feasting room, his face greasy with lardy make-up.

'Ladies and gentlemen,' he heard Uther announce, 'welcome to our play. It is our great honour to present for your entertainment *The Terrible Tragedy of Aurora and Blob.*'

Uther paused for applause. There wasn't any.

'Let us press on,' continued Uther hastily. 'We set our scene in the land of Madeupiya. In this land there lived a handsome young man named Blob.'

'Get on,' hissed Princess Lois, giving Blart a powerful shove.

Blob shot out from behind the arras, stumbled and fell flat on his face.

There was a roar of laughter. Harsh laughter. Laughter that enjoyed watching the suffering and misfortune of others. Blart (now playing Blob) raised his head and quailed at the sight that met his eyes. In front of him was a great table and at that table sat six fearsome soldiers. And sitting in the middle of the soldiers sat Baron Kilbride. A hulking brute of a man dressed in red robes with a contemptuous sneer smeared across his face.

'A handsome young man named Blob,' said Uther, 'who after tripping up by accident stood up again and looked very manly.'

Blob managed to pull himself to his feet but a terrible nervousness overcame him and his legs began to shake.

'What's that on his face?' demanded one of the soldiers.

'Blob was tanned after a trip to the South,' narrated Uther by way of explanation. Perhaps he had gone over-board on the lard. 'Once home he walked about and whistled in a noble fashion.'

Blob tried to obey Uther's instructions but his nervous legs refused to move. So he pursed his lips to whistle. One of Blart's greatest skills was the ability to produce at will a loud and unpleasant whistle. It was not a talent that most of us would boast about but Blart did not have as much choice as most people when it came to talents. But now he found that when he pursed his lips he could produce no sound at all. Blart was suffering from stage fright.

'Blob didn't whistle for long,' narrated Uther. 'Instead he resolved to stay still and hum.'

Blart managed to produce a low hum.

'This play had better improve soon,' said Baron Kilbride.

'While he was standing still and humming,' said Uther,

'the beautiful lady Aurora came wandering by.'

From behind the arras appeared Princess Lois as Aurora.

'She spied Blob and he spied her,' said Uther. 'She was a modest maiden and so she covered her face to avoid showing how handsome she found the noble Blob.'

Princess Lois, not by nature a modest maiden, suddenly became one. She lowered her eyes. A shy smile played on her face.

'Blob was captivated by Aurora's beauty and he showered her with compliments,' narrated Uther.

Blob didn't say anything.

'He showered her with compliments,' repeated Uther.

Blob opened his mouth to speak. No words came out. Instead he burped.

'What is this nonsense?' the Baron said impatiently. 'If it wasn't for the maiden I would have them thrown into the moat.'

Uther took the hint and decided to switch the dramatic focus to Aurora.

'Aurora was overcome with the beauty of the compliments showered on her by the noble Blob and she giggled,' Aurora giggled, 'and simpered,' Aurora simpered, 'and danced nimbly about to show her delight.' Aurora danced nimbly.

The Baron applauded.

'That's more like it,' he told his soldiers. 'I like a bit of nimble dancing.'

'Emboldened by the success of his compliments and dazzled by her maidenly beauty Blob sought a kiss from the beautiful lady, Aurora.'

Blob was still unable to move, so Aurora danced closer to him.

'Their first kiss was modest and tender but hinted at a deep passion,' narrated Uther.

Aurora and Blob looked at each other. Neither had ever anticipated having to kiss the other. Baron Kilbride leant forward in his chair. For the Dark Ages this was hot stuff.

The needs of the drama overcame their reluctance. Aurora shaped her lips into a round red heart. Somehow Blob gained enough control over his body to purse his own lips in response. For the briefest of moments their lips touched.

Some of the lard from Blob's face attached itself to Aurora's nose. It was a tender moment.

'The tenderness of that one kiss revealed to them both that they were bound to spend the rest of their lives together and instantly they became betrothed.'

'He's got to ask her to marry him,' shouted the Baron.

Uther looked at Blob, whose mouth was opening and closing helplessly.

'Their union was so perfect that they needed no words to express their devotion,' said Uther desperately. 'Their kiss was their betrothal.'

'Humph!' said the Baron, unconvinced.

'But Craggle, Aurora's father, was passing by,' narrated Uther quickly before the Baron could dwell on his dissatisfaction.

Capablanca as Craggle appeared from behind the arras.

'He's old enough to be her grandfather,' observed one soldier.

'Her great-grandfather,' remarked another soldier.

'Her great-great-grandfather,' said a third soldier, who was one of those people who never quite realise when a joke's gone too far.

'Quiet,' ordered the Baron.

'Craggle had become a father very late in life,' continued Uther in an attempt to fit Capablanca's appearance successfully into the narrative. 'And therefore he was extra protective. He flew into a rage when he saw Blob kissing his daughter and hit the noble Blob with his staff.'

Blart felt a painful thwack on the back of his head.

'Ow!' said Blob, falling to the floor. 'Get off.'

'Don't hit him, Father,' shrieked Aurora. 'He's my intended.'

'I intend him harm,' said Craggle, and he struck Blob once more with his staff.

There was satisfied applause from the watching Baron and his soldiers.

Capablanca hit Blob again.

'You want to marry my daughter, do you?'

'No,' said Blob, who was not concerned with the drama

making sense and was instead more concerned about not being hit any more.

'End of Act One,' shouted Uther before Blob could do further damage to the story's credibility. 'Time for a five-minute interval.'

There was no applause from the soldiers as the actors fled behind the arras. Instead there were mutterings of discontent from the Baron and his soldiers. Blart's performance as Blob the Hero had made suspending their disbelief very difficult.

Meanwhile, behind the arras there was much whispered criticism.

'You kept hitting me,' hissed Blart.

'I was trying to get you to act,' answered Capablanca.

'And you got lard on me, weasel-features,' said Princess Lois. 'Now I'm all greasy.'

'Did anyone see the tree imp?' asked Beo, who was rather envious of everybody else who'd been acting while he was sitting behind the arras.

'I saw her,' answered Capablanca.

'So did I,' said the Princess.

'I nearly saw her,' said Blart.

'She was in a cage,' said Princess Lois, her freckles seeming to redden with anger. 'A tiny cage – she could hardly move and there was not even a twig for her to stand on.'

'If we can get through the second half of our play then it will be free by tomorrow,' said Uther. 'But Blart you must act more nobly in your final scene and you have to kill Beo and Capablanca.'

'The interval is over,' bellowed Baron Kilbride from his feasting table. 'Get on with Act Two or I'll chuck you in the moat.'

'It is customary for a bell to be rung,' said Uther, 'but in this case I think we can make an exception,' and he dashed out from behind the arras. Blart and the Princess remained behind.

The first scene of Act Two featured Craggle (Capablanca) arranging the marriage of his daughter to Grasper (Beo) a wealthy local merchant. From what Blart could hear nothing seemed to go wrong. Then Princess Lois was rushed out as Aurora to be told of her impending marriage.

'No,' Blart heard her wail. 'I love another.'

'You will marry this merchant.'

'Me,' said Grasper, who perhaps wasn't as good at improvisation as the other two.

'But just when all hope was lost,' announced Uther, 'Blob appeared.'

Blob rushed on to the stage.

'What are you doing here?' demanded Craggle and he hit Blob with his staff squarely on the nose.

'Ow!' said Blob, feeling blood begin to run.

'Blob informed Craggle and Grasper that he was here to claim his bride and would fight to the death if they tried to stop him,' narrated Uther.

Blob opened his mouth to threaten Craggle in exactly the way Uther had described. Unfortunately, when he opened his mouth it was immediately filled by blood. Instead of speaking, Blob coughed violently. A mixture of blood, sweat and lard shot out of Blob's mouth and landed on Aurora.

'Euurrghh!' said Aurora.

'That's the way to treat your fiancée,' shouted the Baron, who as we know was not always delicate in his dealings with his wives.

Uther's ability to improvise narrative did not extend to knowing what to do when the hero coughed bile all over the heroine. In desperation he resorted to the solution employed by many a writer when his plot becomes too outrageous — gratuitous violence and a bloodbath.

'Now they fought to the death,' shouted Uther.

Aurora screamed. Craggle raised his staff, Grasper drew his sword and Blob reached for his dagger.

Chapter 38

*F*irst, Blob stabbed Craggle, but he ensured that his dagger in fact slipped between Craggle's arm and his torso. Then he faced Grasper. They struggled. First Blob seemed to have the upper hand. Then it was Grasper.

'Ten crowns on the fat one,' wagered the Baron.

The Baron had seen many a fight and it was not difficult for his experienced eye to see that the huge Grasper could easily overpower the slight Blob. However, the needs of the story meant that Blob had to win this fight. Not that Grasper seemed to be aware of it. With blows that were impressive for their remarkable realism he clouted Blob repeatedly about the head.

'Ow!' said Blob. 'Stop it.'

'Hit him back, you coward,' shouted the Baron.

'Woe is me,' bemoaned Aurora. 'My love is about to be slain and happiness will be taken from me for ever. I will be forced to get myself to a nunnery!'

Grasper hit Blob again and this time sent him sprawling

backwards on to the floor. Grasper towered over him.

'Blob killed Grasper and claimed Aurora as his bride,' shouted Uther, desperately trying to remind Grasper of the way the story was supposed to go. But Grasper was enjoying hitting Blob far too much to knuckle down to the needs of a happy ending. He raised his sword. Blob cowered beneath him. Nobody was acting any more.

Aurora recognised the situation was desperate. So desperate that she stepped out of character and jumped on to Grasper's back.

'There's a damsel with spirit,' observed the Baron. 'I may marry her at the end of this play.'

But Aurora's strength was not enough to restrain Grasper by herself. Observing this from his position on the floor, where for the purposes of drama he was technically dead, Craggle decided to act. He stood up and tackled Grasper.

'Whoa,' shouted the Baron. 'The father has risen from the dead.'

Still there was not enough power to restrain Grasper, so Uther dived at Grasper's legs.

'Now the narrator's joined in,' remarked the Baron's first officer.

'I thought narrators were supposed to be neutral,' said a puzzled Baron.

At last Grasper was held. Blob grabbed his dagger and thrust it in.

That is, he thrust it into the gap between Grasper's arm

and his torso. Though whether that was where he was actually aiming only Blob knew for sure.

'And so the merchant died,' narrated Uther from beneath Grasper's legs.

Grasper staggered one way, stumbled another and collapsed.

All five questors lay exhausted on the floor. And they still hadn't got to a happy ending. The Baron stood up. It seemed as though they weren't going to be allowed to.

'Enough,' cried the Baron. 'That was undoubtedly the worst play I have ever seen in my life.'

'It hasn't finished yet,' said Uther.

'Oh yes it has,' answered the Baron. 'Your appalling performances are an insult to dramatic tradition and you shall all be summarily thrown into the moat.'

'Hurrah!' said the four officers around the table.

'Apart from the girl,' added the Baron, 'whom I will marry.'

'Hurrah!' repeated the officers.

'Couldn't I be thrown into the moat as well?' asked Princess Lois.

'No,' said the Baron.

'Hurrah!' shouted the officers once more. They were cheering anything now.

'But first,' said the Baron. 'I will teach you something. Get up, all of you.'

The questors picked themselves up from the melee they had collapsed into and stood panting in front of the great dining table. The Baron clambered over it and towered in front of them.

'Your killings were unconvincing,' he announced.

'We could go away and rehearse,' offered Uther quickly.

'When you leave this room it will be to be thrown into the moat,' the Baron repeated. He turned to one of the officers. 'Tie these players' hands up so that they will not be able to swim.'

Beo bristled and prepared to fight but Capablanca hissed at him to stop. Inside this room were five bloodthirsty soldiers, and surrounding the tower were many more. To fight now would be suicide. The questors allowed their hands to be bound.

'All except the girl,' said the Baron. 'I would not harm my betrothed.'

All the officers laughed horribly at that because they knew the fate that had befallen the other women in his life.

Meanwhile the Baron regarded the helpless questors.

'Before you meet your destiny in the moat,' he informed them, 'I am prepared to teach you a little bit about realistic killing on the stage. You.' The Baron indicated one of his officers. 'Over here.'

The officer obediently got out of his chair and clambered over the table. It was obviously considered bad form amongst bloodthirsty soldiers to simply go round the table.

'This is how you kill someone convincingly on the stage,' said the Baron, and he drew his mighty sword and plunged it straight into the heart of the officer.

The officer collapsed backwards, clutching his chest and gurgling.

'Wow,' said Blart. 'That is convincing.'

'Or you could do this,' said the Baron, and he swung round and thrust his sword straight into the neck of another officer, who was sitting dumbstruck at the table. Blood spurted from the horrendous wound and the officer fell from his chair.

Another officer rose from the table and reached for his own weapon.

'Or even this,' announced the Baron, using his sword like a spear and throwing it towards the man who had stood up, impaling him and sending him flying back into the wall, where his lifeless body slumped slowly to the floor.

'Hurrah!' said Blart somewhat tastelessly.

The Baron ignored him.

'Is that all of them, Staunton?' the Baron asked of the one remaining living officer in the room.

Staunton nodded.

'That will teach them to plot against me,' said Baron. 'You will be well rewarded for alerting me to their terrible purpose.'

'Thank you, Baron,' said Staunton.

'Why has he killed his own men?' asked Blart, who was not keeping up with developments at all.

'Because they plotted against me,' snapped the Baron

savagely. 'It is the eternal problem of the bloodthirsty tyrant. You surround yourself with bloodthirsty officers and before you know it they want to be bloodthirsty tyrants too. If I hadn't acted they would have killed me before the cock crowed.'

Capablanca saw an opportunity to save the questors.

'Doesn't this demonstrate the folly of endless slaughter?' he suggested. 'Surely now is the time to stop the killing. By not throwing us into the moat you could make a statement that you have embarked on a more peaceful approach to being a tyrant.'

'A peaceful tyrant?' The Baron's fearsome eyebrows knitted together in anger. 'There is no such thing. If my men down there were to hear that I was embracing peace they would chop me into pieces.'

He laughed raucously at his appalling pun.

'Staunton,' he bellowed. 'Fetch my steward so these appalling actors can be dispatched into the moat.'

Staunton rushed to do the Baron's bidding.

'And tell him to bring a wedding dress when he comes. There should be one hanging in the Lady's bedchamber.'

The Baron regarded Princess Lois with a leer.

'You won't mind the bloodstains around the neck I'm sure.'

Princess Lois gulped. She almost wished she were back in Illyria, being plied with fruit and compliments by Anatoly the Handsome.

Almost, but not quite.

'Whilst we wait for the steward and my wedding dress,' said the Princess, 'can I try killing someone more realistically as you have shown us?'

'Of course,' said the Baron. 'They can die in the moat or they can die here. It matters not to me.'

And so saying the Baron tossed his sword to the Princess, who turned to face the questors. Could it be that the Princess was prepared to kill them in order to improve her chances of surviving for longer with the Baron?

'Who should I practise on?' said the Princess.

'Whoever you dislike most,' answered the Baron.

Princess Lois picked out Blart.

'But we've always been friends,' protested Blart.

'No, we haven't,' maintained the Princess. 'You have been foul since the day we met.'

'Get on with it,' said the Baron. 'I hate it when people delay a killing.'

The Princess raised her sword. Blart tried to look appealing.

'Farewell, ferret-features,' said the Princess, and she brought her sword down and stuck it firmly into Blart.

Everybody gasped.

'No, no, no, no, no,' said the Baron. 'You missed. You've stuck your sword into the tiny gap between his body and his arm. Let me show you.'

It appeared Blart wasn't stabbed at all.

The Baron strode over to the Princess. The Princess pulled the sword out from under Blart's arm.

'Let me have one more go,' she said. 'I'm sure I'll be more accurate next time.'

'Don't try too hard,' said Blart.

'Go on, then,' said the Baron.

'I just need to get the sword right through the heart, don't I?' asked the Princess

'That's right,' agreed the Baron.

'Think of the good times we spent together,' said Blart. 'Think of the jokes we shared.'

The Princess thought.

'I can't remember any,' she said.

And she spun round and stuck her sword firmly into his heart.

Chapter 39

The Baron's heart, that is.

The Baron clutched his chest, made an unpleasant gurgling noise and collapsed dead on the floor. Underestimating a woman had undone him. Princess Lois had struck an unlikely blow for equality.

'That's what you get for trying to marry me,' said the Princess.

'Well done,' said Capablanca. 'Now cut us loose.'

With four swift flashes from the Princess's sword the other questors were freed.

'I thought you were really going to kill me,' said Blart.

'I was,' said the Princess. 'But I missed.'

Blart looked at the Princess. She stared right back at him. Blart couldn't make up his mind whether she meant it or not.

'What have you done?'

At the door was Staunton, the Baron's officer, with a look of horror on his face.

'Quick, Beo,' said Capablanca. 'Stop him.'

But a sudden burst of speed wasn't among Beo's attributes and before he could get to the door Staunton had fled, shouting 'Murder!' at the top of his voice.

There was a great uproar in the courtyard below. Blart and Capablanca rushed to the arrow slit and looked down. News of the killing was spreading through the Baron's soldiers and they were standing, shouting, gesticulating, arming themselves and running into the tower to exact revenge.

'Barricade the door,' shouted Capablanca.

'The table,' suggested Uther.

The questors rushed to the massive table. They pushed. It wouldn't move. They pushed harder – Beo's huge muscles strained, Capablanca's eyes bulged, veins stood out on Uther's neck, beads of perspiration formed on the Princess's forehead and Blart ground his teeth with effort.

For once the questors were truly working together. The huge oak table gave. It moved across the floor until it lay against the door to the great dining room. They heard the feet of the Baron's men thundering up the tower.

'Push against the table,' Beo instructed, throwing his bulk against it.

All the questors obeyed. They braced themselves for the impact. Outside, the Baron's soldiers reached the door. They heaved. The questors pushed back with all their might. The door didn't move.

'Push as hard as you like,' shouted Beo triumphantly. 'You will never defeat us. We have won.'

It was left to Capablanca to point out that being trapped in a tower surrounded by armed soldiers who all wanted to kill you was not commonly regarded as a victory.

'Tush and pish,' said Beo. 'The staircase is too winding for them to use a battering ram. The door will hold. They can't get us.'

'What's that smell?' said Blart.

The questors sniffed.

'It's smoke,' said Uther. 'They've built a fire outside the door. They're going to smoke us out.'

And as he spoke the first curl of smoke crept under the door.

'We're trapped,' said Capablanca. 'The room will fill with smoke and we will be choked to death. Can anybody think of a way out?'

'I can,' said Blart unexpectedly.

Blart's reputation for coming up with workable plans was not high but as more smoke crept under the door they were prepared to try anything.

'I heard this story once,' explained Blart, 'about a woman trapped in a tower. She escaped by growing her hair so long that it stretched to the bottom of the tower, cutting it off, tying it on to something and then climbing down it. We could do that.'

All the questors gaped at Blart in stunned disbelief.

'My hair's only shoulder length,' said the Princess.

Blart sensed that they were not as impressed with his

plan as perhaps they ought to be, and he stalked off to the arrow slit and looked out, feeling misunderstood.

'We've forgotten about the tree imp,' exclaimed Princess Lois suddenly. 'She has been caged for many years. We must allow her to breathe the fresh air of freedom.'

'The fresh air of freedom is rapidly filling with smoke,' observed Uther. He was right – the fire outside was obviously getting stronger. More and more smoke poured into the room.

Ignoring Uther, Princess Lois rushed over to the tree imp's cage.

'Don't be alarmed. We have come to rescue you.'

The tree imp's response was scathing.

'And you're doing a rotten job of it.'

'We're doing our best, Marjoram.'

The tree imp started.

'How do you know my name?'

'There is no time to explain,' said the Princess. 'Can you help us escape?'

'Why should I?' said Marjoram.

'She's even worse than the other one,' said Blart.

Marjoram's eyes opened wider.

'Another tree imp?' she said.

'Yes,' said Blart. 'Just as nasty as you.'

'He's called Sorel,' said Princess Lois urgently.

'I haven't seen another one of my own kind for years,' said Marjoram excitedly. 'I will help you!'

More smoke was coming into the room.

'The door has caught fire,' shouted Beo. 'It will burn through. If the smoke doesn't kill us then the Baron's soldiers will.'

'What help could you be?' said Blart scornfully to Marjoram. 'You are nothing but a tree imp.'

'I could tell you that a section of the left-hand wall is really a door,' said Marjoram. 'And if you push it in just the right place then it will reveal a staircase that leads up to the tower roof.'

'Oh,' said Blart, realising that might help.

'Where is it?' asked Princess Lois.

'Pick up my cage and I'll show you,' Marjoram told her.

Princess Lois did as she was bid. She took Marjoram in her cage over to the wall. Smoke was now billowing into the room and the heat was unbearable.

'We will fight to the death,' shouted Beo through the burning door behind which, waiting on the steps, were scores of the Baron's angry men.

'Left a bit,' said Marjoram as soon as Princess Lois got her cage to the wall. 'Down a bit. And push there.'

Princess Lois pushed. Nothing happened.

'Down a bit more,' instructed Marjoram. 'Push again.'

This time the wall moved. It swung open to reveal a stone staircase.

'Capablanca, Beo, Uther,' shouted Princess Lois. 'Marjoram has shown us a way out. Come on.'

'What about me?' demanded Blart indignantly. 'She wouldn't have helped us if I hadn't been rude to her.'

Princess Lois ignored Blart and ran up the steps carrying the tree imp. Capablanca, Uther and Beo swiftly followed her. Before Blart followed he took a last look round. The door was now burning fiercely and it would not be long before it collapsed and the Baron's soldiers were able to force their way through.

The stone staircase was not too high and soon they emerged on the roof. The combination of the smoke and the sudden rush up the staircase had left them desperate for breath and they all took a moment to take in delicious lung-fuls of clean air. Then they took in their situation.

'We're trapped again,' observed Blart, saying, not for the first time, what nobody else wanted to hear. 'As soon as the door collapses, the Baron's men will charge up here and we will all be cut to pieces.'

'Thank you, Blart,' said Capablanca shortly. 'If you can't say anything useful then go and stand over there.'

Blart was about to refuse but he saw the dangerous look in Beo's eye and decided to do as he was told. He looked over the battlements. The courtyard below was deserted. All the Baron's men were inside the tower, standing squashed together on the high staircase, all waiting for the chance to avenge their master's murder.

A slight figure appeared and began to walk across the courtyard. A slight figure that Blart recognised.

'Stodge!' he shouted.

It was indeed Stodge. He looked up.

'Hello, Stodge,' shouted Blart.

Stodge shook his head.

'What's the matter?' Blart wanted to know.

Stodge looked all around him. Then, apparently having satisfied himself that there was nobody within earshot, he cupped his hands around his mouth.

'I can't talk to you,' Stodge shouted. 'You murdered the Baron. You are going to be hacked into a thousand pieces by the soldiers.'

'It wasn't me,' protested Blart. 'I quite liked the Baron.'

'You're disgusting,' remarked Princess Lois from behind Blart.

Blart ignored her.

'I've got to go now,' shouted Stodge. 'The horses need watering. I hope it doesn't hurt too much when they kill you.'

Stodge headed off across the courtyard towards the stables, and at that moment an idea popped into Blart's head.

'Stodge,' he shouted desperately.

Stodge turned round.

'I would like one final request,' Blart shouted. 'Before I die let me see my horse one more time.'

Even in the distance Blart could see that Stodge looked puzzled.

'I thought you preferred pigs,' he shouted back.

'I do,' Blart assured him sincerely. 'But as there are no

pigs here a horse will have to do. And the horse is called Pig.'

Blart watched as Stodge considered this final request. He thought about it for a moment and then he looked up to the tower and regretfully shook his head.

'I cannot do it,' he said. 'If the soldiers found out they would kill me too.'

And with a forlorn wave he turned away.

'Don't say no!' shouted Blart to Stodge's departing back. 'Just one brief look before I die. Do it for our shared love of pigs.'

Stodge continued to walk away. He did not look back.

Behind Blart things were getting worse. The angry cries of the Baron's soldiers grew louder as they anticipated the ever-nearing moment when they would be able to wreak a terrible vengeance on the questors. Beo had ventured back down the staircase to see what was happening below but all of a sudden he shot back up.

'They are through,' he bellowed. 'The door is gone and they are pushing the table away. In seconds they will be upon us. We must take as many of them with us as we can.'

And so saying the warrior drew his sword.

'If only I had a spell,' cursed Capablanca. 'But all I have is a staff. I will fight with it.'

'I will fight with my dagger,' said Princess Lois.

'And I with mine,' said Uther.

All of them moved towards the entrance to the turret. Blart was inspired by the nobility of his fellow questors to stay as far away from the entrance as possible.

He looked up at the sky. It was a clear deep blue. Blart thought that he could never remember seeing a sky so blue. Was it the last sky he would ever see?

'Here they come,' shouted Beo.

Blart heard the frenzied shouts of the Baron's soldiers below. Their frustration was at an end and they scented blood.

Blart took one last lingering look at the deep blue sky. Then he looked down – to see Stodge the Lad leading Pig the Horse out of the stable.

'I had to let you see him one last time,' shouted Stodge. 'Even though he's not a pig he's called Pig and that's the next best thing.'

'Pig,' shouted Blart, not bothering to thank Stodge. 'Help! We're in danger. Rescue us.'

Blart waved his arms frantically.

Behind him he heard the clash of steel as the first of the Baron's soldiers charged the turret.

'Take that,' he heard Beo shout.

'Help, Pig,' shouted Blart again, and he shook his head as well as waving his arms to try and emphasise the true desperation of the situation.

'He can't understand you,' shouted back Stodge. 'And even if he could he couldn't help you.'

Blart heard a thwack behind him as the wizard's staff connected with one of the Baron's soldiers' heads.

'We can't hold them off for much longer,' yelled Uther.

Down below, Pig suddenly tugged at his reins.

'Whoa!' shouted a startled Stodge.

Pig tugged again.

'Easy,' shouted Stodge.

Stodge was a slight lad and Pig was a massive horse. The third tug dragged the reins from Stodge's hands.

'Hey!' shouted Stodge.

The huge wings unfurled from beneath Pig's belly and began to beat. Stodge watched, dumbfounded. As did Blart. He didn't know how or why but somehow Pig the Horse had sensed his desperation and even now was rising to the rescue.

'Capablanca!' shouted Blart.

Higher rose Pig.

'Don't distract me when I'm fighting to the death, boy,' snapped back the wizard.

'But we're going to be rescued,' said Blart.

'Rescued,' sneered Beo as he dispatched yet another of the Baron's men with a mighty blow. 'We're not going to be rescued.'

Pig the Horse's great wings brought him level with the height of the turret.

'Well, I'm going to be rescued,' said Blart. 'You can come if you want. But if you want to stay and die that's up to you.'

And so saying Blart climbed on to the battlements, took a deep breath and jumped.

Blart landed on Pig's back.

'Hey!' shouted Uther, turning round. 'The boy is getting away.'

He climbed on to the battlements and jumped on to Pig the Horse.

'Cowards,' cried Beo, who was now thoroughly committed to dying in a hopeless cause against overwhelming odds, which he felt was most chivalric. 'Beowulf the Warrior runs from no man.'

Capablanca was not as convinced by the necessity of immediate death.

'We must run now so that we can fight a greater battle later,' he shouted to Beo.

'I cannot retreat,' shouted back Beo.

'You must come and protect Princess Lois,' ordered Capablanca.

'I don't need protecting,' shouted Princess Lois and she emphasised the point by sliding her dagger into the stomach of one of the Baron's men, who was about to deliver a ferocious blow to Beowulf's head.

'You could pretend,' said Capablanca testily.

Any moment the Baron's men would swarm up.

'You'll never make it to being a knight now,' Blart mocked Beo from the safety of Pig the Horse.

Where all Capablanca's sensible persuasion had failed, a vicious taunt succeeded. Beo turned to Capablanca.

'I will not die until I'm a knight,' he declared. 'Let us retreat with honour.'

'One, two, three, flee!' shouted Capablanca.

At exactly the same moment Capablanca, Beo and Princess Lois turned and ran across the turret. The Baron's men were so shocked by this that for one brief moment they paused before pursuing them. But one brief moment was all they needed.

Grabbing the tree imp's cage as she ran, Princess Lois, followed by Capablanca and Beo, clambered the battlements and vaulted on to Pig the Horse.

'Fly,' shouted Blart. 'Fly, fly, fly!'

Pig the Horse beat his wings and the great horse rose higher and higher into the sky. Beneath them the turret filled with the angry cries of the Baron's men. The questors watched them become smaller and smaller and smaller until they were nothing but distant squeaks of indignation.

'I've saved you all again, haven't I?' said Blart.

Chapter 40

Sorel was sitting exactly where they'd left him.

'We would like to introduce you to Marjoram,' said Capablanca, indicating the cage.

'I can't see a tree imp,' said Sorel. This was unfortunately true. As soon as they had reached the outskirts of the forest, Princess Lois, concerned that Marjoram was deprived of her natural habitat, had crammed her cage with twigs and leaves to make her feel at home. Marjoram was now entirely invisible.

'Get these leaves off me,' said a shrill voice. 'What are you trying to do, suffocate me? For five years I hardly see a leaf and then all of a sudden I've got a whole wood on top of me.'

'I was only trying to make you feel more comfortable,' protested Princess Lois, nevertheless removing the offending foliage.

'I can't imagine how bad it would be if you'd wanted me to feel less comfortable,' grumbled Marjoram.

'That sounds like a tree imp,' said Sorel excitedly. 'And from what I can see it looks like a tree imp. Though not a very attractive one.'

'Speak for yourself,' replied Marjoram indignantly. 'You look all gnarled and knotty.'

'How dare you?' rejoined Sorel. 'At least I wasn't stupid enough to get trapped in captivity.'

'I don't believe it,' remarked the Princess to Capablanca. 'We bring together two tree imps after years of solitude and all they can do is be nasty to each other.'

'Don't worry,' Capablanca reassured her authoritatively. 'Conversation between tree imps generally features the hurling of abuse. This is one of the reasons they are verging on extinction.'

'So,' said Uther to Sorel, 'we have kept our part of the bargain, now you must keep yours. Take us to the horse shouter.'

Sorel tried to look grumpy about this but it was obvious to the questors below that he was too excited about insulting a fellow tree imp face to face to brook any delay.

'Follow me,' said Sorel. 'I will move through the branches above and show you the way.'

And with that the tree imp set off.

Through the pathless forest went the questors. They passed great strong trees whose trunks were thicker than a fortress wall and withered trees that were dying and rotting. They clambered over fallen branches and tripped on gnarled roots that rose up out of the ground like the coils of a sea monster. They forded flooded streams, clambered over rocks and up muddy hills, all the time keeping their eyes on the tree imp above them.

'Hurry up,' Sorel urged them whenever they paused to find a gap big enough for Pig to squeeze through.

'I thought the imp said he knew the way,' grumbled Blart. He attempted to jump over another stream, didn't put enough effort in and so landed with a disappointing splosh in the water. 'This is taking ages and I'm getting wet.'

'It's your own fault, mole-face,' snapped Princess Lois, easily jumping over. 'Don't you dare blame the tree imp.'

'I'll blame –' began Blart but he was interrupted by a cry from above.

'Look! The dwelling of Agnes the Horse Shouter.'

Dwelling was a flattering name for what they saw. In a small clearing, branches and leaves had been heaped to create the most primitive shelter Blart had ever seen.

Sorel had descended to a low branch.

'I kept my promise,' he said. 'Now you must release Marjoram.'

Princess Lois didn't need to be asked twice.

'No,' shouted Uther, too late. The cage was open, Marjoram was out and the two tree imps disappeared into the forest, arguing furiously.

'What did you do that for?' demanded Uther. 'That tree imp was worth money.'

Princess Lois regarded the merchant with scorn.

'I will never regret freeing a wild creature,' she answered, 'no matter how much money it is worth.'

'It was priceless,' answered Uther. 'Now that Marjoram has gone, so has Sorel, and without him we have no way of finding our way out of the forest.'

'I thought you were dropping stones behind you to help us find our way out,' said the Princess.

'I stopped because I thought we weren't going to let the tree imp go until we'd been led to the edge of the forest,' answered Uther.

'You didn't tell me,' snapped Princess Lois.

'You didn't tell me you were going to let them go,' snapped back Uther.

'Calm down,' said Capablanca. 'There has been a slight breakdown in communication but nobody was really at fault.'

'I think they were both at fault,' said Blart.

Pig whinnied. The dark forest with its dense vegetation was nothing like the vast open expanses of the land of Nevod where he had grown up, and he didn't like it.

The horse's distress had an effect on the questors that nothing else could have produced. A little ashamed of themselves they pulled back from their argument. For Pig the Horse was the only questor that all the others liked. Well, almost all the others.

'Nobody ever tells the horse to shut up,' said Blart bitterly.

All the questors were about to tell Blart that Pig was a much more pleasant creature than he was but they were interrupted by a very loud snore.

'That's even louder than Beo,' said Blart.

Another snore erupted from Agnes's dwelling place. Birds perching in nearby trees flew off, screeching their disapproval.

'Let's wake her up,' said Beo, who was eager to move the conversation away from a discussion of his own sleeping habits. He strode purposefully across the clearing to Agnes's dwelling place. He paused. Agnes's dwelling place posed a problem for the visitor as it lacked an obvious door to knock on. Beo was not to be put off easily. He pummelled his fist firmly against the structure.

It swiftly emerged that whatever talents Agnes had, building was not one of them. Three powerful blows from Beo's fists left the structure shaking, wobbling and finally crashing down entirely to reveal the lumpy figure of Agnes, lying on her back on a bed of moss.

'What?' said Agnes, waking up as the branches collapsed on to her head.

'Tush and pish,' said Beo. 'I barely touched it.'

'What's going on?' said Agnes, still befuddled by sleep.

'Your house has fallen down,' said Blart helpfully.

'There was a sudden wind,' said Capablanca, deciding that it was probably better not to inform Agnes of the real cause of her sudden homelessness. 'It rushed through the forest and knocked over your house.'

Agnes stood up. She was wearing a threadbare plaid shawl over a ragged green blouse with a hessian skirt.

'You snore really loudly,' Blart told her.

'I don't normally snore,' insisted Agnes. 'But at the moment I have a cold.'

She scrutinised the remnants of her shelter suspiciously.

'A wind, you say?'

'A freak wind,' nodded Capablanca. 'It came out of nowhere.'

'Don't winds normally come from nowhere?' asked Blart unhelpfully.

The wizard ignored him and focused on Agnes. But Agnes was no longer looking at Capablanca. Nor was she considering the remains of her house.

'What's that?'

The questors turned round anxiously. All they saw was Pig the Horse. The questors looked at each other. This was not a good sign.

Chapter 41

'It's a horse,' said Capablanca.

'Called Pig,' added Blart.

'We thought you might like to talk to him,' coaxed Princess Lois.

'Talk to him?' shouted Agnes. 'Of course I don't want to talk him. Get him out of my clearing.'

The questors looked at each other in despair.

'But, madam,' said Uther soothingly, 'is it not the case that you are the legendary Agnes? Your reputation has stretched far and wide.'

Agnes stared at him balefully. Uther reached deeper into his larder of compliments.

'And so we have travelled in a spirit of great humbleness and humility to find Agnes, Agnes the Great, I should say, to see if she considers us worthy to marvel at her gifts and witness her speak to a horse.'

Agnes's stare had become a little less baleful with each honey-covered word that had slipped from Uther's mouth.

'It's not just horses, you know,' Agnes told Uther. 'I can talk to all the animals.'

'All the animals?' said Uther.

'Even pigs?' said Blart.

Agnes nodded wearily as though the memory brought her no joy whatsoever.

'Then we have underestimated you,' said Uther smoothly, 'for which we humbly apologise. We realise now that you should not be known as simply Agnes the Great, but as Agnes the ...'

Uther paused. His larder of compliments seemed to need restocking.

'Very Great?' suggested the Princess.

'Extra Great?' suggested Capablanca.

'Great and a bit more?' suggested Beo.

Agnes began to look a little dubious as the disappointing epithets rolled in.

'Agnes the Superb,' concluded Uther.

Agnes cheered up.

'Agnes the Superb,' she repeated. 'I like the sound of that.'

'And it sounds right because it is true,' agreed Uther. 'If I were to say, for example, "Blart the Superb", then it would sound wrong, wouldn't it?'

'Not to me,' said Blart.

Agnes and the other questors agreed it would sound wrong.

'We must tell everyone that Agnes the Great should no

longer be called Agnes the Great but should instead be called Agnes the Superb,' said Uther. 'And we should do it straight away.'

'Yes,' agreed Agnes the Newly Superb, blinded by the blizzard of compliments.

'For that reason we ask you to speak briefly to Pig the Horse so that we can be numbered among those who really have seen you talk to the animals.'

Agnes the Newly Superb stood up to do as she was bid. And then she remembered something. Her face darkened and she sat down again.

'What is the matter?' asked Uther soothingly.

'I swore I would never do it again,' said Agnes. 'I would never speak to another animal as long as I lived.'

'Why?' asked Capablanca. 'Surely when one has an almost magical power like yours one should be prepared to use it.'

'That is what I thought once,' said Agnes, 'but something changed my mind.'

'What?' asked Princess Lois.

'Dung.'

'Don't use language like that in front of a maiden,' cautioned Beo. 'It is unchivalrous.'

'I don't need protecting from dung, you oaf,' snapped Princess Lois. 'My pet dragons were always making big piles of dung.'

'Not like the piles of dung I've seen,' said Agnes darkly,

and as she spoke it felt as though she was summoning up an awful memory.

'What's wrong with dung?' said Blart. 'My pigs were always leaving piles of it in their sty. I never minded.'

'In their sty,' cried Agnes. 'If the dung had stayed in sties and coops then I wouldn't have minded.'

'You mean your dung came out of its sty?' said Blart. Mobile dung was not a thing anybody wanted to come across.

'No, no, no,' said Agnes. 'The dung didn't move. The people did.'

None of the questors had any idea what Agnes was talking about any more. But Agnes was now deep into her traumatic memory and was not concerned whether people understood her or not.

'At first it wasn't a problem. I lived in a house outside a pretty village. The villagers knew of my gift and they used to come by every now and then to ask me why their dog was barking so much or why their cat wasn't eating, and I used to talk to the animal and find out and tell the owner and everything was fine.'

'There you are,' said Uther. 'That's almost what we'd like you to do with —'

'But then word spread,' said Agnes, cutting off Uther in mid-flow. 'People began to come from far and wide with their animals. "Why won't my cow give milk?", "Why won't my hen lay?", "Is my toad happy?". I tried to help. I tried to talk to all their animals. But each day when I woke in the morning there were more people outside my door, waiting with their animals. And no matter how fast I talked to each one, the queue of people and animals would grow longer. Soon it stretched around my house and into the village. A big queue of animals waiting. And then there was the dung from all the waiting animals. It piled up outside my house. It piled up in the village. The smell was terrible. The villagers, who used to be my friends, blamed me for all this though it was not my fault. One night they came to my house armed with torches and sticks. They stood outside, shouting about me ruining their neighbourhood. They called me names and said I had brought disease to their streets. In vain, did I shout through the window, telling them that I had never wanted all this dung, that I disliked it more than them. But they wouldn't listen. One by one they threw their burning torches at my house. The thatch caught fire. I had no time to gather even my most precious possessions before I had to run from my own home.'

Blart nodded sympathetically.

'I've been chased out of villages too,' he said.

Agnes seemed not to notice this interruption, so deep was she in the recollection of her own misfortune.

'But I survived. And realising that my gift had brought nothing but trouble and misery —'

'And dung,' added Blart.

'— I resolved to hide myself in the middle of the deepest forest and never to use my gift again.'

Agnes finished her story with a shudder.

The questors, recognising that Agnes had found recounting the incident difficult, maintained a respectful silence.

That is, most of the questors.

'I bet pigs were the best animals to talk to,' said Blart.

'Your experiences sound terrible,' said Uther to Agnes with such sincerity that he could only be lying. 'We all sympathise with your predicament and respect completely your decision not to use your gift again.'

Uther paused. The other questors looked confused. Surely if they respected Agnes's decision then they would fail in their quest, Illyria would be invaded, Zoltab would be freed and the world would be destroyed.

'But,' said Uther, 'we would ask you to use your gift just once more.'

'Never,' answered Agnes firmly. 'Did you not hear me say I swore a solemn oath?'

'But —' began Uther.

'Never, never, never,' interrupted Agnes.

Capablanca decided that Uther's insincere compliments had reached the summit of their usefulness and that it was now time for him to take over.

'Agnes,' said the wizard. 'I understand you swore an oath but you must know that this is no ordinary matter. If you do not help us there will be war. Evil forces will rise up and the world will be destroyed.'

'Never, never, never,' repeated Agnes.

Capablanca was dumbfounded. Princess Lois felt that

Capablanca's method was flawed. What would Agnes care about the wider world, she thought, living as she was in a rude shelter in the middle of a forest? She felt that a more personal approach was called for.

'Agnes,' she said, adopting a kindly tone. 'We know that you love animals and would like to talk to them. But you have a fear. A fear that if you start talking to our horse then we would tell others and they would come to see you too and before you knew it there would be dung everywhere.'

Agnes shook a little when she heard the word 'dung'.

'Let us assure you,' said Princess Lois, moving closer to Agnes and placing a comforting hand on her arm, 'that we will tell nobody of our visit. Nobody will ever know that we have met you.'

Princess Lois looked so sweet all of a sudden that Agnes was tempted. She remembered the fun she'd had talking to animals and the way everyone was so impressed by what she could do.

But then she remembered the dung.

'No,' she repeated.

Princess Lois's eyes shrank back to their normal size and her comforting hand dropped from Agnes's arm.

Beo watched Princess Lois's failure.

'When you want a job done I'm the man to do it for you,' he announced and he pulled his giant sword from his scabbard.

'Now,' he said, approaching Agnes, 'we've tried to be nice

and we've tried to be reasonable. And you, being a nasty crone living in a hovel, couldn't appreciate nice and reasonable – which makes me sad. And when I get sad I get angry. And when I get angry I tend to pick up my sword and cleave into pieces the person who made me sad and angry, unless they change their mind and talk to that horse straight away.'

Beo's approach lacked subtlety, but as he approached Agnes, brandishing his sword, none of the questors doubted that it would be effective.

But Agnes was not cowed.

'There are worse things than being cleaved in two.'

'Don't be too sure,' said Beo, raising his sword higher and preparing to slash.

'I will face death before I face dung.'

Agnes raised her head and fearlessly faced Beo's blade.

'Beowulf!' said Capablanca. 'We cannot come into a woman's clearing, knock down her shelter and then kill her simply because she won't help us.'

'Can't we?' said Beo.

'We are not savages,' the wizard reminded him.

The warrior looked dubious.

'I thought you said my shelter blew down in a freak wind,' said Agnes.

'Did we?' said Capablanca, realising his mistake.

'Yes,' said Agnes. 'And I was considering helping you.'

'No, you weren't,' insisted Beo.

'I was,' said Agnes.

'You didn't sound like you were to me,' said Beo.

'Beowulf!' said Capablanca.

The questors looked at each other helplessly. If even death could not persuade Agnes to help them, then nothing could. It was at that moment that Blart produced a freak wind of his own.

Chapter 42

'Is something wrong with your lard?' Blart demanded of Uther.

'Blart!' snapped Capablanca. 'We are trying to save the world. The quality of Uther's lard is entirely unimportant.'

'My lard is fine,' insisted Uther.

'It's doing strange things to my insides,' said Blart.

'There's probably something wrong with your insides, then,' said Uther, who never acknowledged anything he sold was defective.

'I think my insides are about to become outsides,' said Blart.

'What's the boy talking about?' demanded Beo. 'If he wants his insides to become outsides then I've got an unsheathed sword in my hand that will do a fine job of it. One swift cut is all I need.'

'No,' explained Blart. 'I need to –'

'I know what you need to do,' said Capablanca, feeling that even though the quest was not going well it had not yet descended to the level where public discussion of Blart's less attractive physical requirements was necessary. Beo was bound to find it unchivalrous and offensive to the modesty of Princess Lois and soon there'd be blood everywhere.

'Just go into the trees,' said Capablanca.

Blart walked delicately but swiftly towards the trees, which was the point at which Agnes finally understood what was going on.

'No!' she shouted, a terrible desperation in her voice. 'I can't have that horrible boy's dung near my clearing. You must stop him. I'll do anything.'

'Including talk to Pig the Horse for us?' said Uther quickly.

'Anything,' repeated Agnes.

'Blart,' commanded Capablanca. 'Stop.'

Blart paused at the edge of the clearing.

'I'm not sure I can,' he said.

'You can and you will,' ordered Beo. 'All you need is will power.'

'What's that?' asked Blart.

'Your body wants to do something but you use the power of your mind to stop it.'

Blart looked confused. When his body wanted to do something his mind usually went along with it.

'Concentrate, boy,' urged Capablanca. 'The success of the quest may hinge on your movements.'

'Or lack of movements,' added Uther unnecessarily.

Rarely can the world have been so at risk.

Blart screwed up his face and concentrated.

'We must hurry,' said Capablanca to Agnes. 'I don't know how long we can keep your clearing dung free.'

Agnes needed no more encouragement and she rushed across the clearing towards Pig the Horse.

'Beo and the Princess!' said Capablanca. 'You are Blart's oldest friends. Distract him. Keep his mind on higher things.'

Capablanca and Uther followed Agnes to where Pig the Horse was waiting patiently. Reluctantly, Beo and the Princess obeyed the wizard.

'Hello, Blart,' said the Princess.

'Hello, Blart,' said Beo.

'Hello,' answered Blart.

There was an awkward silence. It appeared that despite having spent long periods of time in each other's company, having saved the world once and being in the process of trying to save it again, the three questors had nothing to say to each other.

'Would it help if I threatened to kill you?' said Beo.

Blart shook his head. Down below his insides made strange and ominous noises.

Strange noises were also coming from the other side of the clearing.

Agnes stood in front of Pig the Horse and cleared her throat impressively.

'May I ask respectfully,' said Uther, 'why you are a horse

shouter? I have heard of horse whisperers.'

'I was a horse whisperer when I was young,' replied Agnes. 'But then I became hard of hearing.'

'How does your shouting help your hearing?'

'If you shout at them they shout back,' said Agnes. 'Now let me get on.'

Agnes reached up to Pig's ear and suddenly produced a loud noise that hovered between a bray and a whinny.

Pig did nothing.

Agnes nodded her head vigorously and repeated the noise, only louder this time with a bit more whinny and a little less bray.

Nothing.

'Is there a problem?' said Capablanca.

'Of course there isn't a problem,' said Agnes testily. 'Horses are just like people. They speak a broadly similar language but they have different dialects. I just have to hit upon the one your horse speaks.'

'How many horse dialects are there?' asked Uther.

'Seventy-eight.'

Capablanca looked across the clearing. Blart was sweating with effort. In the battle of mind over matter, the wizard was sure matter was on the verge of winning.

Agnes nodded and brayed, shook her head, whinnied, blew out some air and then brayed.

Pig the Horse did exactly the same.

'Got it,' said Agnes.

'What did the horse say?' said Uther.

'He said, "Hello."'

'You had to do all that to say hello?'

Agnes nodded.

'Horse language is very primitive, so it takes a long time to say anything,' she explained. 'But they do have twenty-seven different words for hay.'

'This is no time for a lesson in horse language,' said Capablanca. 'Ask Pig if he can remember where we took Zoltab the Dark Lord after we captured him.'

Agnes looked shocked.

'Can't I ask him whether he likes his oats?' said Agnes. 'It's what people normally wanted me to ask their horses.'

Capablanca ground his teeth with frustration.

'We have not travelled vast distances at considerable risk to ourselves to find out whether the horse likes its feed. Now ask what I have told you to.'

'It's not that easy,' protested Agnes. 'I don't think I've ever learnt how to say "Zoltab the Dark Lord" in horse language.'

'You must try,' Capablanca told him. 'Can you not sense how important this is?'

'All right,' agreed Agnes. 'But I can't guarantee that it will work.'

And so Agnes embarked upon a long series of whinnies and brays and loud blows through her mouth and shakes of her head and snorts.

After a while she stopped and the Pig the Horse whinnied, brayed and snorted back.

This went on for a long time. All the questors watched in silence, awed by the communication between woman and beast, which none of them had ever witnessed before.

That is, they were awed for a bit and then it got boring. After all, one whinny sounds much like another. And once you've heard one snort you've heard them all.

Still, Agnes persisted and with occasional prompts from Capablanca it looked like progress was being made when Agnes was finally able to report …

'The horse remembers.'

'Hurrah!' shouted Capablanca uncharacteristically. 'What does he remember?'

Many more snorts and whinnies later Agnes turned to the questors once again.

'It is a little confusing,' she announced, 'but the horse remembers going to some big white hills where there wasn't any hay.'

'Big white hills,' said Capablanca thoughtfully.

'The tallest and steepest white hill was so tall and steep that Pig the Horse couldn't land on its top,' continued Agnes. 'So he and you and Zoltab landed lower down and you climbed up it. It was very cold and the white stuff was hard for the horse to climb through, but eventually, tired and exhausted, you reached the summit, where there wasn't any hay.'

'You can edit the hay bits,' said Capablanca irritably.

'Here, you imprisoned Zoltab the Dark Lord and left him no hay.'

'I said edit the hay bits,' said Capablanca.

'You asked me to tell you what the horse said and I'm telling you,' said Agnes. 'He'd like more oats if it could be arranged and he doesn't ever want to go back to the circus. That's everything.'

But Capablanca had stopped listening and was already deep in thought.

'Big white hills and the white was hard to walk through,' the wizard pondered. 'They must be snow-covered mountains.'

Uther nodded.

'And the tallest and steepest mountain is,' the wizard began muttering the names of mountains to himself and shaking his head as he ruled them out one by one. And then suddenly his head stopped shaking.

'I have it,' he declared. 'Zoltab is imprisoned at the summit of Mount Xag.'

Chapter 43

'Mount Xag the Unclimbable,' said Uther.

'My insides feel better now,' announced Blart, but nobody seemed to be listening. Now that Agnes had spoken to Pig the Horse, Blart's insides had become irrelevant. He followed Princess Lois and Beo across the clearing to join the others.

'It cannot be unclimbable if I climbed it,' Capablanca said to Uther.

'Oh, yes,' added Agnes. 'The horse said something I didn't quite understand about a stick and lots of blue light when you were climbing the mountain.'

'I thought you said you'd told me everything,' said Capablanca.

'You got very tetchy about the hay,' said Agnes indignantly. 'So I thought you'd get really angry if I started talking about sticks.'

'The stick must have been your wand,' exclaimed Princess Lois. 'You must have used magic to help you climb.'

'Surely that's cheating,' observed Beo, who was very aware, as a possible knight, that if one was to do a deed of derring-do, such as climbing an unclimbable mountain, then it had to be done properly.

'I had more important concerns than whether I was cheating or not,' said Capablanca. 'I was imprisoning Zoltab the Dark Lord, who, if discovered by his Ministers and minions and rejuvenated to full power, could cast a pall over the entire world.'

'I'm just saying that there are right ways of doing things and wrong ways.'

'I will dispute this no longer,' said Capablanca. 'We must get out of this forest and make our way to Mount Xag, where we will be able to take evidence from Zoltab to prove he has been imprisoned. This will be sufficient to prevent the war between the Grand Alliance and Illyria.'

'Can you have a war when only one side's got an army?' asked Princess Lois.

'Not really,' conceded Capablanca. 'What you usually get is a massacre, but massacre doesn't sound as good, so the winners usually call it a war anyway and the losers tend not to complain because they're dead. We must head north to Mount Xag immediately.'

'Except we can't,' pointed out Uther, 'because the Princess let the tree imps go.'

'Because you didn't drop a path of pebbles,' countered the Princess.

'Let us leave that matter in the past,' said Capablanca. 'I'm sure Agnes can lead us out of the forest.'

Agnes shook her head vigorously.

'No,' she said. 'Nobody mentioned anything about leading you out of the forest. I swore a solemn oath to stay deep in this forest for ever. I cannot help you.'

'But you've already broken one solemn oath today,' said Uther. 'So, when you think about it, your oaths can't really be that solemn.'

'My oaths are as solemn as the next woman's,' protested Agnes. 'I will not break this one.'

Uther was completely unruffled by this refusal. He knew Agnes's weak point and as an experienced merchant he knew that once he found a weak point he could make a deal.

'If you don't help us we will be forced to stay here with nothing but rancid lard to eat. You would be faced with mountains of dung,' he threatened. 'But if you do help you will never see us or a horse ever again.'

Uther offered his hand to shake on the agreement.

Agnes stared at the merchant, horrified by his threat. But she knew she was beaten. She shook his hand. The deal was done.

Chapter 44

'There is no time to waste,' urged Capablanca as they watched Agnes disappear back into the forest. 'We must fly to Mount Xag and find Zoltab's prison. We have only two days before the Grand Alliance invades Illyria and war must be averted.'

'I'm tired,' said Blart. 'Could we have a rest first?'

The temptation to rest was great for the wizard. He was exhausted and his body ached. He looked at the other questors. They too seemed to want a rest. It would be so easy just to collapse into the soft grass and sleep.

But no! Capablanca shook his head angrily at his own weakness. There was no time to waste. The future of Illyria and possibly the future of the world depended on the questors not stopping for a moment. The wizard drew himself up and embarked upon a more rousing call to arms.

'Fellow questors. We are called upon to go once more into the breach. We are tired and yet we must go on. We must stiffen our sinews, summon up our blood, set our teeth and stretch our nostrils wide. We must …'

A repulsive sight abruptly halted Capablanca's speech.

'What is the matter with you, boy?' demanded the wizard.

'I'm doing what you said,' answered Blart. 'I'm stretching my nostrils wide. I was wondering how far they would go.'

Capablanca gave up on his morale-building speech.

'Just get on the horse,' he told the questors. 'We've got a war to stop.'

Once more the questors climbed on to Pig the Horse. Once more Pig the Horse unfurled his great wings from under his belly. Once more they rose into the air. Capablanca directed Pig north and the steady beats of his great wings took them towards Mount Xag and Zoltab and the answers to so many questions. Would they be able to climb Mount Xag? Would they be able to find Zoltab's eternal dungeon? Would Zoltab still be inside it? Would they return in time to prevent the conquest of Illyria? And just how far could Blart's nostrils stretch?

'Faster,' Capablanca urged Pig the Horse. 'Every second saved is crucial.'

'I think I've got a nose bleed,' said Blart.

Nobody paid any attention.

Instead they watched the world pass beneath them. The verdant forests became scrub grass became desert became beach became sea. Bright day dimmed to cold night. Moonlight beamed down on the ocean below, shooting stars flashed across the sky and Pig the Horse's wings beat on, regular and strong. The first warm rays of morning shone from the east as the sun rose, dismissing the puny light provided by the moon and the stars. Below them the sea became land. But no longer a land of yellow sand or green vegetation. Instead there were fierce crags and jagged rocks, trees without leaves and barren plains with no cover. And in the distance there was the white glare of snow. Though the sun was at its height the temperature fell as Pig the Horse continued north. Blart blew steam from his mouth, the Princess pinched her cheeks to bring them warmth, and drops of water in the warrior's beard froze to form shards of ice.

And then they saw them.

White and majestic, the great mountains shot up into the immaculate blue of the sky. Beowulf the Warrior shielded his eyes and shivered at the same time. Never had he seen such terrible beauty.

'Where are we?' he asked Capablanca in a hushed tone.

'Behold,' said the wizard, 'the Xanthean Mountains. The most inhospitable place on earth.'

'Aren't there any quests to nice places?' asked Blart.

Capablanca ignored him.

'We must find the highest peak,' said Capablanca. 'Mount Xag the Unclimbable. We must journey to the top, where Zoltab is imprisoned.'

'Why is it called "the Unclimbable"?' asked Blart.

Capablanca tried to answer casually.

'There are tales of paths that lead to overhanging cliffs,

of thundering death-dealing avalanches that can be triggered by the slightest cough, of mysterious wild beasts with fearsome tusks that roam in packs, ready to disembowel any intruder in their lofty domain.'

'But you climbed it to imprison Zoltab,' said Princess Lois.

'Yes, Princess,' agreed the wizard. 'But you must remember that I used the power of magic to help me. I expect I used the Spell of Heat to warm me, the Spell of Navigation to lead me, the Spell of Invisibility to prevent the wild beasts from seeing me and the Spell of Silence to render any cough noiseless. This time we must climb the mountain without the aid of magic. It will be far more treacherous. We will land on its lower slopes.'

'Couldn't we just land on the top?' said Blart.

'The nearer the summit we land, the greater the risk of starting an avalanche,' explained Capablanca. 'We must land in the foothills, leave Pig behind us to save time, and head for the top on foot.'

'Pig climbed it last time,' protested Blart. 'Why does he get to stay behind?'

'Last time Pig would have been needed to carry Zoltab,' replied Capablanca. 'This time everyone in the party is willing to go.'

'I'm not,' said Blart. 'And you'll probably need someone to stay at the bottom and look after Pig the Horse. I'll do that.'

Capablanca shook his head.

'We must all climb to the summit.'

'But,' protested Blart, 'poor Pig might be captured and returned to the circus while we're gone.'

Capablanca's expression hardened.

'It is most unlikely that the circus will be visiting the foothills of the most inhospitable place in the world.'

Onwards flew Pig towards the Xanthean mountains. As the fearsome peaks grew nearer Blart's excuses as to why he couldn't climb the mountain grew ever more ludicrous.

'I think my cold is turning into a cough and I could easily start an avalanche,' he suggested. Then, 'I have bad circulation in my toes.'

Finally, Blart produced his best excuse of all.

'I was once attacked by a snowman.'

'How did it attack you?' demanded the Princess.

'I don't want to talk about it,' said Blart.

Now they were flying amongst the mountains. The air had a fresh sharp bite Blart had never experienced before. Towering above were white peaks, serene, implacable and utterly merciless. They looked fit to swallow an army without trace, let alone five questors.

Blart heard a deep ominous rumble.

'What's that?' he asked Capablanca, not really sure that he wanted to know the answer.

The wizard responded by pointing towards a nameless peak. Blart squinted through the glare and saw the snow moving, rolling down the mountain stronger and more powerful than any river, covering everything that it swept up with wave upon wave of snow.

'Avalanche!' shouted the wizard through hands cupped for warmth.

Blart turned away from the fearsome sight. But wherever he looked there were white mountains stretching into the distance and reaching high into the sky.

'There!' shouted Capablanca suddenly. 'Mount Xag!'

In front of them, silent and impassive, sat the king of mountains – higher, sharper and more ferocious than any other peak in the range. It was massive in a way that was beyond Blart's puny comprehension.

It lay in wait for them.

Chapter 45

Pig whinnied.

'Farewell, Pig,' said Princess Lois. 'When we return I promise I shall take you back to Illyria and you shall have a life of ease such as no horse in history has ever known.'

She patted the horse and followed the others along the path that led from the foothills upwards towards Mount Xag.

'Are we ready?' said Capablanca.

All the questors nodded. Apart from Blart.

'Remember we must move quickly,' instructed the wizard. 'In cold such as this we will not be able to survive for more than two days. Keep close together. Do not shout. Avoid mysterious creatures with tusks. Let us climb.'

The questors set off. A few moments later they stopped. The path had disappeared under a fresh carpet of snow.

'Hmm,' said Capablanca.

'Oh dear,' said Blart cheerily. 'We'll have to turn back. Nobody can say we didn't try.'

'This could be a good thing,' said Capablanca.

'How can it be a good thing?' demanded Blart. 'There isn't a path any more. We don't know which way to go.'

'You forget,' said Capablanca, 'that many of the paths that crisscross the mountain lead over precipices. It is probably good to be without one.'

The wizard sounded more confident than he felt. A climber doesn't need a path to find himself tumbling over a precipice. He can do that just as well without one.

'It's a mountain,' added Uther. 'One keeps going up until there is no more up to go. Then one is at the top.'

'Unless one has fallen off a cliff before one gets there,' said Blart bitterly.

'There is good visibility,' Capablanca assured him. 'We would see a cliff long before we fell over it. Now, let us have no more talking. Beo, lead the way. We must climb.'

And climb they did. For the rest of the day barely a word was spoken as they trudged steadily through the snow, following in the giant footmarks of Beo the Warrior. Though the air was crisp and the snow was cold, the combination of their movement, a regular bite of Uther's endless supply of lard and the sun above served to keep them warm enough. Up and up and up they walked, sometimes battling against enormous drifts of snow which seemed ready to engulf them, sometimes inching along snow-covered ridges, sharp as knives, that sheared down to deep ravines filled with cold black merciless tarns, and sometimes hurrying beneath frozen waterfalls where icicles hung like deadly daggers ready for the kill.

After hours of ceaseless toil they reached a high plateau that promised easier walking. The questors, whose hearts were fit to burst after exerting so much energy, each breathed a sigh of relief.

'We will sit and rest and have some lard when we have crossed this plain,' said Capablanca.

'Remember it's got to be paid for,' Uther reminded him. 'I'm keeping count of the amount of lard you've all eaten in my head.'

'You will be paid when we return to Illyria,' said Capablanca.

'And it's a delicacy in these parts,' added Uther, 'so I'll have to adjust the price accordingly.'

'You mean your lard is more expensive here than it was in the Baron's castle?' said Blart.

'Of course,' said Uther.

'But it's the same lard.'

'Perhaps,' said Uther. 'Here it is much rarer and so the price has to rise. It's a firm rule of trade. You can't buck the market.'

Blart always found himself puzzled by Uther's explanations of economics. Somehow every rule seemed geared to ensuring that the merchant made lots of money and his customer had to pay the highest price.

'Come on,' said Capablanca, pointing to the other side of the snow-covered plateau. 'Each step brings us closer to our next bite of lard.'

It was not a cry that would have motivated many groups, but the hungry questors rallied to it.

'Follow me!' cried Beo enthusiastically.

'Sssh,' hissed Capablanca. 'Remember avalanches.'

'Follow me,' whispered Beo.

They set off, glad for the first time not to be going uphill. This was like normal walking. This was almost easy. This was …

'Whoa,' shouted the warrior.

'Beo,' hissed Capablanca again. 'No shouting.'

But the warrior was not listening. Instead he was trying to stop with all his might. The snow on which he had placed his front foot suddenly disappeared and the other questors saw why.

A crevasse. One of a mountain's deadliest traps. A gash in the ice just wide enough for a man to fall into but far too deep for him ever to be seen again. Once a man had fallen into a crevasse all that was left to do was to wait for his blood to freeze.

The warrior wobbled precariously. All of his momentum was pushing him into the icy void. He waved his arms in a desperate attempt to pull himself back from the brink. Capablanca and Princess Lois rushed forward to help. But they were too late. Beo's momentum was too great. With a cry of horror he toppled into the deadly blue abyss.

Chapter 46

If Beowulf had been a fit young knight he would never have been seen again. But thanks to a diet largely made up of succulent pies and numerous flagons of ale, he was not. And how grateful he was for each mouthful of pastry and gravy and each draught of ale now. For although he toppled into the crevasse, he did not disappear. Instead he found himself securely wedged.

'Get me out of here,' demanded Beo's top half – the only bit that was visible.

'Say please,' said Blart, who was not going to let an opportunity as good as this go by.

'I say that I'll kill you if you don't,' answered Beowulf gruffly.

'Blart,' said Capablanca sternly. 'You must help your comrade. This is why quests are such valuable things. They demonstrate that by working together we achieve much more than by working apart.'

Blart sighed. He had heard far too many lectures on the

benefits of quests and he knew that the only way to stop them was to do what the wizard was asking. Aware there might be more dangerous crevasses ready to swallow him up he tiptoed gingerly to the edge and, along with the wizard, grabbed hold of one of the warrior's arms. Princess Lois and Uther took the other.

'Pull,' said Capablanca.

They pulled. The warrior didn't move.

'Pull with all your might,' urged Capablanca.

The questors did as they were bid. They pulled, they tugged and they strained, but Beo remained stuck firmly in the crevasse.

'If I was pulling I'd have had myself out in no time,' remarked Beo somewhat ungratefully while the other questors collapsed, exhausted, into the snow.

'He's too fat,' said Blart.

'I have big bones,' protested Beo. 'It runs in my family.'

'We must wait until he gets thinner,' said Uther.

'This is no time for diets,' said Capablanca, shaking his head vigorously. 'We have to get to the top of Mount Xag.'

'I can't feel my legs,' said Beo.

The questors looked at the helpless warrior. Whereas his upper half was out in the sun his lower half was dangling inside the freezing glacier. Frostbite was setting in rapidly. If they didn't get him out fast then he might never walk again. And not to be able to walk when stuck high on Mount Xag was a sentence of death.

The questors were sobered by these thoughts. That is, all the questors except Blart.

'I'm hungry,' he said to Uther. 'Can I have a bite of lard?'

'Of course you can't,' interjected Capablanca. 'One of your comrades is fallen, his legs face an uncertain future. It is not appropriate to be snacking.'

'I don't see why not,' said Blart. 'I don't see why me being hungry is going to help.'

'It is a matter of respect,' said Capablanca. 'When one's comrade is suffering it is appropriate to try and share that suffering a little rather than indulge yourself in the joys of la…' He paused. 'Unless, of course, lard is the answer.'

'You think we should all eat some?' said a puzzled Blart. 'I thought you just said –'

'Not eat it,' said Capablanca. 'Rub it. If we rub it between our hands we will make it warm and soft. Then we can rub it on to Beowulf and he will slide free.'

'Can I eat some first?' asked Blart.

'No,' said Capablanca fiercely. 'Every bit of lard might be necessary to free Beowulf. There is a lot of him to cover.'

'I tell you, it's my big bones,' protested the warrior again. None of his fellow questors listened though. They had already set to work warming up the lard. A casual bystander might have spotted that one of the questors appeared to be surreptitiously eating the portion of the lard he was supposedly preparing to free his comrade. Luckily for Blart, they were high up a desolate mountain and any casual bystander would have frozen to death long ago.

Once the lard was soft enough, the questors forced their hands into the crevasse and coated Beo's midriff with it.

'If we run out of food it's all your fault,' pointed out Blart while applying the lard he hadn't eaten.

'Is everyone ready?' asked Capablanca. 'Then let us pull once more.'

The questors took Beo's arms, braced themselves and pulled. And tugged. And strained.

And dragged the warrior out of the crevasse.

'Hurrah!' shouted the questors, momentarily linked by a fleeting sense of achievement.

But the look on Beo's face suggested that something was still wrong.

'I can't feel my feet,' he said.

'Get his boots off,' Capablanca ordered Blart.

'Why me?' said Blart.

'My hands are old and gnarled,' said the wizard, 'and are not as flexible as they once were.'

'So are mine,' said Uther quickly.

Blart glumly removed the boots. The feet revealed were dirty, smelly and blue.

'My feet aren't that colour,' commented Blart.

'Of course they aren't,' said Capablanca. 'Beo is in the early stages of frostbite. He will lose his toes unless they are massaged back to life.'

Blart sighed. *Here I am*, he thought bitterly, *being forced to*

*rub a warrior's dirty toes in order to save the country of Illyria. A
country I don't even like.*

For a supposedly brave man, Beo made a great deal of
noise while his toes were being rubbed.

'Ooooh!' he shouted.

'Beo,' said Capablanca.

'Aaaah!' replied the warrior.

'You'll set off an avalanche,' warned Capablanca.

'But it hurts,' said Beo.

'They're better now,' said Blart, for his efforts had
restored a healthy pink to Beo's toes.

'We must get on,' said Capablanca, looking across the
white plain they had only just begun to cross. 'This glacier
could be riddled with crevasses, so we must move carefully.'

Under Capablanca's instruction the questors walked in a
straight line. Beo led, using his sword as a stick to check the
reliability of the ground ahead. Before each step he would
sink his sword into the snow. Usually the glacier beneath
stopped it with a judder and then they knew it was safe to
proceed. But sometimes there was no glacier beneath the
snow to stop the thrust of the mighty sword and this meant
that they had located yet another crevasse. Their progress
was slow and laborious and they grew colder and more
irritable.

'My sword is going to be blunt after all this banging,'
lamented Beo.

'Why did you imprison Zoltab in such a cold place?' Blart

demanded of Capablanca. 'Why couldn't you put him somewhere warmer?'

'The more inhospitable the location the less the chance
of his Ministers and minions freeing him to reek a terrible
vengeance on the world.'

'We have heard nothing of Zoltab's minions for many
days,' said Uther. 'We shouldn't worry about them when we
have so much else to concern ourselves with.'

Blart ignored Uther and continued to question the
wizard.

'But when we captured Zoltab the first time you said that
you were going to put an irreversible spell on him which
would keep him imprisoned for ever,' said Blart.

The wizard shook his head.

'You misunderstand magic,' he told Blart a little haughti-
ly. 'It is not constant but is always changing as wizards in
ancient libraries research new spells. So even though the spell
was eternal a Minister could by now have researched a spell
to remove it.'

'But how would they know what spell to reverse?' asked
Princess Lois.

Capablanca coughed.

'There may have been certain banquets held in my honour at the Cavernous Library of Ping when I first returned
after imprisoning Zoltab, where I may have mentioned it.'

'Why would you do that?' demanded the Princess.

'It is important for a great wizard like myself to impart

my knowledge to younger wizards.'

'He was showing off,' translated Blart.

The wizard grew more agitated.

'The young don't understand the first thing about battling against evil,' he said. 'You think you can just defeat evil once and that's it. But evil's not like that. Evil gets angry, evil regroups, evil gets worse and comes back for more.'

'Can evil get worse?' wondered Blart idly.

'Of course evil can get worse,' shouted Capablanca, showing scant regard for the danger of avalanches. 'Why, when I was a young wizard evil wasn't much more than nasty. Evil played by the rules. But with each defeat evil toughens up. It learns. And it comes back nastier than before.'

There was a silence as the questors contemplated an eviller evil. Flakes of snow began to fall around them. So engrossed had they been in their argument that they had not noticed a dark cloud drifting menacingly towards Mount Xag from the east.

'We must make haste,' said Capablanca. 'Soon the light will be fading.'

Beo stabbed his sword into the snow in front of them and they resumed their plodding progress across the glacier. It seemed as if they were trapped in an immense maze to which someone had forgotten to build an exit. But with the aid of Beo's careful prodding they somehow managed to keep moving slowly forward until, with gasps of relief, they stepped safely off the glacier and back on to the solidity of snow-covered rock. They were chilled to their very core and the snow swirling around them was thickening into a blizzard as night fell.

'We must find shelter,' said Capablanca. 'We cannot blunder on in darkness or we will stumble over a cliff.'

'There is no shelter, wizard,' said Uther, shivering angrily. 'And if we stop on the bare mountain then we will freeze to death.'

'I did not know we would be so long delayed by the crevasses,' said Capablanca.

'What's that orange?' said Blart suddenly.

'You see,' said Uther. 'Blart, who has the weakest mind of any of us, is already seeing hallucinations of fruit. Soon the cold will enter all our minds and we will become similarly confused.'

Blart ignored the merchant and pointed.

'Not that kind of orange,' he said.

Capablanca knew that more than once Blart's sharp eyesight had saved the questors, and he followed Blart's finger. For a brief moment he saw the merest flicker of orange. Beo and the Princess saw it too.

A fire.

Not caring for crevasses, not caring for cliffs, the questors scrambled towards it.

Chapter 47

With freezing hands and toes the questors shuffled, stumbled and staggered towards the fire. Blart imagined feeling the heat from its warming flames on his face. So eager was he to be by it that he didn't even wonder who had lit it.

Even when Blart saw that there was a bald-headed figure in a brown habit hunched over the fire he didn't hesitate. He scrambled through the last drift of snow and plonked himself down, holding out his hands so that they were almost licked by the tongues of flame.

'Hello,' said the bald-headed figure, who seemed a little surprised to have a fireside companion. 'Pleased to meet you. I am Votok the Hermit. You are welcome to share my fire, young man, but you'll burn your hands by holding them so close.'

Votok's tone was kindly not critical. Blart looked at him more closely and saw a plump, friendly face which reminded him a little of a particular pig he had fed swill to when he was a small boy. He withdrew his hands to a safe distance.

The Princess now pushed her way through the snow and sat down next to Blart. Beo arrived next with Uther, followed last of all by Capablanca, wheezing from the effort. They sat around the fire, breathing heavily and letting the life-saving heat warm the very marrow of their bones.

Votok the Hermit broke the silence.

'Did you just happen to be passing or is this a special visit?'

More deep breathing and wheezing.

'I was about to heat up a pan of stew for my supper,' said Votok. 'Would anybody like some?'

'Has it got lard in it?' said Blart.

Votok was somewhat taken aback by this question but seemed to see it as an improvement on wheezing and deep breathing.

'No,' he told Blart apologetically. 'I'm afraid it hasn't.'

'Good,' said Blart. 'I'll have lots, please.'

'Perhaps you'd like to follow me into my cave,' said Votok.

Blart shook his head.

'I want to stay by the fire.'

'I have another fire in my cave.'

Blart looked confused.

'What do you want two fires for?' he asked.

Votok smiled.

'The one in my cave keeps me warm and fed,' he

explained. 'The fire out here keeps me safe from the ferocious tusks of the wild beasts that roam the mountains.'

The questors looked around nervously.

'You are all welcome,' continued Votok. 'The stew will take a while to heat up but it means that we will have time to get to know one another.'

With an amiable smile Votok turned and headed into his cave. They all willingly followed him.

If a person is used to living in a barn then a house seems like a palace. Similarly, if a person has expected to spend the night on a blizzard-blasted icy mountain then a simple rock cave with a blazing fire in it feels like a mansion. The questors did not need any extra bidding to make themselves at home.

Votok produced a huge pan filled with stew that he hung over the fire. The questors, whose recent diet had been made up of lard, more lard and extra lard, eyed it greedily.

'I see you are hungry,' said Votok. 'It will not take long.'

'Thank you,' said Capablanca. He was beginning to wonder about Votok. What was he doing here high on an isolated mountain so far from other people yet so near to Zoltab's prison and with an unnecessarily large amount of stew?

The wizard pondered how he could quiz Votok without alerting him to his suspicions.

'I see you have much stew,' he observed.

Votok nodded. He picked up a rough wooden spoon and began to stir.

Capablanca realised that he was going to have to be more direct.

'What brings you and your stew to the mountain?' he asked.

'Didn't you see him last time you came?' said Blart.

Capablanca flashed Blart an angry look. The last thing he wanted was Votok to know that he had been here before.

'You have been here before?' said Votok, looking interested.

Capablanca nodded reluctantly.

'What brought you here?' asked the hermit.

Capablanca couldn't believe it. He was supposed to be asking the questions but now, thanks to Blart, the questions were being asked of him instead.

'I'm a very keen hiker.'

'You are?' Votok sounded surprised.

'I am,' insisted the wizard.

'Forgive me, friend,' said Votok kindly. 'But for a man keen on the mountains, you and your friends are not very well prepared. Your coats are not thick enough and your boots are not sturdy.'

'We're fond of hiking but we're not very good at it,' explained Capablanca. 'I've always wondered why we never seem to get to the top of anything.'

'Ah,' said Votok wisely.

For a while the hermit concentrated on preparing the stew. A hearty aroma filled the air.

'It is nearly done. My young friend will find six bowls and six spoons at the back of the cave.'

Blart didn't respond. Nobody had ever called him 'my young friend' before.

'Ignorant boy,' said Beo. 'Get the bowls before we all starve.'

This time Blart understood.

'Six bowls and six spoons?' said Capablanca even more suspiciously. 'And yet only one of you?'

'It is fortunate, isn't it?' agreed Votok amiably. 'If we had been forced to share one bowl then the meal would have been less enjoyable.'

'Hmmm,' said Capablanca. 'You were about to tell me what you were doing up here.'

'Was I?' said Votok. 'Perhaps when we have food in our bowls then I will explain.'

Capablanca's suspicions grew.

'Tell us before supper,' he said.

However, his comrades overruled him.

'I'm hungry,' announced Blart.

'I'll starve if I don't get some food inside me soon,' agreed Beo.

'Would you like me to add some lard?' suggested Uther.

'What is it with you and lard?' demanded Beo.

'I'm sick of lard,' said Blart firmly.

'I'll remember that,' said Uther. 'When you are hungry

and there is nothing but lard available, I will remember your words.'

'I'll write them down for you if you like,' said Blart, who remembered the agonising stomach pangs he had suffered in the Forest of Arcadia. 'Well, I would if I could write,' he added.

'Calm down, friends,' said Votok. 'An argument before one eats will be sure to bring on indigestion. Let us chew our victuals in harmony.'

He passed a bowl of stew to each of the questors and their mutual hunger ensured that nobody spoke for a while.

'Now,' said Capablanca after the first few mouthfuls had reached his stomach. 'Perhaps you would be good enough to tell us how you came here.'

'Of course,' he said, resting his spoon in his stew. 'When I was a young man I wanted to do something that would help people and make them happy. I considered all the options and decided upon a religious life.'

'Admirable,' said Capablanca, though he did not sound admiring.

'I was most enthused by the prospect of uniting young couples in matrimony,' continued Votok. 'Here I thought that I could find true joy. By joining two people who loved each other together for ever. What could be more important than that?'

'Pigs,' said Blart.

Votok appeared not to hear.

'And so,' said Votok, 'I underwent a religious training. I studied and I fasted. For seven long years I scourged myself.'

'What's that?' asked Blart.

'You whip yourself as a punishment for being bad,' explained Votok.

'Why?' demanded Blart, not understanding this at all.

'We must be punished for doing bad things,' said Votok. 'So I whipped myself for seven years to show how sorry I was.'

'Couldn't you just tell yourself off?' said Blart. 'And then promise yourself not to do it again?'

Votok shook his head. 'It's not like –' he began, but he was cut off by Capablanca, who felt that there were more pressing matters at hand than trying to explain the intricacies of a religious training to Blart.

'You must not worry about the boy's questions,' said the wizard. 'Tell us what brought you to this lonely place.'

'Disillusionment,' answered Votok. 'I believed that marriage was about love. And I discovered it was about business. A maiden would profess love for one man and then another man would come along who had more land and suddenly she would be professing love for him. And then along would come someone with more land and more cows and she would be professing love for him. It seemed to me that marriage was not about the selfless union of hearts and souls but instead about the benefit to be gained from the union of farmhouses.'

'That's how it should be,' said Uther. 'With ten per cent of the wealth of each farm given to the agent who introduced the couple and negotiated the dowry.'

'In vain did I try to explain to the couples that having similarly-sized barns was no basis for a long-lasting commitment,' said Votok. 'I tried to speak of love and companionship.'

'Sentimental nonsense,' commented Uther.

'I'm afraid those that I counselled agreed with you,' said Votok. 'I was exiled for refusing to celebrate marriages that I deemed to be improper. And so I resolved to become a hermit. To live a life away from men and women until they came to see that a couple should marry for love and only love.'

'You'll have a long wait,' predicted Uther.

'My parents wanted me to marry for love,' said Princess Lois.

'Did they?' said Votok, looking encouraged

'But they kept making me meet all these horrible suitors and so I have decided that I'm never going to get married.'

'You can't say that,' said Votok, upset that a young girl could make an important decision like that at such a young age. 'And this is the world that I fled from,' he reflected. 'And it is on that sober note we must retire for the night. You will want a good night's rest if you are to try for the summit tomorrow.'

'Why do you think we want to reach the summit?' asked Capablanca.

'Few hikers set off to climb a mountain merely to get halfway up and then turn round,' said Votok simply. 'I assumed that you wanted to get to the top.'

'Hmm,' said Capablanca. Votok always seemed to have a plausible answer and the wizard wasn't sure that he liked it.

Suddenly, above their heads there was the sound of drumming. It passed over the cave and disappeared.

'What was that?' asked Blart.

'The sound of wild beasts,' answered Votok, 'pursuing some defenceless creature to its death.'

The questors looked nervously towards the entrance to the cave.

'Do not worry,' said Votok. 'The fire will keep them away.'

Nevertheless the sounds of wild beasts nearby rendered the questors silent. Beo determined to raise their spirits.

'Wild beasts do not scare me,' he announced cheerily. 'I will sing a loud and lusty ballad to show I defy them.'

And before they could stop him, he did.

'*A tiger chewed off my right arm*
And I was very upset
He swallowed it whole and growled no thanks
But I will fight on yet.

A lion tore off my left leg
It really made me sore

300

He chomped it to pieces in his mouth
But I will fight once more.

A rhino gored me in the chest
It gave no end of pain
His horn was covered in my blood
But I will fight again.

An angry dragon burnt off my head
The agony was dire
He ate the rest of me in one gulp
I think I might retire.'

Beo finished singing. The other questors were not sure that when menaced by wild beasts a ballad that stressed the various ways they might be maimed and consumed was entirely appropriate. Votok, however, clapped enthusiastically.

'This is the kind of mutual support which so inspired me when I was a novice.'

The questors lay down by the fire. After a hard day's climbing they were all soon asleep, but Blart was awakened several times by the sounds of wild beasts thundering overhead.

Chapter 48

The blizzard had passed. The storm had blown itself out. A brilliant blue sky and pure white snow greeted Blart as he stepped out of Votok's cave. Dazzled by the early morning light he shaded his eyes. High above gleamed the summit of Mount Xag the Unclimbable. Blart felt a thrill at the thought of standing on top of it.

The other questors shuffled out of Votok's cave and, like Blart, they seemed to grow as they emerged into the sunlight, as though they were physically rising to the final challenge that lay ahead.

'Thank you for your hospitality,' said Capablanca to Votok.

The hermit shook each of the questors by the hand.

'I wish you good luck in your quest,' he said.

'Who said we were on a quest?' said Capablanca immediately. He still had his suspicions about the hermit.

'I meant your quest for the summit,' explained Votok mildly.

'Of course you did,' said the wizard.

'May the weather keep fine for you, may the wild beasts not ravage you and may avalanches not sweep you away,' said the hermit warmly. 'Farewell.'

The questors waved their farewells and set off up the mountain. The climb was much easier than on the previous day. The snow had compacted and was firm underneath their feet. True, the air was cold, but the questors made steady progress, their breath pluming white in front of them. They felt warm blood rushing in their veins and each step seemed to energise rather than tire. It was as though Mount Xag, having failed to repel them yesterday, was now accepting defeat gracefully. Each satisfying crunch that the questors' boots made in the snow brought them nearer to the summit.

'Do you think that climbing Mount Xag will be enough to get me a knighthood?' asked Beo as they paused for a break after a couple of hours' walking. 'For it is surely an act of derring-do.'

'You must not think of personal advancement at such a time,' said Capablanca. 'You will only become a knight when you cease to be obsessed by becoming one. A true knight does his chivalrous deeds simply because they are right.'

'You mean I'll only get to be a knight once I stop trying,' said Beo, sounding puzzled.

Capablanca nodded.

'I could get you made a knight tomorrow for a price,' said Uther.

'What do you mean?' demanded Beo. 'The only way to become a knight is to suitably impress a king or a queen.'

Uther shook his head in the face of such naivety. 'It depends on the king or …' he began, but was silenced by the wizard.

'This is no time to debate your sordid bribes,' Capablanca told the merchant forcibly. 'The time for resting is at an end. Let us begin our final climb to the top.'

Inspired by his words the questors rose as one. Well, not quite as one. Blart as usual was a little behind the others. There was just something about him that meant that he didn't ever get up quite as fast as everybody else. Even when he tried.

Together they embarked on the last stretch of their climb. And though the slope of the mountain grew steeper, still they managed to make good progress. Whenever they reached up they found a handhold and whenever they stretched out they found a safe place to put their foot. After all the tribulations of the quest they were at last finding something easier than they had expected it to be. They climbed over cornices, hauled each other up crags and pulled themselves past overhangs. The only frustration as they approached the top of the mountain was that now the summit disappeared behind other snowy mounds. Each time they climbed a mound thinking it was the end of their ascent they found another higher one beyond it, but for once even Blart didn't suggest that they give up. Instead they strode faster and climbed quicker. Up and up and up until there was no more up left.

They were there.

'Behold the summit of Mount Xag,' said Capablanca. 'We are on top of the world.'

The questors looked down. Bathed in brilliant sunshine the landscape spread out below them. Their eyes saw further than any human eyes had seen before. Lakes and rivers sparkled in the distance. All was awe-inspiring and silent.

'Are you sure that bit over there isn't higher?' said Blart, pointing to a mound nearby.

'Of course it isn't,' snapped Capablanca.

'It looks higher to me,' insisted Blart.

'Wizard,' admitted Beo ruefully, 'it looks higher to me too.'

'I don't believe it,' said Princess Lois. 'I think I'm going to have to agree with weasel-features. That bit over there is higher.'

Capablanca looked in irritation at where they were pointing. Uther, who had taken a tiny mirror out of his coat and appeared to be admiring the twirl of his moustache, hastily returned it and agreed that it was indeed higher.

Five minutes later they stood on the true summit.

'Behold the summit of Mount Xag,' said Capablanca. 'Now we are truly at the top of the world.'

Somehow his dramatic statement didn't seem so impressive second time around.

Blart looked back at the peak they had just walked from. 'Maybe that one is higher after all.'

Beo and Princess Lois looked unsure. Uther, who had got the mirror half out of his coat pocket, grumpily shoved it back in again.

'This is the top of the world,' insisted Capablanca.

'How do you know?' said Blart.

'Because I can see that I built a cairn here to show it,' said the wizard, indicating seven stones gathered together in a loose heap.

'That's just a few stones,' said Blart.

'That's what a cairn is,' snapped back Capablanca. 'A pile of stones that marks the top of a mountain.'

'I thought cairns were supposed to be bigger than that,' said Princess Lois doubtfully.

'Perhaps he got tired when he was building it and so that's why it's quite small,' suggested Beo charitably. 'After all, he is quite old.'

Capablanca was getting very irritated by now.

'It's nothing to do with me being old and tired,' he snapped. 'It's to do with the fact that it's been snowing. I probably built a cairn of a perfectly respectable size but most of it has been covered up. If we dig down into the snow I'm sure we will unearth the rest of the cairn, and by digging further still we will bring ourselves face to face with Zoltab.'

Chapter 49

And so the questors dug. It was cold work digging with their bare hands, but with four of them working as hard as they could and Blart working nearly as hard as he could, they soon made progress. In a short time they had unearthed a bigger cairn.

'I told you this was the top,' said Capablanca.

'*I* told *you* it was the top,' maintained Blart. 'If it hadn't been for me we'd have been digging on that peak over there.'

'I see gold,' said the Princess.

'They are the gold bars of Zoltab's prison,' said Capablanca.

Excited, the questors dug faster.

'They're flashing,' said Blart.

'Flashing gold bars signal our triumph,' said the wizard exultantly. 'If the spell had been broken and Zoltab released then they would no longer be flashing. We have got here in time. Zoltab is still imprisoned. The world will remain safe and war can be prevented.'

Something moved beneath the gold bars. Blart felt his legs go very weak, for he recognised the powerful shaven head of Zoltab the Dark Lord. The great head nodded slightly. It appeared that Zoltab was asleep.

Beo continued to shift huge armfuls of snow, revealing more of Zoltab's prison. The Dark Lord's dungeon was nothing but a barren stone cell with a rough wooden bed at one end.

'Now I will be able to prove to my enemies that I was no friend of Zoltab,' said Capablanca. 'Now I will make them give me back my magical power and build me a new chair in the Cavernous Library of Ping. And this time it will be even comfier.'

Blart heard the wizard's words but was mesmerised by the power and size of Zoltab's slumbering figure. He remembered his cold sneer and his pitiless stare. He remembered –

Zoltab's head shot back and he looked straight up. His black unblinking eyes bored into Blart.

'So you're back, are you, boy?'

Even behind enchanted bars Zoltab terrified Blart. He opened his mouth but no words came out.

'Letting Zoltab see you again is as good as signing your own death warrant,' menaced the Dark Lord.

'Don't listen to him, Blart,' said Capablanca with a slight tremor in his voice. 'He is powerless behind the magic bars.'

'Is that you, wizard?' said Zoltab. 'You think your puny spell will hold Zoltab? I will make you swallow those words before I kill you.'

'If anybody is going to be doing killing it will be us,' threatened Beo.

'Oh, and your fat friend has come too,' said Zoltab. 'I have had time to think of many tortures for you. You will be a thinner and sadder man before you die.'

'We're not scared of you,' said Princess Lois, sounding quite scared.

'How touching,' said Zoltab. 'I recognise the voice of my betrothed. So good of you to visit, my dear.'

'I'm not your betrothed,' said Princess Lois defiantly.

A flicker of anger rippled across Zoltab's massive forehead.

'We will be married one day, Princess,' said the Dark Lord. 'I promise you we will.'

Chilled by Zoltab's threats, the questors were silent. Zoltab sensed their weakness.

'It is not easy to face me, is it?' he taunted them. 'For when you look at the true power of Zoltab you know in your hearts that no cheap magician's trick can hold him for long. You know that he will escape and when he does his thirst for revenge will be unquenchable.'

It was as though Zoltab had read their minds. The questors could neither look at him nor each other.

Finally, Capablanca found the strength to speak.

'We have nothing to fear,' he claimed. 'The bars that surround him are unbreakable.'

Blart turned away. As he did so his eyes were caught by a bright flash. Uther was hurriedly pushing a little mirror back into his coat.

'That hurt my eyes,' Blart said to him. 'Why do you –'

'Be quiet,' said Uther angrily. 'Can't a man look his best, even in times of great peril?'

'What's this?' said Beo.

'He was blinding me with his mirror,' complained Blart.

'The boy is a fool,' said Uther. 'I don't have a mirror.'

'He was using it to flash the sun in my eyes,' insisted Blart.

'Don't be stupid, boy,' said Uther.

'I saw him get a mirror out when we were on the last peak,' said Princess Lois.

'I wanted to check if there was something in my teeth,' said Uther desperately. 'That stew last night was very stringy.'

'You lie, merchant,' said Beo. 'That stew was succulent and well-seasoned.'

There was a hunted guilty look in Uther's eyes.

'And I thought you said you didn't have a mirror,' said the Princess.

'I … I …' Uther was lost for an explanation.

'Signalling,' Beo accused Uther. 'You were signalling.'

'Nonsense,' said Uther.

But the warrior hadn't the patience for arguments. He drew his great sword.

'Who were you signalling to?' he demanded.

'What's going on?' asked Capablanca.

'We have a traitor in our midst,' said Beo. 'And if he does not tell us who he was signalling to then I will cleave him into pieces.'

'He lies, wizard,' said Uther, shaking his head vigorously. Too vigorously. There was a clunk as the small mirror fell from his coat.

Beo raised his huge sword.

'I should kill you now.'

'No,' said Capablanca. 'We need answers not corpses. Tell us who you were signalling to and we will spare your life.'

But there was no need for Uther to answer. The answer rose all around them.

Surrounding the peaks of Mount Xag were numerous smaller mountains. And from behind those smaller mountains little black dots were appearing from all directions. North, east, south, west. Each way Blart looked there were black dots.

And as he looked they got bigger.

The black dots were heading their way.

'Who are they?' demanded Beowulf. 'Tell me now or I will kill you.'

'It makes no difference now,' answered Uther. 'Know that they are minions of Zoltab.'

'You are a minion of Zoltab?' said Capablanca.

'I'm nobody's minion,' said Uther defiantly. 'I'm a merchant, as I told you all along.'

'But why are you signalling to them?' demanded the Princess.

'I am concluding a business transaction,' said Uther.

'What do you mean?'

'I was hired to find Zoltab,' said Uther, 'and bring his minions to him. I began by finding Blart in Milkdale, and now you have all led me to him. In a few minutes I will have fulfilled my part of the bargain.'

'You were in league with Zoltab's minions all along?' asked Blart. 'Even when we were playing Muggins in The Happy Hangman?'

Uther nodded.

Blart was dumbfounded by this treachery.

'That's why you kept saying we didn't need to worry about Zoltab's minions,' said Princess Lois.

Uther nodded again.

'How –' began Capablanca, but he was interrupted by a cry from the Princess.

The black dots were flying horses, each of them ridden by two figures clad in the black armour of Zoltab. And from the prison came the rumbling roar of the Dark Lord.

'I will wreak a terrible vengeance on all who have stood against me,' he bellowed.

Closer and closer came the flying horses, their tails streaming out behind them, their black-clad warriors brandishing swords.

'They are getting nearer,' said Blart anxiously. 'Shouldn't

we be leaving?'

He was right. The horses with their fearsome riders flew ever closer to Mount Xag.

'They have made a mistake,' said Capablanca, 'for they cannot land on this small space. The horses wouldn't have time to stop and they would fall over the cliffs and plummet to their deaths.'

The flying army had risen over the peaks of the nearest mountain. Within moments they would be above the questors.

'What did they give you for your treachery?' demanded Beo, turning to Uther.

'They promised to make me the wealthiest man in the world when Zoltab is freed,' Uther replied.

'But the spell that secures Zoltab's cage is irreversible,' said Capablanca. 'Or, at least it . . . it . . . was.'

Uther coughed.

'Exactly,' he told the wizard. 'Zoltab's Ministers have been researching diligently since you spoke so unguardedly at your banquet, and they believe they have found a way to undo it. It may take them some time but they are confident of success.'

Capablanca looked close to despair.

Closer came the flying horses. There were at least fifty of them – a terrifying sight in the clear blue sky.

'Are you sure that we are safe?' asked Blart.

'Of course,' snapped Capablanca. 'They can fly above

our heads but they cannot land.'

It was at this moment that the first rope was lowered from a flying horse. A minion from each horse was preparing to slide down the rope and jump on to the mountain top.

'If only we had a bow,' cried Beo, 'we could shoot them down.'

'What are we going to do?' cried Princess Lois.

'I will fight to the death,' said Beo.

'You always want to fight to the death,' said Blart. 'Why don't we run for our lives instead?'

'Blart's right,' said Capablanca. 'Fifty minions of Zoltab are too many for us. They would kill us and rescue Zoltab. We must flee.'

'But then they'll rescue Zoltab anyway,' said Beo.

'I must have time to think,' said Capablanca. 'Retreat!'

The questors ran from the peak of Mount Xag. Uther, waiting for his payment, watched them go. As they fled, the black-armoured minions landed on the summit and prepared to release their master.

Chapter 50

'Have we been defeated?' asked Blart.

'Never,' growled Beowulf.

'Oh,' said Blart, sounding disappointed. 'I just thought if we'd been defeated then we could go down the mountain and get warm again.'

They had floundered through the snow and down the south face of Mount Xag, twice nearly stumbling over sheer cliffs, until they had found a shallow ice cave. They sat in it, shivering and waiting for Zoltab's minions to find them. But Zoltab's minions did not come. Instead they secured the area surrounding Zoltab's prison. Any other task could wait.

'I must think,' said Capablanca when they realised they were no longer in imminent danger. And so saying the wizard flung his cowl over his head and sank deep into thought.

'We should never have trusted a merchant,' fumed Beo.

'I didn't trust him,' said Blart.

'Why didn't you say anything, weasel-features?' asked the Princess.

'I don't trust any of you,' explained Blart. 'You all seem to get me into trouble all the time.'

The wizard, distracted by their chatter, shook in anger beneath his coat. He knew now that his bottom would never again sit on a personalised chair in the Cavernous Library of Ping.

'What's that?' asked Blart, pointing to a piece of paper that Capablanca's temper had shaken from his pocket.

The wizard picked up the paper.

'The prophecy,' he said. 'I had forgotten all about it.'

'What did it say?' asked Blart.

The wizard read the prophecy again:

> *'There will come a time when friends are enemies and enemies*
>   *are friends*
> *When Zoltab, twice imprisoned, may once more be freed*
> *To destroy the world or be defeated*
> *By the hand of the husband of his betrothed.'*

'What does it mean?' asked Beo.

Capablanca, who could not bear to admit he didn't understand something, didn't answer.

'People think we're Zoltab's friends when really we're his enemies,' said the Princess.

'That is true,' agreed the wizard.

'And Uther was our enemy but pretended to be our friend,' said Blart.

'I understood that bit,' insisted Capablanca irritably. 'So the first line has come to pass. And high up at the summit they are doubtless trying to make the second line come true by freeing Zoltab.'

'But he can be defeated,' said Beo. 'It says so.'

'But that is the part that makes no sense,' said Capablanca. 'It refers to the husband of Zoltab's betrothed. If someone is betrothed to someone then they don't have a husband. This could be the prophecy's gnomic way of saying that nobody can stop Zoltab apart from himself.'

'Why couldn't it just say that?' said Blart.

'I despair of your ever understanding prophecies,' said Capablanca. 'All prophecies are open to multiple interpretation.'

'Why?' demanded Blart.

'Because they are,' said Capablanca firmly.

'If it can mean anything then can I say what it means?' asked Blart.

'It cannot mean anything,' corrected Capablanca angrily. 'It is open to scholarly interpretation. It is not open to pig boys.'

'I'm going to have a go anyway,' said Blart. 'Princess Lois is Zoltab's betrothed, isn't she?'

'I'm not,' said Princess Lois.

'Zoltab may be under the impression you are,' said Capablanca reluctantly. 'At the end of our last quest he did not relinquish his claim on you to be his wife.'

'Well, then,' said Blart. 'She's his betrothed. Whoever marries her is the husband of Zoltab's betrothed and can defeat him.'

'That's prepost ...' began Capablanca. And then he stopped. He read the prophecy once more. He read it twice more.

'I think I've solved it,' announced the wizard.

'Tell us what it means,' said Beo.

'Whoever marries the Princess can defeat Zoltab.'

Blart thought for a moment.

'That's what I —' he protested.

But the wizard cut him off.

'This is no time to argue,' he told Blart sternly. 'The future of the world is at stake. Every second that passes, trying to claim undeserved credit, brings Zoltab's minions a step nearer to releasing their master and unleashing chaos on the world. We must decide.'

'Decide what?' asked Blart.

'Which of you is to marry Princess Lois.'

Chapter 51

'What did you just say?'

Princess Lois's freckles had never looked so menacing.

'You have to get married to either Beo or Blart if we are to succeed in our quest,' said Capablanca. 'Make up your mind.'

For a moment the Princess was speechless. But only for a moment.

'Listen,' she told the wizard. 'I came on this quest to get away from my suitors. I came because I didn't want to get married. And if you think that after travelling vast distances to avoid getting married I'm going to marry one of these two just because you say so, then you are wrong. I am a woman and I will not be told by some old man when to marry and whom to marry.'

'I'm not telling you whom to marry,' pointed out Capablanca desperately. 'I'm giving you a choice.'

'A choice?' Princess Lois glared at the wizard. 'You call a

fat warrior or a stupid pig boy a choice?'

'Princess,' said the wizard. 'I understand your feelings but if you don't agree then Illyria will be destroyed in war and Zoltab will rise and the world will be shrouded in gloom and despair.'

'That's not very good wooing,' interjected Beo.

'What?' snapped Capablanca.

'When you are wooing a maiden,' said Beo, 'it is customary to dwell on her beauty rather than descriptions of the end of the world.'

'We have no time for that,' said the wizard. 'There will be no beauty and no truth if she doesn't agree to marry one of you. I suggest Beo. After all he has great strength. Perhaps once he is married to you that strength will be multiplied enough for him to defeat Zoltab's minions.'

Beo coughed.

'I'm afraid I cannot marry the Princess.'

'Do not worry about your difference in rank,' said the wizard.

'It is not that,' Beo assured him. 'I would be honoured to marry the Princess but I cannot. For I am married already.'

'Who to?'

'I cannot remember,' said Beo.

'What?' said Capablanca. 'Surely a man as chivalric as you can remember his own wife.'

Beo sighed.

'I was young. I had drunk many flagons of mead. I woke

up to find that during the night I had got married. My fellow warriors insisted I celebrate. We drank more flagons of mead. The next time I woke up my wife had gone and I had forgotten her name.'

'Didn't you ask your friends what her name was?' asked the wizard.

'They had drunk more mead than me,' lamented the warrior. 'They can't remember either. All I know is that I am married, but to whom is a mystery.'

'You could marry again,' suggested Blart.

Capablanca shook his head.

'That would not be a proper marriage,' he said. 'And would not fulfil the prophecy.'

'Perhaps you should marry the Princess,' said Beo to Capablanca. 'Perhaps then your magic powers will be restored and you will be able to defeat Zoltab's minions.'

Capablanca shook his head.

'Do not worry about the age difference,' said Beo.

'It is not that,' said the wizard. 'But I cannot marry the Princess. For I am also already married.'

'Who are you married to?' said the warrior, surprised that the wizard, so single-minded in his dedication to ancient lore, might have a wife.

Capablanca drew himself up to his full height.

'I am married to a beautiful witch,' he said.

'You've never mentioned her before,' said Beo.

'We were tragically separated,' said Capablanca and the

hint of a tear glinted in his eye. 'I have not seen her for many years.'

'What happened?' asked Princess Lois.

Capablanca did not answer directly.

'You must understand,' he said, 'that I was a young wizard experimenting with my spells.'

'What happened?' repeated Princess Lois.

'I turned her into a mouse.'

'A mouse!' said Blart. 'You're married to a mouse?'

Capablanca did not reply.

'Couldn't you just turn her back into a beautiful witch?' asked Princess Lois.

Capablanca sighed.

'I would if I could,' he said. 'But she disappeared behind the skirting board and I never saw her again.'

There was a silence while Capablanca and Beowulf dwelt on their disastrous marriages. Then there was a noise as Princess Lois realised what this meant.

'You,' she said, looking at Blart with horror.

'You,' answered Blart.

It wasn't exactly love at first sight.

Chapter 52

Capablanca had to take the Princess to one side of the icy cave and explain to her time and time again the importance of getting married. Finally she was convinced. Blart was easier to convince. He was promised a large pig farm if he did get married and the removal of his head with Beo's sword if he didn't.

'Remember,' said Capablanca as they approached Votok's cave. 'The hermit will not marry you if he does not believe that you truly love one another. Therefore let me do all the talking and just try and look tenderly at one another.'

Blart attempted to look tenderly at Princess Lois. The Princess backed away.

'Couldn't you marry us?' she asked the wizard. 'And then as soon as Blart's done whatever it is he has to do you could unmarry us.'

Capablanca shook his head.

'A wizard cannot perform a marriage,' he said. 'It must be done by a licensed practitioner like Votok the

323

Hermit. And then you must stay married until death parts you.'

Princess Lois looked downcast.

'Look on the bright side,' said Beo, who did not like to see a downcast damsel. 'As soon as you are married Blart has to face Zoltab the Dark Lord, so death could be parting you pretty soon.'

Blart gulped.

Votok was sitting outside his cave.

'Greetings,' he said when he saw the questors.

'Greetings,' said Capablanca.

'We'd like you to perform a marriage for us,' said Beo.

Votok was taken aback by the suddenness of this request.

'But I no longer perform marriages,' he said.

'This isn't like those other marriages,' Beo assured him. 'This is a love match.'

'A most touching love match,' Capablanca continued. 'Two young people, who, at the top of the highest mountain in the world, were suddenly overcome with passion and became engaged on the spot. Look at how they glow with happiness. Surely you would not deny them your legal blessing on their union.'

Blart and Princess Lois attempted to glow with happiness. They didn't succeed. Firstly, because they were both miserable, and secondly, because it was too cold for glowing. But Votok didn't notice their lack of a glow. Instead he spotted something else.

'Weren't there five of you when you left this morning?' he asked.

'Oh,' said Capablanca, remembering Uther and his terrible treachery. All the time he had been suspecting Votok, Uther had been preparing to betray them. 'Yes.'

'Where is your fellow climber?' asked the hermit.

Capablanca was at a loss for a satisfactory answer. Explaining about Zoltab and his minions would take too long.

'He fell off,' said Beo suddenly.

'Fell off?' repeated Votok in shock.

'Just before we reached the top,' said Beo. 'Plummeted to his death. A tragic accident.'

'That's terrible,' said Votok. 'Surely we couldn't countenance a marriage on such a sad day. We should be reflecting on your companion's life.'

'Of course we should,' said Capablanca. 'But it was Uther's last wish that the two of them should be married today.'

'He shouted it out just before he smashed into the bottom of the ice cliff,' added Beo with perhaps more detail than was strictly necessary.

Votok's look of horror changed to one of puzzlement.

'But I thought you said that he fell off before you reached the top and that the young people didn't get engaged until they reached the summit.'

Capablanca and Beo were stumped by this question. Votok looked more and more dubious with each second their silence lasted. Any moment now he would refuse their marriage request and the prophecy would go unfulfilled.

'Blart confided in him,' said Princess Lois.

'Did I?' said Blart.

'Yes,' said Princess Lois. 'You asked him for his advice.'

'What did you ask him?' Votok wanted to know.

Blart tried to think of a satisfactory answer. Without much success.

'I ... I ... I ...'

'Yes?'

'I asked him which knee I should go down on.'

'I beg your pardon?' said Votok.

'When you ask someone to marry you,' said Blart desperately, 'you have to go down on one knee and I wasn't sure which one, so I asked him and he told me.'

Votok considered this response.

'Well,' he said finally, 'if you are truly in love and as it was your companion's last request then I will consent to marry you.'

'Excellent,' said Capablanca. 'Now can we have the shortest service, please? We've got things to do.'

Votok held up his hand.

'Do not be hasty. I said if the young couple are truly in love. I will talk to them alone and if I am satisfied of their

326

mutual devotion then I will marry them.'

'What's mutual devotion?' asked Blart, following Votok and the Princess into the cave.

Capablanca spent some minutes pacing up and down and looking nervously at the sky. The sun shone brightly above him, indicating it was noon. So much had already happened that day and yet so much still had to happen, thought the wizard. The war on Illyria started tomorrow. He cast another worried glance at the cave. What was taking Blart and Princess Lois so long?

Inside the cave, Blart and the Princess were being closely questioned.

'So what kind of things does Blart like?' Votok asked Princess Lois.

'He likes pigs.'

'And do you like pigs?'

'No.'

Votok looked doubtful.

'I could learn to like them, I suppose,' said the Princess.

Votok turned to Blart.

'What does the Princess like?' he asked.

Blart looked blank.

'You can't think of anything?'

Blart shook his head. Votok was about to reach the conclusion that the marriage could not possibly take place because the couple had nothing in common.

'I can think of things she doesn't like,' said Blart. 'She

doesn't like fruit and she doesn't like people being nice and she doesn't like her parents and she doesn't like doors.'

'Doors?' said Votok.

'She's always slamming them,' said Blart.

'You're always making horrid noises,' said Princess Lois.

'You call me names,' said Blart.

'You deserve them.'

For the first time Votok noticed a shared passion in the eyes of Blart and Princess Lois. They continued to insult each other. Each insult was keener than the last and was responded to with gusto. He noticed similar interests in saying nasty things, in pointing out faults and in blaming each other for numerous failures. With each spiteful word that came out of their mouths it became obvious to Votok what was not at all obvious to either Blart or Princess Lois.

They were soul mates.

'I will marry you,' he said.

'What?' said Blart and Princess Lois, who had become so engrossed in their row that they had forgotten he was in the cave with them.

'You were obviously meant to be together. I will marry you.'

Even Blart and Princess Lois were temporarily silenced.

A few minutes later, the sun shone down on Blart and the Princess as they stood in front of Votok's cave while Capablanca and Beo looked anxiously on.

'I now pronounce you man and wife,' said Votok.

'Come on,' said Capablanca immediately. 'We've got to climb back up that mountain.'

'The groom hasn't kissed the bride,' protested Votok.

'We've no time for that,' said the wizard. 'We've got to stop a war and save the world.'

'Go in peace,' said Votok before they rushed off.

'Peace,' laughed Beo. 'That's the last thing we're going in.'

And so Blart and Princess Lois embarked on married life by climbing the unclimbable peak of Mount Xag for the second time in one day. It would not have been most people's choice of honeymoon.

But they had no alternative. Above them the sun moved inexorably towards the west. High up on the peak, against the white of the snow, they could see black figures busy working. At this distance the figures seemed tiny and insignificant, but each of the questors reminded themselves that up close they were heavily armoured minions with fearsome weapons. It seemed madness to be walking towards them. But Capablanca held fast to the power of the prophecy. And Beo held fast to his promise to cleave Blart in two if he tried to run away. Even on his wedding day.

And so they kept climbing once more. But they were not the climbers that they had been earlier in the day. The easy footsteps had become a weary trudge. The bright eyes were dulled as they grimly marched towards their fate.

Had Zoltab's minions succeeded in freeing him?

The answer lay in the cold dead land above them.

Chapter 53

The sun was beginning to slip behind the Xanthian mountains. There was not much daylight left. Far away on the Illyrian border the soldiers of the Grand Alliance prepared to do battle. Nearby, Zoltab's minions toiled to free their master.

The questors had crept up the final slope as close to Zoltab's prison as they could without being seen, and were lying on their fronts in the snow, watching.

'What do we do now?' whispered Beo to Capablanca.

It might have been a slip brought on by tiredness but Capablanca uttered his three least favourite words.

'You don't know?' hissed the Princess. 'You mean I'm married to weasel-features for the rest of my life and you don't even know what to do next?'

'I can only think of one thing,' said Capablanca. 'We must trust to the prophecy. We must follow the husband of Zoltab's betrothed and march on Zoltab's minions.'

Blart remembered that the husband of Zoltab's

betrothed was him.

'I'm not marching on anyone,' he said.

'We have no choice,' said the wizard. 'We have come this far. We cannot do nothing.'

'It will be a worthy way to die,' agreed Beowulf. 'To follow a prophecy and march to our certain doom. Four against fifty. There is a nobility to it.'

'There's a stupidity to it,' said Blart. 'Isn't there, Princess?'

'If I have to spend my life married to you,' answered the Princess, 'it might as well be a short one. I will march too.'

'But ...' protested Blart. They were all mad. Completely and utterly mad. Unfortunately they were on his side.

'Let us stand together,' said Capablanca. 'All for one and one for all.'

'But ...' said Blart again, but even he could see it was hopeless. The wizard, the warrior and the Princess had one thing in common. When they made up their minds there was no changing them.

Together the wizard, the warrior, the Princess and the pig boy stood up.

Two hundred feet away, fifty heavily armoured minions turned towards them.

'You are the husband of Zoltab's betrothed,' Capablanca told Blart. 'You must lead us.'

Blart looked ahead. He saw the black armour of the minions. He saw their swords, their lances, their daggers, their bows and arrows. He saw his doom.

'Take heart,' said Capablanca.

'Courage,' urged Beo.

'You're in my family now,' said the Princess. 'Do not shame our royal name.'

Blart put one foot forward. And so began the questors' final ascent towards the peak of Mount Xag and their destiny.

Zoltab's minions formed a black line and waited. Ever closer marched the questors. They were in the open now and vulnerable to a sudden charge or a bolt from an arrow, but Zoltab's minions did not move. Instead they watched, impassive and terrible like the mountains they stood upon. Each step brought them nearer to the weapons and, with no plan other than a belief in a prediction written on a torn piece of paper, surely their deaths.

'Halt,' said Capablanca when the questors were no further than thirty feet away from Zoltab's minions.

'Halt?' said Beowulf, gripping his mighty sword. 'Don't you mean charge?'

'We must give them a chance to surrender,' said Capablanca.

'Surrender?' said Blart incredulously, looking at the implacable forces lined up in front of him. 'Isn't that what we should be doing?'

The wizard ignored him and addressed the fearsomely armed enemies.

'Minions of Zoltab. Know ye that we are the Questors of Good and Valour.'

'Are we?' said Blart.

'We order you to surrender,' said the wizard boldly.

Harsh derisive laughter came from Zoltab's minions.

Capablanca reached into his pocket and pulled out the prophecy. He held it up in the air. It fluttered slightly in the breeze.

'Know ye that I have here a prophecy which predicts Zoltab's defeat,' he announced. 'Earlier today the prophecy was fulfilled and Zoltab's defeat was assured. The inevitable forces of destiny are now lined up against you. Zoltab will not be freed and there will be no war. This piece of paper guarantees us peace in our time.'

This time there was no harsh derisive laughter from Zoltab's minions. The power of prophecy was well known and coupled with the confidence of Capablanca's speech in the face of such seemingly overwhelming odds they were silenced.

The middle of the minions' line parted to reveal a tall, thin, black-cloaked figure that they had last seen standing by Zoltab's side in the Terrorsium.

The Master.

Zoltab's most senior Minister.

'We meet again,' said the Master softly, but in the silence of the mountain tops his words still reached the questors and they felt their deadly menace.

Capablanca paled at the sight. The Master had outwitted him before.

'It is most irritating,' said the Master, 'to be called away from my sacred task of freeing Zoltab the Dark Lord, which was nearing completion. But I am told you have a prophecy.'

He spoke so calmly that Capablanca, still holding the prophecy high in the air, began to feel a little foolish, and he felt his hand begin to shake. But bravely he fought back his fear.

'I have,' said the wizard. 'It foretells that the husband of Zoltab's betrothed will prevent his escape. Zoltab is not yet free and the husband of Zoltab's betrothed has arrived in time to stop it.'

'Where is the husband of Zoltab's betrothed?' asked the Master.

'Here!' said Capablanca, pushing Blart forward.

There was a short silence.

Then the Master began to laugh. The laughter spread to Zoltab's minions. Louder and louder they laughed. It echoed off the surrounding mountains. And then, just as suddenly as it had begun the laughter stopped.

'Blart the Pig Boy,' said the Master. 'You think he can prevent the release of Zoltab and save the world?'

'I did it before,' said Blart defiantly.

'You were lucky,' said the Master. 'You will have no such luck this time.'

'We have more than luck,' said Capablanca. 'We have a

prophecy.'

'Of course,' said the Master dryly. 'That flimsy torn piece of paper you hold in your hand. Your friend Uther mentioned it to us.'

'He is no friend of ours,' said Beowulf. 'He is a traitor.'

'Whatever he is, he proved most informative.'

'He'll do anything for money,' said the Princess scornfully.

'Oh, we didn't think it necessary to pay him,' replied the Master. 'We have much more effective ways of persuading a man to tell us all he knows. And he told us everything. He told us that you are a wizard so weakened that he can no longer use magic.'

Capablanca looked down in shame.

'And he told us about your prophecy.' The Master paused. 'Or at least, your half a prophecy.'

'Half a prophecy?' said Capablanca. 'How do you know it's half a prophecy?'

The Master reached into his black cloak and pulled out a piece of paper. A piece of paper that was not torn and was twice the size of the one Capablanca held aloft.

'Because I have the full one,' said the Master calmly. 'Would you like to know where I got it?'

Capablanca said nothing but his body seemed to slump in defeat.

'Somebody brought it to me,' continued the Master. 'Somebody I think you know.'

'Uther?' said Capablanca. 'How did …'

'Wrong again, wizard,' said the Master. 'It was not Uther. It was …'

The Master turned round and nodded. From behind the line of fierce minions emerged a bearded figure wearing a dirty cowl. He looked like a younger version of Capablanca, for his beard was not as long and straggly and his coat was not as dirty.

'Teichmann!' gasped Capablanca, his breathing coming in desperate short bursts. 'A wizard! In league with Zoltab's minions! Using his magic for evil! I … I …'

Capablanca was so overcome he could speak no more.

'It is good to see you shocked,' boasted Teichmann in a shrill voice that offended the ears of all who heard it. 'For years as a young wizard I had to look up to you in the Cavernous Library of Ping. That is why I researched so hard to find this prophecy and brought it to the Master. For now you must look up to me.'

'Who are you?' demanded Blart.

'I am Teichmann,' answered the wizard. 'Or am I?'

Suddenly the wizard's face began to change. His cheeks grew wider, his chin doubled, his nose shrank and his beard shrivelled to nothing. A new face appeared. A face Blart recognised.

'Votok!'

'How is married life?' said Votok the Hermit with a kindly smile.

'You have mastered shape shifting,' said Capablanca in disbelief.

'A skill you never could,' said Votok, but this time he spoke with Teichmann's shrill voice. 'But it really isn't too hard to the truly gifted.'

And as if to prove it he returned his face to its original wizard-like features.

'Does that mean I'm not married?' asked Blart.

'No,' said Capablanca. 'You are still married. I told you before that Teichmann was a friar before training as a wizard.'

'You are correct,' said Teichmann. 'But being married will do you no good, pig boy. Zoltab will make your wife a widow before this day is done.'

'But Zoltab will destroy everything,' protested Capablanca.

'Zoltab is the irresistible power on this earth,' said Teichmann. 'The world will be moulded in his image. All who study know this. We wizards must learn to adapt to a new order.'

'You are betraying everything that is good and right,' said Capablanca, but his voice sounded feeble in the cold air.

'I am becoming part of the future,' said Teichmann.

'I never believed a wizard could …' Capablanca's voice trailed off. He seemed to have lost all will for the fight.

'Reunions of old friends so often bring a tear to my eye,' commented the Master scornfully. 'Do you not think, wizard, that the time has come to admit your inferiority. You have half a prophecy while I have the full one. You will always lose to me.'

Blart looked up at Capablanca. The wizard seemed to have no reply to the cruel taunts of his nemesis.

'What does the prophecy say?' demanded Princess Lois.

'It matters not now,' said the Master. 'But before the minions kill you I will let you read it to show the futility of your pathetic hopes. Guard! Bring out their friend. He can deliver it to them.'

One of Zoltab's minions leapt to obey the Master's command. And from behind the grim line of minions emerged Uther.

But it was not the Uther they had seen before. His clothes were torn, his walk was unsteady and he bled from numerous wounds. Contemptuously, the Master handed him the prophecy.

'Take this to your friends. And then you are free to go.'

The weight of the paper seemed almost too much for the merchant to bear, but somehow he began the short walk towards his former comrades. Behind him he left a trail of blood. None of the questors could bear to look and yet none could wrench their eyes from the awful sight.

'Here,' gasped the merchant, thrusting the parchment into the wizard's hand and then collapsing on to the snow.

Looking down the questors could see that Uther was near death. His breathing came in desperate gasps.

For one final time he looked up.

'I remember,' he said. 'I remember …'

And then he stopped. What did he remember? Something that the other questors had forgotten which would allow them to defeat Zoltab's minions? Or something more distant? Some far-off memory of childhood, when life was more than just profit and loss?

'I remember,' he wheezed, 'that you all owe me money.'

Uther's eyes closed and he lay dead on the ground. And so Uther the Merchant suffered the fate of all traders: death took his wealth from him for ever, for there is indeed no pocket in a shroud.

'What does the prophecy say?' demanded Princess Lois.

Capablanca read out the words on the blood-spattered paper in a hopeless monotone:

'There will come a time when friends are enemies and enemies
*   are friends*
When Zoltab, twice imprisoned, may once more be freed
To destroy the world or be defeated
By the hand of the husband of his betrothed.

But if he comes with men he'll fail and die
If he comes with women the same
If he comes alone he'll perish for aye
And Zoltab then will reign.'

Capablanca looked across the snow at the sneering contemptuous face of the Master.

'You see how you have failed,' said the Master. 'The prophecy mocks you. Now you must surrender to me.'

Capablanca was shaking his head.

'I will count to ten and then Zoltab's minions will slaughter you where you stand.'

'What are we going to do?' the Princess asked the wizard.

The contempt of the Master seemed to jolt the last desperate vestige of life from Capablanca.

'We must make the prophecy come to pass,' he answered.

'One … two … three …' counted the Master.

'Take it line by line,' said Capablanca. 'He cannot succeed if he is with men, therefore Beo and I must leave him. And he cannot succeed if he comes with women, 'so the Princess must leave him too.'

'Seven … eight …'

'Do it now,' said Capablanca.

'Desert a comrade?' said Beo. 'Never!'

'We must,' said Capablanca. 'The prophecy is our only hope!'

'Farewell, Blart,' said Princess Lois.

'Nine …'

Capablanca, Beo and Princess Lois began to back away from Blart.

'What about the next line?' said Blart helplessly. 'The line that says that if I'm all alone I'll perish and Zoltab will reign.'

'One line at a time,' shouted Capablanca. 'And I'm still working on that one.'

Blart turned back to face the Master.

'You may have saved the world once, boy. But this time you die.'

Blart didn't want to die.

'Ten!'

On the Master's command Zoltab's minions advanced towards Blart, their grim weapons of death held out in front of them. Blart wanted to run, wanted to shout, wanted to be anywhere other than in this icy waste, facing death. But he could do nothing.

And then there was a sound from behind Blart. A sound that he had heard the night before when he had been lying in Votok's cave. It was a sound that stopped the march of Zoltab's minions.

It was the sound of the Wild Boars of Xanthia.

Up the mountainside they came, huge powerful beasts charging through the snow, smoke billowing from their snouts and their fearsome tusks glistening in the evening light.

The wild boars had sight of their prey and were determined to eat. They would gore every living thing on the slopes of Mount Xag to death and feast on the bloody remnants.

It was a sight that terrified questors and minions alike.

It terrified everyone except Blart.

To Blart they looked like big pigs.

He uttered a low whistle. It echoed off the mountains and it reached the pink ears of the Wild Boars of Xanthia. It seemed that the ferocious creatures were slowing down. Blart repeated the whistle. The closer they got to the summit of Mount Xag the slower they were getting. Again Blart whistled. A slow calming gentle whistle. The Wild Boars of Xanthia trotted towards him and gathered around him, snuffling the ground.

'What are you waiting for?' demanded the Master of Zoltab's minions. 'That boy has stolen Zoltab's bride and come here to try and prevent his release. Kill him!'

Zoltab's minions moved forward.

Blart whistled. This time not a low calming whistle. This time a high-pitched whistle. A call to arms.

As quick as their heads had fallen to snuffling the Wild Boars of Xanthia's snouts rose again. They dug their trotters in the snow, bared their sharp teeth, pointed their tusks in front of them and charged behind their leader.

Blart was not coming with men.

Blart was not coming with women.

Blart was not coming alone.

Blart was coming with pigs.

The prophecy was fulfilled.

Zoltab's minions panicked at the terrible sight. They

turned and fled in front of the grunting onslaught. In vain did the Master urge them to hold their line in the face of the terrible tusks. In vain did he and Teichmann cast spells at the advancing beasts. There were too many of them to be stopped. With cries of anguish the Master and Teichmann were trampled underfoot. And nor did the fleeing minions of Zoltab escape the dreaded tusks. The Wild Boars pursued them and they were caught, gored and chased to their doom off the fearsome cliffs of Mount Xag.

Blart watched Zoltab's minions disappear, one by one.

Capablanca, Beo and Princess Lois emerged from the icy hollows they had dived into.

'You made the prophecy come true,' said Capablanca.

'You have triumphed over tremendous odds,' said Beowulf.

'You have to admit you got lucky,' said Princess Lois.

On the ground in front of him lay the Master's body, blood oozing from a fatal tusk wound to his heart.

'We will take his body back with us as evidence of our defeat of Zoltab and his minions,' said Capablanca. 'Then all will know that we fought against the Dark Lord, war will be averted and we will once more live like free men.'

They were standing just below the summit and from above them they heard an angry cry.

'Master! What has happened? What was that noise? Where have you gone? I command you to release me.'

The questors turned and began the long walk down the mountain, leaving the voice of Zoltab howling in anger to an empty wasteland.

Epilogue

'A toast,' said the King, rising to his feet.

The feasting room of the King and Queen of Illyria was full. All had eaten and drunk well.

'To peace,' said the King.

'To peace!'

The Duke of Northwestmoreland, the Earl of Nethershire and the Prince of Murkstan raised their glasses. The Grand Alliance had been dissolved. The threat of war was past. From outside the feasting room where Pig the Horse was eating his fill of the best hay and oats in the kingdom, there was a neigh of satisfaction.

Capablanca the Grand Wizard raised his glass. An emissary from the Wizards' Committee at the Cavernous Library of Ping had arrived that day, restoring Capablanca's magic powers, conferring on him a new title and informing him that a new, even more comfortable chair was to be constructed in his honour. To triumph over Zoltab and the Master and the traitorous wizard Teichmann without even magic to aid him – Capablanca was once more considered the Greatest Sorcerer in all the World. Only more so.

'Step forward, Beowulf,' said the King.

Beowulf rose from his chair and walked a trifle unsteadily, for he had drunk many flagons of mead, towards the king.

'Now kneel.'

The warrior did as he was bid. The King touched Beowulf's shoulders lightly and he was a warrior no more.

'Arise, Sir Beowulf.'

With some difficulty the knight stood up.

'Hurrah!' cried all at the table.

But a ferocious knocking at the feasting-room door dampened their cheering. The great door swung open. Standing there, his flawless complexion shining in the lantern's flame, was Anatoly the Handsome.

He rushed across the room and flung himself at the feet of Princess Lois.

'Princess,' he said, 'I have searched for you high and low. I have followed your trail to castles and to forests and to mountains, each time arriving just after you departed, and yet still I have followed you to prove my devotion. What has kept me going is the thought of your beautiful face, of your tender white hands, of your ruby lips, of your –'

'Get to the point,' ordered the Princess. 'My pudding is getting cold.'

Anatoly got on with it.

'Having proved my devotion I must ask once more for your hand in marriage and insist that I am not denied.'

There was a silence at the table.

Princess Lois looked down at Anatoly the Handsome. She thought about how married life would be with him. Compliments raining down on her morning, noon and night. She shuddered.

'I'm afraid I can't marry you,' she told Anatoly, 'for I am already married.'

'Who to?' demanded Anatoly the Handsome.

'To him,' said Princess Lois and she pointed across the table at Blart, who, just a moment previously, had dropped custard on his new tunic and was trying to rub it off.

'Him?' said Anatoly, indignantly considering Blart's looks and his manners and his demeanour and concluding that he, Anatoly, was infinitely superior in all regards. 'What can he possibly have to offer that I have not?'

Princess Lois looked at Blart and his custard stain. At least marriage with him meant that she would not be showered with endless meaningless compliments, and for such small mercies she was momentarily grateful. And then she looked back down at Anatoly the Handsome.

'He has just one thing you do not,' she told him.

'What thing?' demanded Anatoly.

'My husband saved the world,' explained Princess Lois. 'Twice. He is a hero.'

Everybody at the table looked at Blart. It was true.

Blart looked up.

'And that's the last time,' he said.

THE END

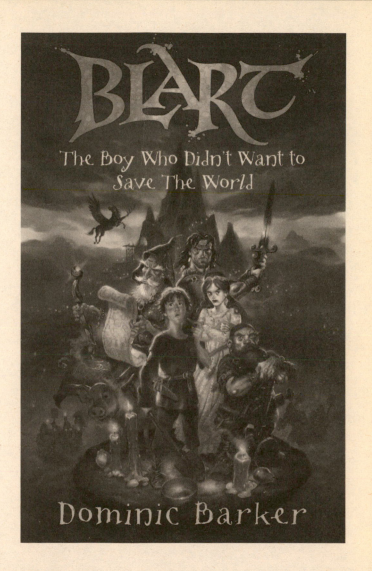

PAUL AUSTER

The New York Trilogy

City of Glass
Ghosts
The Locked Room

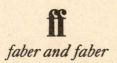

faber and faber

First published in Great Britain in 1987
by Faber and Faber Limited
3 Queen Square London WC1N 3AU
Open market paperback edition first published in 1992
UK paperback edition first published in 1988

Printed and bound in Great Britain by
Mackays of Chatham plc, Chatham, Kent

A CIP record for this book is
available from the British Library

ISBN 0-571-15223-6

24 26 28 29 27 25 23

CONTENTS

City of Glass 1
Ghosts 133
The Locked Room 197

City of Glass

1

It was a wrong number that started it, the telephone ringing three times in the dead of night, and the voice on the other end asking for someone he was not. Much later, when he was able to think about the things that happened to him, he would conclude that nothing was real except chance. But that was much later. In the beginning, there was simply the event and its consequences. Whether it might have turned out differently, or whether it was all predetermined with the first word that came from the stranger's mouth, is not the question. The question is the story itself, and whether or not it means something is not for the story to tell.

As for Quinn, there is little that need detain us. Who he was, where he came from, and what he did are of no great importance. We know, for example, that he was thirty-five years old. We know that he had once been married, had once been a father, and that both his wife and son were now dead. We also know that he wrote books. To be precise, we know that he wrote mystery novels. These works were written under the name of William Wilson, and he produced them at the rate of about one a year, which brought in enough money for him to live modestly in a small New York apartment. Because he spent no more than five or six months on a novel, for the rest of the year he was free to do as he wished. He read many books, he looked at paintings, he went to the movies. In the summer he watched baseball on television; in the winter he went to the opera. More than anything else, however, what he liked to do was walk. Nearly every day, rain or shine, hot or cold, he would leave his apartment to walk through the city – never really going anywhere, but simply going wherever his legs happened to take him.

New York was an inexhaustible space, a labyrinth of endless steps, and no matter how far he walked, no matter how well he

3

came to know its neighbourhoods and streets, it always left him with the feeling of being lost. Lost, not only in the city, but within himself as well. Each time he took a walk, he felt as though he were leaving himself behind, and by giving himself up to the movement of the streets, by reducing himself to a seeing eye, he was able to escape the obligation to think, and this, more than anything else, brought him a measure of peace, a salutary emptiness within. The world was outside of him, around him, before him, and the speed with which it kept changing made it impossible for him to dwell on any one thing for very long. Motion was of the essence, the act of putting one foot in front of the other and allowing himself to follow the drift of his own body. By wandering aimlessly, all places became equal and it no longer mattered where he was. On his best walks, he was able to feel that he was nowhere. And this, finally, was all he ever asked of things: to be nowhere. New York was the nowhere he had built around himself, and he realized that he had no intention of ever leaving it again.

In the past, Quinn had been more ambitious. As a young man he had published several books of poetry, had written plays, critical essays, and had worked on a number of long translations. But quite abruptly, he had given up all that. A part of him had died, he told his friends, and he did not want it coming back to haunt him. It was then that he had taken on the name of William Wilson. Quinn was no longer that part of him that could write books, and although in many ways Quinn continued to exist, he no longer existed for anyone but himself.

He had continued to write because it was the only thing he felt he could do. Mystery novels seemed a reasonable solution. He had little trouble inventing the intricate stories they required, and he wrote well, often in spite of himself, as if without having to make an effort. Because he did not consider himself to be the author of what he wrote, he did not feel responsible for it and therefore was not compelled to defend it in his heart. William Wilson, after all, was an invention, and even though he had been born within Quinn himself, he now led an independent life.

4

Quinn treated him with deference, at times even admiration, but he never went so far as to believe that he and William Wilson were the same man. It was for this reason that he did not emerge from behind the mask of his pseudonym. He had an agent, but they had never met. Their contacts were confined to the mail, for which purpose Quinn had rented a numbered box at the post office. The same was true of the publisher, who paid all fees, monies, and royalties to Quinn through the agent. No book by William Wilson ever included an author's photograph or biographical note. William Wilson was not listed in any writers' directory, he did not give interviews, and all the letters he received were answered by his agent's secretary. As far as Quinn could tell, no one knew his secret. In the beginning, when his friends learned that he had given up writing, they would ask him how he was planning to live. He told them all the same thing: that he had inherited a trust fund from his wife. But the fact was that his wife had never had any money. And the fact was that he no longer had any friends.

It had been more than five years now. He did not think about his son very much anymore, and only recently he had removed the photograph of his wife from the wall. Every once in a while, he would suddenly feel what it had been like to hold the three-year-old boy in his arms – but that was not exactly thinking, nor was it even remembering. It was a physical sensation, an imprint of the past that had been left in his body, and he had no control over it. These moments came less often now, and for the most part it seemed as though things had begun to change for him. He no longer wished to be dead. At the same time, it cannot be said that he was glad to be alive. But at least he did not resent it. He was alive, and the stubbornness of this fact had little by little begun to fascinate him – as if he had managed to outlive himself, as if he were somehow living a posthumous life. He did not sleep with the lamp on anymore, and for many months now he had not remembered any of his dreams.

It was night. Quinn lay in bed smoking a cigarette, listening to the rain beat against the window. He wondered when it would stop and whether he would feel like taking a long walk or a short walk in the morning. An open copy of Marco Polo's *Travels* lay face down on the pillow beside him. Since finishing the latest William Wilson novel two weeks earlier, he had been languishing. His private-eye narrator, Max Work, had solved an elaborate series of crimes, had suffered through a number of beatings and narrow escapes, and Quinn was feeling somewhat exhausted by his efforts. Over the years, Work had become very close to Quinn. Whereas William Wilson remained an abstract figure for him, Work had increasingly come to life. In the triad of selves that Quinn had become, Wilson served as a kind of ventriloquist. Quinn himself was the dummy, and Work was the animated voice that gave purpose to the enterprise. If Wilson was an illusion, he nevertheless justified the lives of the other two. If Wilson did not exist, he nevertheless was the bridge that allowed Quinn to pass from himself into Work. And little by little, Work had become a presence in Quinn's life, his interior brother, his comrade in solitude.

Quinn picked up the Marco Polo and started reading the first page again. 'We will set down things seen as seen, things heard as heard, so that our book may be an accurate record, free from any sort of fabrication. And all who read this book or hear it may do so with full confidence, because it contains nothing but the truth.' Just as Quinn was beginning to ponder the meaning of the sentences, to turn their crisp assurances over in his mind, the telephone rang. Much later, when he was able to reconstruct the events of that night, he would remember looking at the clock, seeing that it was past twelve, and wondering why someone should be calling him at that hour. More than likely, he thought, it was bad news. He climbed out of bed, walked naked to the telephone, and picked up the receiver on the second ring.

'Yes?'

There was a long pause on the other end, and for a moment Quinn thought the caller had hung up. Then, as if from a great distance, there came the sound of a voice unlike any he had ever heard. It was at once mechanical and filled with feeling, hardly more than a whisper and yet perfectly audible, and so even in tone that he was unable to tell if it belonged to a man or a woman.

'Hello?' said the voice.

'Who is this?' asked Quinn.

'Hello?' said the voice again.

'I'm listening,' said Quinn. 'Who is this?'

'Is this Paul Auster?' asked the voice. 'I would like to speak to Mr Paul Auster.'

'There's no one here by that name.'

'Paul Auster. Of the Auster Detective Agency.'

'I'm sorry,' said Quinn. 'You must have the wrong number.'

'This is a matter of utmost urgency,' said the voice.

'There's nothing I can do for you,' said Quinn. 'There is no Paul Auster here.'

'You don't understand,' said the voice. 'Time is running out.'

'Then I suggest you dial again. This is not a detective agency.'

Quinn hung up the phone. He stood there on the cold floor, looking down at his feet, his knees, his limp penis. For a brief moment he regretted having been so abrupt with the caller. It might have been interesting, he thought, to have played along with him a little. Perhaps he could have found out something about the case – perhaps even have helped in some way. 'I must learn to think more quickly on my feet,' he said to himself.

Like most people, Quinn knew almost nothing about crime. He had never murdered anyone, had never stolen anything, and he did not know anyone who had. He had never been inside a police station, had never met a private detective, had never spoken to a criminal. Whatever he knew about these things, he had learned from books, films, and newspapers. He did not, however, consider this to be a handicap. What interested him about the stories he wrote was not their relation to the world but their relation to other stories. Even before he became William Wilson, Quinn had been a devoted reader of mystery novels. He knew that most of them were poorly written, that most could not stand up to even

7

the vaguest sort of examination, but still, it was the form that appealed to him, and it was the rare, unspeakably bad mystery that he would refuse to read. Whereas his taste in other books was rigorous, demanding to the point of narrow-mindedness, with these works he showed almost no discrimination whatsoever. When he was in the right mood, he had little trouble reading ten or twelve of them in a row. It was a kind of hunger that took hold of him, a craving for a special food, and he would not stop until he had eaten his fill.

What he liked about these books was their sense of plenitude and economy. In the good mystery there is nothing wasted, no sentence, no word that is not significant. And even if it is not significant, it has the potential to be so – which amounts to the same thing. The world of the book comes to life, seething with possibilities, with secrets and contradictions. Since everything seen or said, even the slightest, most trivial thing, can bear a connection to the outcome of the story, nothing must be overlooked. Everything becomes essence; the centre of the book shifts with each event that propels it forward. The centre, then, is everywhere, and no circumference can be drawn until the book has come to its end.

The detective is the one who looks, who listens, who moves through this morass of objects and events in search of the thought, the idea that will pull all these things together and make sense of them. In effect, the writer and the detective are interchangeable. The reader sees the world through the detective's eye, experiencing the proliferation of its details as if for the first time. He has become awake to the things around him, as if they might speak to him, as if, because of the attentiveness he now brings to them, they might begin to carry a meaning other than the simple fact of their existence. Private eye. The term held a triple meaning for Quinn. Not only was it the letter 'i,' standing for 'investigator,' it was 'I' in the upper case, the tiny life-bud buried in the body of the breathing self. At the same time, it was also the physical eye of the writer, the eye of the man who looks out from himself into the world and demands that the world reveal itself to him. For five years now, Quinn had been living in the grip of this pun.

He had, of course, long ago stopped thinking of himself as real. If he lived now in the world at all, it was only at one remove, through the imaginary person of Max Work. His detective necessarily had to be real. The nature of the books demanded it. If Quinn had allowed himself to vanish, to withdraw into the confines of a strange and hermetic life, Work continued to live in the world of others, and the more Quinn seemed to vanish, the more persistent Work's presence in that world became. Whereas Quinn tended to feel out of place in his own skin, Work was aggressive, quick-tongued, at home in whatever spot he happened to find himself. The very things that caused problems for Quinn, Work took for granted, and he walked through the mayhem of his adventures with an ease and indifference that never failed to impress his creator. It was not precisely that Quinn wanted to be Work, or even to be like him, but it reassured him to pretend to be Work as he was writing his books, to know that he had it in him to be Work if he ever chose to be, even if only in his mind.

That night, as he at last drifted off to sleep, Quinn tried to imagine what Work would have said to the stranger on the phone. In his dream, which he later forgot, he found himself alone in a room, firing a pistol into a bare white wall.

The following night, Quinn was caught off guard. He had thought the incident was over and was not expecting the stranger to call again. As it happened, he was sitting on the toilet, in the act of expelling a turd, when the telephone rang. It was somewhat later than the previous night, perhaps ten or twelve minutes before one. Quinn had just reached the chapter that tells of Marco Polo's journey from Peking to Amoy, and the book was open on his lap as he went about his business in the tiny bathroom. The ringing of the telephone came as a distinct irritation. To answer it promptly would mean getting up without wiping himself, and he was loath to walk across the apartment in that state. On the other hand, if he finished what he was doing at his normal speed, he would not make it to the phone in time. In spite of this, Quinn found himself reluctant to move. The telephone was not his favourite object, and more than once he had considered getting rid of his. What he disliked most of all was its tyranny. Not only did it have the power to interrupt him against his will, but inevitably he would give in to its command. This time, he decided to resist. By the third ring, his bowels were empty. By the fourth ring, he had succeeded in wiping himself. By the fifth ring, he had pulled up his pants, left the bathroom, and was walking calmly across the apartment. He answered the phone on the sixth ring, but there was no one at the other end. The caller had hung up.

The next night, he was ready. Sprawled out in his bed, perusing the pages of *The Sporting News*, he waited for the stranger to call a third time. Every now and then, when his nerves got the better of him, he would stand up and pace about the apartment. He put on a record – Haydn's opera, *The Man in the Moon* – and listened to it from start to finish. He waited and waited. At two-thirty, he finally gave up and went to sleep.

He waited the next night, and the night after that as well. Just as he was about to abandon his scheme, realizing that he had been wrong in all his assumptions, the telephone rang again. It was May nineteenth. He would remember the date because it was his parents' anniversary – or would have been, had his parents been alive – and his mother had once told him that he had been conceived on her wedding night. This fact had always appealed to him – being able to pinpoint the first moment of his existence – and over the years he had privately celebrated his birthday on that day. This time it was somewhat earlier than on the other two nights – not yet eleven o'clock – and as he reached for the phone he assumed it was someone else.

'Hello?' he said.

Again, there was a silence on the other end. Quinn knew at once that it was the stranger.

'Hello?' he said again. 'What can I do for you?'

'Yes,' said the voice at last. The same mechanical whisper, the

10

same desperate tone. 'Yes. It is needed now. Without delay.'

'What is needed?'

'To speak. Right now. To speak right now. Yes.'

'And who do you want to speak to?'

'Always the same man. Auster. The one who calls himself Paul Auster.'

This time Quinn did not hesitate. He knew what he was going to do, and now that the time had come, he did it.

'Speaking,' he said. 'This is Auster speaking.'

'At last. At last I've found you.' He could hear the relief in the voice, the tangible calm that suddenly seemed to overtake it.

'That's right,' said Quinn. 'At last.' He paused for a moment to let the words sink in, as much for himself as for the other. 'What can I do for you?'

'I need help,' said the voice. 'There is great danger. They say you are the best one to do these things.'

'It depends on what things you mean.'

'I mean death. I mean death and murder.'

'That's not exactly my line,' said Quinn. 'I don't go around killing people.'

'No,' said the voice petulantly. 'I mean the reverse.'

'Someone is going to kill you?'

'Yes, kill me. That's right. I am going to be murdered.'

'And you want me to protect you?'

'To protect me, yes. And to find the man who is going to do it.'

'You don't know who it is?'

'I know, yes. Of course I know. But I don't know where he is.'

'Can you tell me about it?'

'Not now. Not on the phone. There is great danger. You must come here.'

'How about tomorrow?'

'Good. Tomorrow. Early tomorrow. In the morning.'

'Ten o'clock?'

'Good. Ten o'clock.' The voice gave an address on East 69th Street. 'Don't forget, Mr Auster. You must come.'

'Don't worry,' said Quinn. 'I'll be there.'

11

2

The next morning, Quinn woke up earlier than he had in several weeks. As he drank his coffee, buttered his toast, and read through the baseball scores in the paper (the Mets had lost again, two to one, on a ninth inning error), it did not occur to him that he was going to show up for his appointment. Even that locution, *his appointment*, seemed odd to him. It wasn't his appointment, it was Paul Auster's. And who that person was he had no idea.

Nevertheless, as time wore on he found himself doing a good imitation of a man preparing to go out. He cleared the table of the breakfast dishes, tossed the newspaper on the couch, went into the bathroom, showered, shaved, went on to the bedroom wrapped in two towels, opened the closet, and picked out his clothes for the day. He found himself tending toward a jacket and tie. Quinn had not worn a tie since the funerals of his wife and son, and he could not even remember if he still owned one. But there it was, hanging amidst the debris of his wardrobe. He dismissed a white shirt as too formal, however, and instead chose a grey and red check affair to go with the grey tie. He put them on in a kind of trance.

It was not until he had his hand on the doorknob that be began to suspect what he was doing. 'I seem to be going out,' he said to himself. 'But if I am going out, where exactly am I going?' An hour later, as he climbed from the number 4 bus at 70th Street and Fifth Avenue, he still had not answered the question. To one side of him was the park, green in the morning sun, with sharp, fleeting shadows; to the other side was the Frick, white and austere, as if abandoned to the dead. He thought for a moment of Vermeer's *Soldier and Young Girl Smiling*, trying to remember the expression on the girl's face, the exact position of her hands around the cup, the red back of the faceless man. In his mind, he caught a glimpse of the blue map on the wall and the sunlight pouring through the window, so like the sunlight that surrounded him now. He was walking. He was crossing the street and moving eastward. At Madison Avenue he turned right and went south for a block, then turned left and saw where he was. 'I seem to have arrived,' he said to himself. He stood before the building and paused. It suddenly did not seem to matter any more. He felt remarkably calm, as if everything had already happened to him. As he opened the door that would lead him into the lobby, he gave himself one last word of advice. 'If all this is really happening,' he said, 'then I must keep my eyes open.'

It was a woman who opened the apartment door. For some reason, Quinn had not been expecting this, and it threw him off track. Already, things were happening too fast. Before he had a chance to absorb the woman's presence, to describe her to himself and form his impressions, she was talking to him, forcing him to respond. Therefore, even in those first moments, he had lost ground, was starting to fall behind himself. Later, when he had time to reflect on these events, he would manage to piece together his encounter with the woman. But that was the work of memory, and remembered things, he knew, had a tendency to subvert the things remembered. As a consequence, he could never be sure of any of it.

The woman was thirty, perhaps thirty-five; average height at best; hips a touch wide, or else voluptuous, depending on your point of view; dark hair, dark eyes, and a look in those eyes that was at once self-contained and vaguely seductive. She wore a black dress and very red lipstick.

'Mr Auster?' A tentative smile; a questioning tilt to the head.

'That's right,' said Quinn. 'Paul Auster.'

'I'm Virginia Stillman,' the woman began. 'Peter's wife. He's been waiting for you since eight o'clock.'

'The appointment was for ten,' said Quinn, glancing at his watch. It was exactly ten.

'He's been frantic,' the woman explained. 'I've never seen him like this before. He just couldn't wait.'

13

She opened the door for Quinn. As he crossed the threshold and entered the apartment, he could feel himself going blank, as if his brain had suddenly shut off. He had wanted to take in the details of what he was seeing, but the task was somehow beyond him at that moment. The apartment loomed up around him as a kind of blur. He realized that it was large, perhaps five or six rooms, and that it was richly furnished, with numerous art objects, silver ashtrays, and elaborately framed paintings on the walls. But that was all. No more than a general impression – even though he was there, looking at those things with his own eyes.

He found himself sitting on a sofa, alone in the living room. He remembered now that Mrs Stillman had told him to wait there while she went to find her husband. He couldn't say how long it had been. Surely no more than a minute or two. But from the way the light was coming through the windows, it seemed to be almost noon. It did not occur to him, however, to consult his watch. The smell of Virginia Stillman's perfume hovered around him, and he began to imagine what she looked like without any clothes on. Then he thought about what Max Work might have been thinking, had he been there. He decided to light a cigarette. He blew the smoke into the room. It pleased him to watch it leave his mouth in gusts, disperse, and take on new definition as the light caught it.

He heard the sound of someone entering the room behind him. Quinn stood up from the sofa and turned around, expecting to see Mrs Stillman. Instead, it was a young man, dressed entirely in white, with the white-blond hair of a child. Uncannily, in that first moment, Quinn thought of his own dead son. Then, just as suddenly as the thought had appeared, it vanished.

Peter Stillman walked into the room and sat down in a red velvet armchair opposite Quinn. He said not a word as he made his way to his seat, nor did he acknowledge Quinn's presence. The act of moving from one place to another seemed to require all his attention, as though not to think of what he was doing would reduce him to immobility. Quinn had never seen anyone move in such a manner, and he realized at once that this was the same

14

person he had spoken to on the phone. The body acted almost exactly as the voice had: machine-like, fitful, alternating between slow and rapid gestures, rigid and yet expressive, as if the operation were out of control, not quite corresponding to the will that lay behind it. It seemed to Quinn that Stillman's body had not been used for a long time and that all its functions had been relearned, so that motion had become a conscious process, each movement broken down into its component submovements, with the result that all flow and spontaneity had been lost. It was like watching a marionette trying to walk without strings.

Everything about Peter Stillman was white. White shirt, open at the neck; white pants, white shoes, white socks. Against the pallor of his skin, the flaxen thinness of his hair, the effect was almost transparent, as though one could see through to the blue veins behind the skin of his face. This blue was almost the same as the blue of his eyes: a milky blue that seemed to dissolve into a mixture of sky and clouds. Quinn could not image himself addressing a word to this person. It was as though Stillman's presence was a command to be silent.

Stillman settled slowly into his chair and at last turned his attention to Quinn. As their eyes met, Quinn suddenly felt that Stillman had become invisible. He could see him sitting in the chair across from him, but at the same time it felt as though he was not there. It occurred to Quinn that perhaps Stillman was blind. But no, that did not seem possible. The man was looking at him, even studying him, and if recognition did not flicker across his face, it still held something more than a blank stare. Quinn did not know what to do. He sat there dumbly in his seat, looking back at Stillman. A long time passed.

'No questions, please,' the young man said at last. 'Yes. No. Thank you.' He paused for a moment. 'I am Peter Stillman. I say this of my own free will. Yes. That is not my real name. No. Of course, my mind is not all it should be. But nothing can be done about that. No. About that. No, no. Not anymore.

'You sit there and think: who is this person talking to me? What are these words coming from his mouth? I will tell you. Or else I

15

will not tell you. Yes and no. My mind is not all it should be. I say this of my own free will. But I will try. Yes and no. I will try to tell you, even if my mind makes it hard. Thank you.

'My name is Peter Stillman. Perhaps you have heard of me, but more than likely not. No matter. That is not my real name. My real name I cannot remember. Excuse me. Not that it makes a difference. That is to say, anymore.

'This is what is called speaking. I believe that is the term. When words come out, fly into the air, live for a moment, and die. Strange, is it not? I myself have no opinion. No and no again. But still, there are words you will need to have. There are many of them. Many millions I think. Perhaps only three or four. Excuse me. But I am doing well today. So much better than usual. If I can give you the words you need to have, it will be a great victory. Thank you. Thank you a million times over.

'Long ago there was mother and father. I remember none of that. They say: mother died. Who they are I cannot say. Excuse me. But that is what they say.

'No mother, then. Ha ha. Such is my laughter now, my belly burst of mumbo jumbo. Ha ha ha. Big father said: it makes no difference. To me. That is to say, to him. Big father of the big muscles and the boom, boom, boom. No questions now, please.

'I say what they say because I know nothing. I am only poor Peter Stillman, the boy who can't remember. Boo hoo. Willy nilly. Nincompoop. Excuse me. They say, they say. But what does poor little Peter say? Nothing, nothing. Anymore.

'There was this. Dark. Very dark. As dark as very dark. They say: that was the room. As if I could talk about it. The dark, I mean. Thank you.

'Dark, dark. They say for nine years. Not even a window. Poor Peter Stillman. And the boom, boom, boom. The caca piles. The pipi lakes. The swoons. Excuse me. Numb and naked. Excuse me. Anymore.

'There is the dark then. I am telling you. There was food in the dark, yes, mush food in the hush dark room. He ate with his hands. Excuse me. I mean Peter did. And if I am Peter, so much

16

the better. That is to say, so much the worse. Excuse me. I am Peter Stillman. That is not my real name. Thank you.

'Poor Peter Stillman. A little boy he was. Barely a few words of his own. And then no words, and then no one, and then no, no, no. Anymore.

'Forgive me, Mr Auster. I see that I am making you sad. No questions, please. My name is Peter Stillman. That is not my real name. My real name is Mr Sad. What is your name, Mr Auster? Perhaps you are the real Mr Sad, and I am no one.

'Boo hoo. Excuse me. Such is my weeping and wailing. Boo hoo, sob sob. What did Peter do in that room? No one can say. Some say nothing. As for me, I think that Peter could not think. Did he blink? Did he drink? Did he stink? Ha ha ha. Excuse me. Sometimes I am so funny.

'Wimble click crumblechaw beloo. Clack clack bedrack. Numb noise, flacklemuch, chewmanna. Ya, ya, ya. Excuse me. I am the only one who understands these words.

'Later and later and later. So they say. It went on too long for Peter to be right in the head. Never again. No, no, no. They say that someone found me. I do not remember. No, I do not remember what happened when they opened the door and the light came in. No, no, no. I can say nothing about any of this. Anymore.

'For a long time I wore dark glasses. I was twelve. Or so they say. I lived in a hospital. Little by little, they taught me how to be Peter Stillman. They said: you are Peter Stillman. Thank you, I said. Ya, ya, ya. Thank you and thank you. I said.

'Peter was a baby. They had to teach him everything. How to walk, you know. How to eat. How to make caca and pipi in the toilet. That wasn't bad. Even when I bit them, they didn't do the boom, boom, boom. Later, I even stopped tearing off my clothes.

'Peter was a good boy. But it was hard to teach him words. His mouth did not work right. And of course he was not all there in his head. Ba ba ba, he said. And da da da. And wa wa wa. Excuse me. It took more years and years. Now they say to Peter: you can go now, there's nothing more we can do for you. Peter Stillman, you are a human being, they said. It is good to believe what doctors say. Thank you. Thank you so very much.

'I am Peter Stillman. That is not my real name. My real name is Peter Rabbit. In the winter I am Mr White, in the summer I am Mr Green. Think what you like of this. I say it of my own free will. Wimble click crumblechaw beloo. It is beautiful, is it not? I make up words like this all the time. That can't be helped. They just come out of my mouth by themselves. They cannot be translated.

'Ask and ask, It does no good. But I will tell you. I don't want you to be sad, Mr Auster. You have such a kind face. You remind me of a somesuch or a groan, I don't know which. And your eyes look at me. Yes, yes. I can see them. That is very good. Thank you.

'That is why I will tell you. No questions, please. You are wondering about all the rest. That is to say, the father. The terrible father who did all those things to little Peter. Rest assured. They took him to a dark place. They locked him up and left him there. Ha ha ha. Excuse me. Sometimes I am so funny.

'Thirteen years, they said. That is perhaps a long time. But I know nothing of time. I am new every day. I am born when I wake up in the morning, I grow old during the day, and I die at night when I go to sleep. It is not my fault. I am doing so well today. I am doing so much better than I have ever done before.

'For thirteen years the father was away. His name is Peter Stillman too. Strange, is it not? That two people can have the same name? I do not know if that is his real name. But I do not think he is me. We are both Peter Stillman. But Peter Stillman is not my real name. So perhaps I am not Peter Stillman, after all.

'Thirteen years I say. Or they say. It makes no difference. I know nothing of time. But what they tell me is this. Tomorrow is the end of thirteen years. That is bad. Even though they say it is not, it is bad. I am not supposed to remember. But now and then I do, in spite of what I say.

'He will come. That is to say, the father will come. And he will try to kill me. Thank you. But I do not want that. No, no. Not anymore. Peter lives now. Yes. All is not right in his head, but still

18

he lives. And that is something, is it not? You bet your bottom dollar. Ha ha ha.

'I am mostly now a poet. Every day I sit in my room and write another poem. I make up all the words myself, just like when I lived in the dark. I begin to remember things that way, to pretend that I am back in the dark again. I am the only one who knows what the words mean. They cannot be translated. These poems will make me famous. Hit the nail on the head. Ya, ya ya. Beautiful poems. So beautiful the whole world will weep.

'Later perhaps I will do something else. After I am done being a poet. Sooner or later I will run out of words, you see. Everyone has just so many words inside him. And then where will I be? I think I would like to be a fireman after that. And after that a doctor. It makes no difference. The last thing I will be is a high-wire walker. When I am very old and have at last learned how to walk like other people. Then I will dance on the wire, and people will be amazed. Even little children. That is what I would like. To dance on the wire until I die.

'But no matter. It makes no difference. To me. As you can see, I am a rich man. I do not have to worry. No, no. Not about that. You bet your bottom dollar. The father was rich, and little Peter got all his money after they locked him up in the dark. Ha ha ha. Excuse me for laughing. Sometimes I am so funny.

'I am the last of the Stillmans. That was quite a family, or so they say. From old Boston, in case you might have heard of it. I am the last one. There are no others. I am the end of everyone, the last man. So much the better, I think. It is not a pity that it should all end now. It is good for everyone to be dead.

'The father was perhaps not really bad. At least I say so now. He had a big head. As big as very big, which meant there was too much room in there. So many thoughts in that big head of his. But poor Peter, was he not? And in terrible straits indeed. Peter who could not see or say, who could not think or do. Peter who could not. No. Not anything.

'I know nothing of any of this. Nor do I understand. My wife is the one who tells me these things. She says it is important for me

19

to know, even if I do not understand. But even this I do not understand. In order to know, you must understand. Is that not so? But I know nothing. Perhaps I am Peter Stillman, and perhaps I am not. My real name is Peter Nobody. Thank you. And what do you think of that?

'So I am telling you about the father. It is a good story, even if I do not understand it. I can tell it to you because I know the words. And that is something, is it not? To know the words I mean. Sometimes I am so proud of myself! Excuse me. This is what my wife says. She says the father talked about God. That is a funny word to me. When you put it backwards, it spells dog. And a dog is not much like God, is it? Woof woof. Bow wow. Those are dog words. I think they are beautiful. So pretty and true. Like the words I make up.

'Anyway. I was saying. The father talked about God. He wanted to know if God had a language. Don't ask me what this means. I am only telling you because I know the words. The father thought a baby might speak it if the baby saw no people. But what baby was there? Ah. Now you begin to see. You did not have to buy him. Of course, Peter knew some people words. That could not be helped. But the father thought maybe Peter would forget them. After a while. That is why there was so much boom, boom, boom. Every time Peter said a word, his father would boom him. At last Peter learned to say nothing. Ya ya ya. Thank you.

'Peter kept the words inside him. All those days and months and years. There in the dark, little Peter all alone, and the words made noise in his head and kept him company. This is why his mouth does not work right. Poor Peter. Boo hoo. Such are his tears. The little boy who can never grow up.

'Peter can talk like people now. But he still has the other words in his head. They are God's language, and no one else can speak them. They cannot be translated. That is why Peter lives so close to God. That is why he is a famous poet.

'Everything is so good for me now. I can do whatever I like. Any time, any place. I even have a wife. You can see that. I mentioned her before. Perhaps you have even met her. She is beautiful, is she not? Her name is Virginia. That is not her real name. But that makes no difference. To me.

'Whenever I ask, my wife gets a girl for me. They are whores. I put my worm inside them and they moan. There have been so many. Ha ha. They come up here and I fuck them. It feels good to fuck. Virginia gives them money and everyone is happy. You bet your bottom dollar. Ha ha.

'Poor Virginia. She does not like to fuck. That is to say, with me. Perhaps she fucks another. Who can say? I know nothing of this. It makes no difference. But maybe if you are nice to Virginia she will let you fuck her. It would make me happy. For your sake. Thank you.

'So. There are a great many things. I am trying to tell them to you. I know that all is not right in my head. And it is true, yes, and I say this of my own free will, that sometimes I just scream and scream. For no good reason. As if there had to be a reason. But for none that I can see. Or anyone else. No. And then there are the times when I say nothing. For days and days on end. Nothing, nothing, nothing. I forget how to make the words come out of my mouth. Then it is hard for me to move. Ya ya. Or even to see. That is when I become Mr Sad.

'I still like to be in the dark. At least sometimes. It does me good, I think. In the dark I speak God's language and no one can hear me. Do not be angry, please. I cannot help it.

'Best of all, there is the air. Yes. And little by little, I have learned to live inside it. The air and the light, yes, that too, the light that shines on all things and puts them there for my eyes to see. There is the air and the light and this best of all. Excuse me. The air and the light. Yes. When the weather is good, I like to sit by the open window. Sometimes I look out and watch the things below. The street and all the people, the dogs and cars, the bricks of the building across the way. And then there are the times when I close my eyes and just sit there, with the breeze blowing on my face, and the light inside the air, all around me and just beyond my eyes, and the world all red, a beautiful red inside my eyes, with the sun shining on me and my eyes.

'It is true that I rarely go out. It is hard for me, and I am not always to be trusted. Sometimes I scream. Do not be angry with me, please. I cannot help it. Virginia says I must learn how to behave in public. But sometimes I cannot help myself, and the screams just come out of me.

'But I do love going to the park. There are the trees, and the air and the light. There is good in all that, is there not? Yes. Little by little, I am getting better inside myself. I can feel it. Even Dr Wyshnegradsky says so. I know that I am still the puppet boy. That cannot be helped. No, no. Anymore. But sometimes I think I will at last grow up and become real.

'For now, I am still Peter Stillman. That is not my real name. I cannot say who I will be tomorrow. Each day is new, and each day I am born again. I see hope everywhere, even in the dark, and when I die I will perhaps become God.

'There are many more words to speak. But I do not think I will speak them. No. Not today. My mouth is tired now, and I think the time has come for me to go. Of course, I know nothing of time. But that makes no difference. To me. Thank you very much. I know you will save my life, Mr Auster. I am counting on you. Life can last just so long, you understand. Everything else is in the room, with darkness, with God's language, with screams. Here I am of the air, a beautiful thing for the light to shine on. Perhaps you will remember that. I am Peter Stillman. That is not my real name. Thank you very much.'

The speech was over. How long it had lasted Quinn could not say. For it was only now, after the words had stopped, that he realized they were sitting in the dark. Apparently, a whole day had gone by. At some point during Stillman's monologue the sun had set in the room, but Quinn had not been aware of it. Now he could feel the darkness and the silence, and his head was humming with them. Several minutes went by. Quinn thought that perhaps it was up to him to say something now, but he could not be sure. He could hear Peter Stillman breathing heavily in his spot across the room. Other than that, there were no sounds. Quinn could not decide what to do. He thought of several possibilities, but then, one by one, dismissed them from his mind. He sat there in his seat, waiting for the next thing to happen.

The sound of stockinged legs moving across the room finally broke the silence. There was the metal click of a lamp switch, and suddenly the room was filled with light. Quinn's eyes automatically turned to its source, and there, standing beside a table lamp to the left of Peter's chair, he saw Virginia Stillman. The young man was gazing straight ahead, as if asleep with his eyes open. Mrs Stillman bent over, put her arm around Peter's shoulder, and spoke softly into his ear.

'It's time now, Peter,' she said. 'Mrs Saavedra is waiting for you.'

Peter looked up at her and smiled. 'I am filled with hope,' he said.

Virginia Stillman kissed her husband tenderly on the cheek. 'Say goodbye to Mr Auster,' she said.

Peter stood up. Or rather, he began the sad, slow adventure of manoeuvring his body out of the chair and working his way to his feet. At each stage there were relapses, crumplings, catapults back, accompanied by sudden fits of immobility, grunts, words whose meaning Quinn could not decipher.

At last Peter was upright. He stood in front of his chair with an expression of triumph and looked Quinn in the eyes. Then he smiled, broadly and without self-consciousness.

'Goodbye,' he said.

'Goodbye, Peter,' said Quinn.

Peter gave a little spastic wave of the hand and then slowly turned and walked across the room. He tottered as he went, listing first to the right, then to the left, his legs by turns buckling and locking. At the far end of the room, standing in a lighted doorway, was a middle-aged woman dressed in a white nurse's uniform. Quinn assumed it was Mrs Saavedra. He followed Peter Stillman with his eyes until the young man disappeared through the door.

Virginia Stillman sat down across from Quinn, in the same chair her husband had just occupied.

'I could have spared you all that,' she said, 'but I thought it would be best for you to see it with your own eyes.'

'I understand,' said Quinn.

'No, I don't think you do,' the woman said bitterly. 'I don't think anyone can understand.'

Quinn smiled judiciously and then told himself to plunge in. 'Whatever I do or do not understand,' he said, 'is probably beside the point. You've hired me to do a job, and the sooner I get on with it the better. From what I can gather, the case is urgent. I make no claims about understanding Peter or what you might have suffered. The important thing is that I'm willing to help. I think you should take it for what it's worth.'

He was warming up now. Something told him that he had captured the right tone, and a sudden sense of pleasure surged through him, as though he had just managed to cross some internal border within himself.

'You're right,' said Virginia Stillman. 'Of course you're right.'

The woman paused, took a deep breath, and then paused again, as if rehearsing in her mind the things she was about to say. Quinn noticed that her hands were clenched tightly around the arms of the chair.

'I realize,' she went on, 'that most of what Peter says is very confusing – especially the first time you hear him. I was standing in the next room listening to what he said to you. You mustn't assume that Peter always tells the truth. On the other hand, it would be wrong to think he lies.'

'You mean that I should believe some of the things he said and not believe others.'

'That's exactly what I mean.'

'Your sexual habits, or lack of them, don't concern me, Mrs Stillman,' said Quinn. 'Even if what Peter said is true, it makes no difference. In my line of work you tend to meet a little of everything, and if you don't learn to suspend judgement, you'll never get anywhere. I'm used to hearing people's secrets, and I'm also used to keeping my mouth shut. If a fact has no direct bearing on a case, I have no use for it.'

Mrs Stillman blushed. 'I just wanted you to know that what Peter said isn't true.'

Quinn shrugged, took out a cigarette, and lit it. 'One way or the other,' he said, 'it's not important. What I'm interested in are the other things Peter said. I assume they're true, and if they are, I'd like to hear what you have to say about them.'

'Yes, they're true.' Virginia Stillman released her grip on the chair and put her right hand under her chin. Pensive. As if searching for an attitude of unshakeable honesty. 'Peter has a child's way of telling it. But what he said is true.'

'Tell me something about the father. Anything you think is relevant.'

'Peter's father is a Boston Stillman. I'm sure you've heard of the family. There were several governors back in the nineteenth century, a number of Episcopal bishops, ambassadors, a Harvard president. At the same time, the family made a great deal of money in textiles, shipping, and God knows what else. The details are unimportant. Just so long as you have some idea of the background.

'Peter's father went to Harvard, like everyone else in the family. He studied philosophy and religion and by all accounts was quite brilliant. He wrote his thesis on sixteenth- and seventeenth-century theological interpretations of the New World, and then he took a job in the religion department at Columbia. Not long after that, he married Peter's mother. I don't know much about her. From the photographs I've seen, she was very pretty. But delicate – a little like Peter, with those pale blue eyes and white skin. When Peter was born a few years later, the family was living in a large apartment on Riverside Drive. Stillman's academic career was prospering. He rewrote his dissertation and turned it into a book – it did very well – and was made a full professor when he was thirty-four or thirty-five. Then Peter's mother died. Everything about that death is unclear. Stillman claimed that she had died in her sleep, but the evidence seemed to point to suicide. Something to do with an overdose of pills, but of course nothing could be proved. There was even some talk that he had killed her. But those were just rumours, and nothing ever came of it. The whole affair was kept very quiet.

'Peter was just two at the time, a perfectly normal child. After his wife's death, Stillman apparently had little to do with him. A nurse was hired, and for the next six months or so she took complete care of Peter. Then, out of the blue, Stillman fired her. I forget her name – a Miss Barber, I think – but she testified at the trial. It seems that Stillman just came home one day and told her that he was taking charge of Peter's upbringing. He sent in his resignation to Columbia and told them he was leaving the university to devote himself full-time to his son. Money, of course, was no object, and there was nothing anyone could do about it.

'After that, he more or less dropped out of sight. He stayed on in the same apartment, but he hardly ever went out. No one really knows that happened. I think, probably, that he began to believe in some of the far-fetched religious ideas he had written about. It made him crazy, absolutely insane. There's no other way to describe it. He locked Peter in a room in the apartment, covered up the windows, and kept him there for nine years. Try

26

to imagine it, Mr Auster. Nine years. An entire childhood spent in darkness, isolated from the world, with no human contact except an occasional beating. I live with the results of that experiment, and I can tell you the damage was monstrous. What you saw today was Peter at his best. It's taken thirteen years to get him this far, and I'll be damned if I let anyone hurt him again.'

Mrs Stillman stopped to catch her breath. Quinn sensed that she was on the verge of a scene and that one more word might put her over the edge. He had to speak now, or the conversation would run away from him.

'How was Peter finally discovered?' he asked.

Some of the tension went out of the woman. She exhaled audibly and looked Quinn in the eyes.

'There was a fire,' she said.

'An accidental fire or one set on purpose?'

'No one knows.'

'What do you think?'

'I think Stillman was in his study. He kept the records of his experiment there, and I think he finally realized that his work had been a failure. I'm not saying that he regretted anything he had done. But even taking it on his own terms, he knew he had failed. I think he reached some point of final disgust with himself that night and decided to burn his papers. But the fire got out of control, and much of the apartment burned. Luckily, Peter's room was at the other end of a long hall, and the firemen got to him in time.'

'And then?'

'It took several months to sort everything out. Stillman's papers had been destroyed, which meant there was no concrete evidence. On the other hand, there was Peter's condition, the room he had been locked up in, those horrible boards across the windows, and eventually the police put the case together. Stillman was finally brought to trial.'

'What happened in court?'

'Stillman was judged insane and he was sent away.'

'And Peter?'

27

'He also went to a hospital. He stayed there until just two years ago.'

'Is that where you met him?'

'Yes. In the hospital.'

'How?'

'I was his speech therapist. I worked with Peter every day for five years.'

'I don't mean to pry. But how exactly did that lead to marriage?'

'It's complicated.'

'Do you mind telling me about it?'

'Not really. But I don't think you'd understand.'

'There's only one way to find out.'

'Well, to put it simply. It was the best way to get Peter out of the hospital and give him a chance to lead a more normal life.'

'Couldn't you have been made his legal guardian?'

'The procedures were very complicated. And besides, Peter was no longer a minor.'

'Wasn't that an enormous self-sacrifice on your part?'

'Not really. I was married once before – disastrously. It's not something I want for myself any more. At least with Peter there's a purpose to my life.'

'Is it true that Stillman is being released?'

'Tomorrow. He'll be arriving at Grand Central in the evening.'

'And you feel he might come after Peter. Is this just a hunch, or do you have some proof?'

'A little of both. Two years ago, they were going to let Stillman out. But he wrote Peter a letter, and I showed it to the authorities. They decided he wasn't ready to be released, after all.'

'What kind of letter was it?'

'An insane letter. He called Peter a devil boy and said there would be a day of reckoning.'

'Do you still have the letter?'

'No. I gave it to the police two years ago.'

'A copy?'

'I'm sorry. Do you think it's important?'

'It might be.'

'I can try to get one for you if you like.'

'I take it there were no more letters after that one.'

'No more letters. And now they feel Stillman is ready to be discharged. That's the official view, in any case, and there's nothing I can do to stop them. What I think, though, is that Stillman simply learned his lesson. He realized that letters and threats would keep him locked up.'

'And so you're still worried.'

'That's right.'

'But you have no precise idea of what Stillman's plans might be.'

'Exactly.'

'What is it you want me to do?'

'I want you to watch him carefully. I want you to find out what he's up to. I want you to keep him away from Peter.'

'In other words, a kind of glorified tail job.'

'I suppose so.'

'I think you should understand that I can't prevent Stillman from coming to this building. What I can do is warn you about it. And I can make it my business to come here with him.'

'I understand. As long as there's some protection.'

'Good. How often do you want me to check in with you?'

'I'd like you to give me a report every day. Say a telephone call in the evening, around ten or eleven o'clock.'

'No problem.'

'Is there anything else?'

'Just a few more questions. I'm curious, for example, to know how you found out that Stillman will be coming into Grand Central tomorrow evening.'

'I've made it my business to know, Mr Auster. There's too much at stake here for me to leave it to chance. And if Stillman isn't followed from the moment he arrives, he could easily disappear without a trace. I don't want that to happen.'

'What train will he be on?'

'The six forty-one, arriving from Poughkeepsie.'

'I assume you have a photograph of Stillman?'

'Yes, of course.'

'There's also the question of Peter. I'd like to know why you told him about all this in the first place. Wouldn't it have been better to have kept it quiet?'

'I wanted to. But Peter happened to be listening in on the other phone when I got the news of his father's release. There was nothing I could do about it. Peter can be very stubborn, and I've learned it's best not to lie to him.'

'One last question. Who was it who referred you to me?'

'Mrs Saavedra's husband, Michael. He used to be a policeman, and he did some research. He found out that you were the best man in the city for this kind of thing.'

'I'm flattered.'

'From what I've seen of you so far, Mr Auster, I'm sure we've found the right man.'

Quinn took this as his cue to rise. It came as a relief to stretch his legs at last. Things had gone well, far better than he had expected, but his head hurt now, and his body ached with an exhaustion he had not felt in years. If he carried on any longer, he was sure to give himself away.

'My fee is one hundred dollars a day plus expenses,' he said. 'If you could give me something in advance, it would be proof that I'm working for you – which would ensure us a privileged investigator-client relationship. That means everything that passes between us would be in strictest confidence.'

Virginia Stillman smiled, as if at some secret joke of her own. Or perhaps she was merely responding to the possible double meaning of his last sentence. Like so many of the things that happened to him over the days and weeks that followed, Quinn could not be sure of any of it.

'How much would you like?' she asked.

'It doesn't matter. I'll leave that up to you.'

'Five hundred?'

'That would be more than enough.'

'Good. I'll go get my cheque book.' Virginia Stillman stood up and smiled at Quinn again. 'I'll get you a picture of Peter's father, too. I think I know just where it is.'

Quinn thanked her and said he would wait. He watched her leave the room and once again found himself imagining what she would look like without any clothes on. Was she somehow coming on to him, he wondered, or was it just his own mind trying to sabotage him again? He decided to postpone his meditations and take up the subject again later.

Virginia Stillman walked back into the room and said, 'Here's the cheque. I hope I made it out correctly.'

Yes, yes, thought Quinn as he examined the check, everything is tip top. He was pleased with his own cleverness. The cheque, of course, was made out to Paul Auster, which meant that Quinn could not be held accountable for impersonating a private detective without a licence. It reassured him to know that he had somehow put himself in the clear. The fact that he would never be able to cash the cheque did not trouble him. He understood, even then, that he was not doing any of this for money. He slipped the cheque into the inside breast pocket of his jacket.

'I'm sorry there's not a more recent photograph,' Virginia Stillman was saying. 'This one dates from more than twenty years ago. But I'm afraid it's the best I can do.'

Quinn looked at the picture of Stillman's face, hoping for a sudden epiphany, some sudden rush of subterranean knowledge that would help him to understand the man. But the picture told him nothing. It was no more than a picture of a man. He studied it for a moment longer and concluded that it could just as easily have been anyone.

'I'll look at it more carefully when I get home,' he said, putting it into the same pocket where the cheque had gone. 'Taking the passage of time into account, I'm sure I'll be able to recognize him at the station tomorrow.'

'I hope so,' said Virginia Stillman. 'It's terribly important, and I'm counting on you.'

'Don't worry,' said Quinn. 'I haven't let anyone down yet.'

She walked him to the door. For several seconds they stood there in silence, not knowing whether there was something to add or if the time had come to say goodbye. In that tiny interval,

Virginia Stillman suddenly threw her arms around Quinn, sought out his lips with her own, and kissed him passionately, driving her tongue deep inside his mouth. Quinn was so taken off guard that he almost failed to enjoy it.

When he was at last able to breathe again, Mrs Stillman held him at arm's length and said, 'That was to prove that Peter wasn't telling you the truth. It's very important that you believe me.'

'I believe you,' said Quinn. 'And even if I didn't believe you, it wouldn't really matter.'

'I just wanted you to know what I'm capable of.'

'I think I have a good idea.'

She took his right hand in her two hands and kissed it. 'Thank you, Mr Auster. I really do think you're the answer.'

He promised he would call her the next night, and then he found himself walking out the door, taking the elevator downstairs, and leaving the building. It was past midnight when he hit the street.

4

Quinn had heard of cases like Peter Stillman before. Back in the days of his other life, not long after his own son was born, he had written a review of a book about the wild boy of Aveyron, and at the time he had done some research on the subject. As far as he could remember, the earliest account of such an experiment appeared in the writings of Herodotus: the Egyptian pharaoh Psamtik isolated two infants in the seventh century BC and commanded the servant in charge of them never to utter a word in their presence. According to Herodotus, a notoriously unreliable chronicler, the children learned to speak – their first word being the Phrygian word for bread. In the Middle Ages, the Holy Roman Emperor Frederick II repeated the experiment, hoping to discover man's true 'natural language' using similar methods, but the children died before they ever spoke any words. Finally, in what was undoubtedly a hoax, the early sixteenth-century King of Scotland, James IV, claimed that Scottish children isolated in the same manner wound up speaking 'very good Hebrew.'

Cranks and ideologues, however, were not the only ones interested in the subject. Even so sane and sceptical a man as Montaigne considered the question carefully, and in his most important essay, the *Apology for Raymond Sebond*, he wrote: 'I believe that a child who had been brought up in complete solitude, remote from all association (which would be a hard experiment to make), would have some sort of speech to express his ideas. And it is not credible that Nature has denied us this resource that she has given to many other animals . . . But it is yet to be known what language this child would speak; and what has been said about it by conjecture has not much appearance of truth.'

Beyond the cases of such experiments, there were also the cases of accidental isolation – children lost in the woods, sailors marooned on islands, children brought up by wolves – as well as the cases of cruel and sadistic parents who locked up their children, chained them to beds, beat them in closets, tortured them for no other reason than the compulsions of their own madness – and Quinn had read through the extensive literature devoted to these stories. There was the Scottish sailor Alexander Selkirk (thought by some to be the model for Robinson Crusoe) who had lived for four years alone on an island off the coast of Chile and who, according to the ship captain who rescued him in 1708, 'had so much forgot his language for want of use, that we could scarce understand him.' Less than twenty years later, Peter of Hanover, a wild child of about fourteen, who had been discovered mute and naked in a forest outside the German town of Hamelin, was brought to the English court under the special protection of George I. Both Swift and Defoe were given a chance to see him, and the experience led to Defoe's 1726 pamphlet, *Mere Nature Delineated*. Peter never learned to speak, however, and several months later was sent to the country, where he lived to the age of seventy, with no interest in sex, money, or other worldly matters. Then there was the case of Victor, the wild boy of Aveyron, who was found in 1800. Under the patient and meticulous care of Dr Itard, Victor learned some of the rudiments of speech, but he never progressed beyond the level of a small child. Even better known than Victor was Kaspar Hauser, who appeared one afternoon in Nuremberg in 1828, dressed in an outlandish costume and barely able to utter an intelligible sound. He was able to write his name, but in all other respects he behaved like an infant. Adopted by the town and entrusted to the care of a local teacher, he spent his days sitting on the floor playing with toy horses, eating only bread and water. Kaspar nevertheless developed. He became an excellent horseman, became obsessively neat, had a passion for the colours red and white, and by all accounts displayed an extraordinary memory, especially for names and faces. Still, he preferred to remain indoors, shunned bright light and, like Peter of Hanover, never showed any interest in sex or money. As the memory of his past gradually came back to him, he was able to recall how he had spent many years on the floor of a darkened room, fed by a man who never spoke to him or let himself be seen. Not long after these disclosures, Kaspar was murdered by an unknown man with a dagger in a public park.

It had been years now since Quinn had allowed himself to think of these stories. The subject of children was too painful for him, especially children who had suffered, had been mistreated, had died before they could grow up. If Stillman was the man with the dagger, come back to avenge himself on the boy whose life he had destroyed, Quinn wanted to be there to stop him. He knew he could not bring his own son back to life, but at least he could prevent another from dying. It had suddenly become possible for him to do this, and standing there on the street now, the idea of what lay before him loomed up like a terrible dream. He thought of the little coffin that held his son's body and how he had seen it on the day of the funeral being lowered into the ground. That was isolation, he said to himself. That was silence. It did not help, perhaps, that his son's name had also been Peter.

At the corner of 72nd Street and Madison Avenue, he waved down a cab. As the car rattled through the park toward the West Side, Quinn looked out the window and wondered if these were the same trees that Peter Stillman saw when he walked out into the air and the light. He wondered if Peter saw the same things he did, or whether the world was a different place for him. And if a tree was not a tree, he wondered what it really was.

After the cab had dropped him off in front of his house, Quinn realized that he was hungry. He had not eaten since breakfast early that morning. It was strange, he thought, how quickly time had passed in the Stillman apartment. If his calculations were correct, he had been there for more than fourteen hours. Within himself, however, it felt as though his stay had lasted three or four hours at most. He shrugged at the discrepancy and said to himself, 'I must learn to look at my watch more often.'

He retraced his path along 107th Street, turned left on Broadway, and began walking uptown, looking for a suitable place to eat. A bar did not appeal to him tonight – eating in the dark, the press of boozy chatter – although normally he might have welcomed it. As he crossed 112th Street, he saw that the Heights Luncheonette was still open and decided to go in. It was a brightly lit yet dreary place, with a large rack of girlie magazines on one wall, an area for stationery supplies, another area for newspapers, several tables for patrons, and a long Formica counter with swivel stools. A tall Puerto Rican man in a white cardboard chef's hat stood behind the counter. It was his job to make the food, which consisted mainly of gristle-studded hamburger patties, bland sandwiches with pale tomatoes and wilted lettuce, milkshakes, egg creams, and buns. To his right, ensconced behind the cash register, was the boss, a small balding man with curly hair and a concentration camp number tattooed on his forearm, lording it over his domain of cigarettes, pipes, and cigars. He sat there impassively, reading the night owl edition of the next morning's *Daily News*.

The place was almost deserted at that hour. At the back table sat two old men in shabby clothes, one very fat and the other very thin, intently studying the racing forms. Two empty coffee cups sat on the table between them. In the foreground, facing the magazine rack, a young student stood with an open magazine in his hands, staring at the picture of a naked woman. Quinn sat down at the counter and ordered a hamburger and a coffee. As the counterman swung into action, he spoke over his shoulder to Quinn.

'Did you see game tonight, man?'

'I missed it. Anything good to report?'

'What do you think?'

For several years Quinn had been having the same conversation with this man, whose name he did not know. Once, when he had been in the luncheonette, they had talked about baseball, and now, each time Quinn came in, they continued to talk about it. In the winter, the talk was of trades, predictions, memories. During the season, it was always the most recent game. They were both Mets fans, and the hopelessness of that passion had created a bond between them.

The counterman shook his head. 'First two times up, Kingman hits solo shots,' he said. 'Boom, boom. Big mothers – all the way to the moon. Jones is pitching good for once and things don't look too bad. It's two to one, bottom of the ninth. Pittsburgh gets men on second and third, one out, so the Mets go to the bullpen for Allen. He walks the next guy to load them up. The Mets bring the corners in for a force at home, or maybe they can get the double play if it's hit up the middle. Peña comes up and chicken-shits a little grounder to first and the fucker goes through Kingman's legs. Two men score, and that's it, bye-bye New York.'

'Dave Kingman is a turd,' said Quinn, biting into his hamburger.

'But watch out for Foster,' said the counterman.

'Foster's washed up. A has-been. A mean-faced bozo.' Quinn chewed his food carefully, feeling with his tongue for stray bits of bone. 'They should ship him back to Cincinnati by express mail.'

'Yeah,' said the counterman. 'But they'll be tough. Better than last year, anyway.'

'I don't know,' said Quinn, taking another bite. 'It looks good on paper, but what do they really have? Stearns is always getting hurt. They have minor leaguers at second and short, and Brooks can't keep his mind on the game. Mookie's good, but he's raw, and they can't even decide who to put in right. There's still Rusty, of course, but he's too fat to run anymore. And as for the pitching, forget it. You and I could go over to Shea tomorrow and get hired as the top two starters.'

'Maybe I make you the manager,' said the counterman. 'You could tell those fuckers where to get off.'

'You bet your bottom dollar,' said Quinn.

After he finished eating, Quinn wandered over to the stationery shelves. A shipment of new notebooks had come in, and the pile was impressive, a beautiful array of blues and greens and reds and yellows. He picked one up and saw that the pages had the narrow lines he preferred. Quinn did all his writing with a pen, using a typewriter only for final drafts, and he was always on the lookout for good spiral notebooks. Now that he had embarked on the Stillman case, he felt that a new notebook was in order. It would be helpful to have a separate place to record his thoughts, his observations, and his questions. In that way, perhaps, things might not get out of control.

He looked through the pile, trying to decide which one to pick. For reasons that were never made clear to him, he suddenly felt an irresistible urge for a particular red notebook at the bottom. He pulled it out and examined it, gingerly fanning the pages with his thumb. He was at a loss to explain to himself why he found it so appealing. It was a standard eight and a half by eleven notebook with one hundred pages. But something about it seemed to call out to him – as if its unique destiny in the world was to hold the words that came from his pen. Almost embarrassed by the intensity of his feelings, Quinn tucked the red notebook under his arm, walked over to the cash register, and bought it.

Back in his apartment a quarter of an hour later, Quinn removed the photograph of Stillman and the cheque from his jacket pocket and placed them carefully on his desk. He cleared the debris from the surface – dead matches, cigarette butts, eddies of ash, spent ink cartridges, a few coins, ticket stubs, doodles, a dirty handkerchief – and put the red notebook in the centre. Then he drew the shades in the room, took off all his clothes, and sat down at the desk. He had never done this before, but it somehow seemed appropriate to be naked at this moment. He sat there for twenty or thirty seconds, trying not to move, trying not to do anything but breathe. Then he opened the red notebook. He picked up his pen and wrote his initials, DQ (for Daniel Quinn), on the first page. It was the first time in more than five years that he had put his own name in one of his notebooks. He stopped to consider this fact for a moment but then dismissed it as irrelevant. He turned the page. For several moments he studied its blankness, wondering if he was not a bloody fool. Then he pressed his pen against the top line and made the first entry in the red notebook.

Stillman's face. Or: Stillman's face as it was twenty years ago. Impossible to know whether the face tomorrow will resemble it. It is certain, however, that this is not the face of a madman. Or is this not a legitimate statement? To my eyes, at least, it seems benign, if not downright pleasant. A hint of tenderness around the mouth even. More than likely blue eyes, with a tendency to water. Thin hair even then, so perhaps gone now, and what remains gray, or even white. He bears an odd familiarity: the meditative type, no doubt high-strung, someone who might stutter, fight with himself to stem the flood of words rushing from his mouth.

Little Peter. Is it necessary for me to imagine it, or can I accept it on faith? The darkness. To think of myself in that room, screaming. I am

39

reluctant. Nor do I think I even want to understand it. To what end? This is not a story, after all. It is a fact, something happening in the world, and I am supposed to do a job, one little thing, and I have said yes to it. If all goes well, it should even be quite simple. I have not been hired to understand – merely to act. This is something new. To keep it in mind, at all costs.

And yet, what is it that Dupin says in Poe? 'An identification of the reasoner's intellect with that of his opponent.' But here it would apply to Stillman senior. Which is probably even worse.

As for Virginia, I am in a quandary. Not just the kiss, which might be explained by any number of reasons; not what Peter said about her, which is unimportant. Her marriage? Perhaps. The complete incongruity of it. Could it be that she's in it for the money? Or somehow working in collaboration with Stillman? That would change everything. But, at the same time, it makes no sense. For why would she have hired me? To have a witness to her apparent good intentions? Perhaps. But that seems too complicated. And yet: why do I feel she is not to be trusted?

Stillman's face, again. Thinking for these past few minutes that I have seen it before. Perhaps years ago in the neighbourhood – before the time of his arrest.

To remember what it feels like to wear other people's clothes. To begin with that, I think. Assuming I must. Back in the old days, eighteen, twenty years ago, when I had no money and friends would give me things to wear. J's old overcoat in college, for example. And the strange sense I would have of climbing into his skin. That is probably a start.

And then, most important of all: to remember who I am. To remember who I am supposed to be. I do not think this is a game. On the other hand, nothing is clear. For example: who are you? And if you think you know, why do you keep lying about it? I have no answer. All I can say is this: listen to me. My name is Paul Auster. That is not my real name.

Quinn spent the next morning at the Columbia library with Stillman's book. He arrived early, the first one there as the doors opened, and the silence of the marble halls comforted him, as though he had been allowed to enter some crypt of oblivion. After flashing his alumni card at the drowsing attendant behind the desk, he retrieved the book from the stacks, returned to the third floor, and then settled down in a green leather armchair in one of the smoking rooms. The bright May morning lurked outside like a temptation, a call to wander aimlessly in the air, but Quinn fought it off. He turned the chair around, positioning himself with his back to the window, and opened the book.

The Garden and the Tower: Early Visions of the New World was divided into two parts of approximately equal length, 'The Myth of Paradise' and 'The Myth of Babel'. The first concentrated on the discoveries of the explorers, beginning with Columbus and continuing on through Raleigh. It was Stillman's contention that the first men to visit America believed they had accidentally found paradise, a second Garden of Eden. In the narrative of his third voyage, for example, Columbus wrote: 'For I believe that the earthly Paradise lies here, which no one can enter except by God's leave.' As for the people of this land, Peter Martyr would write as early as 1505: 'They seem to live in that golden world of which old writers speak so much, wherein men lived simply and innocently, without enforcement of laws, without quarrelling, judges, or libels, content only to satisfy nature.' Or, as the ever-present Montaigne would write more than half a century later: 'In my opinion, what we actually see in these nations not only surpasses all the pictures which the poets have drawn of the Golden Age, and all their inventions representing the then happy state of mankind, but also the conception and desire of philosophy itself.' From the very beginning, according to Stillman, the discovery of the New World was the quickening impulse of utopian thought, the spark that gave hope to the perfectibility of human life – from Thomas More's book of 1516 to Gerónimo de Mendieta's prophecy, some years later, that America would become an ideal theocratic state, a veritable City of God.

There was, however, an opposite point of view. If some saw the Indians as living in prelapsarian innocence, there were others who judged them to be savage beasts, devils in the form of men. The discovery of cannibals in the Caribbean did nothing to assuage this opinion. The Spaniards used it as a justification to exploit the natives mercilessly for their own mercantile ends. For if you do not consider the man before you to be human, there are few restraints of conscience on your behaviour towards him. It was not until 1537, with the papal bull of Paul III, that the Indians were declared to be true men possessing souls. The debate nevertheless went on for several hundred years, culminating on the one hand in the 'noble savage' of Locke and Rousseau – which laid the theoretical foundations of democracy in an independent America – and, on the other hand, in the campaign to exterminate the Indians, in the undying belief that the only good Indian was a dead Indian.

The second part of the book began with a new examination of the fall. Relying heavily on Milton and his account in *Paradise Lost* – as representing the orthodox Puritan position – Stillman claimed that it was only after the fall that human life as we know it came into being. For if there was no evil in the Garden, neither was there any good. As Milton himself put it in the *Areopagitica*, 'It was out of the rind of one apple tasted that good and evil leapt forth into the world, like two twins cleaving together.' Stillman's gloss on this sentence was exceedingly thorough. Alert to the possibility of puns and word play throughout, he showed how the word 'taste' was actually a reference to the Latin word 'sapere,' which means both 'to taste' and 'to know' and therefore contains a subliminal reference to the tree of knowledge: the source of the apple whose taste brought forth knowledge into the world, which is to say, good and evil. Stillman also dwelled on the paradox of the word 'cleave,' which means both 'to join together' and 'to break apart,' thus embodying two equal and opposite significations, which in turn embodies a view of language that Stillman found to be present in all of Milton's work. In *Paradise Lost*, for example, each key word has two meanings – one before the fall and one after the fall. To illustrate his point, Stillman isolated several of those words – sinister, serpentine, delicious – and showed how their prelapsarian use was free of moral connotations, whereas their use after the fall was shaded, ambiguous, informed by a knowledge of evil. Adam's one task in the Garden had been to invent language, to give each creature and thing its name. In that state of innocence, his tongue had gone straight to the quick of the world. His words had not been merely appended to the things he saw, they had revealed their essences, had literally brought them to life. A thing and its name were interchangeable. After the fall, this was no longer true. Names became detached from things; words devolved into a collection of arbitrary signs; language had been severed from God. The story of the Garden, therefore, not only records the fall of man, but the fall of language.

Later in the Book of Genesis there is another story about language. According to Stillman, the Tower of Babel episode was an exact recapitulation of what happened in the Garden – only expanded, made general in its significance for all mankind. The story takes on special meaning when its placement in the book is considered: chapter eleven of Genesis, verses one through nine. This is the very last incident of prehistory in the Bible. After that, the Old Testament is exclusively a chronicle of the Hebrews. In other words, the Tower of Babel stands as the last image before the true beginning of the world.

Stillman's commentaries went on for many pages. He began with a historical survey of the various exegetical traditions concerning the story, elaborated on the numerous misreadings that had grown up around it, and ended with a lengthy catalogue of

legends from the Aggadah (a compendium of rabbinical interpretations not connected with legal matters). It was generally
accepted, wrote Stillman, that the Tower had been built in the
year 1996 after the creation, a scant three hundred and forty years
after the Flood, 'lest we be scattered abroad upon the face of the
whole earth'. God's punishment came as a response to this
desire, which contradicted a command that had appeared earlier
in Genesis: 'Be fertile and increase, fill the earth and master it.' By
destroying the Tower, therefore, God condemned man to obey
this injunction. Another reading, however, saw the Tower as a
challenge against God. Nimrod, the first ruler of all the world,
was designated as the Tower's architect: Babel was to be a shrine
that symbolized the universality of his power. This was the
Promethean view of the story, and it hinged on the phrases
'whose top may reach unto heaven' and 'let us make a name'. The
building of the Tower became the obsessive, overriding passion
of mankind, more important finally than life itself. Bricks became
more precious than people. Women labourers did not even stop
to give birth to their children; they secured the newborn in their
aprons and went right on working. Apparently, there were three
different groups involved in the construction: those who wanted
to dwell in heaven, those who wanted to wage war against God,
and those who wanted to worship idols. At the same time, they
were united in their efforts – 'And the whole earth was of one
language, and of one speech' – and the latent power of a united
mankind outraged God. 'And the Lord said, Behold, the people
is one, and they have all one language; and this they begin to do:
and now nothing will be restrained from them, which they have
imagined to do.' This speech is a conscious echo of the words God
spoke on expelling Adam and Eve from the Garden: 'Behold, the
man is become one of us, to know good and evil; and now, lest he
put forth his hand, and take also of the tree of life, and eat, and
live forever – Therefore the Lord God sent him forth from the
garden of Eden . . .' Still another reading held that the story was
intended merely as a way of explaining the diversity of peoples
and languages. For if all men were descended from Noah and his

sons, how was it possible to account for the vast differences among cultures? Another, similar reading contended that the story was an explanation of the existence of paganism and idolatry – for until this story all men are presented as being monotheistic in their beliefs. As for the Tower itself, legend had it that one third of the structure sank into the ground, one third was destroyed by fire, and one third was left standing. God attacked it in two ways in order to convince man that the destruction was a divine punishment and not the result of chance. Still, the part left standing was so high that a palm tree seen from the top of it appeared no larger than a grasshopper. It was also said that a person could walk for three days in the shadow of the Tower without ever leaving it. Finally – and Stillman dwelled upon this at great length – whoever looked upon the ruins of the Tower was believed to forget everything he knew.

What all this had to do with the New World Quinn could not say. But then a new chapter started, and suddenly Stillman was discussing the life of Henry Dark, a Boston clergyman who was born in London in 1649 (on the day of Charles I's execution), came to America in 1675, and died in a fire in Cambridge, Massachusetts in 1691.

According to Stillman, as a young man Henry Dark had served as private secretary to John Milton – from 1669 until the poet's death five years later. This was news to Quinn, for he seemed to remember reading somewhere that the blind Milton had dictated his work to one of his daughters. Dark, he learned, was an ardent Puritan, a student of theology, and a devoted follower of Milton's work. Having met his hero one evening at a small gathering, he was invited to pay a call the following week. That led to further calls, until eventually Milton began to entrust Dark with various small tasks: taking dictation, guiding him through the streets of London, reading to him from the works of the ancients. In a 1672 letter written by Dark to his sister in Boston, he mentioned long discussions with Milton on the finer points of Biblical exegesis. Then Milton died, and Dark was disconsolate. Six months later, finding England a desert, a land that offered him nothing, he

45

decided to emigrate to America. He arrived in Boston in the summer of 1675.

Little was known of his first years in the New World. Stillman speculated that he might have travelled westward, foraging out into uncharted territory, but no concrete evidence could be found to support this view. On the other hand, certain references in Dark's writings indicated an intimate knowledge of Indian customs, which led Stillman to theorize that Dark might possibly have lived among one of the tribes for a period of time. Be that as it may, there was no public mention of Dark until 1682, when his name was entered in the Boston marriage registry as having taken one Lucy Fitts as his bride. Two years later, he was listed as heading a small Puritan congregation on the outskirts of the city. Several children were born to the couple, but all them died in infancy. A son John, however, born in 1686, survived. But in 1691 the boy was reported to have fallen accidentally from a second-story window and perished. Just one month later, the entire house went up in flames, and both Dark and his wife were killed.

Henry Dark would have passed into the obscurity of early American life if not for one thing: the publication of a pamphlet in 1690 entitled *The New Babel*. According to Stillman, this little work of sixty-four pages was the most visionary account of the new continent that had been written up to that time. If Dark had not died so soon after its appearance, its effect would no doubt have been greater. For, as it turned out, most of the copies of the pamphlet were destroyed in the fire that killed Dark. Stillman himself had been able to discover only one – and that by accident in the attic of his family's house in Cambridge. After years of diligent research, he had concluded that this was the only copy still in existence.

The New Babel, written in bold, Miltonic prose, presented the case for the building of paradise in America. Unlike the other writers on the subject, Dark did not assume paradise to be a place that could be discovered. There were no maps that could lead a man to it, no instruments of navigation that could guide a man to its shores. Rather, its existence was immanent within man himself: the idea of a beyond he might someday create in the here and now. For utopia was nowhere – even, as Dark explained, in its 'wordhood.' And if man could bring forth this dreamed-of place, it would only be by building it with his own two hands.

Dark based his conclusions on a reading of the Babel story as a prophetic work. Drawing heavily on Milton's interpretation of the fall, he followed his master in placing an inordinate importance on the role of language. But he took the poet's ideas one step further. If the fall of man also entailed a fall of language, was it not logical to assume that it would be possible to undo the fall, to reverse its effects by undoing the fall of language, by striving to recreate the language that was spoken in Eden? If man could learn to speak this original language of innocence, did it not follow that he would thereby recover a state of innocence within himself? We had only to look at the example of Christ, Dark argued, to understand that this was so. For was Christ not a man, a creature of flesh and blood? And did not Christ speak this prelapsarian language? In Milton's *Paradise Regained*, Satan speaks with 'double-sense deluding', whereas Christ's 'actions to his words accord, his words / To his large heart give utterance due, his heart / Contains of good, wise, just, the perfect shape.' And had God not 'now sent his living Oracle / Into the World to teach his final will, / And sends his Spirit of Truth henceforth to dwell / In pious Hearts, an inward Oracle / To all Truth requisite for me to know'? And, because of Christ, did the fall not have a happy outcome, was it not a *felix culpa*, as doctrine instructs? Therefore, Dark contended, it would indeed be possible for man to speak the original language of innocence and to recover, whole and unbroken, the truth within himself.

Turning to the Babel story, Dark then elaborated his plan and announced his vision of things to come. Quoting from the second verse of Genesis 11 – 'And it came to pass, as they journeyed from the east, that they found a plain in the land of Shi-nar; and they dwelt there' – Dark stated that this passage proved the westward movement of human life and civilization. For the city of Babel – or Babylon – was situated in Mesopotamia, far east of the land of the

Hebrews. If Babel lay to the west of anything, it was Eden, the original site of mankind. Man's duty to scatter himself across the whole earth – in response to God's command to 'be fertile . . . and fill the earth' – would inevitably move along a western course. And what more Western land in all Christendom, Dark asked, than America? The movement of English settlers to the New World, therefore, could be read as the fulfilment of the ancient commandment. America was the last step in the process. Once the continent had been filled, the moment would be ripe for a change in the fortunes of mankind. The impediment to the building of Babel – that man must fill the earth – would be eliminated. At that moment it would again be possible for the whole earth to be of one language and one speech. And if that were to happen, paradise could not be far behind.

Just as Babel had been built three hundred and forty years after the Flood, so it would be, Dark predicted, exactly three hundred and forty years after the arrival of the Mayflower at Plymouth that the commandment would be carried out. For surely it was the Puritans, God's newly chosen people, who held the destiny of mankind in their hands. Unlike the Hebrews, who had failed God by refusing to accept his son, these transplanted Englishmen would write the final chapter of history before heaven and earth were joined at last. Like Noah in his ark, they had travelled across the vast oceanic flood to carry out their holy mission.

Three hundred and forty years, according to Dark's calculations, meant that in 1960 the first part of the settlers work would have been done. At that point, the foundations would have been laid for the real work that was to follow: the building of the new Babel. Already, Dark wrote, he saw encouraging signs in the city of Boston, for there, as nowhere else in the world, the chief construction material was brick – which, as set forth in verse three of Genesis 11, was specified as the construction material of Babel. In the year 1960, he stated confidently, the new Babel would begin to go up, its very shape aspiring toward the heavens, a symbol of the resurrection of the human spirit. History would be written in reverse. What had fallen would be raised up; what had been broken would be made whole. Once completed, the Tower would be large enough to hold every inhabitant of the New World. There would be a room for each person, and once he entered that room, he would forget everything he knew. After forty days and forty nights, he would emerge a new man, speaking God's language, prepared to inhabit the second, everlasting paradise.

So ended Stillman's synopsis of Henry Dark's pamphlet, dated 20 December 1690, the seventieth anniversary of the landing of the Mayflower.

Quinn let out a little sigh and closed the book. The reading room was empty. He leaned forward, put his head in his hands, and closed his eyes. '1960,' he said aloud. He tried to conjure up an image of Henry Dark, but nothing came to him. In his mind he saw only fire, a blaze of burning books. Then, losing track of his thoughts and where they had been leading him, he suddenly remembered that 1960 was the year that Stillman had locked up his son.

He opened the red notebook and set it squarely on his lap. Just as he was about to write in it, however, he decided that he had had enough. He closed the red notebook, got up from his chair, and returned Stillman's book to the front desk. Lighting a cigarette at the bottom of the stairs, he left the library and walked out into the May afternoon.

He made it to Grand Central well in advance. Stillman's train was not due to arrive until six forty-one, but Quinn wanted time to study the geography of the place, to make sure that Stillman would not be able to slip away from him. As he emerged from the subway and entered the great hall, he saw by the clock that it was just past four. Already the station had begun to fill with the rush hour crowd. Making his way through the press of oncoming bodies, Quinn made a tour of the numbered gates, looking for hidden staircases, unmarked exits, dark alcoves. He concluded that a man determined to disappear could do so without much trouble. He would have to hope that Stillman had not been warned that he would be there. If that were the case, and Stillman managed to elude him, it would mean that Virginia Stillman was responsible. There was no one else. It solaced him to know that he had an alternate plan if things went awry. If Stillman did not show up, Quinn would go straight to 69th Street and confront Virginia Stillman with what he knew.

As he wandered through the station, he reminded himself of who he was supposed to be. The effect of being Paul Auster, he had begun to learn, was not altogether unpleasant. Although he still had the same body, the same mind, the same thoughts, he felt as though he had somehow been taken out of himself, as if he no longer had to walk around with the burden of his own consciousness. By a simple trick of the intelligence, a deft little twist of naming, he felt incomparably lighter and freer. At the same time, he knew it was all an illusion. But there was a certain comfort in that. He had not really lost himself; he was merely pretending, and he could return to being Quinn whenever he wished. The fact that there was now a purpose to his being Paul Auster – a purpose that was becoming more and more important to him – served as a kind of moral justification for the charade and absolved him of having to defend his lie. For imagining himself as Auster had become synonymous in his mind with doing good in the world.

He wandered through the station, then, as if inside the body of Paul Auster, waiting for Stillman to appear. He looked up at the vaulted ceiling of the great hall and studied the fresco of constellations. There were light bulbs representing the stars and line drawings of the celestial figures. Quinn had never been able to grasp the connection between the constellations and their names. As a boy he had spent many hours under the night sky trying to tally the clusters of pinprick lights with the shapes of bears, bulls, archers, and water carriers. But nothing had ever come of it, and he had felt stupid, as though there were a blind spot in the centre of his brain. He wondered if the young Auster had been any better at it than he was.

Across the way, occupying the greater part of the station's east wall, was the Kodak display photograph, with its bright, unearthly colors. The scene that month showed a street in some New England fishing village, perhaps Nantucket. A beautiful spring light shone on the cobblestones, flowers of many colors stood in window boxes along the house fronts, and far down at the end of the street was the ocean, with its white waves and blue, blue water. Quinn remembered visiting Nantucket with his wife long ago, in her first month of pregnancy, when his son was no more than a tiny almond in her belly. He found it painful to think of that now, and he tried to suppress the pictures that were forming in his head. 'Look at it through Auster's eyes,' he said to himself, 'and don't think of anything else.' He turned his attention to the photograph again and was relieved to find his thoughts wandering to the subject of whales, to the expeditions that had set out from Nantucket in the last century, to Melville and the opening pages of *Moby Dick*. From there his mind drifted off to the accounts he had read of Melville's last years – the taciturn old man working in the New York customs house, with no readers, forgotten by everyone. Then, suddenly, with great clarity and precision, he saw Bartleby's window and the blank brick wall before him.

Someone tapped him on the arm, and as Quinn wheeled to meet the assault, he saw a short, silent man holding out a green and red ballpoint pen to him. Stapled to the pen was a little white paper flag, one side of which read: 'This good article is the Courtesy of a DEAF MUTE. Pay any price. Thank you for your help.' On the other side of the flag there was a chart of the manual alphabet – LEARN TO SPEAK TO YOUR FRIENDS – that showed the hand positions for each of the twenty-six letters. Quinn reached into his pocket and gave the man a dollar. The deaf mute nodded once very briefly and then moved on, leaving Quinn with the pen in his hand.

It was now past five o'clock. Quinn decided he would be less vulnerable in another spot and removed himself to the waiting room. This was generally a grim place, filled with dust and people with nowhere to go, but now, with the rush hour at full force, it had been taken over by men and women with briefcases, books, and newspapers. Quinn had trouble finding a seat. After searching for two or three minutes, he finally found a place on one of the benches, wedging himself between a man in a blue suit and a plump young woman. The man was reading the sports section of the *Times*, and Quinn glanced over to read the account of the Mets' loss the night before. He had made it to the third or fourth paragraph when the man turned slowly toward him, gave him a vicious stare, and jerked the paper out of view.

After that, a strange thing happened. Quinn turned his attention to the young woman on his right, to see if there was any reading material in that direction. Quinn guessed her age at around twenty. There were several pimples on her left cheek, obscured by a pinkish smear of pancake makeup, and a wad of chewing gum was crackling in her mouth. She was, however, reading a book, a paperback with a lurid cover, and Quinn leaned ever so slightly to his right to catch a glimpse of the title. Against all his expectations, it was a book he himself had written – *Suicide Squeeze* by William Wilson, the first of the Max Work novels.

Quinn had often imagined this situation: the sudden, unexpected pleasure of encountering one of his readers. He had even imagined the conversation that would follow: he, suavely diffident as the stranger praised the book, and then, with great reluctance and modesty, agreeing to autograph the title page, 'since you insist'. But now that the scene was taking place, he felt quite disappointed, even angry. He did not like the girl sitting next to him, and it offended him that she should be casually skimming the pages that had cost him so much effort. His impulse was to tear the book out of her hands and run across the station with it.

He looked at her face again, trying to hear the words she was sounding out in her head, watching her eyes as they darted back and forth across the page. He must have been looking too hard, for a moment later she turned to him with an irritated expression on her face and said, 'You got a problem, mister?'

Quinn smiled weakly. 'No problem,' he said. 'I was just wondering if you liked the book.'

The girl shrugged. 'I've read better and I've read worse.'

Quinn wanted to drop the conversation right there, but something in him persisted. Before he could get up and leave, the words were already out of his mouth. 'Do you find it exciting?'

The girl shrugged again and cracked her gum loudly. 'Sort of. There's a part where the detective gets lost that's kind of scary.'

'Is he a smart detective?'

'Yeah, he's smart. But he talks too much.'

'You'd like more action?'

'I guess so.'

'If you don't like it, why do you go on reading?'

'I don't know.' The girl shrugged once again. 'It passes the time, I guess. Anyway, it's no big deal. It's just a book.'

He was about to tell her who he was, but then he realized that it made no difference. The girl was beyond hope. For five years he had kept William Wilson's identity a secret, and he wasn't about to give it away now, least of all to an imbecile stranger. Still, it was painful, and he struggled desperately to swallow his pride. Rather than punch the girl in the face, he abruptly stood up from his seat and walked away.

At six-thirty he posted himself in front of gate twenty-four. The train was due to arrive on time, and from his vantage in the centre of the doorway, Quinn judged that his chances of seeing Stillman were good. He took out the photograph from his pocket and studied it again, paying special attention to the eyes. He remembered having read somewhere that the eyes were the one feature of the face that never changed. From childhood to old age they remained the same, and a man with the head to see it could theoretically look into the eyes of a boy in a photograph and recognize the same person as an old man. Quinn had his doubts, but this was all he had to go on, his only bridge to the present. Once again, however, Stillman's face told him nothing.

The train pulled into the station, and Quinn felt the noise of it shoot through his body: a random, hectic din that seemed to join with his pulse, pumping his blood in raucous spurts. His head then filled with Peter Stillman's voice, as a barrage of nonsense words clattered against the walls of his skull. He told himself to stay calm. But that did little good. In spite of what he had been expecting of himself at this moment, he was excited.

The train was crowded, and as the passengers started filling the ramp and walking towards him, they quickly became a mob. Quinn flapped the red notebook nervously against his right thigh, stood on his tiptoes, and peered into the throng. Soon the people were surging around him. There were men and women, children and old people, teenagers and babies, rich people and poor people, black men and white women, white men and black women, Orientals and Arabs, men in brown and gray and blue and green, women in red and white and yellow and pink, children in sneakers, children in shoes, children in cowboy boots, fat people and thin people, tall people and short people, each one different from all the others, each one irreducibly himself. Quinn watched them all, anchored to his spot, as if his whole being had been exiled to his eyes. Each time an elderly man approached, he braced himself for it to be Stillman. They came and went too quickly for him to indulge in disappointment, but in each old face he seemed to find an augur of what the real Stillman would be like, and he rapidly shifted his expectations with each new face, as if the accumulation of old men was heralding the imminent arrival of Stillman himself. For one brief instant Quinn thought, 'So this is what detective work is like.' But other than that he thought nothing. He watched. Immobile among the moving crowd, he stood there and watched.

With about half the passengers now gone, Quinn had his first sight of Stillman. The resemblance to the photograph seemed unmistakable. No, he had not gone bald, as Quinn had thought he would. His hair was white, and it lay on his head uncombed, sticking up here and there in tufts. He was tall, thin, without question past sixty, somewhat stooped. Inappropriately for the season, he wore a long, brown overcoat that had gone to seed, and he shuffled slightly as he walked. The expression on his face seemed placid, midway between a daze and thoughtfulness. He did not look at the things around him, nor did they seem to interest him. He had one piece of luggage, a once beautiful but now battered leather suitcase with a strap around it. Once or twice as he walked up the ramp he put the suitcase down and rested for a moment. He seemed to be moving with effort, a bit thrown by the crowd, uncertain whether to keep up with it or to let the others pass him by.

Quinn backed off several feet, positioning himself for a quick move to the left or right, depending on what happened. At the same time, he wanted to be far enough away so that Stillman would not feel he was being followed.

As Stillman reached the threshold of the station, he put his bag down once again and paused. At that moment Quinn allowed himself a glance to Stillman's right, surveying the rest of the crowd to be doubly sure he had made no mistakes. What happened then defied explanation. Directly behind Stillman, heaving into view just inches behind his right shoulder, another man stopped, took a lighter out of his pocket, and lit a cigarette. His face was the exact twin of Stillman's. For a second Quinn thought it was an illusion, a kind of aura thrown off by the electromagnetic currents in Stillman's body. But no, this other Stillman moved, breathed, blinked his eyes; his actions were clearly independent of the first Stillman. The second Stillman had a prosperous air about him. He was dressed in an expensive blue suit; his shoes were shined; his white hair was combed; and in his eyes there was the shrewd look of a man of the world. He, too, was carrying a single bag: an elegant black suitcase, about the same size as the other Stillman's.

Quinn froze. There was nothing he could do now that would not be a mistake. Whatever choice he made – and he had to make a choice – would be arbitrary, a submission to chance. Uncertainty would haunt him to the end. At that moment, the two Stillmans started on their way again. The first turned right, the second turned left. Quinn craved an amoeba's body, wanting to cut himself in half and run off in two directions at once. 'Do something,' he said to himself, 'do something now, you idiot.'

For no reason, he went to his left, in pursuit of the second Stillman. After nine or ten paces, he stopped. Something told him he would live to regret what he was doing. He was acting out of spite, spurred on to punish the second Stillman for confusing him. He turned around and saw the first Stillman shuffling off in the other direction. Surely this was his man. This shabby creature, so broken down and disconnected from his surroundings – surely this was the mad Stillman. Quinn breathed deeply, exhaled with a trembling chest, and breathed in again. There was no way to know: not this, not anything. He went after the first Stillman, slowing his pace to match the old man's, and followed him to the subway.

It was nearly seven o'clock now, and the crowds had begun to thin out. Although Stillman seemed to be in a fog, he nevertheless knew where he was going. The professor went straight for the subway staircase, paid his money at the token booth below, and waited calmly on the platform for the Times Square Shuttle.

Quinn began to lose his fear of being noticed. He had never seen anyone so lost in his own thoughts. Even if he stood directly in front of him, he doubted that Stillman would be able to see him.

They travelled to the West Side on the shuttle, walked through the dank corridors of the 42nd Street station, and went down another set of stairs to the IRT trains. Seven or eight minutes later they boarded the Broadway express, careened uptown for two long stops, and got off at 96th Street. Slowly making their way up the final staircase, with several pauses as Stillman set down his bag and caught his breath, they surfaced on the corner and entered the indigo evening. Stillman did not hesitate. Without stopping to get his bearings, he began walking up Broadway along the east side of the street. For several minutes Quinn toyed with the irrational conviction that Stillman was walking toward his house on 107th Street. But before he could indulge himself in a full-blown panic, Stillman stopped at the corner of 99th Street, waited for the light to change from red to green, and crossed over to the other side of Broadway. Halfway up the block there was a small fleabag for down-and-outs, the Hotel Harmony. Quinn had passed it many times before, and he was familiar with the winos and vagabonds who hung around the place. It surprised him to see Stillman open the front door and enter the lobby. Somehow he had assumed the old man would have found more comfortable lodgings. But as Quinn stood outside the glass-panelled door and saw the professor walk up to the desk, write what was undoubtedly his name in the guest book, pick up his bag and disappear into the elevator, he realized that this was where Stillman meant to stay.

Quinn waited outside for the next two hours, pacing up and down the block, thinking that Stillman would perhaps emerge to look for dinner in one of the local coffee shops. But the old man did not appear, and at last Quinn decided he must have gone to sleep. He put in a call to Virginia Stillman from a pay booth on the corner, gave her a full report of what had happened, and then headed home to 107th Street.

The next morning, and for many mornings to follow, Quinn posted himself on a bench in the middle of the traffic island at Broadway and 99th Street. He would arrive early, never later than seven o'clock, and sit there with a take-out coffee, a buttered roll, and an open newspaper on his lap, watching the glass door of the hotel. By eight o'clock Stillman would come out, always in his long brown overcoat, carrying a large, old-fashioned carpet bag. For two weeks this routine did not vary. The old man would wander through the streets of the neighbourhood, advancing slowly, sometimes by the merest of increments, pausing, moving on again, pausing once more, as though each step had to be weighed and measured before it could take its place among the sum total of steps. Moving in this manner was difficult for Quinn. He was used to walking briskly, and all this starting and stopping and shuffling began to be a strain, as though the rhythm of his body was being disrupted. He was the hare in pursuit of the tortoise, and again and again he had to remind himself to hold back.

What Stillman did on these walks remained something of a mystery to Quinn. He could, of course, see with his own eyes what happened, and all these things he dutifully recorded in his red notebook. But the meaning of these things continued to elude him. Stillman never seemed to be going anywhere in particular, nor did he seem to know where he was. And yet, as if by conscious design, he kept to a narrowly circumscribed area, bounded on the north by 110th Street, on the south by 72nd Street, on the west by Riverside Park, and on the east by Amsterdam Avenue. No matter how haphazard his journeys seemed to be – and each day his itinerary was different – Stillman never crossed these borders. Such precision baffled Quinn, for in all other respects Stillman seemed to be aimless.

As he walked, Stillman did not look up. His eyes were permanently fixed on the pavement, as though he were searching for something. Indeed, every now and then he would stoop down, pick some object off the ground, and examine it closely, turning it over and over in his hand. It made Quinn think of an archaeologist inspecting a shard at some prehistoric ruin. Occasionally, after poring over an object in this way, Stillman would toss it back onto the sidewalk. But more often than not he would open his bag and lay the object gently inside it. Then, reaching into one of his coat pockets, he would remove a red notebook – similar to Quinn's but smaller – and write in it with great concentration for a minute or two. Having completed this operation, he would return the notebook to his pocket, pick up his bag, and continue on his way.

As far as Quinn could tell, the objects Stillman collected were valueless. They seemed to be no more than broken things, discarded things, stray bits of junk. Over the days that passed, Quinn noted a collapsible umbrella shorn of its material, the severed head of a rubber doll, a black glove, the bottom of a shattered light bulb, several pieces of printed matter (soggy magazines, shredded newspapers), a torn photograph, anonymous machinery parts, and sundry other clumps of flotsam he could not identify. The fact that Stillman took this scavenging seriously intrigued Quinn, but he could do no more than observe, write down what he saw in the red notebook, hover stupidly on the surface of things. At the same time, it pleased him to know that Stillman also had a red notebook, as if this formed a secret link between them. Quinn suspected that Stillman's red notebook contained answers to the questions that had been accumulating in his mind, and he began to plot various stratagems for stealing it from the old man. But the time had not yet come for such a step.

Other than picking up objects from the street, Stillman seemed to do nothing. Every now and then he would stop somewhere for a meal. Occasionally he would bump into someone and mumble an apology. Once a car nearly ran over him as he was crossing the street. Stillman did not talk to anyone, did not go into any stores, did not smile. He seemed neither happy nor sad. Twice, when his scavenging haul had been unusually large, he returned to the hotel in the middle of the day and then re-emerged a few minutes later with an empty bag. On most days he spent at least several hours in Riverside Park, walking methodically along the macadam footpaths or else thrashing through the bushes with a stick. His quest for objects did not abate amidst the greenery. Stones, leaves, and twigs all found their way into his bag. Once, Quinn observed, he even stooped down for a dried dog turd, sniffed it carefully, and kept it. It was in the park, too, that Stillman rested. In the afternoon, often following his lunch, he would sit on a bench and gaze out across the Hudson. Once, on a particularly warm day, Quinn saw him sprawled out on the grass asleep. When darkness came, Stillman would eat dinner at the Apollo Coffee Shop on 97th Street and Broadway and then return to his hotel for the night. Not once did he try to contact his son. This was confirmed by Virginia Stillman, whom Quinn called each night after returning home.

The essential thing was to stay involved. Little by little, Quinn began to feel cut off from his original intentions, and he wondered now if he had not embarked on a meaningless project. It was possible, of course, that Stillman was merely biding his time, lulling the world into lethargy before striking. But that would assume he was aware of being watched, and Quinn felt that was unlikely. He had done his job well so far, keeping at a discrete distance from the old man, blending into the traffic of the street, neither calling attention to himself nor taking drastic measures to keep himself hidden. On the other hand, it was possible that Stillman had known all along that he would be watched – had even known it in advance – and therefore had not taken the trouble to discover who the particular watcher was. If being followed was a certainty, what did it matter? A watcher, once discovered, could always be replaced by another.

This view of the situation comforted Quinn, and he decided to believe in it, even though he had no grounds for belief. Either Stillman knew what he was doing or he didn't. And if he didn't, then Quinn was going nowhere, was wasting his time. How much better it was to believe that all his steps were actually to some purpose. If this interpretation required knowledge on Stillman's part, then Quinn would accept this knowledge as an article of faith, at least for the time being.

There remained the problem of how to occupy his thoughts as he followed the old man. Quinn was used to wandering. His excursions through the city had taught him to understand the connectedness of inner and outer. Using aimless motion as a technique of reversal, on his best days he could bring the outside in and thus usurp the sovereignty of inwardness. By flooding himself with externals, by drowning himself out of himself, he had managed to exert some small degree of control over his fits of despair. Wandering, therefore, was a kind of mindlessness. But following Stillman was not wandering. Stillman could wander, he could stagger like a blindman from one spot to another, but this was a privilege denied to Quinn. For he was obliged now to concentrate on what he was doing, even if it was next to nothing. Time and again his thoughts would begin to drift, and soon thereafter his steps would follow suit. This meant that he was constantly in danger of quickening his pace and crashing into Stillman from behind. To guard against this mishap he devised several different methods of deceleration. This first was to tell himself that he was no longer Daniel Quinn. He was Paul Auster now, and with each step he took he tried to fit more comfortably into the strictures of that transformation. Auster was no more than a name to him, a husk without content. To be Auster meant being a man with no interior, a man with no thoughts. And if there were no thoughts available to him, if his own inner life had been made inaccessible, then there was no place for him to retreat to. As Auster he could not summon up any memories or fears, any dreams or joys, for all these things, as they pertained to Auster, were a blank to him. He consequently had to remain solely on his own surface, looking outward for sustenance. To keep his eyes fixed on Stillman, therefore, was not merely a distraction from the train of his thoughts, it was the only thought he allowed himself to have.

For a day or two this tactic was mildly successful, but eventually even Auster began to droop from the monotony. Quinn realized that he needed something more to keep himself occupied, some little task to accompany him as he went about his work. In the end, it was the red notebook that offered him salvation. Instead of merely jotting down a few casual comments, as he had done the first few days, he decided to record every detail about Stillman he possibly could. Using the pen he had bought from the deaf mute, he set about his task with diligence. Not only did he take note of Stillman's gestures, describe each object he selected or rejected for his bag, and keep an accurate timetable for all events, but he also set down with meticulous care an exact itinerary of Stillman's divagations, noting each street he followed, each turn he made, and each pause that occurred. In addition to keeping him busy, the red notebook slowed Quinn's pace. There was no danger now of overtaking Stillman. The problem, rather, was to keep up with him, to make sure he did not vanish. For walking and writing were not easily compatible activities. If for the past five years Quinn had spent his days doing the one and the other, now he was trying to do them both at the same time. In the beginning he made many mistakes. It was especially difficult to write without looking at the page, and he often discovered that he had written two or even three lines on top of each other, producing a jumbled, illegible palimpsest. To look at the page, however, meant stopping, and this would increase his chances of losing Stillman. After a time, he decided that it was basically a questions of position. He experimented with the notebook in front of him at a forty-five degree angle, but he found his left wrist soon tired. After that, he tried keeping the notebook directly in front of his face, eyes peering over it like some Kilroy come to life, but this proved impractical. Next, he tried propping the notebook on his right arm several inches above his elbow and supporting the back of the notebook with his left palm. But this cramped his writing hand and made writing on the bottom half of the page impossible. Finally, he decided to rest the notebook on his left hip, much as an artist holds his palette. This was an improvement. The carrying no longer caused a strain, and his right hand could hold the pen unencumbered by other duties. Although this method also had its drawbacks, it seemed to be the most comfortable arrangement over the long haul. For Quinn was now able to divide his attention almost equally between Stillman and his writing, glancing now up at the one, now down at the other, seeing the thing and writing about it in the same fluid gesture. With the deaf mute's pen in his right hand and the red notebook on his left hip, Quinn went on following Stillman for another nine days.

His nightly conversations with Virginia Stillman were brief. Although the memory of the kiss was still sharp in Quinn's mind, there had been no further romantic developments. At first, Quinn had expected something to happen. After such a promising start, he felt certain that he would eventually find Mrs Stillman in his arms. But his employer had rapidly retreated behind the mask of business and not once had referred to that isolated moment of passion. Perhaps Quinn had been misguided in his hopes, momentarily confusing himself with Max Work, a man who never failed to profit from such situations. Or perhaps it was simply that Quinn was beginning to feel his loneliness more keenly. It had been a long time since a warm body had been beside him. For the fact was, he had started lusting after Virginia Stillman the moment he saw her, well before the kiss took place. Nor did her current lack of encouragement prevent him from continuing to imagine her naked. Lascivious pictures marched through Quinn's head each night, and although the chances of their becoming real seemed remote, they remained a pleasant diversion. Much later, long after it was too late, he realized that deep inside he had been nurturing the chivalric hope of solving the case so brilliantly, of removing Peter Stillman from danger so swiftly and irrevocably, that he would win Mrs Stillman's desire for as long as he wanted it. That, of course, was a mistake. But of all the mistakes Quinn made from beginning to end, it was no worse than any other.

It was the thirteenth day since the case had begun. Quinn returned home that evening out of sorts. He was discouraged, ready to abandon ship. In spite of the games he had been playing with himself, in spite of the stories he had made up to keep himself going, there seemed to be no substance to the case. Stillman was a crazy old man who had forgotten his son. He could be followed to the end of time, and still nothing would happen. Quinn picked up the phone and dialled the Stillman apartment.

'I'm about ready to pack it in,' he said to Virginia Stillman. 'From all I've seen, there's no threat to Peter.'

'That's just what he wants us to think,' the woman answered. 'You have no idea how clever he is. And how patient.'

'He might be patient, but I'm not. I think you're wasting your money. And I'm wasting my time.'

'Are you sure he hasn't seen you? That could make all the difference.'

'I wouldn't stake my life on it, but yes, I'm sure.'

'What are you saying, then?'

'I'm saying you have nothing to worry about. At least for now. If anything happens later, contact me. I'll come running at the first sign of trouble.'

After a pause Virginia Stillman said, 'You could be right.' Then, after another pause, 'But just to reassure me a little, I wonder if we could compromise.'

'It depends on what you have in mind.'

'Just this. Give it a few more days. To make absolutely certain.'

'On one condition,' said Quinn. 'You've got to let me do it in my own way. No more restraints. I have to be free to talk to him, to question him, to get to the bottom of it once and for all.'

'Wouldn't that be risky?'

'You don't have to worry. I'm not going to tip our hand. He won't even guess who I am or what I'm up to.'

'How will you manage that?'

'That's my problem. I have all kinds of tricks up my sleeve. You just have to trust me.'

'All right, I'll go along. I don't suppose it will hurt.'

'Good. I'll give it a few more days, and then we'll see where we stand.'

'Mr Auster?'

'Yes?'

'I'm terribly grateful. Peter has been in such good shape these past two weeks, and I know it's because of you. He talks about you all the time. You're like . . . I don't know . . . a hero to him.'

'And how does Mrs Stillman feel?'

'She feels much the same way.'

'That's good to hear. Maybe someday she'll allow me to feel grateful to her.'

'Anything is possible, Mr Auster. You should remember that.'

'I will. I'd be a fool not to.'

Quinn made a light supper of scrambled eggs and toast, drank a bottle of beer, and then settled down at his desk with the red notebook. He had been writing in it now for many days, filling page after page with his erratic, jostled hand, but he had not yet had the heart to read over what he had written. Now that the end at last seemed in sight, he thought he might hazard a look.

Much of it was hard going, especially in the early parts. And when he did manage to decipher the words, it did not seem to have been worth the trouble. 'Picks up pencil in middle of block. Examines, hesitates, puts in bag . . . Buys sandwich in deli . . . Sits on bench in park and reads through red notebook.' These sentences seemed utterly worthless to him.

It was all a question of method. If the object was to understand Stillman, to get to know him well enough to be able to anticipate what he would do next, Quinn had failed. He had started with a limited set of facts: Stillman's background and profession, the imprisonment of his son, his arrest and hospitalization, a book of bizarre scholarship written while he was supposedly still sane,

65

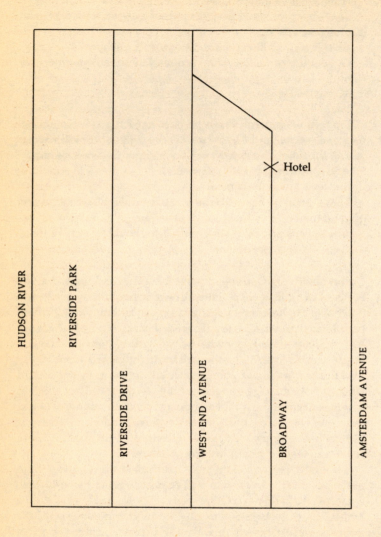

and above all Virginia Stillman's certainty that he would now try to harm his son. But the facts of the past seemed to have no bearing on the facts of the present. Quinn was deeply disillusioned. He had always imagined that the key to good detective work was a close observation of details. The more accurate the scrutiny, the more successful the results. The implication was that human behaviour could be understood, that beneath the infinite façade of gestures, tics, and silences, there was finally a coherence, an order, a source of motivation. But after struggling to take in all these surface effects, Quinn felt no closer to Stillman than when he first started following him. He had lived Stillman's life, walked at his pace, seen what he had seen, and the only thing he felt now was the man's impenetrability. Instead of narrowing the distance that lay between him and Stillman, he had seen the old man slip away from him, even as he remained before his eyes.

For no particular reason that he was aware of, Quinn turned to a clean page of the red notebook and sketched a little map of the area Stillman had wandered in.

Then, looking carefully through his notes, he began to trace with his pen the movements Stillman had made on a single day – the first day he had kept a full record of the old man's wanderings. The result was as follows:

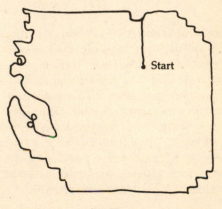

Quinn was struck by the way Stillman had skirted around the edge of the territory, not once venturing into the centre. The diagram looked a little like a map of some imaginary state in the Midwest. Except for the eleven blocks up Broadway at the start, and the series of curlicues that represented Stillman's meanderings in Riverside Park, the picture also resembled a rectangle. On the other hand, given the quadrant structure of New York streets, it might also have been a zero or the letter 'O'.

Quinn went on to the next day and decided to see what would happen. The results were not at all the same.

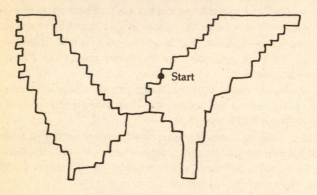

This picture made Quinn think of a bird, a bird of prey perhaps, with its wings spread, hovering aloft in the air. A moment later, this reading seemed far-fetched to him. The bird vanished, and in its stead there were only two abstract shapes, linked by the tiny bridge Stillman had formed by walking west on 83rd Street. Quinn paused for a moment to ponder what he was doing. Was he scribbling nonsense? Was he feeble-mindedly frittering away the evening, or was he trying to find something? Either response, he realized, was unacceptable. If he was simply killing time, why had he chosen such a painstaking way to do it? Was he so muddled that he no longer had the courage to think? On the other hand, if he was not merely diverting himself, what was he actually up to? It seemed to him that he was looking for a sign. He was ransacking the chaos of Stillman's movements for some glimmer of cogency. This implied only one thing: that he continued to disbelieve the arbitrariness of Stillman's actions. He wanted there to be a sense to them, no matter how obscure. This, in itself, was unacceptable. For it meant that Quinn was allowing himself to deny the facts, and this, as he well knew, was the worst thing a detective could do.

Nevertheless, he decided to go on with it. It was not late, not even eleven o'clock yet, and the truth was that it could do no harm. The results of the third map bore no resemblance to the other two.

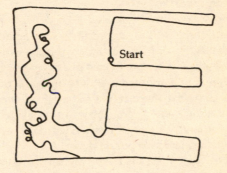

There no longer seemed to be a question about what was happening. If he discounted the squiggles from the park, Quinn felt certain that he was looking at the letter 'E'. Assuming the first diagram had in fact represented the letter 'O,' then it seemed legitimate to assume that the bird wing of the second formed the letter 'W'. Of course, the letters O-W-E spelled a word, but Quinn was not ready to draw any conclusions. He had not begun his inventory until the fifth day of Stillman's travels, and the identities of the first four letters were anyone's guess. He regretted not having started sooner, knowing now that the mystery of those four days was irretrievable. But perhaps he would be able to make up for the past by plunging forward. By coming to the end, perhaps he could intuit the beginning.

The next day's diagram seemed to yield a shape that resembled the letter 'R'. As with the others, it was complicated by numerous irregularities, approximations, and ornate embellishments in the park. Still clinging to a semblance of objectivity, Quinn tried to look at it as if he had not been anticipating a letter of the alphabet. He had to admit that nothing was sure: it could well have been meaningless. Perhaps he was looking for pictures in the clouds, as he had done as a small boy. And yet, the coincidence was too striking. If one map had resembled a letter, perhaps even two, he might have dismissed it as a quirk of chance. But four in a row was stretching it too far.

The next day gave him a lopsided 'O', a doughnut crushed on one side with three or four jagged lines sticking out the other. Then came a tidy 'F', with the customary rococo swirls to the side. After that there was a 'B' that looked like two boxes haphazardly placed on top of one another, with packing excelsior brimming over the edges. Next there was a tottering 'A' that somewhat resembled a ladder, with graded steps on each side. And finally there was a second 'B': precariously tilted on a perverse single point, like an upside-down pyramid.

Quinn then copied out the letters in order: OWEROFBAB. After fiddling with them for a quarter of an hour, switching them around, pulling them apart, rearranging the sequence, he returned to the original order and wrote them out in the following manner: OWER OF BAB. The solution seemed so grotesque that his nerve almost failed him. Making all due allowances for the fact that he had missed the first four days and that Stillman had not yet finished, the answer seemed inescapable: THE TOWER OF BABEL.

Quinn's thoughts momentarily flew off to the concluding pages of *A. Gordon Pym* and to the discovery of the strange hieroglyphs on the inner wall of the chasm – letters inscribed into the earth itself, as though they were trying to say something that could no longer be understood. But on second thought this did not seem apt. For Stillman had not left his message anywhere. True, he had created the letters by the movement of his steps, but they had not been written down. It was like drawing a picture in the air with your finger. The image vanishes as you are making it. There is no result, no trace to mark what you have done.

And yet, the pictures did exist – not in the streets where they had been drawn, but in Quinn's red notebook. He wondered if Stillman had sat down each night in his room and plotted his course for the following day or whether he had improvised as he had gone along. It was impossible to know. He also wondered what purpose this writing served in Stillman's mind. Was it merely some sort of note to himself, or was it intended as a message to others? At the very least, Quinn concluded, it meant that Stillman had not forgotten Henry Dark.

Quinn did not want to panic. In an effort to restrain himself, he tried to imagine things in the worst possible light. By seeing the worst, perhaps it would not be as bad as he thought. He broke it down as follows. First: Stillman was indeed plotting something against Peter. Response: that had been the premise in any case. Second: Stillman had known he would be followed, had known his movements would be recorded, had known his message would be deciphered. Response: that did not change the essential fact – that Peter had to be protected. Third: Stillman was far more dangerous than previously imagined. Response: that did not mean he could get away with it.

This helped somewhat. But the letters continued to horrify Quinn. The whole thing was so oblique, so fiendish in its circumlocutions, that he did not want to accept it. Then doubts came, as if on command, filling his head with mocking, sing-song voices. He had imagined the whole thing. The letters were not letters at all. He had seen them only because he had wanted to see them. And even if the diagrams did form letters, it was only a fluke. Stillman had nothing to do with it. It was all an accident, a hoax he had perpetrated on himself.

He decided to go to bed, slept fitfully, woke up, wrote in the red notebook for half an hour, went back to bed. His last thought before he went to sleep was that he probably had two more days, since Stillman had not yet completed his message. The last two letters remained – the 'E' and the 'L'. Quinn's mind dispersed. He arrived in a neverland of fragments, a place of wordless things and thingless words. Then, struggling through his torpor one last time, he told himself that El was the ancient Hebrew for God.

In his dream, which he later forgot, he found himself in the town dump of his childhood, sifting through a mountain of rubbish.

The first meeting with Stillman took place in Riverside Park. It was mid-afternoon, a Saturday of bicycles, dog-walkers, and children. Stillman was sitting alone on a bench, staring out at nothing in particular, the little red notebook on his lap. There was light everywhere, an immense light that seemed to radiate outward from each thing the eye caught hold of, and overhead, in the branches of the trees, a breeze continued to blow, shaking the leaves with a passionate hissing, a rising and falling that breathed on as steadily as surf.

Quinn had planned his moves carefully. Pretending not to notice Stillman, he sat down on the bench beside him, folded his arms across his chest, and stared out in the same direction as the old man. Neither of them spoke. By his later calculations, Quinn estimated that this went on for fifteen or twenty minutes. Then, without warning, he turned his head toward the old man and looked at him point blank, stubbornly fixing his eyes on the wrinkled profile. Quinn concentrated all his strength in his eyes, as if they could begin to burn a hole in Stillman's skull. This stare went on for five minutes.

At last Stillman turned to him. In a surprisingly gentle tenor voice he said, 'I'm sorry, but it won't be possible for me to talk to you.'

'I haven't said anything,' said Quinn.

'That's true,' said Stillman. 'But you must understand that I'm not in the habit of talking to strangers.'

'I repeat,' said Quinn, 'that I haven't said anything.'

'Yes, I heard you the first time. But aren't you interested in knowing why?'

'I'm afraid not.'

'Well put. I can see you're a man of sense.'

Quinn shrugged, refusing to respond. His whole being now exuded indifference.

Stillman smiled brightly at this, leaned toward Quinn, and said in a conspiratorial voice, 'I think we're going to get along.'

'That remains to be seen,' said Quinn after a long pause.

Stillman laughed – a brief, booming 'haw' – and then continued. 'It's not that I dislike strangers *per se*. It's just that I prefer not to speak to anyone who does not introduce himself. In order to begin, I must have a name.'

'But once a man gives you his name, he's no longer a stranger.'

'Exactly. That's why I never talk to strangers.'

Quinn had been prepared for this and knew how to answer. He was not going to let himself be caught. Since he was technically Paul Auster, that was the name he had to protect. Anything else, even the truth, would be an invention, a mask to hide behind and keep him safe.

'In that case,' he said, 'I'm happy to oblige you. My name is Quinn.'

'Ah,' said Stillman reflectively, nodding his head. 'Quinn.'

'Yes, Quinn. Q-U-I-N-N.'

'I see. Yes, yes, I see. Quinn. Hmmm. Yes. Very interesting. Quinn. A most resonant word. Rhymes with twin, does it not?'

'That's right. Twin.'

'And sin, too, if I'm not mistaken.'

'You're not.'

'And also in – one n – or inn – two. Isn't that so?'

'Exactly.'

'Hmmm. Very interesting. I see many possibilities for this word, this Quinn, this . . . quintessence . . . of quiddity. Quick, for example. And quill. And quack. And quirk. Hmmm. Rhymes with grin. Not to speak of kin. Hmmm. Very interesting. And win. And fin. And din. And gin. And pin. And tin. And bin. Even rhymes with djinn. Hmmm. And if you say it right, with been. Hmmm. Yes, very interesting. I like your name enormously, Mr Quinn. It flies off in so many little directions at once.'

'Yes, I've often noticed that myself.'

'Most people don't pay attention to such things. They think of words as stones, as great unmoveable objects with no life, as monads that never change.'

'Stones can change. They can be worn away by wind or water. They can erode. They can be crushed. You can turn them into shards, or gravel, or dust.'

'Exactly. I could tell you were a man of sense right away, Mr Quinn. If you only knew how many people have misunderstood me. My work has suffered because of it. Suffered terribly.'

'Your work?'

'Yes, my work. My projects, my investigations, my experiments.'

'Ah.'

'Yes. But in spite of all the setbacks, I have never really been daunted. At present, for example, I am engaged in one of the most important things I have ever done. If all goes well, I believe I will hold the key to a series of major discoveries.'

'The key?'

'Yes, the key. A thing that opens locked doors.'

'Ah.'

'Of course, for the time being I'm merely collecting data, gathering evidence so to speak. Then I will have to coordinate my findings. It's highly demanding work. You wouldn't believe how hard – especially for a man of my age.'

'I can imagine.'

'That's right. There's so much to do, and so little time to do it. Every morning I get up at dawn. I have to be outside in all kinds of weather, constantly on the move, forever on my feet, going from one place to the next. It wears me out, you can be sure of that.'

'But it's worth it.'

'Anything for the truth. No sacrifice is too great.'

'Indeed.'

'You see, no one has understood what I have understood. I'm the first. I'm the only one. It puts a great burden of responsibility on me.'

'The world on your shoulders.'

75

'Yes, so to speak. The world, or what is left of it.'

'I hadn't realized it was as bad as that.'

'It's that bad. Maybe even worse.'

'Ah.'

'You see, the world is in fragments, sir. And it's my job to put it back together again.'

'You've taken on quite a bit.'

'I realize that. But I'm merely looking for the principle. That's well within the scope of one man. If I can lay the foundation, other hands can do the work of restoration itself. The important thing is the premise, the theoretical first step. Unfortunately, there is no one else who can do this.'

'Have you made much progress?'

'Enormous strides. In fact, I feel now that I'm on the verge of a significant breakthrough.'

'I'm reassured to hear it.'

'It's a comforting thought, yes. And it's all because of my cleverness, the dazzling clarity of my mind.'

'I don't doubt it.'

'You see, I've understood the need to limit myself. To work within a terrain small enough to make all results conclusive.'

'The premise of the premise, so to speak.'

'That's it, exactly. The principle of the principle, the method of operation. You see, the world is in fragments, sir. Not only have we lost our sense of purpose, we have lost the language whereby we can speak of it. These are no doubt spiritual matters, but they have their analogue in the material world. My brilliant stroke has been to confine myself to physical things, to the immediate and tangible. My motives are lofty, but my work now takes place in the realm of the everyday. That's why I'm so often misunderstood. But no matter. I've learned to shrug these things off.'

'An admirable response.'

'The only response. The only one worthy of a man of my stature. You see, I am in the process of inventing a new language. With work such as that to do, I can't be bothered by the stupidity of others. In any case, it's all part of the disease I'm trying to cure.'

'A new language?'

'Yes. A language that will at last say what we have to say. For our words no longer correspond to the world. When things were whole, we felt confident that our words could express them. But little by little these things have broken apart, shattered, collapsed into chaos. And yet our words have remained the same. They have not adapted themselves to the new reality. Hence, every time we try to speak of what we see, we speak falsely, distorting the very thing we are trying to represent. It's made a mess of everything. But words, as you yourself understand, are capable of change. The problem is how to demonstrate this. That is why I now work with the simplest means possible – so simple that even a child can grasp what I am saying. Consider a word that refers to a thing – "umbrella", for example. When I say the word "umbrella", you see the object in your mind. You see a kind of stick, with collapsible metal spokes on top that form an armature for a waterproof material which, when opened, will protect you from the rain. This last detail is important. Not only is an umbrella a thing, it is a thing that performs a function – in other words, expresses the will of man. When you stop to think of it, every object is similar to the umbrella, in that it serves a function. A pencil is for writing, a shoe is for wearing, a car is for driving. Now, my question is this. What happens when a thing no longer performs its function? Is it still the thing, or has it become something else? When you rip the cloth off the umbrella, is the umbrella still an umbrella? You open the spokes, put them over your head, walk out into the rain, and you get drenched. Is it possible to go on calling this object an umbrella? In general, people do. At the very limit, they will say the umbrella is broken. To me this is a serious error, the source of all our troubles. Because it can no longer perform its function, the umbrella has ceased to be an umbrella. It might resemble an umbrella, it might once have been an umbrella, but now it has changed into something else. The word, however, has remained the same. Therefore, it can no longer express the thing. It is imprecise; it is false; it hides the thing it is supposed to reveal. And if we cannot even name a common, everyday object that we hold in our hands, how can we expect to speak of the things that truly concern us? Unless we can begin to embody the notion of change in the words we use, we will continue to be lost.'

'And your work?'

'My work is very simple. I have come to New York because it is the most forlorn of places, the most abject. The brokenness is everywhere, the disarray is universal. You have only to open your eyes to see it. The broken people, the broken things, the broken thoughts. The whole city is a junk heap. It suits my purpose admirably. I find the streets an endless source of material, an inexhaustible storehouse of shattered things. Each day I go out with my bag and collect objects that seem worthy of investigation. My samples now number in the hundreds – from the chipped to the smashed, from the dented to the squashed, from the pulverized to the putrid.'

'What do you do with these things?'

'I give them names.'

'Names?'

'I invent new words that will correspond to the things.'

'Ah. Now I see. But how do you decide? How do you know if you've found the right word?'

'I never make a mistake. It's a function of my genius.'

'Could you give me an example?'

'Of one of my words?'.

'Yes.'

'I'm sorry, but that won't be possible. It's my secret, you understand. Once I've published my book, you and the rest of the world will know. But for now I have to keep it to myself.

'Classified information.'

'That's right. Top secret.'

'I'm sorry.'

'You shouldn't be too disappointed. It won't be long now before I've put my findings in order. Then great things will begin to happen. It will be the most important event in the history of mankind.'

*

The second meeting took place a little past nine o'clock the following morning. It was Sunday, and Stillman had emerged from the hotel an hour later than usual. He walked the two blocks to his customary breakfast place, the Mayflower Cafe, and sat down in a corner booth at the back. Quinn, growing bolder now, followed the old man into the restaurant and sat down in the same booth, directly opposite him. For a minute or two Stillman seemed not to notice his presence. Then, looking up from his menu, he studied Quinn's face in an abstract sort of way. He apparently did not recognize him from the day before.

'Do I know you?' he asked.

'I don't think so,' said Quinn. 'My name is Henry Dark.'

'Ah,' Stillman nodded. 'A man who begins with the essential. I like that.'

'I'm not one to beat around the bush,' said Quinn.

'The bush? What bush might that be?'

'The burning bush, of course.'

'Ah, yes. The burning bush. Of course.' Stillman looked at Quinn's face – a little more carefully now, but also with what seemed to be a certain confusion. 'I'm sorry,' he went on, 'but I don't remember your name. I recall that you gave it to me not long ago, but now it seems to be gone.'

'Henry Dark,' said Quinn.

'So it is. Yes, now it comes back to me. Henry Dark.' Stillman paused for a long moment and then shook his head. 'Unfortunately, that's not possible, sir.'

'Why not?'

'Because there is no Henry Dark.'

'Well, perhaps I'm another Henry Dark. As opposed to the one who doesn't exist.'

'Hmmm. Yes, I see your point. It is true that two people sometimes have the same name. It's quite possible that your name is Henry Dark. But you're not *the* Henry Dark.'

'Is he a friend of yours?'

Stillman laughed, as if at a good joke. 'Not exactly,' he said.

79

'You see, there never was any such person as Henry Dark. I made him up. He's an invention.'

'No,' said Quinn, with feigned disbelief.

'Yes. He's a character in a book I once wrote. A figment.'

'I find that hard to accept.'

'So did everyone else. I fooled them all.'

'Amazing. Why in the world did you do it?'

'I needed him, you see. I had certain ideas at the time that were too dangerous and controversial. So I pretended they had come from someone else. It was a way of protecting myself.'

'How did you decide on the name Henry Dark?'

'It's a good name, don't you think? I like it very much. Full of mystery, and at the same time quite proper. It suited my purpose well. And besides, it had a secret meaning.'

'The allusion to darkness?'

'No, no. Nothing so obvious. It was the initials, HD. That was very important.'

'How so?'

'Don't you want to guess?'

'I don't think so.'

'Oh, do try. Make three guesses. If you don't get it then, I'll tell you.'

Quinn paused for a moment, trying to give it his best effort. 'HD,' he said. 'For Henry David? As in Henry David Thoreau.'

'Not even close.'

'How about HD pure and simple? For the poet Hilda Doolittle.'

'Worse than the first one.'

'All right, one more guess. HD. H . . . and D . . . Just a moment . . . How about . . . Just a moment . . . Ah . . . Yes, here we are. H for the weeping philosopher, Heraclitus . . . and D for the laughing philosopher, Democritus. Heraclitus and Democritus . . . the two poles of the dialectic.'

'A very clever answer.'

'Am I right?'

'No, of course not. But a clever answer just the same.'

'You can't say I didn't try.'

'No, I can't. That's why I'm going to reward you with the correct answer. Because you tried. Are you ready?'

'Ready.'

'The initials HD in the name Henry Dark refer to Humpty Dumpty.'

'Who?'

'Humpty Dumpty. You know who I mean. The egg.'

'As in "Humpty Dumpty sat on a wall?" '

'Exactly.'

'I don't understand.'

'Humpty Dumpty: the purest embodiment of the human condition. Listen carefully, sir. What is an egg? It is that which has not yet been born. A paradox, is it not? For how can Humpty Dumpty be alive if he has not been born? And yet, he is alive – make no mistake. We know that because he can speak. More than that, he is a philosopher of language. "When *I* use a word, Humpty Dumpty said, in rather a scornful tone, it means just what I choose it to mean – neither more nor less. The question is, said Alice, whether you *can* make words mean so many different things. The question is, said Humpty Dumpty, which is to be master – that's all." '

'Lewis Carroll.'

'*Through the Looking Glass*, chapter six.'

'Interesting.'

'It's more than interesting, sir. It's crucial. Listen carefully, and perhaps you will learn something. In his little speech to Alice, Humpty Dumpty sketches the future of human hopes and gives the clue to our salvation: to become masters of the words we speak, to make language answer our needs, Humpty Dumpty was a prophet, a man who spoke truths the world was not ready for.'

'A man?'

'Excuse me. A slip of the tongue. I mean an egg. But the slip is instructive and helps to prove my point. For all men are eggs, in a manner of speaking. We exist, but we have not yet achieved the form that is our destiny. We are pure potential, an example of the not-yet-arrived. For man is a fallen creature – we know that from Genesis. Humpty Dumpty is also a fallen creature. He falls from his wall, and no one can put him back together again – neither the king, nor his horses, nor his men. But that is what we must all now strive to do. It is our duty as human beings: to put the egg back together again. For each of us, sir, is Humpty Dumpty. And to help him is to help ourselves.'

'A convincing argument.'

'It's impossible to find a flaw in it.'

'No cracks in the egg.'

'Exactly.'

'And, at the same time, the origin of Henry Dark.'

'Yes. But there is more to it than that. Another egg, in fact.'

'There's more than one?'

'Good heavens, yes. There are millions of them. But the one I have in mind is particularly famous. It's probably the most celebrated egg of all.'

'You're beginning to lose me.'

'I'm speaking of Columbus's egg.'

'Ah, yes. Of course.'

'You know the story?'

'Everyone does.'

'It's charming, is it not? When faced with the problem of how to stand an egg on its end, he merely tapped slightly on the bottom, cracking the shell just enough to create a certain flatness that would support the egg when he removed his hand.'

'It worked.'

'Of course it worked. Columbus was a genius. He sought paradise and discovered the New World. It is still not too late for it to become paradise.'

'Indeed.'

'I admit that things have not worked out too well yet. But there is still hope. Americans have never lost their desire to discover new worlds. Do you remember what happened in 1969?'

'I remember many things. What do you have in mind?'

'Men walked on the moon. Think of that, dear sir. Men walked on the moon!'

'Yes, I remember. According to the President, it was the greatest event since creation.'

'He was right. The only intelligent thing that man ever said. And what do you suppose the moon looks like?'

'I have no idea.'

'Come, come, think again.'

'Oh yes. Now I see what you mean.'

'Granted, the resemblance is not perfect. But it is true that in certain phases, especially on a clear night, the moon does look very much like an egg.'

'Yes. Very much like.'

At that moment, a waitress appeared with Stillman's breakfast and set it on the table before him. The old man eyed the food with relish. Decorously lifting a knife with his right hand, he cracked the shell of his soft-boiled egg and said, 'As you can see, sir, I leave no stone unturned.'

The third meeting took place later that same day. The afternoon was well advanced: the light like gauze on the bricks and leaves, the shadows lengthening. Once again, Stillman retreated to Riverside Park, this time to the edge of it, coming to rest on a knobby outcrop at 84th Street known as Mount Tom. On this same spot, in the summers of 1843 and 1844, Edgar Allan Poe had spent many long hours gazing out at the Hudson. Quinn knew this because he had made it his business to know such things. As it turned out, he had often sat there himself.

He felt little fear now about doing what he had to do. He circled the rock two or three times, but failed to get Stillman's attention. Then he sat down next to the old man and said hello. Incredibly, Stillman did not recognize him. This was the third time Quinn had presented himself, and each time it was as though Quinn had been someone else. He could not decide whether this was a good sign or bad. If Stillman was pretending, he was an actor like no other in the world. For each time Quinn had appeared, he had done it by surprise. And yet Stillman had not even blinked. On the other hand, if Stillman really did not recognize him, what did this mean? Was it possible for anyone to be so impervious to the things he saw?

The old man asked him who he was.

'My name is Peter Stillman,' said Quinn.

'That's my name,' answered Stillman. 'I'm Peter Stillman.'

'I'm the other Peter Stillman,' said Quinn.

'Oh. You mean my son. Yes, that's possible. You look just like him. Of course, Peter is blond and you are dark. Not Henry Dark, but dark of hair. But people change, don't they? One minute we're one thing, and then another another.'

'Exactly.'

'I've often wondered about you, Peter. Many times I've thought to myself, "I wonder how Peter is getting along." '

'I'm much better now, thank you.'

'I'm glad to hear it. Someone once told me you had died. It made me very sad.'

'No, I've made a complete recovery.'

'I can see that. Fit as a fiddle. And you speak so well, too.'

'All words are available to me now. Even the ones most people have trouble with. I can say them all.'

'I'm proud of you, Peter.'

'I owe it all to you.'

'Children are a great blessing. I've always said that. An incomparable blessing.'

'I'm sure of it.'

'As for me, I have my good days and my bad days. When the bad days come, I think of the ones that were good. Memory is a great blessing, Peter. The next best thing to death.'

'Without a doubt.'

'Of course, we must live in the present, too. For example, I am currently in New York. Tomorrow, I could be somewhere else. I travel a great deal, you see. Here today, gone tomorrow. It's part of my work.'

'It must be stimulating.'

'Yes, I'm very stimulated. My mind never stops.'

'That's good to hear.'

'The years weigh heavily, it's true. But we have so much to be thankful for. Time makes us grow old, but it also gives us the day and the night. And when we die, there is always someone to take our place.'

'We all grow old.'

'When you're old, perhaps you'll have a son to comfort you.'

'I would like that.'

'Then you would be as fortunate as I have been. Remember, Peter, children are a great blessing.'

'I won't forget.'

'And remember, too, that you shouldn't put all your eggs in one basket. Conversely, don't count your chickens before they hatch.'

'No. I try to take things as they come.'

'Last of all, never say a thing you know in your heart is not true.'

'I won't.'

'Lying is a bad thing. It makes you sorry you were ever born. And not to have been born is a curse. You are condemned to live outside time. And when you live outside time, there is no day and night. You don't even get a chance to die.'

'I understand.'

'A lie can never be undone. Even the truth is not enough. I am a father, and I know about these things. Remember what happened to the father of our country. He chopped down the cherry tree, and then he said to his father, "I cannot tell a lie." Soon thereafter, he threw the coin across the river. These two stories are crucial events in American history. George Washington chopped down the tree, and then he threw away the money. Do you understand? He was telling us an essential truth. Namely, that money doesn't grow on trees. This is what made our country great, Peter. Now George Washington's picture is on every dollar bill. There is an important lesson to be learned from all this.'

'I agree with you.'

'Of course, it's unfortunate that the tree was cut down. That tree was the Tree of Life, and it would have made us immune to death. Now we welcome death with open arms, especially when we are old. But the father of our country knew his duty. He could not do otherwise. That is the meaning of the phrase, "Life is a bowl of cherries." If the tree had remained standing, we would have had eternal life.'

'Yes, I see what you mean.'

'I have many such ideas in my head. My mind never stops. You were always a clever boy, Peter, and I'm glad you understand.'

'I can follow you perfectly.'

'A father must always teach his son the lessons he has learned. In that way knowledge is passed down from generation to generation, and we grow wise.'

'I won't forget what you've told me.'

'I'll be able to die happily now, Peter.'

'I'm glad.'

'But you mustn't forget anything.'

'I won't, father. I promise.'

The next morning, Quinn was in front of the hotel at his usual time. The weather had finally changed. After two weeks of resplendent skies, a drizzle now fell on New York, and the streets were filled with the sound of wet, moving tyres. For an hour Quinn sat on the bench, protecting himself with a black umbrella, thinking Stillman would appear at any moment. He worked his way through his roll and coffee, read the account of the Mets' Sunday loss, and still there was no sign of the old man. Patience, he said to himself, and began to tackle the rest of the paper. Forty minutes passed. He reached the financial section and was about to read an analysis of a corporate merger when the rain suddenly intensified. Reluctantly, he got up from his bench and removed himself to a doorway across the street from the hotel. He stood there in his clammy shoes for an hour and a half. Was Stillman sick, he wondered? Quinn tried to imagine him lying in his bed, sweating out a fever. Perhaps the old man had died during the night and his body had not yet been discovered. Such things happened, he told himself.

Today was to have been the crucial day, and Quinn had made elaborate and meticulous plans for it. Now his calculations were for naught. It disturbed him that he had not taken this contingency into account.

Still, he hesitated. He stood there under his umbrella, watching the rain slide off it in small, fine drops. By eleven o'clock he had begun to formulate a decision. Half an hour later he crossed the street, walked forty paces down the block, and entered Stillman's hotel. The place stank of cockroach repellant and dead cigarettes. A few of the tenants, with nowhere to go in the rain, were sitting in the lobby, sprawled out on orange plastic chairs. The place seemed blank, a hell of stale thoughts.

A large black man sat behind the front desk with his sleeves rolled up. One elbow was on the counter, and his head was propped in his open hand. With his other hand he turned the pages of a tabloid newspaper, barely pausing to read the words. He looked bored enough to have been there all his life.

'I'd like to leave a message for one of your guests,' Quinn said.

The man looked up at him slowly, as if wishing him to disappear.

'I'd like to leave a message for one of your guests,' Quinn said again.

'No guests here,' said the man. 'We call them residents.'

'For one of your residents, then. I'd like to leave a message.'

'And just who might that be, bub?'

'Stillman. Peter Stillman.'

The man pretended to think for a moment, then shook his head. 'Nope. Can't recall anyone by that name.'

'Don't you have a register?'

'Yeah, we've got a book. But it's in the safe.'

'The safe? What are you talking about?'

'I'm talking about the book, bub. The boss likes to keep it locked up in the safe.'

'I don't suppose you know the combination?'

'Sorry. The boss is the only one.'

Quinn sighed, reached into his pocket, and pulled out a five dollar bill. He slapped it on the counter and kept his hand on top of it.

'I don't suppose you happen to have a copy of the book, do you?' he asked.

'Maybe,' said the man. 'I'll have to look in my office.'

The man lifted up the newspaper, which was lying open on the counter. Under it was the register.

'A lucky break,' said Quinn, releasing his hand from the money.

'Yeah, I guess today's my day,' answered the man, sliding the bill along the surface of the counter, whisking it over the edge, and putting it in his pocket. 'What did you say your friend's name was again?'

'Stillman. An old man with white hair.'

'The gent in the overcoat?'

'That's right.'

'We call him the Professor.'

'That's the man. Do you have a room number? He checked in about two weeks ago.'

The clerk opened the register, turned the pages, and ran his finger down the column of names and numbers. 'Stillman,' he said. 'Room 303. He's not here anymore.'

'What?'

'He checked out.'

'What are you talking about?'

'Listen, bub, I'm telling you what it says here. Stillman checked out last night. He's gone.'

'That's the craziest thing I ever heard.'

'I don't care what it is. It's all down here in black and white.'

'Did he give a forwarding address.'

'Are you kidding?'

'What time did he leave?'

'Have to ask Louie, the night man. He comes on at eight.'

'Can I see the room?'

88

'Sorry. I rented it myself this morning. The guy's up there asleep.'

'What did he look like?'

'For five bucks you've got a lot of questions.'

'Forget it,' said Quinn, waving his hand desperately. 'It doesn't matter.'

He walked back to his apartment in a downpour, getting drenched in spite of his umbrella. So much for functions, he said to himself. So much for the meaning of words. He threw the umbrella onto the floor of his living room in disgust. Then he took off his jacket and flung it against the wall. Water splattered everywhere.

He called Virginia Stillman, too embarrassed to think of doing anything else. At the moment she answered, he nearly hung up the phone.

'I lost him,' he said.

'Are you sure?'

'He checked out of his room last night. I don't know where he is.'

'I'm scared, Paul.'

'Have you heard from him?'

'I don't know. I think so, but I'm not sure.'

'What does that mean?'

'Peter answered the phone this morning while I was taking my bath. He won't tell me who it was. He went into his room, closed the shades, and refuses to speak.'

'But he's done that before.'

'Yes. That's why I'm not sure. But it hasn't happened in a long time.'

'It sounds bad.'

'That's what I'm afraid of.'

'Don't worry. I have a few ideas. I'll get to work on them right away.'

'How will I reach you?'

'I'll call you every two hours, no matter where I am.'

'Do you promise?'

'Yes, I promise.'

'I'm so scared, I can't stand it.'

'It's all my fault. I made a stupid mistake, and I'm sorry.'

'No, I don't blame you. No one can watch a person twenty-four hours a day. It's impossible. You'd have to be inside his skin.'

'That's just the trouble. I thought I was.'

'It's not too late now, is it?'

'No. There's still plenty of time. I don't want you to worry.'

'I'll try not to.'

'Good. I'll be in touch.'

'Every two hours?'

'Every two hours.'

He had finessed the conversation rather nicely. In spite of everything, he had managed to keep Virginia Stillman calm. He found it hard to believe, but she still seemed to trust him. Not that it would be of any help. For the fact was, he had lied to her. He did not have several ideas. He did not have even one.

Stillman was gone now. The old man had become part of the city. He was a speck, a punctuation mark, a brick in an endless wall of bricks. Quinn could walk through the streets every day for the rest of his life, and still he would not find him. Everything had been reduced to chance, a nightmare of numbers and probabilities. There were no clues, no leads, no moves to be made.

Quinn backtracked in his mind to the beginning of the case. His job had been to protect Peter, not to follow Stillman. That had simply been a method, a way of trying to predict what would happen. By watching Stillman, the theory was that he would learn what his intentions were toward Peter. He had followed the old man for two weeks. What, then, could he conclude? Not much. Stillman's behaviour had been too obscure to give any hints.

There were, of course, certain extreme measures that they could take. He could suggest to Virginia Stillman that she get an unlisted telephone number. That would eliminate the disturbing calls, at least temporarily. If that failed, she and Peter could move. They could leave the neighbourhood, perhaps leave the city altogether. At the very worst, they could take on new identities, live under different names.

This last thought reminded him of something important. Until now, he realized, he had never seriously questioned the circumstances of his hiring. Things had happened too quickly, and he had taken it for granted that he would fill in for Paul Auster. Once he had taken the leap into that name, he had stopped thinking about Auster himself. If this man was as good a detective as the Stillmans thought he was, perhaps he would be able to help with the case. Quinn would make a clean breast of it, Auster would forgive him, and together they would work to save Peter Stillman.

He looked through the yellow pages for the Auster Detective Agency. There was no listing. In the white pages, however, he found the name. There was one Paul Auster in Manhattan, living on Riverside Drive – not far from Quinn's own house. There was no mention of a detective agency, but that did not necessarily mean anything. It could be that Auster had so much work he didn't need to advertise. Quinn picked up the phone and was about to dial when he thought better of it. This was too important a conversation to leave to the phone. He did not want to run the risk of being brushed off. Since Auster did not have an office, that meant he worked at home. Quinn would go there and talk to him face to face.

The rain had stopped now, and although the sky was still grey, far to the west Quinn could see a tiny shaft of light seeping through the clouds. As he walked up Riverside Drive, he became aware of the fact that he was no longer following Stillman. It felt as though he had lost half of himself. For two weeks he had been tied by an invisible thread to the old man. Whatever Stillman had done, he had done; wherever Stillman had gone, he had gone. His body was not accustomed to this new freedom, and for the first few blocks he walked at the old shuffling pace. The spell was over, and yet his body did not know it.

Auster's building was in the middle of the long block that ran between 116th and 119th Streets, just south of Riverside Church and Grant's Tomb. It was a well-kept place, with polished doorknobs and clean glass, and it had an air of bourgeois sobriety that appealed to Quinn at that moment. Auster's apartment was on the eleventh floor, and Quinn rang the buzzer, expecting to hear a voice speak to him through the intercom. But the door buzzer answered him without any conversation. Quinn pushed the door open, walked through the lobby, and rode the elevator to the eleventh floor.

It was a man who opened the apartment door. He was a tall dark fellow in his mid-thirties, with rumpled clothes and a two-day beard. In his right hand, fixed between his thumb and first two fingers, he held an uncapped fountain pen, still poised in a writing position. The man seemed surprised to find a stranger standing before him.

'Yes?' he asked tentatively.

Quinn spoke in the politest tone he could muster. 'Were you expecting someone else?'

'My wife, as a matter of fact. That's why I rang the buzzer without asking who it was.'

'I'm sorry to disturb you,' Quinn apologized. 'But I'm looking for Paul Auster.'

'I'm Paul Auster,' said the man.

'I wonder if I could talk to you. It's quite important.'

'You'll have to tell me what it's about first.'

'I hardly know myself.' Quinn gave Auster an earnest look. 'It's complicated, I'm afraid. Very complicated.'

'Do you have a name?'

'I'm sorry. Of course I do. Quinn.'

'Quinn what.'

'Daniel Quinn.'

The name seemed to suggest something to Auster, and he paused for a moment abstractedly, as if searching through his memory. 'Quinn,' he muttered to himself. 'I know that name from somewhere.' He went silent again, straining harder to dredge up the answer. 'You aren't a poet, are you?'

'I used to be,' said Quinn. 'But I haven't written poems for a long time now.'

'You did a book several years ago, didn't you? I think the title was *Unfinished Business*. A little book with a blue cover.'

'Yes. That was me.'

'I liked it very much. I kept hoping to see more of your work. In fact, I even wondered what had happened to you.'

'I'm still here. Sort of.'

Auster opened the door wider and gestured for Quinn to enter the apartment. It was a pleasant enough place inside: oddly shaped, with several long corridors, books cluttered everywhere,

93

pictures on the walls by artists Quinn did not know, and a few children's toys scattered on the floor – a red truck, a brown bear, a green space monster. Auster led him to the living room, gave him a frayed upholstered chair to sit in, and then went off to the kitchen to fetch some beer. He returned with two bottles, placed them on a wooden crate that served as the coffee table, and sat down on the sofa across from Quinn.

'Was it some kind of literary thing you wanted to talk about?' Auster began.

'No,' said Quinn. 'I wish it was. But this has nothing to do with literature.'

'With what, then?'

Quinn paused, looked around the room without seeing anything, and tried to start. 'I have a feeling there's been a terrible mistake. I came here looking for Paul Auster, the private detective.'

'The what?' Auster laughed, and in that laugh everything was suddenly blown to bits. Quinn realized that he was talking nonsense. He might just as well have asked for Chief Sitting Bull – the effect would have been no different.

'The private detective,' he repeated softly.

'I'm afraid you've got the wrong Paul Auster.'

'You're the only one in the book.'

'That might be,' said Auster. 'But I'm not a detective.'

'Who are you then? What do you do?'

'I'm a writer.'

'A writer?' Quinn spoke the word as though it were a lament.

'I'm sorry,' Auster said. 'But that's what I happen to be.'

'If that's true, then there's no hope. The whole thing is a bad dream.'

'I have no idea what you're talking about.'

Quinn told him. He began at the beginning and went through the entire story, step by step. The pressure had been building up in him since Stillman's disappearance that morning, and it came out of him now as a torrent of words. He told of the phone calls for Paul Auster, of his inexplicable acceptance of the case, of his meeting with Peter Stillman, of his conversation with Virginia Stillman, of his reading Stillman's book, of his following Stillman from Grand Central Station, of Stillman's daily wanderings, of the carpet bag and the broken objects, of the disquieting maps that formed letters of the alphabet, of his talks with Stillman, of Stillman's disappearance from the hotel. When he had come to the end, he said, 'Do you think I'm crazy?'

'No,' said Auster, who had listened attentively to Quinn's monologue. 'If I had been in your place, I probably would have done the same thing.'

These words came as a great relief to Quinn, as if, at long last, the burden was no longer his alone. He felt like taking Auster in his arms and declaring his friendship for life.

'You see,' said Quinn, 'I'm not making it up. I even have proof.' He took out his wallet and removed the five hundred dollar cheque that Virginia Stillman had written two weeks earlier. He handed it to Auster. 'You see,' he said. 'It's even made out to you.'

Auster looked the cheque over carefully and nodded. 'It seems to be a perfectly normal cheque.'

'Well, it's yours,' said Quinn. 'I want you to have it.'

'I couldn't possibly accept it.'

'It's of no use to me.' Quinn looked around the apartment and gestured vaguely. 'Buy yourself some more books. Or a few toys for your kid.'

'This is money you've earned. You deserve to have it yourself.' Auster paused for a moment. 'There's one thing I'll do for you, though. Since the cheque is in my name, I'll cash it for you. I'll take it to my bank tomorrow morning, deposit it in my account, and give you the money when it clears.'

Quinn did not say anything.

'All right?' Auster asked. 'Is it agreed?'

'All right,' said Quinn at last. 'We'll see what happens.'

Auster put the cheque on the coffee table, as if to say the matter had been settled. Then he leaned back on the sofa and looked Quinn in the eyes. 'There's a much more important question than the cheque,' he said. 'The fact that my name has been mixed up in this. I don't understand it at all.'

'I wondered if you've had any trouble with your phone lately. Wires sometimes get crossed. A person tries to call a number, and even though he dials correctly, he gets someone else.'

'Yes, that's happened to me before. But even if my phone was broken, that doesn't explain the real problem. It would tell us why the call went to you, but not why they wanted to speak to me in the first place.'

'Is it possible that you know the people involved?'

'I've never heard of the Stillmans.'

'Maybe someone wanted to play a practical joke on you.'

'I don't hang around with people like that.'

'You never know.'

'But the fact is, it's not a joke. It's a real case with real people.'

'Yes,' said Quinn after a long silence. 'I'm aware of that.'

They had come to the end of what they could talk about. Beyond that point there was nothing: the random thoughts of men who knew nothing. Quinn realized that he should be going. He had been there almost an hour, and the time was approaching for his call to Virginia Stillman. Nevertheless, he was reluctant to move. The chair was comfortable, and the beer had gone slightly to his head. This Auster was the first intelligent person he had spoken to in a long time. He had read Quinn's old work, he had admired it, he had been looking forward to more. In spite of everything, it was impossible for Quinn not to feel glad of this.

They sat there for a short time without saying anything. At last, Auster gave a little shrug, which seemed to acknowledge that they had come to an impasse. He stood up and said, 'I was about to make some lunch for myself. It's no trouble making it for two.'

Quinn hesitated. It was as though Auster had read his thoughts, divining the thing he wanted most – to eat, to have an excuse to stay a while. 'I really should be going,' he said. 'But yes, thank you. A little food can't do any harm.'

'How does a ham omelette sound?'

'Sounds good.'

Auster retreated to the kitchen to prepare the food. Quinn would have liked to offer to help, but he could not budge. His body felt like a stone. For want of any other idea, he closed his eyes. In the past, it had sometimes comforted him to make the world disappear. This time, however, Quinn found nothing interesting inside his head. It seemed as though things had ground to a halt in there. Then, from the darkness, he began to hear a voice, a chanting, idiotic voice that sang the same sentence over and over again: 'You can't make an omelette without breaking eggs.' He opened his eyes to make the words stop.

There was bread and butter, more beer, knives and forks, salt and pepper, napkins, and omelettes, two of them, oozing on white plates. Quinn ate with crude intensity, polishing off the meal in what seemed a matter of seconds. After that, he made a great effort to be calm. Tears lurked mysteriously behind his eyes, and his voice seemed to tremble as he spoke, but somehow he managed to hold his own. To prove that he was not a self-obsessed ingrate, he began to question Auster about his writing. Auster was somewhat reticent about it, but at last he conceded that he was working on a book of essays. The current piece was about *Don Quixote*.

'One of my favourite books, said Quinn.

'Yes, mine too. There's nothing like it.'

Quinn asked him about the essay.

'I suppose you could call it speculative, since I'm not really out to prove anything. In fact, it's all done tongue-in-cheek. An imaginative reading, I guess you could say.'

'What's the gist?'

'It mostly has to do with the authorship of the book. Who wrote it, and how it was written.'

'Is there any question?'

'Of course not. But I mean the book inside the book Cervantes wrote, the one he imagined he was writing.'

'Ah.'

'It's quite simple. Cervantes, if you remember, goes to great lengths to convince the reader that he is not the author. The book, he says, was written in Arabic by Cid Hamete Benengeli. Cervantes describes how he discovered the manuscript by chance one day in the market at Toledo. He hires someone to translate it for him into Spanish, and thereafter he presents himself as no more than the editor of the translation. In fact, he cannot even vouch for the accuracy of the translation itself.'

'And yet he goes on to say,' Quinn added, 'that Cid Hamete Benengeli's is the only true version of Don Quixote's story. All the other versions are frauds, written by impostors. He makes a great point of insisting that everything in the book really happened in the world.'

'Exactly. Because the book after all is an attack on the dangers of the make-believe. He couldn't very well offer a work of the imagination to do that, could he? He had to claim that it was real.'

'Still, I've always suspected that Cervantes devoured those old romances. You can't hate something so violently unless a part of you also loves it. In some sense, Don Quixote was just a stand-in for himself.'

'I agree with you. What better portrait of a writer than to show a man who has been bewitched by books?'

'Precisely.'

'In any case, since the book is supposed to be real, it follows that the story has to be written by an eyewitness to the events that take place in it. But Cid Hamete, the acknowledged author, never makes an appearance. Not once does he claim to be present at what happens. So, my question is this: who is Cid Hamete Benengeli?'

'Yes, I see what you're getting at.'

'The theory I present in the essay is that he is actually a combination of four different people. Sancho Panza is of course the witness. There's no other candidate – since he is the only one who accompanies Don Quixote on all his adventures. But Sancho can neither read nor write. Therefore, he cannot be the author. On the other hand, we know that Sancho has a great gift for language. In spite of his inane malapropisms, he can talk circles around everyone else in the book. It seems perfectly possible to me that he dictated the story to someone else – namely, to the barber and the priest, Don Quixote's good friends. They put the story into proper literary form – in Spanish – and then turned the manuscript over to Simon Carasco, the bachelor from Salamanca, who proceeded to translate it into Arabic. Cervantes found the translation, had it rendered back into Spanish, and then published the book, *The Adventures of Don Quixote.*'

'But why would Sancho and the others go to all that trouble?'

'To cure Don Quixote of his madness. They want to save their friend. Remember, in the beginning they burn his books of chivalry, but that has no effect. The Knight of the Sad Countenance does not give up his obsession. Then, at one time or another, they all go out looking for him in various disguises – as a woman in distress, as the Knight of the Mirrors, as the Knight of the White Moon – in order to lure Don Quixote back home. In the end, they are actually successful. The book was just one of their ploys. The idea was to hold a mirror up to Don Quixote's madness, to record each of his absurd and ludicrous delusions, so that when he finally read the book himself, he would see the error of his ways.'

'I like that.'

'Yes. But there's one last twist. Don Quixote, in my view, was not really mad. He only pretended to be. In fact, he orchestrated the whole thing himself. Remember: throughout the book Don Quixote is preoccupied by the question of posterity. Again and again he wonders how accurately his chronicler will record his adventures. This implies knowledge on his part; he knows beforehand that this chronicler exists. And who else is it but Sancho Panza, the faithful squire whom Don Quixote has chosen for exactly this purpose? In the same way, he chose the three others to play the roles he destined for them. It was Don Quixote who engineered the Benengeli quartet. And not only did he select the authors, it was probably he who translated the Arabic manuscript back into Spanish. We shouldn't put it past him. For a man so skilled in the art of disguise, darkening his skin and donning the clothes of a Moor could not have been very difficult. I like to imagine that scene in the marketplace at Toledo. Cervantes hiring Don Quixote to decipher the story of Don Quixote himself. There's great beauty to it.'

'But you still haven't explained why a man like Don Quixote would disrupt his tranquil life to engage in such an elaborate hoax.'

'That's the most interesting part of all. In my opinion, Don Quixote was conducting an experiment. He wanted to test the gullibility of his fellow men. Would it be possible, he wondered, to stand up before the world and with the utmost conviction spew out lies and nonsense? To say that windmills were knights, that a barber's basin was a helmet, that puppets were real people? Would it be possible to persuade others to agree with what he said, even though they did not believe him? In other words, to what extent would people tolerate blasphemies if they gave them amusement? The answer is obvious, isn't it? To any extent. For the proof is that we still read the book. It remains highly amusing to us. And that's finally all anyone wants out of a book – to be amused.'

Auster leaned back on the sofa, smiled with a certain ironic pleasure, and lit a cigarette. The man was obviously enjoying himself, but the precise nature of that pleasure eluded Quinn. It seemed to be a kind of soundless laughter, a joke that stopped short of its punchline, a generalized mirth that had no object. Quinn was about to say something in response to Auster's theory, but he was not given the chance. Just as he opened his mouth to speak, he was interrupted by a clattering of keys at the front door, the sound of the door opening and then slamming shut, and a burst of voices. Auster's face perked up at the sound. He rose from his seat, excused himself to Quinn, and walked quickly towards the door.

Quinn heard laughter in the hallway, first from a woman and then from a child – the high and the higher, a staccato of ringing shrapnel – and then the basso rumbling of Auster's guffaw. The child spoke: 'Daddy, look what I found!' And then the woman explained that it had been lying on the street, and why not, it seemed perfectly okay. A moment later he heard the child running towards him down the hall. The child shot into the living room, caught sight of Quinn, and stopped dead in his tracks. He was a blond-haired boy of five or six.

'Good afternoon,' said Quinn.

The boy, rapidly withdrawing into shyness, managed no more than a faint hello. In his left hand he held a red object that Quinn could not identify. Quinn asked the boy what it was.

'It's a yoyo,' he answered, opening his hand to show him. 'I found it on the street.'

'Does it work?'

The boy gave an exaggerated pantomime shrug. 'Dunno. Siri can't do it. And I don't know how.'

Quinn asked him if he could try, and the boy walked over and put it in his hand. As he examined the yoyo, he could hear the child breathing beside him, watching his every move. The yoyo was plastic, similar to the ones he had played with years ago, but more elaborate somehow, an artifact of the space age. Quinn fastened the loop at the end of the string around his middle finger, stood up, and gave it a try. The yoyo gave off a fluted, whistling sound as it descended, and sparks shot off inside it. The boy gasped, but then the yoyo stopped, dangling at the end of its line.

'A great philosopher once said,' muttered Quinn, 'that the way up and the way down are one and the same.'

'But you didn't make it go up,' said the boy. 'It only went down.'

'You have to keep trying.'

Quinn was rewinding the spool for another attempt when Auster and his wife entered the room. He looked up and saw the woman first. In that one brief moment he knew that he was in trouble. She was a tall, thin blonde, radiantly beautiful, with an energy and happiness that seemed to make everything around her invisible. It was too much for Quinn. He felt as though Auster were taunting him with the things he had lost, and he responded with envy and rage, a lacerating self-pity. Yes, he too would have liked to have this wife and this child, to sit around all day spouting drivel about old books, to be surrounded by yoyos and ham omelettes and fountain pens. He prayed to himself for deliverance.

Auster saw the yoyo in his hand and said, 'I see you've already met. Daniel,' he said to the boy, 'this is Daniel.' And then to Quinn, with that same ironic smile, 'Daniel, this is Daniel.'

The boy burst out laughing and said, 'Everybody's Daniel!'

'That's right,' said Quinn. 'I'm you, and you're me.'

'And around and around it goes,' shouted the boy, suddenly spreading his arms and spinning around the room like a gyroscope.

'And this,' said Auster, turning to the woman, 'is my wife, Siri.'

The wife smiled her smile, said she was glad to meet Quinn as though she meant it, and then extended her hand to him. He shook it, feeling the uncanny slenderness of her bones, and asked if her name was Norwegian.

'Not many people know that,' she said.

'Do you come from Norway?'

'Indirectly,' she said. 'By way of Northfield, Minnesota.' And then she laughed her laugh, and Quinn felt a little more of himself collapse.

'I know this is sort of last minute,' Auster said, 'but if you have some time to spare, why don't you stay and have dinner with us?'

'Ah,' said Quinn, struggling to keep himself in check. 'That's very kind. But I really must be going. I'm late as it is.'

He made one last effort, smiling at Auster's wife and waving goodbye to the boy. 'So long, Daniel,' he said, walking towards the door.

The boy looked at him from across the room and laughed again. 'Goodbye myself!' he said.

Auster accompanied him to the door. He said, 'I'll call you as soon as the cheque clears. Are you in the book?'

'Yes,' said Quinn. 'The only one.'

'If you need me for anything,' said Auster, 'just call. I'll be happy to help.'

Auster reached out to shake hands with him, and Quinn realized that he was still holding the yoyo. He placed it in Auster's right hand, patted him gently on the shoulder, and left.

Quinn was nowhere now. He had nothing, he knew nothing, he knew that he knew nothing. Not only had he been sent back to the beginning, he was now before the beginning, and so far before the beginning that it was worse than any end he could imagine.

His watch read nearly six. Quinn walked home the way he had come, lengthening his strides with each new block. By the time he came to his street, he was running. It's June second, he told himself. Try to remember that. This is New York, and tomorrow will be June third. If all goes well, the following day will be the fourth. But nothing is certain.

The hour had long since passed for his call to Virginia Stillman, and he debated whether to go through with it. Would it be possible to ignore her? Could he abandon everything now, just like that? Yes, he said to himself, it was possible. He could forget about the case, get back to his routine, write another book. He could take a trip if he liked, even leave the country for a while. He could go to Paris, for example. Yes, that was possible. But anywhere would do, he thought, anywhere at all.

He sat down in his living room and looked at the walls. They had once been white, he remembered, but now they had turned a curious shade of yellow. Perhaps one day they would drift further into dinginess, lapsing into grey, or even brown, like some piece of ageing fruit. A white wall becomes a yellow wall becomes a gray wall, he said to himself. The paint becomes exhausted, the city encroaches with its soot, the plaster crumbles within. Changes, then more changes still.

He smoked a cigarette, and then another, and then another. He looked at his hands, saw that they were dirty, and got up to wash them. In the bathroom, with the water running in the sink, he decided to shave as well. He lathered his face, took out a clean blade, and started scraping off his beard. For some reason, he found it unpleasant to look in the mirror and kept trying to avoid himself with his eyes. You're getting old, he said to himself, you're turning into an old fart. Then he went into the kitchen, ate a bowl of cornflakes, and smoked another cigarette.

It was seven o'clock now. Once again, he debated whether to call Virginia Stillman. As he turned the question over in his mind, it occurred to him that he no longer had an opinion. He saw the argument for making the call, and at the same time he saw the argument for not making it. In the end, it was etiquette that decided. It would not be fair to disappear without telling her first. After that, it would be perfectly acceptable. As long as you tell people what you are going to do, he reasoned, it doesn't matter. Then you are free to do what you want.

The number, however, was busy. He waited five minutes and dialled again. Again, the number was busy. For the next hour Quinn alternated between dialling and waiting, always with the same result. At last he called the operator and asked whether the phone was out of order. There would be a charge of thirty cents, he was told. Then came a crackling in the wires, the sound of further dialling, more voices. Quinn tried to imagine what the operators looked like. Then the first woman spoke to him again: the number was busy.

Quinn did not know what to think. There were so many possibilities, he could not even begin. Stillman? The phone off the hook? Someone else altogether?

He turned on the television and watched the first two innings of the Mets game. Then he dialled once again. Same thing. In the top of the third St Louis scored on a walk, a stolen base, an infield out, and a sacrifice fly. The Mets matched that run in their half of the inning on a double by Wilson and a single by Youngblood. Quinn realized that he didn't care. A beer commercial came on, and he turned off the sound. For the twentieth time he tried to reach Virginia Stillman, and for the twentieth time the same thing happened. In the top of the fourth St Louis scored five runs, and

Quinn turned off the picture as well. He found his red notebook, sat down at his desk, and wrote steadily for the next two hours. He did not bother to read over what he had written. Then he called Virginia Stillman and got another busy signal. He slammed the receiver down so hard that the plastic cracked. When he tried to call again, he could no longer get a dial tone. He stood up, went into the kitchen, and made another bowl of cornflakes. Then he went to bed.

In his dream, which he later forgot, he found himself walking down Broadway, holding Auster's son by the hand.

Quinn spent the following day on his feet. He started early, just after eight o'clock, and did not stop to consider where he was going. As it happened, he saw many things that day he had never noticed before.

Every twenty minutes he would go into a phone booth and call Virginia Stillman. As it had been the night before, so it was today. By now Quinn expected the number to be busy. It no longer even bothered him. The busy signal had become a counterpoint to his steps, a metronome beating steadily inside the random noises of the city. There was comfort in the thought that whenever he dialled the number, the sound would be there for him, never swerving in its denial, negating speech and the possibility of speech, as insistent as the beating of a heart. Virginia and Peter Stillman were shut off from him now. But he could soothe his conscience with the thought that he was still trying. Whatever darkness they were leading him into, he had not abandoned them yet.

He walked down Broadway to 72nd Street, turned east to Central Park West, and followed it to 59th Street and the statue of Columbus. There he turned east once again, moving along Central Park South until Madison Avenue, and then cut right, walking downtown to Grand Central Station. After circling haphazardly for a few blocks, he continued south for a mile, came to the juncture of Broadway and Fifth Avenue at 23rd Street, paused to look at the Flatiron Building, and then shifted course, taking a

westward turn until he reached Seventh Avenue, at which point
he veered left and progressed further downtown. At Sheridan
Square he turned east again, ambling down Waverly Place,
crossing Sixth Avenue, and continuing on to Washington
Square. He walked through the arch and made his way south
among the crowds, stopping momentarily to watch a juggler
perform on a slack rope stretched between a light pole and a tree
trunk. Then he left the little park at its downtown east corner,
went through the university housing project with its patches of
green grass, and turned right at Houston Street. At West Broadway he turned again, this time to the left, and proceeded onward
to Canal. Angling slightly to his right, he passed through a vest
pocket park and swung around to Varick Street, walked by
number 6, where he had once lived, and then regained his
southern course, picking up West Broadway again where it
merged with Varick. West Broadway took him to the base of the
World Trade Centre and on into the lobby of one of the towers,
where he made his thirteenth call of the day to Virginia Stillman.
Quinn decided to eat something, entered one of the fast food
places on the ground floor, and leisurely consumed a sandwich
as he did some work in the red notebook. Afterwards, he walked
east again, wandering through the narrow streets of the financial
district, and then headed further south, towards Bowling Green,
where he saw the water and the seagulls above it, careening in
the midday light. For a moment he considered taking a ride on
the Staten Island Ferry, but then thought better of it and began
tracking his way to the north. At Fulton Street he slid to his right
and followed the north-eastward path of East Broadway, which
led through the miasma of the Lower East Side and then up into
Chinatown. From there he found the Bowery, which carried him
along to Fourteenth Street. He then hooked left, cut diagonally
through Union Square, and continued uptown along Park
Avenue South. At 23rd Street he jockeyed north. A few blocks
later he jutted right again, went one block to the east, and then
walked up Third Avenue for a while. At 32nd Street he turned
right, came upon Second Avenue, turned left, moved uptown

another three blocks, and then turned right one last time, whereupon he met up with First Avenue. He then walked the remaining seven blocks to the United Nations and decided to take a short rest. He sat down on a stone bench in the plaza and breathed deeply, idling in the air and the light with closed eyes. Then he opened the red notebook, took the deaf mute's pen from his pocket, and began a new page.

For the first time since he had bought the red notebook, what he wrote that day had nothing to do with the Stillman case. Rather, he concentrated on the things he had seen while walking. He did not stop to think about what he was doing, nor did he analyse the possible implications of this uncustomary act. He felt an urge to record certain facts, and he wanted to put them down on paper before he forgot them.

Today, as never before: the tramps, the down-and-outs, the shopping-bag ladies, the drifters and drunks. They range from the merely destitute to the wretchedly broken. Wherever you turn, they are there, in good neighbourhoods and bad.

Some beg with a semblance of pride. Give me this money, they seem to say, and soon I will be back there with the rest of you, rushing back and forth on my daily rounds. Others have given up hope of ever leaving their tramphood. They lie there sprawled out on the sidewalk with their hat, or cup, or box, not even bothering to look up at the passerby, too defeated even to thank the ones who drop a coin beside them. Still others try to work for the money they are given: the blind pencil sellers, the winos who wash the windshield of your car. Some tell stories, usually tragic accounts of their own lives, as if to give their benefactors something for their kindness – even if only words.

Others have real talents. The old black man today, for example, who tap-danced while juggling cigarettes – still dignified, clearly once a vaudevillian, dressed in a purple suit with a green shirt and a yellow tie, his mouth fixed in a half-remembered stage smile. There are also the pavement chalk artists and musicians: saxaphonists, electric guitarists, fiddlers. Occasionally, you will even come across a genius, as I did today:

A clarinettist of no particular age, wearing a hat that obscured his face, and sitting cross-legged on the sidewalk, in the manner of a snake-charmer. Directly in front of him were two wind-up monkeys, one with a tambourine and the other with a drum. With the one shaking and the other banging, beating out a weird and precise syncopation, the man would improvise endless tiny variations on his instrument, his body swaying stiffly back and forth, energetically miming the monkeys' rhythm. He played jauntily and with flair, crisp and looping figures in the minor mode, as if glad to be there with his mechanical friends, enclosed in the universe he had created, never once looking up. It went on and on, always finally the same, and yet the longer I listened the harder I found it to leave.

To be inside that music, to be drawn into the circle of its repetitions: perhaps that is a place where one could finally disappear.

But beggars and performers make up only a small part of the vagabond population. They are the aristocracy, the elite of the fallen. Far more numerous are those with nothing to do, with nowhere to go. Many are drunks – but that term does not do justice to the devastation they embody. Hulks of despair, clothed in rags, their faces bruised and bleeding, they shuffle through the streets as though in chains. Asleep in doorways, staggering insanely through traffic, collapsing on sidewalks – they seem to be everywhere the moment you look for them. Some will starve to death, others will die of exposure, still others will be beaten or burned or tortured.

For every soul lost in this particular hell, there are several others locked inside madness – unable to exit to the world that stands at the threshold of their bodies. Even though they seem to be there, they cannot be counted as present. The man, for example, who goes everywhere with a set of drumsticks, pounding the pavement with them in a reckless, nonsensical rhythm, stooped over awkwardly as he advances along the street, beating and beating away at the cement. Perhaps he thinks he is doing important work. Perhaps, if he did not do what he did, the city would fall apart. Perhaps the moon would spin out of its orbit and come crashing into the earth. There are the ones who talk to themselves, who mutter, who scream, who curse, who groan, who tell themselves stories as if to someone else. The man

I saw today, sitting like a heap of garbage in front of Grand Central Station, the crowds rushing past him, saying in a loud, panic-stricken voice: 'Third Marines . . . eating bees . . . the bees crawling out of my mouth.' Or the woman shouting at an invisible companion: 'And what if I don't want to! What if I just fucking don't want to!'

There are the women with their shopping bags and the men with their cardboard boxes, hauling their possessions from one place to the next, forever on the move, as if it mattered where they were. There is the man wrapped in the American flag. There is the woman with a Hallowe'en mask on her face. There is the man in a ravaged overcoat, his shoes wrapped in rags, carrying a perfectly pressed white shirt on a hanger – still sheathed in the dry-cleaner's plastic. There is the man in a business suit with bare feet and a football helmet on his head. There is the woman whose clothes are covered from head to toe with Presidential campaign buttons. There is the man who walks with his face in his hands, weeping hysterically and saying over and over again: 'No, no, no. He's dead. He's not dead. No, no, no. He's dead. He's not dead.'

Baudelaire: Il me semble que je serais toujours bien là où je ne suis pas. In other words: It seems to me that I will always be happy in the place where I am not. Or, more bluntly: Wherever I am not is the place where I am myself. Or else, taking the bull by the horns: Anywhere out of the world.

It was almost evening. Quinn closed the red notebook and put the pen in his pocket. He wanted to think a little more about what he had written but found he could not. The air around him was soft, almost sweet, as though it no longer belonged to the city. He stood up from the bench, stretched his arms and legs, and walked to a phone booth, where he called Virginia Stillman again. Then he went to dinner.

In the restaurant he realized that he had come to a decision about things. Without his even knowing it, the answer was already there for him, sitting fully formed in his head. The busy signal, he saw now, had not been arbitrary. It had been a sign, and it was telling him that he could not yet break his connection with the case, even if he wanted to. He had tried to contact Virginia Stillman in order to tell her that he was through, but the fates had not allowed it. Quinn paused to consider this. Was 'fate' really the word he wanted to use? It seemed like such a ponderous and old-fashioned choice. And yet, as he probed more deeply into it, he discovered that was precisely what he meant to say. Or, if not precisely, it came closer than any other term he could think of. Fate in the sense of what was, of what happened to be. It was something like the word 'it' in the phrase 'it is raining' or 'it is night.' What that 'it' referred to Quinn had never known. A generalized condition of things as they were, perhaps; the state of is-ness that was the ground on which the happenings of the world took place. He could not be any more definite than that. But perhaps he was not really searching for anything definite.

It was fate, then. Whatever he thought of it, however much he might want it to be different, there was nothing he could do about it. He had said yes to a proposition, and now he was powerless to undo that yes. That meant only one thing: he had to go through with it. There could not be two answers. It was either this or that. And so it was, whether he liked it or not.

The business about Auster was clearly a mistake. Perhaps there had once been a private detective in New York with that name. The husband of Peter's nurse was a retired policeman – therefore not a young man. In his day there had no doubt been an Auster with a good reputation, and he had naturally thought of him when called upon to provide a detective. He had looked in the telephone book, had found only one person with that name and assumed he had the right man. Then he gave the number to the Stillmans. At that point, the second mistake had occurred. There had been a foul-up in the lines, and somehow his number had got crossed with Auster's. That kind of thing happened every day. And so he had received the call – which anyway had been destined for the wrong man. It all made perfect sense.

One problem still remained. If he was unable to contact Virginia Stillman – if, as he believed, he was meant *not* to contact her

– how exactly was he to proceed? His job was to protect Peter, to make sure that no harm came to him. Did it matter what Virginia Stillman thought he was doing as long as he did what he was supposed to do? Ideally, an operative should maintain close contact with his client. That had always been one of Max Work's principles. But was it really necessary? As long as Quinn did his job, how could it matter? If there were any misunderstandings, surely they could be cleared up once the case was settled.

He could proceed, then, as he wished. He would no longer have to telephone Virginia Stillman. He could abandon the oracular busy signal once and for all. From now on, there would be no stopping him. It would be impossible for Stillman to come near Peter without Quinn knowing about it.

Quinn paid up his cheque, put a mentholated toothpick in his mouth, and began walking again. He did not have far to go. Along the way, he stopped at a twenty-four hour Citibank and checked his balance with the automatic teller. There were three hundred and forty-nine dollars in his account. He withdrew three hundred, put the cash in his pocket, and continued uptown. At 57th Street he turned left and walked to Park Avenue. There he turned right and went on walking north until 69th Street, at which point he turned onto the Stillmans' block. The building looked the same as it had on the first day. He glanced up to see if there were any lights on in the apartment, but he could not remember which windows were theirs. The street was utterly quiet. No cars drove down it, no people passed. Quinn stepped across to the other side, found a spot for himself in a narrow alleyway, and settled in for the night.

A long time passed. Exactly how long it is impossible to say. Weeks certainly, but perhaps even months. The account of this period is less full than the author would have liked. But information is scarce, and he has preferred to pass over in silence what could not be definitely confirmed. Since this story is based entirely on facts, the author feels it his duty not to overstep the bounds of the verifiable, to resist at all costs the perils of invention. Even the red notebook, which until now has provided a detailed account of Quinn's experiences, is suspect. We cannot say for certain what happened to Quinn during this period, for it is at this point in the story that he began to lose his grip.

He remained for the most part in the alley. It was not uncomfortable once he got used to it, and it had the advantage of being well hidden from view. From there he could observe all the comings and goings at the Stillmans' building. No one left and no one entered without his seeing who it was. In the beginning, it surprised him that he saw neither Virginia nor Peter. But there were many delivery men constantly coming and going, and eventually he realized that it was not necessary for them to leave the building. Everything could be brought to them. It was then that Quinn understood that they, too, were holing up, waiting inside their apartment for the case to end.

Little by little, Quinn adapted to his new life. There were a number of problems to be faced, but one by one he managed to solve them. First of all, there was the question of food. Because utmost vigilance was required of him, he was reluctant to leave his post for any length of time. It tormented him to think that something might happen in his absence, and he made every effort to minimize the risks. He had read somewhere that between 3.30 and 4.30 am there were more people asleep in their beds than at any other time. Statistically speaking, the chances were best that nothing would happen during that hour, and therefore Quinn chose it as the time to do his shopping. On Lexington Avenue not far north there was an all-night grocery, and at three-thirty every morning Quinn would walk there at a brisk pace (for the exercise, and also to save time) and buy whatever he needed for the next twenty-four hours. It turned out not to be much – and, as it happened, he needed less and less as time went on. For Quinn learned that eating did not necessarily solve the problem of food. A meal was no more than a fragile defence against the inevitability of the next meal. Food itself could never answer the question of food: it only delayed the moment when the question would have to be asked in earnest. The greatest danger, therefore, was in eating too much. If he took in more than he should, his appetite for the next meal increased, and thus more food was needed to satisfy him. By keeping a close and constant watch on himself, Quinn was gradually able to reverse the process. His ambition was to eat as little as possible, and in this way to stave off his hunger. In the best of all worlds, he might have been able to approach absolute zero, but he did not want to be overly ambitious in his present circumstances. Rather, he kept the total fast in his mind as an ideal, a state of perfection he could aspire to but never achieve. He did not want to starve himself to death – and he reminded himself of this every day – he simply wanted to leave himself free to think of the things that truly concerned him. For now, that meant keeping the case uppermost in his thoughts. Fortunately, this coincided with his other major ambition: to make the three hundred dollars last as long as he could. It goes without saying that Quinn lost a good deal of weight during this period.

His second problem was sleep. He could not stay awake all the time, and yet that was really what the situation required. Here, too, he was forced to make certain concessions. As with eating, Quinn felt that he could make do with less than he was accustomed to. Instead of the six to eight hours of sleep he was used to getting, he decided to limit himself to three or four. Adjusting to this was difficult, but far more difficult was the problem of how to distribute these hours so as to maintain maximum vigilance. Clearly, he could not sleep for three or four hours in a row. The risks were simply too great. Theoretically, the most efficient use of the time would be to sleep for thirty seconds every five or six minutes. That would reduce his chances of missing something almost to nil. But he realized that this was physically impossible. On the other hand, using this impossibility as a kind of model, he tried to train himself into taking a series of short naps, alternating between sleeping and waking as often as he could. It was a long struggle, demanding discipline and concentration, for the longer the experiment went on, the more exhausted he became. In the beginning, he tried for sequences of forty-five minutes each, then gradually reduced them to thirty minutes. Towards the end, he had begun to manage the fifteen-minute nap with a fair amount of success. He was helped in his efforts by a near-by church, whose bells rang every fifteen minutes – one stroke on the quarter-hour, two strokes on the half-hour, three strokes on the three-quarter-hour, and four strokes on the hour, followed by the appropriate number of strokes for the hour itself. Quinn lived by the rhythm of that clock, and eventually he had trouble distinguishing it from his own pulse. Starting at midnight, he would begin his routine, closing his eyes and falling asleep before the clock had struck twelve. Fifteen minutes later he would wake, at the half-hour double stroke fall asleep, and at the three-quarter-hour triple stroke wake once more. At three-thirty he would go off for his food, return by four o'clock, and then go to sleep again. His dreams during this period were few. When they did occur, they were strange: brief visions of the immediate – his hands, his shoes, the brick wall beside him. Nor was there ever a moment when he was not dead tired.

His third problem was shelter, but this was more easily solved than the other two. Fortunately, the weather remained warm, and as late spring moved into summer, there was little rain. Every now and then there was a shower, and once or twice a downpour with thunder and lightning, but all in all it was not bad, and

Quinn never stopped giving thanks for his luck. At the back of the alley there was a large metal bin for garbage, and whenever it rained at night Quinn would climb into it for protection. Inside, the smell was overpowering, and it would permeate his clothes for days on end, but Quinn preferred it to getting wet, for he did not want to run the risk of catching cold or falling ill. Happily, the lid had been bent out of shape and did not fit tightly over the bin. In one corner there was a gap of six or eight inches that formed a kind of air hole for Quinn to breathe through – sticking his nose out into the night. By standing on his knees on top of the garbage and leaning his body against one wall of the bin, he found that he was not altogether uncomfortable.

On clear nights he would sleep under the bin, positioning his head in such a way that the moment he opened his eyes he could see the front door of Stillmans' building. As for emptying his bladder, he usually did this in the far corner of the alley, behind the bin and with his back to the street. His bowels were another matter, and for this he would climb into the bin to ensure privacy. There were also a number of plastic garbage cans beside the bin, and from one of these Quinn was usually able to find sufficiently clean newspaper to wipe himself, although once, in an emergency, he was forced to use a page from the red notebook. As for washing and shaving, these were two of the things that Quinn learned to live without.

How he managed to keep himself hidden during this period is a mystery. But it seems that no one discovered him or called his presence to the attention of the authorities. No doubt he learned early on the schedule of the garbage collectors and made sure to be out of the alley when they came. Likewise the building superintendent, who deposited the trash each evening in the bin and the cans. Remarkable as it seems, no one ever noticed Quinn. It was as though he had melted into the walls of the city.

The problems of housekeeping and material life occupied a certain portion of each day. For the most part, however, Quinn had time on his hands. Because he did not want anyone to see him, he had to avoid other people as systematically as he could.

He could not look at them, he could not talk to them, he could not think about them. Quinn had always thought of himself as a man who liked to be alone. For the past five years, in fact, he had actively sought it. But it was only now, as his life continued in the alley, that he began to understand the true nature of solitude. He had nothing to fall back on anymore but himself. And of all the things he discovered during the days he was there, this was the one he did not doubt: that he was falling. What he did not understand, however, was this: in that he was falling, how could he be expected to catch himself as well? Was it possible to be at the top and the bottom at the same time? It did not seem to make sense.

He spent many hours looking up at the sky. From his position at the back of the alley, wedged in between the bin and the wall, there were few other things to see, and as the days passed he began to take pleasure in the world overhead. He saw that, above all, the sky was never still. Even on cloudless days, when the blue seemed to be everywhere, there were constant little shifts, gradual disturbances as the sky thinned out and grew thick, the sudden whitenesses of planes, birds, and flying papers. Clouds complicated the picture, and Quinn spent many afternoons studying them, trying to learn their ways, seeing if he could not predict what would happen to them. He became familiar with the cirrus, the cumulus, the stratus, the nimbus, and all their various combinations, watching for each one in its turn, and seeing how the sky would change under its influence. Clouds, too, introduced the matter of colour, and there was a wide range to contend with, spanning from black to white, with an infinity of greys between. These all had to be investigated, measured, and deciphered. On top of this, there were the pastels that formed whenever the sun and the clouds interracted at certain times of day. The spectrum of variables was immense, the result depending on the temperatures of the different atmosphere levels, the types of clouds present in the sky, and where the sun happened to be at that particular moment. From all this came the reds and pinks that Quinn liked so much, the purples and vermilions, the oranges and lavenders, the golds and feathery persimmons. Nothing lasted for long. The colours would soon disperse, merging with others and moving on or fading as the night appeared. Almost always there was a wind to hasten these events. From where he sat in the alley, Quinn could rarely feel it, but by watching its effect on the clouds, he could gauge its intensity and the nature of the air it carried. One by one, all weathers passed over his head, from sunshine to storms, from gloom to radiance. There were the dawns and dusks to observe, the midday transformations, the early evenings, the nights. Even in its blackness, the sky did not rest. Clouds drifted through the dark, the moon was forever in a different form, the wind continued to blow. Sometimes a star even settled into Quinn's patch of sky, and as he looked up he would wonder if it was still there, or if it had not burned out long ago.

The days therefore came and went. Stillman did not appear. Quinn's money ran out at last. For some time he had been steeling himself for this moment, and towards the end he hoarded his funds with maniacal precision. No penny was spent without first judging the necessity of what he thought he needed, without first weighing all the consequences, pro and con. But not even his most stringent economies could halt the march of the inevitable.

It was some time in mid-August when Quinn discovered that he no longer could hold out. The author has confirmed this date through diligent research. It is possible, however, that this moment occurred as early as late July, or as late as early September, since all investigations of this sort must make allowances for a certain margin for error. But, to the best of his knowledge, having considered the evidence carefully and sifted through all apparent contradictions, the author places the following events in August, somewhere between the twelfth and twenty-fifth of the month.

Quinn had almost nothing now – a few coins that amounted to less than a dollar. He was certain that money had arrived for him during his absence. It was simply a matter of retrieving the cheques from his mailbox at the post office, taking them to the bank, and cashing them. If all went well, he could be back to East 69th Street within a few hours. We will never know the agonies he suffered at having to leave his spot.

He did not have enough money to take the bus. For the first time in many weeks, then, he began to walk. It was odd to be on his feet again, moving steadily from one place to the next, swinging his arms back and forth, feeling the pavement under the soles of his shoes. And yet there he was, walking west on 69th Street, turning right on Madison Avenue, and beginning to make his way north. His legs were weak, and he felt as though his head were made of air. He had to stop every now and then to catch his breath, and once, on the brink of falling, he had to grab hold of a lamp post. He found that things went better if he lifted his feet as little as possible, shuffling forward with slow, sliding steps. In this way he could conserve his strength for the corners, where he had to balance himself carefully before and after each step up and down from the curb.

At 84th Street he paused momentarily in front of a shop. There was a mirror on the façade, and for the first time since he had begun his vigil, Quinn saw himself. It was not that he had been afraid to confront his own image. Quite simply, it had not occurred to him. He had been too busy with his job to think about himself, and it was as though the question of his appearance had ceased to exist. Now, as he looked at himself in the shop mirror, he was neither shocked nor disappointed. He had no feeling about it at all, for the fact was that he did not recognize the person he saw there as himself. He thought that he had spotted a stranger in the mirror, and in that first moment he turned around sharply to see who it was. But there was no one near him. Then he turned back to examine the mirror more carefully. Feature by feature, he studied the face in front of him and slowly began to notice that this person bore a certain resemblance to the man he had always thought of as himself. Yes, it seemed more than likely that this was Quinn. Even now, however, he was not upset. The transformation in his appearance had been so drastic that he could not help but be fascinated by it. He had turned into a bum. His clothes were discoloured, disheveled, debauched by filth. His face was covered by a thick black beard with tiny flecks of grey in it. His hair was long and tangled, matted into tufts behind his ears, and crawling down in curls almost to his shoulders. More than anything else, he reminded himself of Robinson Crusoe, and he marvelled at how quickly these changes had taken place in him. It had been no more than a matter of months, and in that time he had become someone else. He tried to remember himself as he had been before, but he found it difficult. He looked at this new Quinn and shrugged. It did not really matter. He had been one thing before, and now he was another. It was neither better nor worse. It was different, and that was all.

He continued uptown for several more blocks, then turned left, crossed Fifth Avenue, and walked along the wall of Central Park. At 96th Street he entered the park and found himself glad to be among the grass and trees. Late summer had exhausted much of the greenness, and here and there the ground showed through in brown, dusty patches. But the trees overhead were still filled with leaves, and everywhere there was a sparkling of light and shade that struck Quinn as miraculous and beautiful. It was late morning, and the heavy heat of the afternoon lay several hours off.

Halfway through the park Quinn was overtaken by an urge to rest. There were no streets here, no city blocks to mark the stages of his progress, and it seemed to him suddenly that he had been walking for hours. Making it to the other side of the park felt as though it would take another day or two of dogged hiking. He went on for a few more minutes, but at last his legs gave out. There was an oak tree not far from where he stood, and Quinn went for it now, staggering in the way a drunk gropes for his bed after an all-night binge. Using the red notebook as a pillow, he lay down on a grassy mound just north of the tree and fell asleep. It was the first unbroken sleep he had had in months, and he did not wake until it was morning again.

His watch said that it was nine-thirty, and he cringed to think

120

of the time he had lost. Quinn stood up and began loping towards the west, amazed that his strength was back, but cursing himself for the hours he had wasted in getting it. He was beyond consolation. No matter what he did now, he felt that he would always be too late. He could run for a hundred years, and still he would arrive just as the doors were closing.

He emerged from the park at 96th Street and continued west. At the corner of Columbus Avenue he saw a telephone booth, which suddenly reminded him of Auster and the five hundred dollar cheque. Perhaps he could save time by collecting the money now. He could go directly to Auster, put the cash in his pocket, and avoid the trip to the post office and the bank. But would Auster have the cash on hand? If not, perhaps they could arrange to meet at Auster's bank.

Quinn entered the booth, dug into his pocket, and removed what money was left: two dimes, a quarter, and eight pennies. He dialled information for the number, got his dime back in the coin return box, deposited the dime again, and dialled. Auster picked up on the third ring.

'Quinn here,' said Quinn.

He heard a groan on the other end. 'Where the hell have you been hiding?' There was irritation in Auster's voice. 'I've called you a thousand times.'

'I've been busy. Working on the case.'

'The case?'

'The case. The Stillman case. Remember?'

'Of course I remember.'

'That's why I'm calling. I want to come for the money now. The five hundred dollars.'

'What money?'

'The cheque, remember? The cheque I gave you. The one made out to Paul Auster.'

'Of course I remember. But there is no money. That's why I've been trying to call you.'

'You had no right to spend it,' Quinn shouted, suddenly beside himself. 'That money belonged to me.'

121

'I didn't spend it. The cheque bounced.'

'I don't believe you.'

'You can come here and see the letter from the bank, if you want. It's sitting here on my desk. The cheque was no good.'

'That's absurd.'

'Yes, it is. But it hardly matters now, does it?'

'Of course it matters. I need the money to go on with the case.'

'But there is no case. It's all over.'

'What are you talking about?'

'The same thing you are. The Stillman case.'

'But what do you mean "it's over?" I'm still working on it.'

'I can't believe it.'

'Stop being so goddamn mysterious. I don't have the slightest idea what you're talking about.'

'I don't believe you don't know. Where the hell have you been? Don't you read the newspapers?'

'Newspapers? Goddamnit, say what you mean. I don't have time to read newspapers.'

There was a silence on the other end, and for a moment Quinn felt that the conversation was over, that he had somehow fallen asleep and had just now woken up to find the telephone in his hand.

'Stillman jumped off the Brooklyn Bridge,' Auster said. 'He committed suicide two and a half months ago.'

'You're lying.'

'It was all over the papers. You can check for yourself.'

Quinn said nothing.

'It was your Stillman,' Auster went on. 'The one who used to be a Professor at Columbia. They say he died in mid-air, before he even hit the water.'

'And Peter? What about Peter?'

'I have no idea.'

'Does anybody know?'

'Impossible to say. You'd have to find that out yourself.'

'Yes, I suppose so,' said Quinn.

Then, without saying goodbye to Auster, he hung up. He took

122

the other dime and used it to call Virginia Stillman. He still knew the number by heart.

A mechanical voice spoke the number back to him and announced that it had been disconnected. The voice then repeated the message, and afterwards the line went dead.

Quinn could not be sure what he felt. In those first moments, it was as though he felt nothing, as though the whole thing added up to nothing at all. He decided to postpone thinking about it. There would be time for that later, he thought. For now, the only thing that seemed to matter was going home. He would return to his apartment, take off his clothes, and sit in a hot bath. Then he would look through the new magazines, play a few records, do a little housecleaning. Then, perhaps, he would begin to think about it.

He walked back to 107th Street. The keys to his house were still in his pocket, and as he unlocked his front door and walked up the three flights to his apartment, he felt almost happy. But then he stepped into the apartment, and that was the end of that.

Everything had changed. It seemed like another place altogether, and Quinn thought he must have entered the wrong apartment by mistake. He backed into the hall and checked the number on the door. No, he had not been wrong. It was his apartment; it was his key that had opened the door. He walked back inside and took stock of the situation. The furniture had been rearranged. Where there had once been a table there was now a chair. Where there had once been a sofa there was now a table. There were new pictures on the walls, a new rug was on the floor. And his desk? He looked for it but could not find it. He studied the furniture more carefully and saw that it was not his. What had been there the last time he was in the apartment had been removed. His desk was gone, his books were gone, the child drawings of his dead son were gone. He went from the living room to the bedroom. His bed was gone, his bureau was gone. He opened the top drawer of the bureau that was there. Women's underthings lay tangled in random clumps: panties, bras, slips.

The next drawer held women's sweaters. Quinn went no further than that. On a table near the bed there was a framed photograph of a blond, beefy-faced young man. Another photograph showed the same young man smiling, standing in the snow with his arm around an insipid looking girl. She, too, was smiling. Behind them there was a ski slope, a man with two skiis on his shoulder, and the blue winter sky.

Quinn went back to the living room and sat down in a chair. He saw a half-smoked cigarette with lipstick on it in an ashtray. He lit it up and smoked it. Then he went into the kitchen, opened the refrigerator, and found some orange juice and a loaf of bread. He drank the juice, ate three slices of bread, and then returned to the living room, where he sat down in the chair again. Fifteen minutes later he heard footsteps coming up the stairs, a jangling of keys outside the door, and then the girl from the photograph entered the apartment. She was wearing a white nurse's uniform and held a brown grocery bag in her arms. When she saw Quinn, she dropped the bag and screamed. Or else she screamed first and then dropped the bag. Quinn could never be sure which. The bag ripped open when it hit the floor, and milk gurgled in a white path toward the edge of the rug.

Quinn stood up, raised his hand in a gesture of peace, and told her not to worry. He wasn't going to hurt her. The only thing he wanted to know was why she was living in his apartment. He took the key from his pocket and held it up in the air, as if to prove his good intentions. It took him a while to convince her, but at last her panic subsided.

That did not mean she had begun to trust him or that she was any less afraid. She hung by the open door, ready to make a dash for it at the first sign of trouble. Quinn held his distance, not wanting to make things worse. His mouth kept talking, explaining again and again that she was living in his house. She clearly did not believe one word of it, but she listened in order to humour him, no doubt hoping that he would talk himself out and finally leave.

'I've been living here for a month,' she said. 'It's my apartment. I signed a year's lease.'

'But why do I have the key?' Quinn asked for the seventh or eighth time. 'Doesn't that convince you?'

'There are hundreds of ways you could have got that key.'

'Didn't they tell you there was someone living here when you rented the place?'

'They said it was a writer. But he disappeared, hadn't paid his rent in months.'

'That's me!' shouted Quinn. 'I'm the writer!'

The girl looked him over coldly and laughed. 'A writer? That's the funniest thing I ever heard. Just look at you. I've never seen a bigger mess in all my life.'

'I've had some difficulties lately,' muttered Quinn, by way of explanation. 'But it's only temporary.'

'The landlord told me he was glad to get rid of you anyway. He doesn't like tenants who don't have jobs. They use too much heat and run down the fixtures.'

'Do you know what happened to my things?'

'What things?'

'My books. My furniture. My papers.'

'I have no idea. They probably sold what they could and threw the rest away. Everything was cleared out before I moved in.'

Quinn let out a deep sigh. He had come to the end of himself. He could feel it now, as though a great truth had finally dawned in him. There was nothing left.

'Do you realize what this means?' he asked.

'Frankly, I don't care,' the girl said. 'It's your problem, not mine. I just want you to get out of here. Right now. This is my place, and I want you out. If you don't leave, I'm going to call the police and have you arrested.'

It didn't matter anymore. He could stand there arguing with the girl for the rest of the day, and still he wouldn't get his apartment back. It was gone, he was gone, everything was gone. He stammered something inaudible, excused himself for taking up her time, and walked past her out the door.

Because it no longer mattered to him what happened, Quinn was not surprised that the front door at 69th Street opened without a key. Nor was he surprised when he reached the ninth floor and walked down the corridor to the Stillmans' apartment that that door should be open as well. Least of all did it surprise him to find the apartment empty. The place had been stripped bare, and the rooms now held nothing. Each one was identical to every other: a wooden floor and four white walls. This made no particular impression on Quinn. He was exhausted, and the only thing he could think of was closing his eyes.

He went to one of the rooms at the back of the apartment, a small space that measured no more than ten feet by six feet. It had one wire-mesh window that gave on to a view of the airshaft, and of all the rooms it seemed to be the darkest. Within this room there was a second door which led to a windowless cubicle that contained a toilet and a sink. Quinn put the red notebook on the floor, removed the deaf mute's pen from his pocket, and tossed it onto the red notebook. Then he took off his watch and put it in his pocket. After that he took off all his clothes, opened the window, and one by one dropped each thing down the airshaft: first his right shoe, then his left shoe; one sock, and then the other sock; his shirt, his jacket, his underpants, his pants. He did not look out to watch them fall, nor did he check to see where they landed. Then he closed the window, lay down in the centre of the floor, and went to sleep.

It was dark in the room when he woke up. Quinn could not be sure how much time had passed – whether it was the night of that day or the night of the next. It was even possible, he thought, that it was not night at all. Perhaps it was merely dark inside the room, and outside, beyond the window, the sun was shining. For several moments he considered getting up and going to the window to see, but then he decided it did not matter. If it was not night now, he thought, then night would come later. That was certain, and whether he looked out the window or not, the answer would be the same. On the other hand, if it was in fact night here in New York, then surely the sun was shining somewhere else. In China, for example, it was no doubt mid-afternoon, and the rice farmers were mopping sweat from their brows. Night and day were no more than relative terms; they did not refer to an absolute condition. At any given moment, it was always both. The only reason we did not know it was because we could not be in two places at the same time.

Quinn also considered getting up and going to another room, but then he realized that he was quite happy where he was. It was comfortable here in the spot he had chosen, and he found that he enjoyed lying on his back with his eyes open, looking up at the ceiling – or what would have been the ceiling, had he been able to see it. Only one thing was lacking for him, and that was the sky. He realized that he missed having it overhead, after so many days and nights spent in the open. But he was inside now, and no matter what room he chose to camp in, the sky would remain hidden, inaccessible even at the farthest limit of sight.

He thought he would stay there until he no longer could. There would be water from the sink to quench his thirst, and that would buy him some time. Eventually, he would get hungry and have to eat. But he had been working for so long now at wanting so little that he knew this moment was still several days off. He decided not to think about it until he had to. There was no sense in worrying, he thought, no sense in troubling himself with things that did not matter.

He tried to think about the life he had lived before the story began. This caused many difficulties, for it seemed so remote to him now. He remembered the books he had written under the name of William Wilson. It was strange, he thought, that he had done that, and he wondered now why he had. In his heart, he realized that Max Work was dead. He had died somewhere on the way to his next case, and Quinn could not bring himself to feel sorry. It all seemed so unimportant now. He thought back to his desk and the thousands of words he had written there. He thought back to the man who had been his agent and realized he could not remember his name. So many things were disappearing now, it was difficult to keep track of them. Quinn tried to work his way through the Mets' lineup, position by position, but his mind was beginning to wander. The centrefielder, he remembered, was Mookie Wilson, a promising young player whose real name was William Wilson. Surely there was something interesting in that. Quinn pursued the idea for a few moments but then abandoned it. The two William Wilsons cancelled each other out, and that was all. Quinn waved goodbye to them in his mind. The Mets would finish in last place again, and no one would suffer.

The next time he woke up, the sun was shining in the room. There was a tray of food beside him on the floor, the dishes steaming with what looked like a roast beef dinner. Quinn accepted this fact without protest. He was neither surprised nor disturbed by it. Yes, he said to himself, it is perfectly possible that food should have been left here for me. He was not curious to know how or why this had taken place. It did not even occur to him to leave the room to look through the rest of the apartment for an answer. Rather, he examined the food on the tray more closely and saw that in addition to two large slices of roast beef there were seven little roast potatoes, a plate of asparagus, a fresh roll, a salad, a carafe of red wine, and wedges of cheese and a pear for dessert. There was a white linen napkin, and the silverware was of the finest quality. Quinn ate the food – or half of it, which was as much as he could manage.

After his meal, he began to write in the red notebook. He continued writing until darkness returned to the room. There was a small light fixture in the middle of the ceiling and a switch for it by the door, but the thought of using it did not appeal to Quinn. Not long after that he fell asleep again. When he woke up, there was sunlight in the room and another tray of food beside him on the floor. He ate what he could of the food and then went back to writing in the red notebook.

For the most part his entries from this period consisted of marginal questions concerning the Stillman case. Quinn wondered, for example, why he had not bothered to look up the newspaper reports of Stillman's arrest in 1969. He examined the problem of whether the moon landing of that same year had been connected in any way with what had happened. He asked himself why he had taken Auster's word for it that Stillman was dead. He tried to think about eggs and wrote out such phrases as 'a good egg', 'egg on his face', 'to lay an egg', 'to be as like as two eggs'. He wondered what would have happened if he had followed the second Stillman instead of the first. He asked himself why Christopher, the patron saint of travel, had been decanonized by the Pope in 1969, just at the time of the trip to the moon. He thought through the question of why Don Quixote had not simply wanted to write books like the ones he loved – instead of living out their adventures. He wondered why he had the same initials as Don Quixote. He considered whether the girl who had moved into his apartment was the same girl he had seen in Grand Central Station reading his book. He wondered if Virginia Stillman had hired another detective after he failed to get in touch with her. He asked himself why he had taken Auster's word for it that the cheque had bounced. He thought about Peter Stillman and wondered if he had ever slept in the room he was in now. He wondered if the case was really over or if he was not somehow still working on it. He wondered what the map would look like of all the steps he had taken in his life and what word it would spell.

When it was dark, Quinn slept, and when it was light he ate the food and wrote in the red notebook. He could never be sure how much time passed during each interval, for he did not concern himself with counting the days or the hours. It seemed to him, however, that little by little the darkness had begun to win out over the light, that whereas in the beginning there had been a predominance of sunshine, the light had gradually become fainter and more fleeting. At first, he attributed this to a change of season. The equinox had surely passed already, and perhaps the solstice was approaching. But even after winter had come and the process should theoretically have started to reverse itself, Quinn observed that the periods of dark nevertheless kept gaining on the periods of light. It seemed to him that he had less and less time to eat his food and write in the red notebook. Eventually, it seemed to him that these periods had been reduced to a matter of minutes. Once, for example, he finished his food and discovered that there was only enough time to write three sentences in the red notebook. The next time there was light, he could only manage two sentences. He began to skip his meals in order to devote himself to the red notebook, eating only when he felt he could no longer hold out. But the time continued to diminish, and soon he was able to eat no more than a bite or two before the darkness came back. He did not think of turning on the electric light, for he had long ago forgotten it was there.

This period of growing darkness coincided with the dwindling of pages in the red notebook. Little by little, Quinn was coming to the end. At a certain point, he realized that the more he wrote the sooner the time would come when he could no longer write anything. He began to weigh his words with great care, struggling to express himself as economically and clearly as possible. He regretted having wasted so many pages at the beginning of the red notebook, and in fact felt sorry that he had bothered to write about the Stillman case at all. For the case was far behind him now, and he no longer bothered to think about it. It had been a bridge to another place in his life, and now that he had crossed it, its meaning had been lost. Quinn no longer had any interest in himself. He wrote about the stars, the earth, his hopes for mankind. He felt that his words had been severed from him, that now they were a part of the world at large, as real and specific as a stone, or a lake, or a flower. They no longer had anything to do with him. He remembered the moment of his birth and how he had been pulled gently from his mother's womb. He remembered the infinite kindness of the world and all the people he had ever loved. Nothing mattered now but the beauty of all this. He wanted to go on writing about it, and it pained him to know that this would not be possible. Nevertheless, he tried to face the end of the red notebook with courage. He wondered if he had it in him to write without a pen, if he could learn to speak instead, filling the darkness with his voice, speaking the words into the air, into the walls, into the city, even if the light never came back again.

The last sentence of the red notebook reads: 'What will happen when there are no more pages in the red notebook?'

At this point the story grows obscure. The information has run out, and the events that follow this last sentence will never be known. It would be foolish even to hazard a guess.

I returned home from my trip to Africa in February, just hours before a snowstorm began to fall on New York. I called my friend Auster that evening, and he urged me to come over to see him as soon as I could. There was something so insistent in his voice that I dared not refuse, even though I was exhausted.

At his apartment, Auster explained to me what little he knew about Quinn, and then he went on to describe the strange case he had accidently become involved in. He had become obsessed by it, he said, and he wanted my advice about what he should do. Having heard him out, I began to feel angry that he had treated Quinn with such indifference. I scolded him for not having taken a greater part in events, for not having done something to help a man who was so obviously in trouble.

Auster seemed to take my words to heart. In fact, he said, that was why he had asked me over. He had been feeling guilty and needed to unburden himself. He said that I was the only person he could trust.

He had spent the last several months trying to track down Quinn, but with no success. Quinn was no longer living in his apartment, and all attempts to reach Virginia Stillman had failed. It was then that I suggested that we take a look at the Stillman apartment. Somehow, I had an intuition that this was where Quinn had wound up.

We put on our coats, went outside, and took a cab to East 69th Street. The snow had been falling for an hour, and already the roads were treacherous. We had little trouble getting into the building – slipping through the door with one of the tenants who was just coming home. We went upstairs and found the door to what had once been the Stillmans' apartment. It was unlocked. We stepped in cautiously and discovered a series of bare, empty rooms. In a small room at the back, impeccably clean as all the other rooms were, the red notebook was lying on the floor. Auster picked it up, looked through it briefly, and said that it was Quinn's. Then he handed it to me and said that I should keep it. The whole business had upset him so much that he was afraid to keep it himself. I said that I would hold on to it until he was ready to read it, but he shook his head and told me that he never wanted to see it again. Then we left and walked out into the snow. The city was entirely white now, and the snow kept falling, as though it would never end.

As for Quinn, it is impossible for me to say where he is now. I have followed the red notebook as closely as I could, and any inaccuracies in the story should be blamed on me. There were moments when the text was difficult to decipher, but I have done my best with it and have refrained from any interpretations. The red notebook, of course, is only half the story, as any sensitive reader will understand. As for Auster, I am convinced that he behaved badly throughout. If our friendship has ended, he has only himself to blame. As for me, my thoughts remain with Quinn. He will be with me always. And wherever he may have disappeared to, I wish him luck.

Ghosts

First of all there is Blue. Later there is White, and then there is Black, and before the beginning there is Brown. Brown broke him in, Brown taught him the ropes, and when Brown grew old, Blue took over. That is how it begins. The place is New York, the time is the present, and neither one will ever change. Blue goes to his office every day and sits at his desk, waiting for something to happen. For a long time nothing does, and then a man named White walks through the door, and that is how it begins.

The case seems simple enough. White wants Blue to follow a man named Black and to keep an eye on him for as long as necessary. While working for Brown, Blue did many tail jobs, and this one seems no different, perhaps even easier than most.

Blue needs the work, and so he listens to White and doesn't ask many questions. He assumes it's a marriage case and that White is a jealous husband. White doesn't elaborate. He wants a weekly report, he says, sent to such and such a postbox number, typed out in duplicate on pages so long and so wide. A cheque will be sent each week to Blue in the mail. White then tells Blue where Black lives, what he looks like, and so on. When Blue asks White how long he thinks the case will last, White says he doesn't know. Just keep sending the reports, he says, until further notice.

To be fair to Blue, he finds it all a little strange. But to say that he has misgivings at this point would be going too far. Still, it's impossible for him not to notice certain things about White. The black beard, for example, and the overly bushy eyebrows. And then there is the skin, which seems inordinately white, as though covered with powder. Blue is no amateur in the art of disguise, and it's not difficult for him to see through this one. Brown was his teacher, after all, and in his day Brown was the best in the business. So Blue begins to think he was wrong, that the case has nothing to do with marriage. But he gets no farther than this, for White is still speaking to him, and Blue must concentrate on following his words.

Everything has been arranged, White says. There's a small apartment directly across the street from Black's. I've already rented it, and you can move in there today. The rent will be paid for until the case is over.

Good idea, says Blue, taking the key from White. That will eliminate the legwork.

Exactly, White answers, stroking his beard.

And so it's settled. Blue agrees to take the job, and they shake hands on it. To show his good faith, White even gives Blue an advance of ten fifty-dollar bills.

That is how it begins, then. The young Blue and a man named White, who is obviously not the man he appears to be. It doesn't matter, Blue says to himself after White has left. I'm sure he has his reasons. And besides, it's not my problem. The only thing I have to worry about is doing my job.

It is 3 February 1947. Little does Blue know, of course, that the case will go on for years. But the present is no less dark than the past, and its mystery is equal to anything the future might hold. Such is the way of the world: one step at a time, one word and then the next. There are certain things that Blue cannot possibly know at this point. For knowledge comes slowly, and when it comes, it is often at great personal expense.

White leaves the office, and a moment later Blue picks up the phone and calls the future Mrs Blue. I'm going under cover, he tells his sweetheart. Don't worry if I'm out of touch for a little while. I'll be thinking of you the whole time.

Blue takes a small grey satchel down from the shelf and packs it with his thirty-eight, a pair of binoculars, a notebook, and other tools of the trade. Then he tidies his desk, puts his papers in order, and locks up the office. From there he goes to the apartment that White has rented for him. The address is unimportant. But let's say Brooklyn Heights, for the sake of argument. Some quiet, rarely travelled street not far from the bridge – Orange

Street perhaps. Walt Whitman handset the first edition of *Leaves of Grass* on this street in 1855, and it was here that Henry Ward Beecher railed against slavery from the pulpit of his red-brick church. So much for local colour.

It's a small studio apartment on the third floor of a four-storey brownstone. Blue is happy to see that it's fully equipped, and as he walks around the room inspecting the furnishings, he discovers that everything in the place is new: the bed, the table, the chair, the rug, the linens, the kitchen supplies, everything. There is a complete set of clothes hanging in the closet, and Blue, wondering if the clothes are meant for him, tries them on and sees that they fit. It's not the biggest place I've ever been in, he says to himself, pacing from one end of the room to the other, but it's cosy enough, cosy enough.

He goes back outside, crosses the street, and enters the opposite building. In the entryway he searches for Black's name on one of the mailboxes and finds it: Black – 3rd floor. So far so good. Then he returns to his room and gets down to business.

Parting the curtains of the window, he looks out and sees Black sitting at a table in his room across the street. To the extent that Blue can make out what is happening, he gathers that Black is writing. A look through the binoculars confirms that he is. The lenses, however, are not powerful enough to pick up the writing itself, and even if they were, Blue doubts that he would be able to read the handwriting upside down. All he can say for certain, therefore, is that Black is writing in a notebook with a red fountain pen. Blue takes out his own notebook and writes: 3 Feb. 3pm Black writing at his desk.

Now and then Black pauses in his work and gazes out the window. At one point, Blue thinks that he is looking directly at him and ducks out of the way. But on closer inspection he realizes that it is merely a blank stare, signifying thought rather than seeing, a look that makes things invisible, that does not let them in. Black gets up from his chair every once in a while and disappears to a hidden spot in the room, a corner Blue supposes, or perhaps the bathroom, but he is never gone for very long, always returning promptly to the desk. This goes on for several hours, and Blue is none the wiser for his efforts. At six o'clock he writes the second sentence in his notebook: This goes on for several hours.

It's not so much that Blue is bored, but that he feels thwarted. Without being able to read what Black has written, everything is a blank so far. Perhaps he's a madman, Blue thinks, plotting to blow up the world. Perhaps that writing has something to do with his secret formula. But Blue is immediately embarrassed by such a childish notion. It's too early to know anything, he says to himself, and for the time being he decides to suspend judgement.

His mind wanders from one small thing to another, eventually settling on the future Mrs Blue. They were planning to go out tonight, he remembers, and if it hadn't been for White showing up at the office today and this new case, he would be with her now. First the Chinese restaurant on 39th Street, where they would have wrestled with the chopsticks and held hands under the table, and then the double feature at the Paramount. For a brief moment he has a startlingly clear picture of her face in his mind (laughing with lowered eyes, feigning embarrassment), and he realizes that he would much rather be with her than sitting in this little room for God knows how long. He thinks about calling her up on the phone for a chat, hesitates, and then decides against it. He doesn't want to seem weak. If she knew how much he needed her, he would begin to lose his advantage, and that wouldn't be good. The man must always be the stronger one.

Black has now cleared his table and replaced the writing materials with dinner. He sits there chewing slowly, staring out the window in that abstracted way of his. At the sight of food, Blue realizes that he is hungry and hunts through the kitchen cabinet for something to eat. He settles on a meal of canned stew and soaks up the gravy with a slice of white bread. After dinner he has some hope that Black will be going outside, and he is encouraged when he sees a sudden flurry of activity in Black's room. But all comes to nothing. Fifteen minutes later, Black is sitting at his desk again, this time reading a book. A lamp is on beside him, and Blue has a clearer view of Black's face than before. Blue estimates Black's age to be the same as his, give or take a year or two. That is to say, somewhere in his late twenties or early thirties. He finds Black's face pleasant enough, with nothing to distinguish it from a thousand other faces one sees every day. This is a disappointment to Blue, for he is still secretly hoping to discover that Black is a madman. Blue looks through the binoculars and reads the title of the book that Black is reading. *Walden*, by Henry David Thoreau. Blue has never heard of it before and writes it down carefully in his notebook.

So it goes for the rest of the evening, with Black reading and Blue watching him read. As time passes, Blue grows more and more discouraged. He's not used to sitting around like this, and with the darkness closing in on him now, it's beginning to get on his nerves. He likes to be up and about, moving from one place to another, doing things. I'm not the Sherlock Holmes type, he would say to Brown, whenever the boss gave him a particularly sedentary task. Give me something I can sink my teeth into. Now, when he himself is the boss, this is what he gets: a case with nothing to do. For to watch someone read and write is in effect to do nothing. The only way for Blue to have a sense of what is happening is to be inside Black's mind, to see what he is thinking, and that of course is impossible. Little by little, therefore, Blue lets his own mind drift back to the old days. He thinks of Brown and some of the cases they worked on together, savouring the memory of their triumphs. There was the Redman Affair, for example, in which they tracked down the bank-teller who had embezzled a quarter of a million dollars. For that one Blue pretended to be a bookie and lured Redman into placing a bet with him. The money was traced back to the bills missing from the bank, and the man got what was coming to him. Even better was the Gray Case. Gray had been missing for over a year, and his wife was ready to give him up for dead. Blue searched through all the normal channels and came up empty. Then, one day, as he was about to file his final report, he stumbled on Gray in a bar, not two blocks from where the wife was sitting, convinced he would never return. Gray's name was now Green, but Blue knew it was Gray in spite of this, for he had been carrying around a photograph of the man for the past three months and knew his face by heart. It turned out to be amnesia. Blue took Gray back to his wife, and although he didn't remember her and continued to call himself Green, he found her to his liking and some days later proposed marriage. So Mrs Gray became Mrs Green, married to the same man a second time, and while Gray never remembered the past – and stubbornly refused to admit that he had forgotten anything – that did not seem to stop him from living comfortably in the present. Whereas Gray had worked as an engineer in his former life, as Green he now kept the job as bartender in the bar two blocks away. He liked mixing the drinks, he said, and talking to the people who came in, and he couldn't imagine doing anything else. I was born to be a bartender, he announced to Brown and Blue at the wedding party, and who were they to object to what a man chose to do with his life?

Those were the good old days, Blue says to himself now, as he watches Black turn off the light in his room across the street. Full of strange twists and amusing coincidences. Well, not every case can be exciting. You've got to take the good with the bad.

Blue, ever the optimist, wakes up the next morning in a cheerful mood. Outside, snow is falling on the quiet street, and everything has turned white. After watching Black eat his breakfast at the table by the window and read a few more pages of *Walden*, Blue sees him to retreat to the back of the room and then return to the window dressed in his overcoat. The time is shortly after eight o'clock. Blue reaches for his hat, his coat, his muffler and boots, hastily scrambles into them, and gets downstairs to the street less than a minute after Black. It is a windless morning, so still that he can hear the snow falling on the branches of the trees. No one else is about, and Black's shoes have made a perfect set of tracks on the white pavement. Blue follows the tracks around the corner and then sees Black ambling down the next street, as if enjoying the weather. Not the behaviour of a man about to escape, Blue thinks, and accordingly he slows his pace. Two streets later, Black enters a small grocery store, stays ten or twelve minutes, and then comes out with two heavily loaded brown paper bags. Without noticing Blue, who is standing in a doorway across the street, he begins retracing his steps towards Orange Street. Stocking up for the storm, Blue says to himself. Blue then decides to risk losing contact with Black and goes into the store himself to do the same. Unless it's a decoy, he thinks, and Black is planning to dump the groceries and take off, it's fairly certain that he's on his way home. Blue therefore does his own shopping, stops in next door to buy a newspaper and several magazines, and then returns to his room on Orange Street. Sure enough, Black is already at his desk by the window, writing in the same notebook as the day before.

Because of the snow, visibility is poor, and Blue has trouble deciphering what is happening in Black's room. Even the binoculars don't help much. The day remains dark, and through the endlessly falling snow, Black appears to be no more than a shadow. Blue resigns himself to a long wait and then settles down with his newspapers and magazines. He is a devoted reader of *True Detective* and tries never to miss a month. Now, with time on his hands, he reads the new issue thoroughly, even pausing to read the little notices and ads on the back pages. Buried among the feature stories on gangbusters and secret agents, there is one short article that strikes a chord in Blue, and even after he finishes the magazine, he finds it difficult not to keep thinking about it. Twenty-five years ago, it seems, in a patch of woods outside Philadelphia, a little boy was found murdered. Although the police promptly began work on the case, they never managed to come up with any clues. Not only did they have no suspects, they could not even identify the boy. Who he was, where he had come from, why he was there – all these questions remained unanswered. Eventually, the case was dropped from the active file, and if not for the coroner who had been assigned to do the autopsy on the boy, it would have been forgotten altogether. This man, whose name was Gold, became obsessed by the murder. Before the child was buried, he made a death mask of his face, and from then on devoted whatever time he could to the mystery. After twenty years, he reached retirement age, left his job, and began spending every moment on the case. But things did not go well. He made no headway, came not one step closer to solving the crime. The article in *True Detective* describes how he is now offering a reward of two thousand dollars to anyone who can provide information about the little boy. It also includes a grainy, retouched photograph of the man holding the death mask in his hands. The look in his eyes is so haunted and imploring that Blue can scarcely turn his own eyes away. Gold is growing old now, and he is afraid that he will die before he solves the case. Blue is deeply moved by this. If it were possible, he would like nothing better than to drop what he's doing and try to help Gold. There aren't enough men like that, he thinks. If the boy were Gold's son, then it would make sense: revenge, pure and simple, and anyone can understand that. But the boy was a complete stranger to him, and so there's nothing personal about it, no hint of a secret motive. It is this thought that so affects Blue. Gold refuses to accept a world in which the murderer of a child can go unpunished, even if the murderer himself is now dead, and he is willing to sacrifice his own life and happiness to right the wrong. Blue then thinks about the little boy for a while, trying to imagine what really happened, trying to feel what the boy must have felt, and then it dawns on him that the murderer must have been one of the parents, for otherwise the boy would have been reported as missing. That only makes it worse, Blue thinks, and as he begins to grow sick at the thought of it, fully understanding now what Gold must feel all the time, he realizes that twenty-five years ago he too was a little boy and that had the boy lived he would be Blue's age now. It could have been me, Blue thinks. I could have been that little boy. Not knowing what else to do, he cuts out the picture from the magazine and tacks it onto the wall above his bed.

So it goes for the first days. Blue watches Black, and little of anything happens. Black writes, reads, eats, takes brief strolls through the neighbourhood, seems not to notice that Blue is there. As for Blue, he tries not to worry. He assumes that Black is lying low, biding his time until the right moment comes. Since Blue is only one man, he realizes that constant vigilance is not expected of him. After all, you can't watch someone twenty-four hours a day. There has to be time for you to sleep, to eat, to do your laundry, and so on. If White wanted Black to be watched around the clock, he would have hired two or three men, not one. But Blue is only one, and more than what is possible he cannot do.

Still, he does begin to worry, in spite of what he tells himself. For if Black must be watched, then it would follow that he must be watched every hour of every day. Anything less than constant surveillance would be as no surveillance at all. It would not take much, Blue reasons, for the entire picture to change. A single moment's inattention – a glance to the side of him, a pause to scratch his head, the merest yawn – and presto, Black slips away and commits whatever heinous act he is planning to commit. And yet, there will necessarily be such moments, hundreds and even thousands of them every day. Blue finds this troubling, for no matter how often he turns this problem over inside himself, he gets no closer to solving it. But that is not the only thing that troubles him.

Until now, Blue has not had much chance for sitting still, and this new idleness has left him at something of a loss. For the first time in his life, he finds that he has been thrown back on himself, with nothing to grab hold of, nothing to distinguish one moment from the next. He has never given much thought to the world inside him, and though he always knew it was there, it has remained an unknown quantity, unexplored and therefore dark, even to himself. He has moved rapidly along the surface of things for as long as he can remember, fixing his attention on these surfaces only in order to perceive them, sizing up one and then passing on to the next, and he has always taken pleasure in the world as such, asking no more of things than that they be there. And until now they have been, etched vividly against the daylight, distinctly telling him what they are, so perfectly themselves and nothing else that he has never had to pause before them or look twice. Now, suddenly, with the world as it were removed from him, with nothing much to see but a vague shadow by the name of Black, he finds himself thinking about things that have never occurred to him before, and this, too, has begun to trouble him. If thinking is perhaps too strong a word at this point, a slightly more modest term – speculation, for example – would not be far from the mark. To speculate, from the Latin *speculatus*, meaning mirror or looking glass. For in spying out at Black across the street, it is as though Blue were looking into a mirror, and instead of merely watching another, he finds that he is also watching himself. Life has slowed down so drastically for him that Blue is now able to see things that have previously escaped his attention. The trajectory of the light that passes through the room each day, for example, and the way the sun at certain hours will reflect the snow on the far corner of the ceiling in his room. The beating of his heart, the sound of his breath, the blinking of his eyes – Blue is now aware of these tiny events, and try as he might to ignore them, they persist in his mind like a nonsensical phrase repeated over and over again. He knows it cannot be true, and yet little by little this phrase seems to be taking on a meaning.

Of Black, of White, of the job he has been hired to do, Blue now begins to advance certain theories. More than just helping to pass the time, he discovers that making up stories can be a pleasure in itself. He thinks that perhaps White and Black are brothers and that a large sum of money is at stake – an inheritance, for example, or the capital invested in a partnership. Perhaps White wants to prove that Black is incompetent, have him committed to an institution, and take control of the family fortune himself. But Black is too clever for that and has gone into hiding, waiting for the pressure to ease up. Another theory that Blue puts forward has White and Black as rivals, both of them racing toward the same goal – the solution to a scientific problem, for example – and White wants Black watched in order to be sure he isn't

outsmarted. Still another story has it that White is a renegade
agent from the FBI or some espionage organization, perhaps
foreign, and has struck out on his own to conduct some peri-
pheral investigation not necessarily sanctioned by his superiors.
By hiring Blue to do his work for him, he can keep the surveillance of Black a secret and at the same time continue to perform
his normal duties. Day by day, the list of these stories grows, with
Blue sometimes returning in his mind to an early story to add
certain flourishes and details and at other times starting over
again with something new. Murder plots, for instance, and kid-
napping schemes for giant ransoms. As the days go on, Blue
realizes there is no end to the stories he can tell. For Black is no
more than a kind of blankness, a hole in the texture of things, and
one story can fill this hole as well as any other.

Blue does not mince words, however. He knows that more
than anything else he would like to learn the real story. But at this
early stage he also knows that patience is called for. Bit by bit,
therefore, he begins to dig in, and with each day that passes he
finds himself a little more comfortable with his situation, a little
more resigned to the fact that he is in for the long haul.

Unfortunately, thoughts of the future Mrs Blue occasionally
disturb his growing peace of mind. Blue misses her more than
ever, but he also senses somehow that things will never be the
same again. Where this feeling comes from he cannot tell. But
while he feels reasonably content whenever he confines his
thoughts to Black, to his room, to the case he is working on,
whenever the future Mrs Blue enters his consciousness, he is
seized by a kind of panic. All of a sudden, his calm turns to
anguish, and he feels as though he is falling into some dark,
cave-like place, with no hope of finding a way out. Nearly every
day he has been tempted to pick up the phone and call her,
thinking that perhaps a moment of real contact would break the
spell. But the days pass, and still he doesn't call. This, too, is
troubling to him, for he cannot remember a time in his life when
he has been so reluctant to do a thing he so clearly wants to do.
I'm changing, he says to himself. Little by little, I'm no longer the

145

same. This interpretation reassures him somewhat, at least for a while, but in the end it only leaves him feeling stranger than before. The days pass, and it becomes difficult for him not to keep seeing pictures of the future Mrs Blue in his head, especially at night, and there in the darkness of his room, lying on his back with his eyes open, he reconstructs her body piece by piece, beginning with her feet and ankles, working his way up her legs and along her thighs, climbing from her belly toward her breasts, and then, roaming happily among the softness, dipping down to her buttocks and then up again along her back, at last finding her neck and curling forward to her round and smiling face. What is she doing now? he sometimes asks himself. And what does she think of all this? But he can never come up with a satisfactory answer. If he is able to invent a multitude of stories to fit the facts concerning Black, with the future Mrs Blue all is silence, confusion, and emptiness.

The day comes for him to write his first report. Blue is an old hand at such compositions and has never had any trouble with them. His method is to stick to outward facts, describing events as though each word tallied exactly with the thing described, and to question the matter no further. Words are transparent for him, great windows that stand between him and the world, and until now they have never impeded his view, have never even seemed to be there. Oh, there are moments when the glass gets a trifle smudged and Blue has to polish it in one spot or another, but once he finds the right word, everything clears up. Drawing on the entries he has made previously in his notebook, sifting through them to refresh his memory and to underscore pertinent remarks, he tries to fashion a coherent whole, discarding the slack and embellishing the gist. In every report he has written so far, action holds forth over interpretation. For example: The subject walked from Columbus Circle to Carnegie Hall. No references to the weather, no mention of the traffic, no stab at trying to guess what the subject might be thinking. The report confines itself to known and verifiable facts, and beyond this limit it does not try to go.

146

Faced with the facts of the Black case, however, Blue grows aware of his predicament. There is the notebook, of course, but when he looks through it to see what he has written, he is disappointed to find such paucity of detail. It's as though his words, instead of drawing out the facts and making them sit palpably in the world, have induced them to disappear. This has never happened to Blue before. He looks out across the street and sees Black sitting at his desk as usual. Black, too, is looking through the window at that moment, and it suddenly occurs to Blue that he can no longer depend on the old procedures. Clues, legwork, investigative routine – none of this is going to matter anymore. But then, when he tries to imagine what will replace these things, he gets nowhere. At this point, Blue can only surmise what the case is not. To say what it is, however, is completely beyond him.

Blue sets his typewriter on the table and casts about for ideas, trying to apply himself to the task at hand. He thinks that perhaps a truthful account of the past week would include the various stories he has made up for himself concerning Black. With so little else to report, these excursions into the make-believe would at least give some flavour of what has happened. But Blue brings himself up short, realizing that they have nothing really to do with Black. This isn't the story of my life, after all, he says. I'm supposed to be writing about him, not myself.

Still, it looms as a perverse temptation, and Blue must struggle with himself for some time before fighting it off. He goes back to the beginning and works his way through the case, step by step. Determined to do exactly what has been asked of him, he painstakingly composes the report in the old style, tackling each detail with such care and aggravating precision that many hours go by before he manages to finish. As he reads over the results, he is forced to admit that everything seems accurate. But then why does he feel so dissatisfied, so troubled by what he has written? He says to himself: what happened is not really what happened. For the first time in his experience of writing reports, he discovers that words do not necessarily work, that it is possible for them to obscure the things they are trying to say. Blue looks around the room and fixes his attention on various objects, one after the other. He sees the lamp and says to himself, lamp. He sees the bed and says to himself, bed. He sees the notebook and says to himself, notebook. It will not do to call the lamp a bed, he thinks, or the bed a lamp. No, these words fit snugly around the things they stand for, and the moment Blue speaks them, he feels a deep satisfaction, as though he has just proved the existence of the world. Then he looks out across the street and sees Black's window. It is dark now, and Black is asleep. That's the problem, Blue says to himself, trying to find a little courage. That and nothing else. He's there, but it's impossible to see him. And even when I do see him it's as though the lights are out.

He seals up his report in an envelope and goes outside, walks to the corner and drops it into the mailbox. I may not be the smartest person in the world, he says to himself, but I'm doing my best, I'm doing my best.

After that, the snow begins to melt. The next morning, the sun is shining brightly, clusters of sparrows are chirping in the trees, and Blue can hear the pleasant dripping of water from the edge of the roof, the branches, the lampposts. Spring suddenly does not seem far away. Another few weeks, he says to himself, and every morning will be like this one.

Black takes advantage of the weather to wander farther afield than previously, and Blue follows. Blue is relieved to be moving again, and as Black continues on his way, Blue hopes the journey will not end before he's had a chance to work out the kinks. As one would imagine, he has always been an ardent walker, and to feel his legs striding along through the morning air fills him with happiness. As they move through the narrow streets of Brooklyn Heights, Blue is encouraged to see that Black keeps increasing his distance from home. But then, his mood suddenly darkens. Black begins to climb the staircase that leads to the walkway across the Brooklyn Bridge, and Blue gets it into his head that he's planning to jump. Such things happen, he tells himself. A man goes to the top of the bridge, gives a last look to the world through

148

the wind and the clouds, and then leaps out over the water, bones cracking on impact, his body broken apart. Blue gags on the image, tells himself to stay alert. If anything starts to happen, he decides, he will step out from his role as neutral bystander and intervene. For he does not want Black to be dead – at least not yet.

It has been many years since Blue crossed the Brooklyn Bridge on foot. The last time was with his father when he was a boy, and the memory of that day comes back to him now. He can see himself holding his father's hand and walking at his side, and as he hears the traffic moving along the steel bridge-road below, he can remember telling his father that the noise sounded like the buzzing of an enormous swarm of bees. To his left is the Statue of Liberty; to his right is Manhattan, the buildings so tall in the morning sun they seem to be figments. His father was a great one for facts, and he told Blue the stories of all the monuments and skyscrapers, vast litanies of detail – the architects, the dates, the political intrigues – and how at one time the Brooklyn Bridge was the tallest structure in America. The old man was born the same year the bridge was finished, and there was always that link in Blue's mind, as though the bridge were somehow a monument to his father. He liked the story he was told that day as he and Blue Senior walked home over the same wooden planks he was walking on now, and for some reason he never forgot it. How John Roebling, the designer of the bridge, got his foot crushed between the dock pilings and a ferry boat just days after finishing the plans and died from gangrene in less than three weeks. He didn't have to die, Blue's father said, but the only treatment he would accept was hydrotherapy, and that proved useless, and Blue was struck that a man who had spent his life building bridges over bodies of water so that people wouldn't get wet should believe that the only true medicine consisted in immersing oneself in water. After John Roebling's death, his son Washington took over as chief engineer, and that was another curious story. Washington Roebling was just thirty-one at the time, with no building experience except for the wooden bridges he designed during the Civil War, but he proved to be even more brilliant than his father. Not long after construction began on the Brooklyn Bridge, however, he was trapped for several hours during a fire in one of the underwater caissons and came out of it with a severe case of the bends, an excruciating disease in which nitrogen bubbles gather in the bloodstream. Nearly killed by the attack, he was thereafter an invalid, unable to leave the top floor room where he and his wife set up house in Brooklyn Heights. There Washington Roebling sat every day for many years, watching the progress of the bridge through a telescope, sending his wife down every morning with his instructions, drawing elaborate colour pictures for the foreign workers who spoke no English so they would understand what to do next, and the remarkable thing was that the whole bridge was literally in his head: every piece of it had been memorized, down to the tiniest bits of steel and stone, and though Washington Roebling never set foot on the bridge, it was totally present inside him, as though by the end of all those years it had somehow grown into his body.

Blue thinks of this now as he makes his way across the river, watching Black ahead of him and remembering his father and his boyhood out in Gravesend. The old man was a cop, later a detective at the 77th precinct, and life would have been good, Blue thinks, if it hadn't been for the Russo Case and the bullet that went through his father's brain in 1927. Twenty years ago, he says to himself, suddenly appalled by the time that has passed, wondering if there is a heaven, and if so whether or not he will get to see his father again after he dies. He remembers a story from one of the endless magazines he has read this week, a new monthly called *Stranger than Fiction*, and it seems somehow to follow from all the other thoughts that have just come to him. Somewhere in the French Alps, he recalls, a man was lost skiing twenty or twenty-five years ago, swallowed up by an avalanche, and his body was never recovered. His son, who was a little boy at the time, grew up and also became a skier. One day in the past year he went skiing, not far from the spot where his father was lost – although he did not know this. Through the minute and persistent displacements of the ice over the decades since his father's death, the terrain was now completely different from what it had been. All alone there in the mountains, miles away from any other human being, the son chanced upon a body in the ice – a dead body, perfectly intact, as though preserved in suspended animation. Needless to say, the young man stopped to examine it, and as he bent down and looked at the face of the corpse, he had the distinct and terrifying impression that he was looking at himself. Trembling with fear, as the article put it, he inspected the body more closely, all sealed away as it was in the ice, like someone on the other side of a thick window, and saw that it was his father. The dead man was still young, even younger than his son was now, and there was something awesome about it, Blue felt, something so odd and terrible about being older than your own father, that he actually had to fight back tears as he read the article. Now, as he nears the end of the bridge, these same feelings come back to him, and he wishes to God that his father could be there, walking over the river and telling him stories. Then, suddenly aware of what his mind is doing, he wonders why he has turned so sentimental, why all these thoughts keep coming to him, when for so many years they have never even occured to him. It's all part of it, he thinks, embarrassed at himself for being like this. That's what happens when you have no one to talk to.

He comes to the end and sees that he was wrong about Black. There will be no suicides today, no jumping from bridges, no leaps into the unknown. For there goes his man, as blithe and unperturbed as anyone can be, descending the stairs of the walkway and travelling along the street that curves around City Hall, then moving north along Centre Street past the courthouse and other municipal buildings, never once slackening his pace, continuing on through Chinatown and beyond. These divagations last several hours, and at no point does Blue have the sense that Black is walking to any purpose. He seems rather to be airing his lungs, walking for the pure pleasure of walking, and as the journey goes on Blue confesses to himself for the first time that he is developing a certain fondness for Black.

At one point Black enters a bookstore and Blue follows him in. There Black browses for half an hour or so, accumulating a small pile of books in the process, and Blue, with nothing better to do, browses as well, all the while trying to keep his face hidden from Black. The little glances he takes when Black seems not to be looking give him the feeling that he has seen Black before, but he can't remember where. There's something about the eyes, he says to himself, but that's as far as he gets, not wanting to call attention to himself and not really sure if there's anything to it.

A minute later, Blue comes across a copy of *Walden* by Henry David Thoreau. Flipping through the pages, he is surprised to discover that the name of the publisher is Black: 'Published for the Classics Club by Walter J. Black, Inc., Copyright 1942.' Blue is momentarily jarred by this coincidence, thinking that perhaps there is some message in it for him, some glimpse of meaning that could make a difference. But then, recovering from the jolt, he begins to think not. It's a common enough name, he says to himself – and besides, he knows for a fact that Black's name is not Walter. Could be a relative though, he adds, or maybe even his father. Still turning this last point over in his mind, Blue decides to buy the book. If he can't read what Black writes, at least he can read what he reads. A long shot, he says to himself, but who knows that it won't give him some hint of what the man is up to.

So far so good. Black pays for his books, Blue pays for his book, and the walk continues. Blue keeps looking for some pattern to emerge, for some clue to drop in his path that will lead him to Black's secret. But Blue is too honest a man to delude himself, and he knows that no rhyme or reason can be read into anything that's happened so far. For once, he is not discouraged by this. In fact, as he probes more deeply into himself, he realizes that on the whole he feels rather invigorated by it. There is something nice about being in the dark, he discovers, something thrilling about not knowing what is going to happen next. It keeps you alert, he thinks, and there's no harm in that, is there? Wide awake and on your toes, taking it all in, ready for anything.

A few moments after thinking this thought, Blue is finally

offered a new development, and the case takes on its first twist. Black turns a corner in midtown, walks halfway down the block, hesitates briefly, as if searching for an address, backtracks a few paces, moves on again, and several seconds later enters a restaurant. Blue follows him in, thinking nothing much of it, since it's lunchtime after all, and people have to eat, but it does not escape him that Black's hesitation seems to indicate that he's never been here before, which in turn might mean that Black has an appointment. It's a dark place inside, fairly crowded, with a group of people clustered around the bar in front, lots of chatter and the clinking of silverware and plates in the background. It looks expensive, Blue thinks, with wood panelling on the walls and white tablecloths, and he decides to keep his bill as low as he can. Tables are available, and Blue takes it as a good omen when he is seated within eyeshot of Black, not obtrusively close, but not so far as not to be able to watch what he does. Black tips his hand by asking for two menus, and three or four minutes later breaks into a smile when a woman walks across the room, approaches Black's table, and kisses him on the cheek before sitting down. The woman's not bad, Blue thinks. A bit on the lean side for his taste, but not bad at all. Then he thinks: now the interesting part begins.

Unfortunately, the woman's back is turned to Blue, so he can't watch her face as the meal progresses. As he sits there eating his Salisbury steak, he thinks that maybe his first hunch was the right one, that it's a marriage case after all. Blue is already imagining the kinds of things he will write in his next report, and it gives him pleasure to contemplate the phrases he will use to describe what he is seeing now. By having another person in the case, he knows that certain decisions have to be made. For example: should he stick with Black or divert his attention to the woman? This could possibly accelerate matters a bit, but at the same time it could mean that Black would be given the chance to slip away from him, perhaps for good. In other words, is the meeting with the woman a smoke-screen or the real thing? Is it a part of the case or not, is it an essential or contingent fact? Blue ponders these questions for a while and concludes that it's too early to tell. Yes, it could be one thing, he tells himself. But it could also be another.

About midway through the meal, things seem to take a turn for the worse. Blue detects a look of great sadness in Black's face, and before he knows it the woman seems to be crying. At least that is what he can gather from the sudden change in the position of her body: her shoulders slumped, her head leaning forward, her face perhaps covered by her hands, the slight shuddering along her back. It could be a fit of laughter, Blue reasons, but then why would Black be so miserable? It looks as though the ground has just been cut out from under him. A moment later, the woman turns her face away from Black, and Blue gets a glimpse of her in profile: tears without question, he thinks, as he watches her dab her eyes with a napkin and sees a smudge of wet mascara glistening on her cheek. She stands up abruptly and walks off in the direction of the ladies' room. Again Blue has an unobstructed view of Black, and seeing that sadness in his face, that look of absolute dejection, he almost begins to feel sorry for him. Black glances in Blue's direction, but clearly he's not seeing anything, and then, an instant later, he buries his face in his hands. Blue tries to guess what is happening, but it's impossible to know. It looks like it's over between them, he thinks, it has the feeling of something that's come to an end. And yet, for all that, it could just be a tiff.

The woman returns to the table looking a little better, and then the two of them sit there for a few minutes without saying anything, leaving their food untouched. Black sighs once or twice, looking off into the distance, and finally calls for a cheque. Blue does the same and then follows the two of them out of the restaurant. He notes that Black has his hand on her elbow, but that could just be a reflex, he tells himself, and probably means nothing. They walk down the street in silence, and at the corner Black waves down a cab. He opens the door for the woman, and before she climbs in he touches her very gently on the cheek. She gives him a brave little smile in return, but still they don't say a word. Then she sits down in the back seat, Black shuts the door, and the cab takes off.

Black walks around for a few minutes, pausing briefly in front of a travel agency window to study a poster of the White Mountains, and then climbs into a cab himself. Blue gets lucky again and manages to find another cab just seconds later. He tells the driver to follow Black's cab and then sits back as the two yellow cars make their way slowly through the traffic downtown, across the Brooklyn Bridge, and finally to Orange Street. Blue is shocked by the fare and kicks himself mentally for not following the woman instead. He should have known that Black was going home.

His mood brightens considerably when he enters his building and finds a letter in his mailbox. It can only be one thing, he tells himself, and sure enough, as he walks upstairs and opens the envelope, there it is: the first cheque, a postal money order for the exact amount settled on with White. He finds it a bit perplexing, however, that the method of payment should be anonymous. Why not a personal cheque from White? This leads Blue to toy with the thought that White is a renegade agent after all, eager to cover his tracks and therefore making sure there will be no record of the payments. Then, removing his hat and overcoat and stretching out on the bed, Blue realizes that he's a little disappointed not to have had some comment about the report. Considering how hard he struggled to get it right, a word of encouragement would have been welcomed. The fact that the money was sent means that White was not dissatisfied. But still – silence is not a rewarding response, no matter what it means. If that's the way it is, Blue says to himself, I'll just have to get used to it.

The days go by, and once again things settle down to the barest of routines. Black writes, reads, shops in the neighbourhood, visits the post office, takes an occasional stroll. The woman does not reappear, and Black makes no further excursions to Manhattan. Blue begins to think that any day he will get a letter telling him the case is closed. The woman is gone, he reasons, and that could be the end of it. But nothing of the sort happens. Blue's meticulous description of the scene in the restaurant draws no special response from White, and week after week the cheques continue to arrive on time. So much for love, Blue says to himself. The woman never meant anything. She was just a diversion.

In this early period, Blue's state of mind can best be described as one of ambivalence and conflict. There are moments when he feels so completely in harmony with Black, so naturally at one with the other man, that to anticipate what Black is going to do, to know when he will stay in his room and when he will go out, he need merely look into himself. Whole days go by when he doesn't even bother to look through the window or follow Black onto the street. Now and then, he even allows himself to make solo expeditions, knowing full well that during the time he is gone Black will not have budged from his spot. How he knows this remains something of a mystery to him, but the fact is that he is never wrong, and when the feeling comes over him, he is beyond all doubt and hesitation. On the other hand, not all moments are like these. There are times when he feels totally removed from Black, cut off from him in a way that is so stark and absolute that he begins to lose the sense of who he is. Loneliness envelops him, shuts him in, and with it comes a terror worse than anything he has ever known. It puzzles him that he should switch so rapidly from one state to another, and for a long time he goes back and forth between extremes, not knowing which one is true and which one false.

After a stretch of particularly bad days, he begins to long for some companionship. He sits down and writes a detailed letter to Brown, outlining the case and asking for his advice. Brown has retired to Florida, where he spends most of his time fishing, and Blue knows that it will take quite a while before he receives an answer. Still, the day after he mails the letter, he begins looking forward to the reply with an eagerness that soon grows to obsession. Each morning, about an hour before the mail is delivered, he plants himself by the window, watching for the postman to round the corner and come into view, pinning all his hopes on what Brown will say to him. What he is expecting from this letter is not certain. Blue does not even ask the question, but surely it is something monumental, some luminous and extraordinary words that will bring him back to the world of the living.

As the days and weeks go by without any letter from Brown, Blue's disappointment grows into an aching, irrational desperation. But that is nothing compared to what he feels when the letter finally comes. For Brown does not even address himself to what Blue wrote. It's good to hear from you, the letter begins, and good to know you're working so hard. Sounds like an interesting case. Can't say I miss any of it, though. Here it's the good life for me – get up early and fish, spend some time with the wife, read a little, sleep in the sun, nothing to complain about. The only thing I don't understand is why I didn't move down here years ago.

The letter goes on in that vein for several pages, never once broaching the subject of Blue's torments and anxieties. Blue feels betrayed by the man who was once like a father to him, and when he finishes the letter he feels empty, the stuffing all knocked out of him. I'm on my own, he thinks, there's no one to turn to anymore. This is followed by several hours of despondency and self-pity, with Blue thinking once or twice that maybe he'd be better off dead. But eventually he works his way out of the gloom. For Blue is a solid character on the whole, less given to dark thoughts than most, and if there are moments when he feels the world is a foul place, who are we to blame him for it? By the time supper rolls around, he has even begun to look on the bright side. This is perhaps his greatest talent: not that he does not despair, but that he never despairs for very long. It might be a good thing after all, he says to himself. It might be better to stand alone than to depend on anyone else. Blue thinks about his for a while and decides there is something to be said for it. He is no longer an apprentice. There is no master above him anymore. I'm my own man, he says to himself. I'm my own man, accountable to no one but myself.

Inspired by this new approach to things, he discovers that he has as last found the courage to contact the future Mrs Blue. But when he picks up the phone and dials her number, there is no answer. This is a disappointment, but he remains undaunted. I'll try again some other time, he says. Some time soon.

The days continue to pass. Once again Blue falls into step with Black, perhaps even more harmoniously than before. In doing so, he discovers the inherent paradox of his situation. For the closer he feels to Black, the less he finds it necessary to think about him. In other words, the more deeply entangled he becomes, the freer he is. What bogs him down is not involvement but separation. For it is only when Black seems to drift away from him that he must go out looking for him, and this takes time and effort, not to speak of struggle. At those moments when he feels closest to Black, however, he can even begin to lead the semblance of an independent life. At first he is not very daring in what he allows himself to do, but even so he considers it a kind of triumph, almost an act of bravery. Going outside, for example, and walking up and down the block. Small as it might be, this gesture fills him with happiness, and as he moves back and forth along Orange Street in the lovely spring weather, he is glad to be alive in a way he has not felt in years. At one end there is a view of the river, the harbour, the Manhattan skyline, the bridges. Blue finds all this beautiful, and on some days he even allows himself to sit for several minutes on one of the benches and look out at the boats. In the other direction there is the church, and sometimes Blue goes to the small grassy yard to sit for a while, studying the bronze statue of Henry Ward Beecher. Two slaves are holding on to Beecher's legs, as though begging him to help them, to make them free at last, and in the brick wall behind there is a porcelain relief of Abraham Lincoln. Blue cannot help but feel inspired by these images, and each time he comes to the churchyard his head fills with noble thoughts about the dignity of man.

Little by little, he becomes more bold in his strayings from Black. It is 1947, the year that Jackie Robinson breaks in with the Dodgers, and Blue follows his progress closely, remembering the churchyard and knowing there is more to it than just baseball. One bright Tuesday afternoon in May, he decides to make an excursion to Ebbetts Field, and as he leaves Black behind in his room on Orange Street, hunched over his desk as usual with his pen and papers, he feels no cause for worry, secure in the fact that everything will be exactly the same when he returns. He rides the subway, rubs shoulders with the crowd, feels himself lunging towards a sense of the moment. As he takes his seat at the ball park, he is struck by the sharp clarity of the colours around him: the green grass, the brown dirt, the white ball, the blue sky above. Each thing is distinct from every other thing, wholly separate and defined, and the geometric simplicity of the pattern impresses Blue with its force. Watching the game, he finds it difficult to take his eyes off Robinson, lured constantly by the blackness of the man's face, and he thinks it must take courage to do what he is doing, to be alone like that in front of so many strangers, with half of them no doubt wishing him to be dead. As the game moves along, Blue finds himself cheering whatever Robinson does, and when the black man steals a base in the third inning he rises to his feet, and later, in the seventh, when Robinson doubles off the wall in left, he actually pounds the back of the man next to him for joy. The Dodgers pull it out in the ninth with a sacrifice fly, and as Blue shuffles off with the rest of the crowd and makes his way home, it occurs to him that Black did not cross his mind even once.

But ball games are only the beginning. On certain nights, when it is clear to Blue that Black will not be going anywhere, he slips out to a bar not far away for a beer or two, enjoying the conversations he sometimes has with the bartender, whose name is Red, and who bears an uncanny resemblance to Green, the bartender from the Gray Case so long ago. A blowsy tart named Violet is often there, and once or twice Blue gets her tipsy enough to get invited back to her place around the corner. He knows that she likes him well enough because she never makes him pay for it, but he also knows that it has nothing to do with love. She calls him honey and her flesh is soft and ample, but whenever she has one drink too many she begins to cry, and then Blue has to console her, and he secretly wonders if it's worth the trouble. His guilt towards the future Mrs Blue is scant, however, for he justifies these sessions with Violet by comparing himself to a soldier at war in another country. Every man needs a little comfort, especially when his number could be up tomorrow. And besides, he isn't made of stone, he says to himself.

More often than not, however, Blue will bypass the bar and go to the movie theatre several blocks away. With summer coming on now and the heat beginning to hover uncomfortably in his little room, it's refreshing to be able to sit in the cool theatre and watch the feature show. Blue is fond of the movies, not only for the stories they tell and the beautiful women he can see in them, but for the darkness of the theatre itself, the way the pictures on the screen are somehow like the thoughts inside his head whenever he closes his eyes. He is more or less indifferent to the kinds of movies he sees, whether comedies or dramas, for example, or whether the film is shot in black and white or in colour, but he has a particular weakness for movies about detectives, since there is a natural connection, and he is always gripped by these stories more than by others. During this period he sees a number of such movies and enjoys them all: *Lady in the Lake, Fallen Angel, Dark Passage, Body and Soul, Ride the Pink Horse, Desperate*, and so on. But for Blue there is one that stands out from the rest, and he likes it so much that he actually goes back the next night to see it again.

It's called *Out of the Past*, and it stars Robert Mitchum as an ex-private eye who is trying to build a new life for himself in a small town under an assumed name. He has a girl friend, a sweet country girl named Ann, and runs a gas station with the help of a deaf-and-dumb boy, Jimmy, who is firmly devoted to him. But the past catches up with Mitchum, and there's little he can do about it. Years ago, he had been hired to look for Jane Greer, the mistress of gangster Kirk Douglas, but once he found her they fell in love and ran off together to live in secret. One thing led to another – money was stolen, a murder was committed – and eventually Mitchum came to his senses and left Greer, finally understanding the depth of her corruption. Now he is being blackmailed by Douglas and Greer into committing a crime, which itself is merely a set-up, for once he figures out what is happening, he sees that they are planning to frame him for another murder. A complicated story unfolds, with Mitchum desperately trying to extricate himself from the trap. At one point, he returns to the small town where he lives, tells Ann that he's innocent, and again persuades her of his love. But it's really too late, and Mitchum knows it. Towards the end, he manages to convince Douglas to turn in Greer for the murder she committed, but at that moment Greer enters the room, calmly takes out a gun, and kills Douglas. She tells Mitchum that they belong to each other, and he, fatalistic to the last, appears to go along. They decide to escape the country together, but as Greer goes to pack her bag, Mitchum picks up the phone and calls the police. They get into the car and drive off, but soon they come to a police roadblock. Greer, seeing that she's been double-crossed, pulls a gun from her bag and shoots Mitchum. The police then open fire on the car and Greer is killed as well. After that, there's one last scene – the next morning, back in the small town of Bridgeport. Jimmy is sitting on a bench outside the gas station, and Ann walks over and sits down beside him. Tell me one thing, Jimmy, she says, I've got to know this one thing: was he running away with her or not? The boy thinks for a moment, trying to decide between truth and kindness. Is it more important to preserve his friend's good name or to spare the girl? All this happens in no more than an instant. Looking into the girl's eyes, he nods his head, as if to say yes, he was in love with Greer after all. Ann pats Jimmy's arm and thanks him, then walks off to her former boyfriend, a straight-arrow local policeman who always despised Mitchum. Jimmy looks up at the gas station sign with Mitchum's name on it, gives a little salute of friendship, and then turns away and walks down the road. He is the only one who knows the truth, and he will never tell.

For the next few days, Blue goes over this story many times in his head. It's a good thing, he decides, that the movie ends with the deaf mute boy. The secret is buried, and Mitchum will remain an outsider, even in death. His ambition was simple enough: to become a normal citizen in a normal American town, to marry the girl next door, to live a quiet life. It's strange, Blue thinks, that the new name Mitchum chooses for himself is Jeff Bailey. This is remarkably close to the name of another character in a movie he saw the previous year with the future Mrs Blue – George Bailey, played by James Stewart in *It's a Wonderful Life*. That story was also about small town America, but from the opposite point of view: the frustrations of a man who spends his whole life trying to escape. But in the end he comes to understand that his life has been a good one, that he has done the right thing all along. Mitchum's Bailey would no doubt like to be the same man as Stewart's Bailey. But in his case the name is false, a product of wishful thinking. His real name is Markham – or, as Blue sounds it out to himself, mark him – and that is the whole point. He has been marked by the past, and once that happens, nothing can be done about it. Something happens, Blue thinks, and then it goes on happening forever. It can never be changed, can never be otherwise. Blue begins to be haunted by this thought, for he sees it as a kind of warning, a message delivered up from within himself, and try as he does to push it away, the darkness of this thought does not leave him.

One night, therefore, Blue finally turns to his copy of *Walden*. The time has come, he says to himself, and if he doesn't make an effort now, he knows that he never will. But the book is not a simple business. As Blue begins to read, he feels as though he is entering an alien world. Trudging through swamps and brambles, hoisting himself up gloomy screes and treacherous cliffs, he feels like a prisoner on a forced march, and his only thought is to escape. He is bored by Thoreau's words and finds it difficult to concentrate. Whole chapters go by, and when he comes to the end of them he realizes that he has not retained a thing. Why would anyone want to go off and live alone in the woods? What's all this about planting beans and not drinking coffee or eating meat? Why all these interminable descriptions of birds? Blue thought that he was going to get a story, or at least have something like a story, but this is no more than blather, an endless harangue about nothing at all.

It would be unfair to blame him, however. Blue has never read much of anything except newspapers and magazines, and an occasional adventure novel when he was a boy. Even experienced and sophisticated readers have been known to have trouble with *Walden*, and no less a figure than Emerson once wrote in his journal that reading Thoreau made him feel nervous and wretched. To Blue's credit, he does not give up. The next day he begins again, and this second go-through is somewhat less rocky than the first. In the third chapter he comes across a sentence that finally says something to him – Books must be read as deliberately and reservedly as they were written – and suddenly he understands that the trick is to go slowly, more slowly than he has ever gone with the words before. This helps to some extent, and certain passages begin to grow clear: the business about clothes in the beginning, the battle between the red ants and the black ants, the argument against work. But Blue still finds it painful, and though he grudgingly admits that Thoreau is perhaps not as stupid as he thought, he begins to resent Black for putting him through this torture. What he does not know is that were he to find the patience to read the book in the spirit in which it asks to be read, his entire life would begin to change, and little by little he would come to a full understanding of his situation – that is to say, of Black, of White, of the case, of everything that concerns him. But lost chances are as much a part of life as chances taken, and a story cannot dwell on what might have been. Throwing the book aside in disgust, Blue puts on his coat (for it is fall now) and goes out for a breath of air. Little does he realize that this is the beginning of the end. For something is about to happen, and once it happens, nothing will ever be the same again.

He goes to Manhattan, wandering farther from Black than at any time before, venting his frustration in movement, hoping to calm himself down by exhausting his body. He walks north, alone in his thoughts, not bothering to take in the things around him. On East 26th Street his left shoelace comes undone, and it is precisely then, as he bends down to tie it, crouching on one knee, that the sky falls on top of him. For who should he glimpse at just that moment but the future Mrs Blue. She is coming up the street with her two arms linked through the right arm of a man Blue has never seen before, and she is smiling radiantly, engrossed in what the man is saying to her. For several moments Blue is so at a loss that he doesn't know whether to bend his head farther down and hide his face or stand up and greet the woman whom he now understands – with a knowledge as sudden and irrevocable as the slamming of a door – will never be his wife. As it turns out, he manages neither – first ducking his head, but then discovering a second later that he wants her to recognize him, and when he sees she will not, being so wrapped up in her companion's talk, Blue abruptly rises from the pavement when they are no more than six feet away from him. It is as though some spectre has suddenly materialized in front of her, and the ex-future Mrs Blue gives out a little gasp, even before she sees who the spectre is. Blue speaks her name, in a voice that seems strange to him, and she stops dead in her tracks. Her face registers the shock of seeing Blue – and then, rapidly, her expression turns to one of anger.

You! she says to him. You!

Before he has the chance to say a word, she disentangles herself from her companion's arm and begins pounding Blue's chest with her fists, screaming insanely at him, accusing him of one foul crime after another. It is all Blue can do to repeat her name over and over, as though trying desperately to distinguish between the woman he loves and the wild beast who is now attacking him. He feels totally defenceless, and as the onslaught continues, he begins to welcome each new blow as just punishment for his behaviour. The other man soon puts a stop to it, however, and though Blue is tempted to take a swing at him, he is too stunned to act quickly enough, and before he knows it the man has led away the weeping ex-future Mrs Blue down the street and around the corner, and that's the end of it.

This brief scene, so unexpected and devastating, turns Blue

inside out. By the time he regains his composure and manages to return home, he realizes that he has thrown away his life. It's not her fault, he says to himself, wanting to blame her but knowing he can't. He might have been dead for all she knew, and how can he hold it against her for wanting to live? Blue feels tears forming in his eyes, but more than grief he feels anger at himself for being such a fool. He has lost whatever chance he might have had for happiness, and if that is the case, then it would not be wrong to say that this is truly the beginning of the end.

Blue gets back to his room on Orange Street, lies down on his bed, and tries to weigh the possibilities. Eventually, he turns his face to the wall and encounters the photograph of the coroner from Philadelphia, Gold. He thinks of the sad blankness of the unsolved case, the child lying in his grave with no name, and as he studies the death mask of the little boy, he begins to turn an idea over in his mind. Perhaps there are ways of getting close to Black, he thinks, ways that need not give him away. God knows there must be. Moves that can be made, plans that can be set in motion – perhaps two or three at the same time. Never mind the rest, he tells himself. It's time to turn the page.

His next report is due the day after tomorrow, and so he sits down to it now in order to get it mailed off on schedule. For the past few months his reports have been exceedingly cryptic, no more than a paragraph or two, giving the bare bones and nothing else, and this time he does not depart from the pattern. However, at the bottom of the page he interjects an obscure comment as a kind of test, hoping to elicit something more than silence from White: Black seems ill. I'm afraid he might be dying. Then he seals up the report, saying to himself that this is only the beginning.

Two days hence, Blue hastens early in the morning to the Brooklyn Post Office, a great castle of a building within eyeshot of the Manhattan Bridge. All of Blue's reports have been addressed to box number one thousand and one, and he walks over to it now as though by accident, sauntering past it and unobtrusively peeking inside to see if the report has come. It has. Or at least a letter is there – a solitary white envelope tilted at a forty-five degree angle in the narrow cubby – and Blue has no reason to suspect it's any letter other than his own. He then begins a slow circular walk around the area, determined to remain until White or someone working for White appears, his eyes fixed on the huge wall of numbered boxes, each box with a different combination, each one holding a different secret. People come and go, open boxes and close them, and Blue keeps wandering in his circle, pausing every now and then in some random spot and then moving on. Everything seems brown to him, as though the fall weather outside has penetrated the room, and the place smells pleasantly of cigar smoke. After several hours he begins to get hungry, but he does not give in to the call of his stomach, telling himself it's now or never and therefore holding his ground. Blue watches everyone who approaches the bank of post boxes, zeroing in on each person who skirts the vicinity of one thousand and one, aware of the fact that if it's not White who comes for the reports it could be anyone – an old woman, a young child, and consequently he must take nothing for granted. But none of these possibilities comes to anything, for the box remains untouched throughout, and though Blue momentarily and successively spins a story for each candidate who comes near, trying to imagine how that person might be connected to White and or Black, what role he or she might play in the case, and so on, one by one he is forced to dismiss them back into the oblivion from which they have come.

Just past noon, at a moment when the post office begins to get crowded – an influx of people on their lunch break rushing through to mail letters, buy stamps, attend to business of one sort or another – a man with a mask on his face walks through the door. Blue doesn't notice him at first, what with so many others coming through the door at the same time, but as the man separates himself from the crowd and begins walking toward the numbered post boxes, Blue finally catches sight of the mask – a mask of the sort that children wear on Hallowe'en, made of rubber and portraying some hideous monster with gashes in his forehead and bleeding eyeballs and fangs for teeth. The rest of him is perfectly ordinary (grey tweed overcoat, red scarf wrapped around his neck), and Blue senses in this first moment that the man behind the mask is White. As the man continues walking toward the area of box one thousand and one, this sense grows to conviction. At the same time, Blue also feels that the man is not really there, that even though he knows he is seeing him, it is more than likely that he is the only one who can. On this point, however, Blue is wrong, for as the masked man continues moving across the vast marble floor, Blue sees a number of people laughing and pointing at him – but whether this is better or worse he cannot say. The masked man reaches box one thousand and one, spins the combination wheel back and forth and back again, and opens the box. As soon as Blue sees that this is definitely his man, he begins making a move toward him, not really sure of what he is planning to do, but in the back of his mind no doubt intending to grab hold of him and tear the mask of his face. But the man is too alert, and once he has pocketed the envelope and locked the box, he gives a quick glance around the room, sees Blue approaching, and makes a dash for it, heading for the door as fast as he can. Blue runs after him, hoping to catch him from behind and tackle him, but he gets tangled momentarily in a crowd of people at the door, and by the time he manages to get through it, the masked man is bounding down the stairs, landing on the sidewalk, and running down the street. Blue continues in pursuit, even feels he is gaining ground, but then the man reaches the corner, where a bus just happens to be pulling out from a stop, and so he conveniently leaps aboard, and Blue is left in the lurch, all out of breath and standing there like an idiot.

Two days later, when Blue receives his cheque in the mail, there is finally a word from White. No more funny business, it says, and though it's not much of a word, for all that Blue is glad to have received it, happy to have cracked White's wall of silence at last. It's not clear to him, however, whether the message refers to the last report or to the incident in the post office. After thinking it over for a while, he decides that it makes no difference. One way or another, the key to the case is action. He must go on disrupting things wherever he can, a little here, a little there, chipping away at each conundrum until the whole structure begins to weaken, until one day the whole rotten business comes toppling to the ground.

Over the next few weeks, Blue returns to the post office several times, hoping to catch another glimpse of White. But nothing comes of it. Either the report is already gone from the box when he gets there, or White does not show up. The fact that this area of the post office is open twenty-four hours a day leaves Blue with few options. White is on to him now, and he will not make the same mistake twice. He will simply wait until Blue is gone before going to the box, and unless Blue is willing to spend his entire life in the post office, there's no way he can expect to sneak up on White again.

The picture is far more complicated than Blue ever imagined. For almost a year now, he has thought of himself as essentially free. For better or worse he had been doing his job, looking straight ahead of him and studying Black, waiting for a possible opening, trying to stick with it, but through it all he has not given a single thought to what might be going on behind him. Now, after the incident with the masked man and the further obstacles that have ensued, Blue no longer knows what to think. It seems perfectly plausible to him that he is also being watched, observed by another in the same way that he has been observing Black. If that is the case, then he has never been free. From the very start he has been the man in the middle, thwarted in front and hemmed in on the rear. Oddly enough, this thought reminds him of some sentences from *Walden*, and he searches through his notebook for the exact phrasing, fairly certain that he has written them down. We are not where we are, he finds, but in a false position. Through an infirmity of our natures, we suppose a case, and put ourselves into it, and hence are in two cases at the same time, and it is doubly difficult to get out. This makes sense to Blue, and though he is beginning to feel a little frightened, he thinks that perhaps it is not too late for him to do something about it.

The real problem boils down to identifying the nature of the problem itself. To start with, who poses the greater threat to him, White or Black? White has kept up his end of the bargain: the cheques have come on time every week, and to turn against him now, Blue knows, would be to bite the hand that feeds him. And yet White is the one who set the case in motion – thrusting Blue into an empty room, as it were, and then turning off the light and locking the door. Ever since, Blue has been groping about in the darkness, feeling blindly for the light switch, a prisoner of the case itself. All well and good, but why would White do such a thing? When Blue comes up against this question, he can no longer think. His brain stops working, he can get no farther than this.

Take Black, then. Until now he has been the entire case, the apparent cause of all his troubles. But if White is really out to get Blue and not Black, then perhaps Black has nothing to do with it, perhaps he is no more than an innocent bystander. In that case, it is Black who occupies the position Blue has assumed all along to be his, and Blue who takes the role of Black. There is something to be said for this. On the other hand, it is also possible that Black is somehow working in league with White and that together they have conspired to do Blue in.

If so, what are they doing to him? Nothing very terrible, finally – at least not in any absolute sense. They have trapped Blue into doing nothing, into being so inactive as to reduce his life to almost no life at all. Yes, says Blue to himself, that's what it feels like: like nothing at all. He feels like a man who has been condemned to sit in a room and go on reading a book for the rest of his life. This is strange enough – to be only half alive at best, seeing the world only through words, living only through the lives of others. But if the book were an interesting one, perhaps it wouldn't be so bad. He could get caught up in the story, so to speak, and little by little begin to forget himself. But this book offers him nothing. There is no story, no plot, no action – nothing but a man sitting alone in a room and writing a book. That's all there is, Blue realizes, and he no longer wants any part of it. But how to get out? How to get out of the room that is the book that will go on being written for as long as he stays in the room?

As for Black, the so-called writer of this book, Blue can no longer trust what he sees. Is it possible that there really is such a man – who does nothing, who merely sits in his room and writes? Blue has followed him everywhere, has tracked him down into the remotest corners, has watched him so hard that his eyes seem to be failing him. Even when he does leave his room, Black never goes anywhere, never does much of anything: grocery shopping, an occasional haircut, a trip to the movies, and so on. But mostly he just wanders around the streets, looking at odd bits of scenery, clusters of random data, and even this happens only in spurts. For a while it will be buildings – craning his neck to catch a glimpse of the roofs, inspecting doorways, running his hands slowly over the stone façades. And then, for a week or two, it will be public statues, or the boats in the river, or the signs in the street. Nothing more than that, with scarcely a word to anyone, and no meetings with others except for that one lunch with the woman in tears by now so long ago. In one sense, Blue knows everything there is to know about Black: what kind of soap he buys, what newspapers he reads, what clothes he wears, and each of these things he has faithfully recorded in his notebook. He has learned a thousand facts, but the only thing they have taught him is that he knows nothing. For the fact remains that none of this is possible. It is not possible for such a man as Black to exist.

Consequently, Blue begins to suspect that Black is no more than a ruse, another one of White's hirelings, paid by the week to sit in that room and do nothing. Perhaps all that writing is merely a sham – page after page of it: a list of every name in the phone book, for example, or each word from the dictionary in alphabetical order, or a handwritten copy of *Walden*. Or perhaps they are not even words, but senseless scribbles, random marks of a pen, a growing heap of nonsense and confusion. This would make White the real writer then – and Black no more than his stand-in, a fake, an actor with no substance of his own. Then there are the times, following through with this thought, that Blue believes the only logical explanation is that Black is not one man but several. Two, three, four look-alikes who play the role of Black for Blue's benefit, each one putting in his allotted time and then going back to the comforts of hearth and home. But this is a thought too monstrous for Blue to contemplate for very long. Months go by, and at last he says to himself out loud: I can't breathe anymore. This is the end. I'm dying.

It is midsummer, 1948. Finally mustering the courage to act, Blue reaches into his bag of disguises and casts about for a new identity. After dismissing several possibilities, he settles on an old man who used to beg on the corners of his neighbourhood when he was a boy – a local character by the name of Jimmy Rose – and decks himself out in the garb of tramphood: tattered woollen clothes, shoes held together with string to prevent the soles from flapping, a weathered carpetbag to hold his belongings, and then, last of all, a flowing white beard and long white hair. These final details give him the look of an Old Testament prophet. Blue as Jimmy Rose is not a scrofulous down-and-outer so much as a wise fool, a saint of penury living in the margins of society. A trifle daft perhaps, but harmless: he exudes a sweet indifference to the world around him, for since everything has happened to him already, nothing can disturb him anymore.

Blue posts himself in a suitable spot across the street, takes a fragment of a broken magnifying glass from his pocket, and begins reading a crumpled day-old newspaper that he has salvaged from one of the nearby garbage cans. Two hours later, Black appears, walking down the steps of his house and then turning in Blue's direction. Black pays no attention to the bum – either lost in his own thoughts or ignoring him on purpose – and so as he begins to approach, Blue addresses him in a pleasant voice.

Can you spare some change, mister?

Black stops, looks over the dishevelled creature who has just spoken, and gradually relaxes into a smile as he realizes he is not in danger. Then he reaches into his pocket, pulls out a coin, and puts it in Blue's hand.

171

Here you are, he says.

God bless you, says Blue.

Thank you, answers Black, touched by the sentiment.

Never fear, says Blue. God blesses all.

And with that word of reassurance, Black tips his hat to Blue and continues on his way.

The next afternoon, once again in bum's regalia, Blue waits for Black in the same spot. Determined to keep the conversation going a little longer this time, now that he has won Black's confidence, Blue finds that the problem is taken out of his hands when Black himself shows an eagerness to linger. It is late in the day by now, not yet dusk but no longer afternoon, the twilight hour of slow changes, of glowing bricks and shadows. After greeting the bum cordially and giving him another coin, Black hesitates a moment, as though debating whether to take the plunge, and then says:

Has anyone ever told you that you look just like Walt Whitman?

Walt who? answers Blue, remembering to play his part.

Walt Whitman. A famous poet.

No, says Blue. I can't say I know him.

You wouldn't know him, says Black. He's not alive anymore. But the resemblance is remarkable.

Well, you know what they say, says Blue. Every man has his double somewhere. I don't see why mine can't be a dead man.

The funny thing, continues Black, is that Walt Whitman used to work on this street. He printed his first book right here, not far from where we're standing.

You don't say, says Blue, shaking his head pensively. It makes you stop and think, doesn't it?

There are some odd stories about Whitman, Black says, gesturing to Blue to sit down on the stoop of the building behind them, which he does, and then Black does the same, and suddenly it's just the two of them out there in the summer light together, chatting away like two old friends about this and that.

Yes, says Black, settling in comfortably to the langour of the

172

moment, a number of very curious stories. The one about Whitman's brain, for example. All his life Whitman believed in the science of phrenology – you know, reading the bumps on the skull. It was very popular at the time.

Can't say I've ever heard of it, replies Blue.

Well, that doesn't matter, says Black. The main thing is that Whitman was interested in brains and skulls – thought they could tell you everything about a man's character. Anyway, when Whitman lay dying over there in New Jersey about fifty or sixty years ago, he agreed to let them perform an autopsy on him after he was dead.

How could he agree to it after he was dead?

Ah, good point. I didn't say it right. He was still alive when he agreed. He just wanted them to know that he didn't mind if they opened him up later. What you might call his dying wish.

Famous last words.

That's right. A lot of people thought he was a genius, you see, and they wanted to take a look at his brain to find out if there was anything special about it. So, the day after he died, a doctor removed Whitman's brain – cut it right out of his head – and had it sent to the American Anthropometric Society to be measured and weighed.

Like a giant cauliflower, interjects Blue.

Exactly. Like a big grey vegetable. But this is where the story gets interesting. The brain arrives at the laboratory, and just as they're about to work on it, one of the assistants drops it on the floor.

Did it break?

Of course it broke. A brain isn't very tough, you know. It splattered all over the place, and that was that. The brain of America's greatest poet got swept up and thrown out with the garbage.

Blue, remembering to respond in character, emits several wheezing laughs – a good imitation of an old codger's mirth. Black laughs, too, and by now the atmosphere has thawed to such an extent that no one could ever know they were not lifelong chums.

It's sad to think of poor Walt lying in his grave, though, says Black. All alone and without any brains.

Just like that scarecrow, says Blue.

Sure enough, says Black. Just like the scarecrow in the land of Oz.

After another good laugh, Black says: And then there's the story of the time Thoreau came to visit Whitman. That's a good one, too.

Was he another poet?

Not exactly. But a great writer just the same. He's the one who lived alone in the woods.

Oh yes, says Blue, not wanting to carry his ignorance too far. Someone once told me about him. Very fond of nature he was. Is that the man you mean?

Precisely, answers Black. Henry David Thoreau. He came down from Massachusetts for a little while and paid a call on Whitman in Brooklyn. But the day before that he came right here to Orange Street.

Any particular reason?

Plymouth Church. He wanted to hear Henry Ward Beecher's sermon.

A lovely spot, says Blue, thinking of the pleasant hours he has spent in the grassy yard. I like to go there myself.

Many great men have gone there, says Black. Abraham Lincoln, Charles Dickens – they all walked down this street and went into the church.

Ghosts.

Yes, there are ghosts all around us.

And the story?

It's really very simple. Thoreau and Bronson Alcott, a friend of his, arrived at Whitman's house on Myrtle Avenue, and Walt's mother sent them up to the attic bedroom he shared with his mentally retarded brother, Eddy. Everything was just fine. They shook hands, exchanged greetings, and so on. But then, when they sat down to discuss their views of life, Thoreau and Alcott noticed a full chamber pot right in the middle of the floor. Walt was of course an expansive fellow and paid no attention, but the two New Englanders found it hard to keep talking with a bucket of excrement in front of them. So eventually they went downstairs to the parlour and continued the conversation there. It's a minor detail, I realize. But still, when two great writers meet, history is made, and it's important to get all the facts straight. That chamber pot, you see, somehow reminds me of the brains on the floor. And when you stop to think about it, there's a certain similarity of form. The bumps and convolutions, I mean. There's a definite connection. Brains and guts, the insides of a man. We always talk about trying to get inside a writer to understand his work better. But when you get right down to it, there's not much to find in there – at least not much that's different from what you'd find in anyone else.

You seem to know a lot about these things, says Blue, who's beginning to lose the thread of Black's argument.

It's my hobby, says Black. I like to know how writers live, especially American writers. It helps me to understand things.

I see, says Blue, who sees nothing at all, for with each word Black speaks, he finds himself understanding less and less.

Take Hawthorne, says Black. A good friend of Thoreau's, and probably the first real writer America ever had. After he graduated from college, he went back to his mother's house in Salem, shut himself up in his room, and didn't come out for twelve years.

What did he do in there?

He wrote stories.

Is that all? He just wrote?

Writing is a solitary business. It takes over your life. In some sense, a writer has no life of his own. Even when he's there, he's not really there.

Another ghost.

Exactly.

Sounds mysterious.

It is. But Hawthorne wrote great stories, you see, and we still read them now, more than a hundred years later. In one of them, a man named Wakefield decides to play a joke on his wife. He tells her that he has to go away on a business trip for a few days, but instead of leaving the city, he goes around the corner, rents a room, and just waits to see what will happen. He can't say for sure why he's doing it, but he does it just the same. Three or four days go by, but he doesn't feel ready to return home yet, and so he stays on in the rented room. The days turn into weeks, the weeks turn into months. One day Wakefield walks down his old street and sees his house decked out in mourning. It's his own funeral, and his wife has become a lonely widow. Years go by. Every now and then he crosses paths with his wife in town, and once, in the middle of a large crowd, he actually brushes up against her. But she doesn't recognize him. More years pass, more than twenty years, and little by little Wakefield has become an old man. One rainy night in autumn, as he's taking a walk through the empty streets, he happens to pass by his old house and peeks through the window. There's a nice warm fire burning in the fireplace, and he thinks to himself: how pleasant it would be if I were in there right now, sitting in one of those cosy chairs by the hearth instead of standing out here in the rain. And so, without giving it any more thought than that, he walks up the steps of the house and knocks on the door.

And then?

That's it. That's the end of the story. The last thing we see is the door opening and Wakefield going inside with a crafty smile on his face.

And we never know what he says to his wife?

No. That's the end. Not another word. But he moved in again, we know that much, and remained a loving spouse until death.

By now the sky has begun to darken overhead, and night is fast approaching. A last glimmer of pink remains in the west, but the day is as good as done. Black, taking his cue from the darkness, stands up from his spot and extends his hand to Blue.

It's been a pleasure talking to you, he says. I had no idea we'd been sitting here so long.

The pleasure's been mine, says Blue, relieved that the

conversation is over, for he knows that it won't be long now before his beard begins to slip, what with the summer heat and his nerves making him perspire into the glue.

My name is Black, says Black, shaking Blue's hand.

Mine's Jimmy, says Blue. Jimmy Rose.

I'll remember this little talk of ours for a long time, Jimmy, says Black.

I will, too, says Blue. You've given me a lot to think about.

God bless you, Jimmy Rose, says Black.

And God bless you, sir, says Blue.

And then, with one last handshake, they walk off in opposite directions, each one accompanied by his own thoughts.

Later that night, when Blue returns to his room, he decides that he had best bury Jimmy Rose now, get rid of him for good. The old tramp has served a purpose, but beyond this point it would not be wise to go.

Blue is glad to have made this initial contact with Black, but the encounter did not quite have the desired effect, and all in all he feels rather shaken by it. For even though the talk had nothing to do with the case, Blue cannot help feeling that Black was actually referring to it all along – talking in riddles, so to speak, as though trying to tell Blue something, but not daring to say it out loud. Yes, Black was more than friendly, his manner was altogether pleasant, but still Blue cannot get rid of the thought that the man was on to him from the start. If so, then Black is surely one of the conspirators – for why else would he have gone on talking to Blue as he did? Not from loneliness, certainly. Assuming that Black is for real, then loneliness cannot be an issue. Everything about his life to this point has been part of a determined plan to remain alone, and it would be absurd to read his willingness to talk as an effort to escape the throes of solitude. Not at this late date, not after more than a year of avoiding all human contact. If Black is finally resolved to break out of his hermetic routine, then why would he begin by talking to a broken-down old man on a street corner? No, Black knew that he was talking to Blue. And if he knew that, then he knows who Blue is. No two ways about it, Blue says to himself: he knows everything.

When the time comes for him to write his next report, Blue is forced to confront this dilemma. White never said anything about making contact with Black. Blue was to watch him, no more, no less, and he wonders now if he has not in fact broken the rules of his assignment. If he includes the conversation in his report, then White might object. On the other hand, if he does not put it in, and if Black is indeed working with White, then White will know immediately that Blue is lying. Blue mulls this over for a long time, but for all that he gets no closer to finding a solution. He's stuck, one way or the other, and he knows it. In the end, he decides to leave it out, but only because he still puts some meagre hope in the fact that he has guessed wrong and that White and Black are not in it together. But this last little stab at optimism comes to naught. Three days after sending in the sanitized report, his weekly cheque comes in the mail, and inside the envelope there is also a note that says, Why do you lie?, and then Blue has proof beyond any shadow of a doubt. And from that moment on, Blue lives with the knowledge that he is drowning.

The next night he follows Black into Manhattan on the subway, dressed in his normal clothes, no longer feeling he has to hide anything. Black gets off at Times Square and wanders around for a while in the bright lights, the noise, the crowds of people surging this way and that. Blue, watching him as though his life depended on it, is never more than three or four steps behind him. At nine o'clock, Black enters the lobby of the Algonquin Hotel, and Blue follows him in. There's quite a crowd milling about, and tables are scarce, so when Black sits down in a corner nook that just that moment has become free, it seems perfectly natural for Blue to approach and politely ask if he can join him. Black has no objection and gestures with an indifferent shrug of the shoulders for Blue to take the chair opposite. For several minutes they say nothing to each other, waiting for someone to take their orders, in the meantime watching the women walk by in their summer dresses, inhaling the different perfumes that flit behind them in the air, and Blue feels no rush to jump into things, content to bide his time and let the business take its course. When the waiter at last comes to ask their pleasure, Black orders a Black and White on the rocks, and Blue cannot help but take this as a secret message that the fun is about to begin, all the while marvelling at Black's effrontery, his crassness, his vulgar obsession. For the sake of symmetry Blue orders the same drink. As he does so, he looks Black in the eyes, but Black gives nothing away, looking back at Blue with utter blankness, dead eyes that seem to say there is nothing behind them and that no matter how hard Blue looks, he will never find a thing.

This gambit nevertheless breaks the ice, and they begin by discussing the merits of various brands of scotch. Plausibly enough, one thing leads to another, and as they sit there chatting about the inconveniences of the New York summer season, the decor of the hotel, the Algonquin Indians who lived in the city long ago when it was all woods and fields, Blue slowly evolves into the character he wants to play for the night, settling on a jovial blowhard by the name of Snow, a life insurance salesman from Kenosha, Wisconsin. Play dumb, Blue tells himself, for he knows that it would make no sense to reveal who he is, even though he knows that Black knows. It's got to be hide and seek, he says, hide and seek to the end.

They finish their first drink and order another round, followed by yet another, and as the talk ambles from actuarial tables to the life expectancies of men in different professions, Black lets fall a remark that turns the conversation in another direction.

I suppose I wouldn't be very high up on your list, he says.

Oh? says Blue having no idea what to expect. What kind of work do you do?

I'm a private detective, says Black, point blank, all cool and collected, and for a brief moment Blue is tempted to throw his drink in Black's face, he's that peeved, that burned at the man's gall.

You don't say! Blue exclaims, quickly recovering and managing to feign a bumpkin's surprise. A private detective. Imagine that.

In the flesh. Just think of what the wife will say when I tell her. Me in New York having drinks with a private eye. She'll never believe it.

What I'm trying to say, says Black rather abruptly, is that I don't imagine my life expectancy is very great. At least not according to your statistics.

Probably not, Blue blusters on. But think of the excitement! There's more to life than living a long time, you know. Half the men in America would give ten years off their retirement to live the way you do. Cracking cases, living by your wits, seducing women, pumping bad guys full of lead – God, there's a lot to be said for it.

That's all make-believe, says Black. Real detective work can be pretty dull.

Well, every job has its routines, Blue continues. But in your case at least you know that all the hard work will eventually lead to something out of the ordinary.

Sometimes yes, sometimes no. But most of the time it's no. Take the case I'm working on now. I've been at it for more than a year already, and nothing could be more boring. I'm so bored that sometimes I think I'm losing my mind.

How so?

Well, figure it out yourself. My job is to watch someone, no one in particular as far as I can tell, and send in a report about him every week. Just that. Watch this guy and write about it. Not one damned thing more.

What's so terrible about that?

He doesn't do anything, that's what. He just sits in his room all day and writes. It's enough to drive you crazy.

It could be that he's leading you along. You know, lulling you to sleep before springing into action.

That's what I thought at first. But now I'm sure that nothing's going to happen – not ever. I can feel it in my bones.

That's too bad, says Blue sympathetically. Maybe you should resign from the case.

I'm thinking about it. I'm also thinking that maybe I should chuck the whole business and go into something else. Some other line of work. Sell insurance, maybe, or run off to join the circus.

I never realized it could get as bad as that, says Blue, shaking his head. But tell me, why aren't you watching your man now? Shouldn't you be keeping an eye on him?

That's just the point, answers Black, I don't even have to bother anymore. I've been watching him for so long now that I know him better than I know myself. All I have to do is think about him, and I know what he's doing, I know where he is, I know everything. It's come to the point that I can watch him with my eyes closed.

Do you know where he is now?

At home. The same as usual. Sitting in his room and writing.

What's he writing about?

I'm not sure, but I have a pretty good idea. I think he's writing about himself. The story of his life. That's the only possible answer. Nothing else would fit.

So why all the mystery?

I don't know, says Black, and for the first time his voice betrays some emotion, catching ever so slightly on the words.

It all boils down to one question, then, doesn't it? says Blue, forgetting all about Snow now and looking Black straight in the eyes. Does he know you're watching him or not?

Black turns away, unable to look at Blue anymore, and says with a suddenly trembling voice: Of course he knows. That's the whole point, isn't it? He's got to know, or else nothing makes sense.

Why?

Because he needs me, says Black, still looking away. He needs my eye looking at him. He needs me to prove he's alive.

Blue sees a tear fall down Black's cheek, but before he can say anything, before he can begin to press home his advantage, Black stands up hastily and excuses himself, saying that he has to make a telephone call. Blue waits in his chair for ten or fifteen minutes, but he knows that he's wasting his time. Black won't be back. The conversation is over, and no matter how long he sits there, nothing more will happen tonight.

Blue pays for the drinks and then heads back to Brooklyn. As he turns down Orange Street, he looks up at Black's window and sees that everything is dark. No matter, says Blue, he'll return before long. We haven't come to the end yet. The party is only beginning. Wait until the champagne is opened, and then we'll see what's what.

Once inside, Blue paces back and forth, trying to plot his next move. It seems to him that Black has finally made a mistake, but he is not quite certain. For in spite of the evidence, Blue cannot shrug the feeling that it was all done on purpose, and that Black has now begun to call out to him, leading him along, so to speak, urging him on towards whatever end he is planning.

Still, he has broken through to something, and for the first time since the case began he is no longer standing where he was. Ordinarily, Blue would be celebrating this little triumph of his, but it turns out that he is in no mood for patting himself on the back tonight. More than anything else, he feels sad, he feels drained of enthusiasm, he feels disappointed in the world. Somehow, the facts have finally let him down, and he finds it hard not to take it personally, knowing full well that however he might present the case to himself, he is a part of it, too. Then he walks to the window, looks out across the street, and sees that the lights are now on in Black's room.

He lies down on his bed and thinks: goodbye, Mr White. You were never really there, were you? There never was such a man as White. And then: poor Black. Poor soul. Poor blighted no one. And then, as his eyes grow heavy and sleep begins to wash over him, he thinks how strange it is that everything has its own colour. Everything we see, everything we touch – everything in the world has its own colour. Struggling to stay awake a little longer, he begins to make a list. Take blue for example, he says. There are bluebirds and blue jays and blue herons. There are cornflowers and periwinkles. There is noon over New York. There are blueberries, huckleberries, and the Pacific Ocean.

There are blue devils and blue ribbons and blue bloods. There is a voice singing the blues. There is my father's police uniform. There are blue laws and blue movies. There are my eyes and my name. He pauses, suddenly at a loss for more blue things, and then moves on to white. There are seagulls, he says, and terns and storks and cockatoos. There are the walls of this room and the sheets on my bed. There are lilies-of-the-valley, carnations, and the petals of daisies. There is the flag of peace and Chinese death. There is mother's milk and semen. There are my teeth. There are the whites of my eyes. There are white bass and white pines and white ants. There is the President's house and white rot. There are white lies and white heat. Then, without hesitating, he moves on to black, beginning with black books, the black market, and the Black Hand. There is night over New York, he says. There are the Chicago Black Sox. There are blackberries and crows, blackouts and black marks, Black Tuesday and the Black Death. There is blackmail. There is my hair. There is the ink that comes out of a pen. There is the world a blind man sees. Then, finally growing tired of the game, he begins to drift, saying to himself that there is no end to it. He falls asleep, dreams of things that happened long ago, and then, in the middle of the night, wakes up suddenly and begins pacing the room again, thinking about what he will do next.

Morning comes, and Blue starts busying himself with another disguise. This time it's the Fuller brush man, a trick he has used before, and for the next two hours he patiently goes about giving himself a bald head, a moustache, and age lines around his eyes and mouth, sitting in front of his little mirror like an old-time vaudevillian on tour. Shortly after eleven o'clock, he gathers up his case of brushes and walks across the street to Black's building. Picking the lock on the front door is child's play for Blue, no more than a matter of seconds, and as he slips into the hallway he can't help feeling something of the old thrill. No tough stuff, he reminds himself, as he starts climbing the stairs to Black's floor. This visit is only to get a look inside, to stake out the room for future reference. Still, there's an excitement to the moment that

Blue can't quite suppress. For it's more than just seeing the room, he knows – it's the thought of being there himself, of standing inside those four walls, of breathing the same air as Black. From now on, he thinks, everything that happens will affect everything else. The door will open, and after that Black will be inside of him forever.

He knocks, the door opens, and suddenly there is no more distance, the thing and the thought of the thing are one and the same. Then it's Black who is there, standing in the doorway with an uncapped fountain pen in his right hand, as though interrupted in his work, and yet with a look in his eyes that tells Blue he's been expecting him, resigned to the hard truth, but no longer seeming to care.

Blue launches into his patter about the brushes, pointing to the case, offering apologies, asking admittance, all in the same breath, with that rapid salesman's pitch he's done a thousand times before. Black calmly lets him in, saying he might be interested in a toothbrush, and as Blue steps across the sill, he goes rattling on about hair brushes and clothes brushes, anything to keep the words flowing, for in that way he can leave the rest of himself free to take in the room, observe the observable, think, all the while diverting Black from his true purpose.

The room is much as he imagined it would be, though perhaps even more austere. Nothing on the walls, for example, which surprises him a little, since he always thought there would be a picture or two, an image of some kind just to break the monotony, a nature scene perhaps, or else a portrait of someone Black might once have loved. Blue was always curious to know what the picture would be, thinking it might be a valuable clue, but now that he sees there is nothing, he understands that this is what he should have expected all along. Other than that, there's precious little to contradict his former notions. It's the same monk's cell he saw in his mind: the small, neatly made bed in one corner, the kitchenette in another corner, everything spotless, not a crumb to be seen. Then, in the centre of the room facing the window, the wooden table with a single stiffbacked wooden chair. Pencils, pens, a typewriter. A bureau, a night table, a lamp. A bookcase on the north wall, but no more than several books in it: *Walden*, *Leaves of Grass*, *Twice-Told Tales*, a few others. No telephone, no radio, no magazines. On the table, neatly stacked around the edges, piles of paper: some blank, some written on, some typed, some in longhand. Hundreds of pages, perhaps thousands. But you can't call this a life, thinks Blue. You can't really call it anything. It's a no man's land, the place you come to at the end of the world.

They look through the toothbrushes, and Black finally chooses a red one. From there they start examining the various clothes brushes, with Blue giving demonstrations on his own suit. For a man as neat as yourself, says Blue, I should think you'd find it indispensable. But black says he's managed so far without one. On the other hand, maybe he'd like to consider a hair brush, and so they go through the possibilities in the sample case, discussing the different sizes and shapes, the different kinds of bristles, and so on. Blue is already done with his real business, of course, but he goes through the motions nevertheless, wanting to do the thing right, even if it doesn't matter. Still, after Black has paid for the brushes and Blue is packing up his case to go, he can't resist making one little remark. You seem to be a writer, he says, gesturing to the table, and Black says yes, that's right, he's a writer.

It looks like a big book, Blue continues.

Yes, says Black. I've been working on it for many years.

Are you almost finished?

I'm getting there, Black says thoughtfully. But sometimes it's hard to know where you are. I think I'm almost done, and then I realize I've left out something important, and so I have to go back to the beginning again. But yes, I do dream of finishing it one day. One day soon, perhaps.

I hope I get a chance to read it, says Blue.

Anything is possible, says Black. But first of all, I've got to finish it. There are days when I don't even know if I'll live that long.

Well, we never know, do we? says Blue, nodding philosophically. One day we're alive, and the next day we're dead. It happens to all of us.

Very true, says Black. It happens to all of us.

They're standing by the door now, and something in Blue wants to go on making inane remarks of this sort. Playing the buffoon is enjoyable, he realizes, but at the same time there's an urge to toy with Black, to prove that nothing has escaped him – for deep down Blue wants Black to know that he's just as smart as he is, that he can match wits with him every step of the way. But Blue manages to fight back the impulse and hold his tongue, nodding politely in thanks for the sales, and then makes his exit. That's the end of the Fuller brush man, and less than an hour later he is discarded into the same bag that holds the remains of Jimmy Rose. Blue knows that no more disguises will be needed. The next step is inevitable, and the only thing that matters now is to choose the right moment.

But three nights later, when he finally gets his chance, Blue realizes that he's scared. Black goes out at nine o'clock, walks down the street, and vanishes around the corner. Although Blue knows that this is a direct signal, that Black is practically begging him to make his move, he also feels that it could be a set-up, and now, at the last possible moment, when only just before he was filled with confidence, almost swaggering with a sense of his own power, he sinks into a fresh torment of self-doubt. Why should he suddenly begin to trust Black? What earthly cause could there be for him to think they are both working on the same side now? How has this happened, and why does he find himself so obsequiously at Black's bidding once again? Then, from out of the blue, he begins to consider another possibility. What if he just simply left? What if he stood up, went out the door, and walked away from the whole business? He ponders this thought for a while, testing it out in his mind, and little by little he begins to tremble, overcome by terror and happiness, like a slave stumbling onto a vision of his own freedom. He imagines himself somewhere else, far away from here, walking through the woods and swinging an axe over his shoulder. Alone and free, his own man at last. He would build his life from the bottom up, an exile, a pioneer, a pilgrim in the new world. But that is as far as he gets. For no sooner does he begin to walk through these woods in the middle of nowhere than he feels that Black is there too, hiding behind some tree, stalking invisibly through some thicket, waiting for Blue to lie down and close his eyes before sneaking up on him and slitting his throat. It goes on and on, Blue thinks. If he doesn't take care of Black now, there will never be any end to it. This is what the ancients called fate, and every hero must submit to it. There is no choice, and if there is anything to be done, it is only the one thing that leaves no choice. But Blue is loath to acknowledge it. He struggles against it, he rejects it, he grows sick at heart. But that is only because he already knows, and to fight it is already to have accepted it, to want to say no is already to have said yes. And so Blue gradually comes round, at last giving in to the necessity of the thing to be done. But that is not to say he does not feel afraid. From this moment on, there is only one word that speaks for Blue, and that word is fear.

He has wasted valuable time, and now he must rush forth onto the street, hoping feverishly it is not too late. Black will not be gone forever, and who knows if he is not lurking around the corner, just waiting for the moment to pounce? Blue races up the steps of Black's building, fumbles awkwardly as he picks the front door lock, continually glancing over his shoulder, and then goes up the stairs to Black's floor. The second lock gives him more trouble than the first, though theoretically it should be simpler, an easy job even for the rawest beginner. This clumsiness tells Blue that he's losing control, letting it all get the better of him; but even though he knows it, there's little he can do but ride it out and hope that his hands will stop shaking. But it goes from bad to worse, and the moment he sets foot in Black's room, he feels everything go dark inside him, as though the night were pressing through his pores, sitting on top of him with a tremendous weight, and at the same time his head seems to be growing, filling with air as though about to detach itself from his body and float away. He takes one more step into the room and then blacks out, collapsing to the floor like a dead man.

His watch stops with the fall, and when he comes to he doesn't know how long he's been out. Dimly at first, he regains consciousness with a sense of having been here before, perhaps long ago, and as he sees the curtains fluttering by the open window and the shadows moving strangely on the ceiling, he thinks that he is lying in bed at home, back when he was a little boy, unable to sleep during the hot summer nights, and he imagines that if he listens hard enough he will be able to hear the voices of his mother and father talking quietly in the next room. But this lasts only a moment. He begins to feel the ache in his head, to register the disturbing queasiness in his stomach, and then, finally seeing where he is, to relive the panic that gripped him the moment he entered the room. He scrambles shakily to his feet, stumbling once or twice in the process, and tells himself he can't stay here, he's got to be going, yes, and right away. He grabs hold of the doorknob, but then, remembering suddenly why he came here in the first place, snatches the flashlight from his pocket and turns it on, waving it fitfully around the room until the light falls by chance on a pile of papers stacked neatly at the edge of Black's desk. Without thinking twice, Blue gathers up the papers with his free hand, saying to himself it doesn't matter, this will be a start, and then makes his way to the door.

Back in his room across the street, Blue pours himself a glass of brandy, sits down on his bed, and tells himself to be calm. He drinks off the brandy sip by sip and then pours himself another glass. As his panic begins to subside, he is left with a feeling of shame. He's botched it, he tells himself, and that's the long and the short of it. For the first time in his life he has not been equal to the moment, and it comes as a shock to him – to see himself as a failure, to realize that at bottom he's a coward.

He picks up the papers he has stolen, hoping to distract himself from these thoughts. But this only compounds the problem, for once he begins to read them, he sees they are nothing more than his own reports. There they are, one after the other, the weekly accounts, all spelled out in black and white, meaning nothing, saying nothing, as far from the truth of the case as silence would have been. Blue groans when he sees them, sinking down deep within himself, and then, in the face of what he finds there, begins to laugh, at first faintly, but with growing force, louder and louder, until he is gasping for breath, almost choking on it, as though trying to obliterate himself once and for all. Taking the papers firmly in his hand, he flings them up to the ceiling and watches the pile break apart, scatter, and come fluttering to the ground, page by miserable page.

It is not certain that Blue ever really recovers from the events of this night. And even if he does, it must be noted that several days go by before he returns to a semblance of his former self. In that time he does not shave, he does not change his clothes, he does not even contemplate stirring from his room. When the day comes for him to write his next report, he does not bother. It's finished now, he says, kicking one of the old reports on the floor, and I'll be damned if I ever write one of those again.

For the most part, he either lies on his bed or paces back and forth in his room. He looks at the various pictures he has tacked onto the walls since starting the case, studying each one in its turn, thinking about it for as long as he can, and then passing on to the next. There is the coroner from Philadelphia, Gold, with the death mask of the little boy. There is a snow-covered mountain, and in the upper right hand corner of the photograph, an inset of the French skier, his face enclosed in a small box. There is the Brooklyn Bridge, and next to it the two Roeblings, father and son. There is Blue's father, dressed in his police uniform and receiving a medal from the mayor of New York, Jimmy Walker. Again there is Blue's father, this time in his street clothes, standing with his arm around Blue's mother in the early days of their marriage, the two of them smiling brightly into the camera. There is a picture of Brown with his arm around Blue, taken in front of their office on the day Blue was made a partner. Below it there is an action shot of Jackie Robinson sliding into second base. Next to that there is a portrait of Walt Whitman. And finally,

189

directly to the poet's left, there is a movie still of Robert Mitchum from one of the fan magazines: gun in hand, looking as though the world is about to cave in on him. There is no picture of the ex-future Mrs Blue, but each time Blue makes a tour of his little gallery, he pauses in front of a certain blank spot on the wall and pretends that she, too, is there.

For several days, Blue does not bother to look out the window. He has enclosed himself so thoroughly in his own thoughts that Black no longer seems to be there. The drama is Blue's alone, and if Black is in some sense the cause of it, it's as though he has already played his part, spoken his lines, and made his exit from the stage. For Blue at this point can no longer accept Black's existence, and therefore he denies it. Having penetrated Black's room and stood there alone, having been, so to speak, in the sanctum of Black's solitude, he cannot respond to the darkness of that moment except by replacing it with a solitude of his own. To enter Black, then, was the equivalent of entering himself, and once inside himself, he can no longer conceive of being anywhere else. But this is precisely where Black is, even though Blue does not know it.

One afternoon, therefore, as if by chance, Blue comes closer to the window than he has in many days, happens to pause in front of it, and then, as if for old time's sake, parts the curtains and looks outside. The first thing he sees is Black – not inside his room, but sitting on the stoop of his building across the street, looking up at Blue's window. Is he finished, then? Blue wonders. Does this mean it's over?

Blue retrieves his binoculars from the back of the room and returns to the window. Bringing them into focus on Black, he studies the man's face for several minutes, first one feature and then another, the eyes, the lips, the nose, and so on, taking the face apart and then putting it back together. He is moved by the depth of Black's sadness, the way the eyes looking up at him seem so devoid of hope, and in spite of himself, caught unawares by this image, Blue feels compassion rising up to him, a rush of pity for that forlorn figure across the street. He wishes it were not so, however, wishes he had the courage to load his gun, take aim at Black, and fire a bullet through his head. He'd never know what hit him, Blue thinks, he'd be in heaven before he touched the ground. But as soon as he has played out this little scene in his mind, he begins to recoil from it. No, he realizes, that's not what he wishes at all. If not that, then – what? Still struggling against the surge of tender feelings, saying to himself that he wants to be left alone, that all he wants is peace and quiet, it gradually dawns on him that he has in fact been standing there for several minutes wondering if there is not some way that he might help Black, if it would not be possible for him to offer his hand in friendship. That would certainly turn the tables, Blue thinks, that would certainly stand the whole business on its head. But why not? Why not do the unexpected? To knock on the door, to erase the whole story – it's no less absurd than anything else. For the fact of the matter is, all the fight has been taken out of Blue. He no longer has the stomach for it. And, to all appearances, neither does Black. Just look at him, Blue says to himself. He's the saddest creature in the world. And then, the moment he says these words, he understands that he's also talking about himself.

Long after Black leaves the steps, therefore, turning around and re-entering the building, Blue goes on staring at the vacant spot. An hour or two before dusk, he finally turns from the window, sees the disorder he has allowed his room to fall into, and spends the next hour straightening things up – washing the dishes, making the bed, putting away his clothes, removing the old reports from the floor. Then he goes into the bathroom, takes a long shower, shaves, and puts on fresh clothes, selecting his best blue suit for the occasion. Everything is different for him now, suddenly and irrevocably different. There is no more dread, no more trembling. Nothing but a calm assurance, a sense of rightness in the thing he is about to do.

Shortly after nightfall, he adjusts his tie one last time before the mirror and then leaves the room, going outside, crossing the street, and entering Black's building. He knows that Black is there, since a small lamp is on in his room, and as he walks up the stairs he tries to imagine the expression that will come over Black's face when he tells him what he has in mind. He knocks twice on the door, very politely, and then hears Black's voice from within: The door's open. Come in.

It is difficult to say exactly what Blue was expecting to find – but in all events, it was not this, not the thing that confronts him the moment he steps into the room. Black is there, sitting on his bed, and he's wearing the mask again, the same one Blue saw on the man in the post office, and in his right hand he's holding a gun, a thirty-eight revolver, enough to blow a man apart at such close range, and he's pointing it directly at Blue. Blue stops in his tracks, says nothing. So much for burying the hatchet, he thinks. So much for turning the tables.

Sit down in the chair, Blue, says Black, gesturing with the gun to the wooden desk chair. Blue has no choice, and so he sits – now facing Black, but too far away to make a lunge at him, too awkwardly positioned to do anything about the gun.

I've been waiting for you, says Black. I'm glad you finally made it.

I figured as much, answers Blue.

Are you surprised?

Not really. At least not at you. Myself maybe – but only because I'm so stupid. You see, I came here tonight in friendship.

But of course you did, says Black, in a slightly mocking voice. Of course we're friends. We've been friends from the beginning, haven't we? The very best of friends.

If this is how you treat your friends, says Blue, then lucky for me I'm not one of your enemies.

Very funny.

That's right, I'm the original funny man. You can always count on a lot of laughs when I'm around.

And the mask – aren't you going to ask me about the mask?

I don't see why. If you want to wear that thing, it's not my problem.

But you have to look at it, don't you?

Why ask questions when you already know the answer?

It's grotesque, isn't it?

Of course it's grotesque.

And frightening to look at.

Yes, very frightening.

Good. I like you, Blue. I always knew you were the right one for me. A man after my own heart.

If you stopped waving that gun around, maybe I'd start feeling the same about you.

I'm sorry, I can't do that. It's too late now.

Which means?

I don't need you anymore, Blue.

It might not be so easy to get rid of me, you know. You got me into this, and now you're stuck with me.

No, Blue, you're wrong. Everything is over now.

Stop the doubletalk.

It's finished. The whole thing is played out. There's nothing more to be done.

Since when?

Since now. Since this moment.

You're out of your mind.

No, Blue. If anything, I'm in my mind, too much in my mind. It's used me up, and now there's nothing left. But you know that, Blue, you know that better than anyone.

So why don't you just pull the trigger?

When I'm ready, I will.

And then walk out of here leaving my body on the floor? Fat chance.

Oh no, Blue. You don't understand. It's going to be the two of us together, just like always.

But you're forgetting something, aren't you?

Forgetting what?

You're supposed to tell me the story. Isn't that how it's supposed to end? You tell me the story, and then we say goodbye.

You know it already, Blue. Don't you understand that? You know the story by heart.

Then why did you bother in the first place?

Don't ask stupid questions.

And me – what was I there for? Comic relief?

No, Blue, I've needed you from the beginning. If it hadn't been for you, I couldn't have done it.

Needed me for what?

To remind me of what I was supposed to be doing. Every time I looked up, you were there, watching me, following me, always in sight, boring into me with your eyes. You were the whole world to me, Blue, and I turned you into my death. You're the one thing that doesn't change, the one thing that turns everything inside out.

And now there's nothing left. You've written your suicide note, and that's the end of it.

Exactly.

You're a fool. You're a goddamned, miserable fool.

I know that. But no more than anyone else. Are you going to sit there and tell me that you're smarter than I am? At least I know what I've been doing. I've had my job to do, and I've done it. But you're nowhere, Blue. You've been lost from the first day.

Why don't you pull the trigger, then, you bastard? says Blue, suddenly standing up and pounding his chest in anger, daring Black to kill him. Why don't you shoot me now and get it over with?

Blue then takes a step towards Black, and when the bullet doesn't come, he takes another, and then another, screaming at the masked man to shoot, no longer caring if he lives or dies. A moment later, he's right up against him. Without hesitating he swats the gun out of Black's hand, grabs him by the collar, and yanks him to his feet. Black tries to resist, tries to struggle against Blue, but Blue is too strong for him, all crazy with the passion of his anger, as though turned into someone else, and as the first blows begin to land on Black's face and groin and stomach, the man can do nothing, and not long after that he's out cold on the floor. But that does not prevent Blue from continuing the assault, batttering the unconscious Black with his feet, picking him up and banging his head on the floor, pelting his body with one punch after another. Eventually, when Blue's fury begins to abate and he sees what he has done, he cannot say for certain whether Black is alive or dead. He removes the mask from Black's face and puts his ear against his mouth, listening for the sound of Black's breath. There seems to be something, but he can't tell if it's coming from Black or himself. If he's alive now, Blue thinks, it won't be for long. And if he's dead, then so be it.

Blue stands up, his suit all in tatters, and begins collecting the pages of Black's manuscript from the desk. This takes several minutes. When he has all of them, he turns off the lamp in the corner and leaves the room, not even bothering to give Black a last look.

It's past midnight when Blue gets back to his room across the street. He puts the manuscript down on the table, goes into the bathroom, and washes the blood off his hands. Then he changes his clothes, pours himself a glass of Scotch, and sits down at the table with Black's book. Time is short. They'll be coming before he knows it, and then there will be hell to pay. Still, he does not let this interfere with the business at hand.

He reads the story right through, every word of it from beginning to end. By the time he finishes, dawn has come, and the room has begun to brighten. He hears a bird sing, he hears footsteps going down the street, he hears a car driving across the Brooklyn Bridge. Black was right, he says to himself. I knew it all by heart.

But the story is not yet over. There is still the final moment, and that will not come until Blue leaves the room. Such is the way of the world: not one moment more, not one moment less. When Blue stands up from his chair, puts on his hat, and walks through the door, that will be the end of it.

Where he goes after that is not important. For we must remember that all this took place more than thirty years ago, back in the days of our earliest childhood. Anything is possible, therefore. I myself prefer to think that he went far away, boarding a train that morning and going out West to start a new life. It is even possible that America was not the end of it. In my secret dreams, I like to think of Blue booking passage on some ship and sailing to China. Let it be China, then, and we'll leave it at that. For now is the moment that Blue stands up from his chair, puts on his hat, and walks through the door. And from this moment on, we know nothing.

The Locked Room

1

It seems to me now that Fanshawe was always there. He is the place where everything begins for me, and without him I would hardly know who I am. We met before we could talk, babies crawling through the grass in diapers, and by the time we were seven we had pricked our fingers with pins and made ourselves blood brothers for life. Whenever I think of my childhood now, I see Fanshawe. He was the one who was with me, the one who shared my thoughts, the one I saw whenever I looked up from myself.

But that was a long time ago. We grew up, went off to different places, drifted apart. None of that is very strange, I think. Our lives carry us along in ways we cannot control, and almost nothing stays with us. It dies when we do, and death is something that happens to us every day.

Seven years ago this November, I received a letter from a woman named Sophie Fanshawe. 'You don't know me,' the letter began, 'and I apologize for writing to you like this out of the blue. But things have happened, and under the circumstances I don't have much choice.' It turned out that she was Fanshawe's wife. She knew that I had grown up with her husband, and she also knew that I lived in New York, since she had read many of the articles I had published in magazines.

The explanation came in the second paragraph, very bluntly, without any preamble. Fanshawe had disappeared, she wrote, and it was more than six months since she had last seen him. Not a word in all that time, not the slightest clue as to where he might be. The police had found no trace of him, and the private detective she hired to look for him had come up empty-handed. Nothing was sure, but the facts seemed to speak for themselves: Fanshawe was probably dead; it was pointless to think he would be coming back. In the light of all this, there was something important she needed to discuss with me, and she wondered if I would agree to see her.

This letter caused a series of little shocks in me. There was too much information to absorb all at once; too many forces were pulling me in different directions. Out of nowhere, Fanshawe had suddenly reappeared in my life. But no sooner was his name mentioned than he had vanished again. He was married, he had been living in New York – and I knew nothing about him any more. Selfishly, I felt hurt that he had not bothered to get in touch with me. A phone call, a post card, a drink to catch up on old times – it would not have been difficult to arrange. But the fault was equally my own. I knew where Fanshawe's mother lived, and if I had wanted to find him, I could easily have asked her. The fact was that I had let go of Fanshawe. His life had stopped the moment we went our separate ways, and he belonged to the past for me now, not to the present. He was a ghost I carried around inside me, a prehistoric figment, a thing that was no longer real. I tried to remember the last time I had seen him, but nothing was clear. My mind wandered for several minutes and then stopped short, fixing on the day his father died. We were in high school then and could not have been more than seventeen years old.

I called Sophie Fanshawe and told her I would be glad to see her whenever it was convenient. We decided on the following day, and she sounded grateful, even though I explained to her that I had not heard from Fanshawe and had no idea where he was.

She lived in a red-brick tenement in Chelsea, an old walk-up building with gloomy stairwells and peeling paint on the walls. I climbed the five flights to her floor, accompanied by the sounds of radios and squabbles and flushing toilets that came from the apartments on the way up, paused to catch my breath, and then knocked. An eye looked through the peephole in the door, there was a clatter of bolts being turned, and then Sophie Fanshawe was standing before me, holding a small baby in her left arm. As she smiled at me and invited me in, the baby tugged at her long brown hair. She ducked away gently from the attack, took hold of her child with her two hands, and turned him face front towards me. This was Ben, she said, Fanshawe's son, and he had been born just three-and-a-half months ago. I pretended to admire the baby, who was waving his arms and drooling whitish spittle down his chin, but I was more interested in his mother. Fanshawe had been lucky. The woman was beautiful, with dark, intelligent eyes, almost fierce in their steadiness. Thin, not more than average height, and with something slow in her manner, a thing that made her both sensual and watchful, as though she looked out on the world from the heart of a deep inner vigilance. No man would have left this woman of his own free will – especially not when she was about to have his child. That much was certain to me. Even before I stepped into the apartment, I knew that Fanshawe had to be dead.

It was a small railroad flat with four rooms, sparsely furnished, with one room set aside for books and a work table, another that served as the living room, and the last two for sleeping. The place was well-ordered, shabby in its details, but on the whole not uncomfortable. If nothing else, it proved that Fanshawe had not spent his time making money. But I was not one to look down my nose at shabbiness. My own apartment was even more cramped and dark than this one, and I knew what it was to struggle each month to come up with the rent.

Sophie Fanshawe gave me a chair to sit in, made me a cup of coffee, and then sat down on the tattered blue sofa. With the baby on her lap, she told me the story of Fanshawe's disappearance.

They had met in New York three years ago. Within a month they had moved in together, and less than a year after that they were married. Fanshawe was not an easy man to live with, she said, but she loved him, and there had never been anything in his behaviour to suggest that he did not love her. They had been happy together; he had been looking forward to the birth of the baby; there was no bad blood between them. One day in April he told her that he was going to New Jersey for the afternoon to see his mother, and then he did not come back. When Sophie called her mother-in-law late that night, she learned that Fanshawe had never made the visit. Nothing like this had ever happened before, but Sophie decided to wait it out. She didn't want to be one of those wives who panicked whenever her husband failed to show up, and she knew that Fanshawe needed more breathing room than most men. She even decided not to ask any questions when he returned home. But then a week went by, and then another week, and at last she went to the police. As she expected, they were not overly concerned about her problem. Unless there was evidence of a crime, there was little they could do. Husbands, after all, deserted their wives every day, and most of them did not want to be found. The police made a few routine inquiries, came up with nothing, and then suggested that she hire a private detective. With the help of her mother-in-law, who offered to pay the costs, she engaged the services of a man named Quinn. Quinn worked doggedly on the case for five or six weeks, but in the end he begged off, not wanting to take any more of their money. He told Sophie that Fanshawe was most likely still in the country, but whether alive or dead he could not say. Quinn was no charlatan. Sophie found him sympathetic, a man who genuinely wanted to help, and when he came to her that last day she realized it was impossible to argue against his verdict. There was nothing to be done. If Fanshawe had decided to leave her, he would not have stolen off without a word. It was not like him to shy away from the truth, to back down from unpleasant confrontations. His disappearance could therefore mean only one thing: that some terrible harm had come to him.

Still, Sophie went on hoping that something would turn up. She had read about cases of amnesia, and for a while this took hold of her as a desperate possibility: the thought of Fanshawe staggering around somewhere not knowing who he was, robbed of his life but nevertheless alive, perhaps on the verge of returning to himself at any moment. More weeks passed and then the end of her pregnancy began to approach. The baby was due in less than a month – which meant that it could come at any time –

and little by little the unborn child began to take up all her thoughts, as though there was no more room inside her for Fanshawe. These were the words she used to describe the feeling – no more room inside her – and then she went on to say that this probably meant that in spite of everything she was angry at Fanshawe, angry at him for having abandoned her, even though it wasn't his fault. This statement struck me as brutally honest. I had never heard anyone talk about personal feelings like that – so unsparingly, with such disregard for conventional pieties – and as I write this now, I realize that even on that first day I had slipped through a hole in the earth, that I was falling into a place where I had never been before.

One morning, Sophie continued, she woke up after a difficult night and understood that Fanshawe would not be coming back. It was a sudden, absolute truth, never again to be questioned. She cried then, and went on crying for a week, mourning Fanshawe as though he were dead. When the tears stopped, however, she found herself without regrets. Fanshawe had been given to her for a number of years, she decided, and that was all. Now there was the child to think about, and nothing else really mattered. She knew this sounded rather pompous – but the fact was that she continued to live with this sense of things, and it continued to make life possible for her.

I asked her a series of questions, and she answered each one calmly, deliberately, as though making an effort not to colour the responses with her own feelings. How they had lived, for example, and what work Fanshawe had done, and what had happened to him in the years since I had last seen him. The baby started fussing on the sofa, and without any pause in the conversation, Sophie opened her blouse and nursed him, first on one breast and then on the other.

She could not be sure of anything prior to her first meeting with Fanshawe, she said. She knew that he had dropped out of college after two years, had managed to get a deferment from the army, and wound up working on a ship of some sort for a while. An oil tanker, she thought, or perhaps a freighter. After that, he had

203

lived in France for several years – first in Paris, then as the caretaker of a farmhouse in the South. But all this was quite dim to her, since Fanshawe had never talked much about the past. At the time they met, he had not been back in America more than eight or ten months. They literally bumped into each other – the two of them standing by the door of a Manhattan bookshop one wet Saturday afternoon, looking through the window and waiting for the rain to stop. That was the beginning, and from that day until the day Fanshawe disappeared, they had been together nearly all the time.

Fanshawe had never had any regular work, she said, nothing that could be called a real job. Money didn't mean much to him, and he tried to think about it as little as possible. In the years before he met Sophie, he had done all kinds of things – the stint in the merchant marine, working in a warehouse, tutoring, ghost writing, waiting on tables, painting apartments, hauling furniture for a moving company – but each job was temporary, and once he had earned enough to keep himself going for a few months, he would quit. When he and Sophie began living together, Fanshawe did not work at all. She had a job teaching music in a private school, and her salary could support them both. They had to be careful, of course, but there was always food on the table, and neither of them had any complaints.

I did not interrupt. It seemed clear to me that this catalogue was only a beginning, details to be disposed of before turning to the business at hand. Whatever Fanshawe had done with his life, it had little connection with this list of odd jobs. I knew this immediately, in advance of anything that was said. We were not talking about just anyone, after all. This was Fanshawe, and the past was not so remote that I could not remember who he was.

Sophie smiled when she saw that I was ahead of her, that I knew what was coming. I think she had expected me to know, and this merely confirmed that expectation, erasing any doubts she might have had about asking me to come. I knew without having to be told, and that gave me the right to be there, to be listening to what she had to say.

'He went on with his writing,' I said. 'He became a writer, didn't he?'

Sophie nodded. That was exactly it. Or part of it, in any case. What puzzled me was why I have never heard of him. If Fanshawe was a writer, then surely I would have run across his name somewhere. It was my business to know about these things, and it seemed unlikely that Fanshawe, of all people, would have escaped my attention. I wondered if he had been unable to find a publisher for his work. It was the only question that seemed logical.

No, Sophie said, it was more complicated than that. He had never tried to publish. At first, when he was very young, he was too timid to send anything out, feeling that his work was not good enough. But even later, when his confidence had grown, he discovered that he preferred to stay in hiding. It would distract him to start looking for a publisher, he told her, and when it came right down to it, he would much rather spend his time on the work itself. Sophie was upset by this indifference, but whenever she pressed him about it, he would answer with a shrug: there's no rush, sooner or later he would get around to it.

Once or twice, she actually thought of taking matters into her own hands and smuggling a manuscript out to a publisher, but she never went through with it. There were rules in a marriage that couldn't be broken, and no matter how wrong-headed his attitude was, she had little choice but to go along with him. There was a great quantity of work, she said, and it maddened her to think of it just sitting there in the closet, but Fanshawe deserved her loyalty, and she did her best to say nothing.

One day, about three or four months before he disappeared, Fanshawe came to her with a compromise gesture. He gave her his word that he would do something about it within a year, and to prove that he meant it, he told her that if for any reason he failed to keep up his end of the bargain, she was to take all his manuscripts to me and put them in my hands. I was the guardian of his work, he said, and it was up to me to decide what should happen to it. If I thought it was worth publishing, he would give in to my judgement. Furthermore, he said, if anything should happen to him in the meantime, she was to give me the manuscripts at once and allow me to make all the arrangements, with the understanding that I would receive twenty-five per cent of any money the work happened to earn. If I thought his writings were not worth publishing, however, then I should return the manuscripts to Sophie, and she was to destroy them, right down to the last page.

These pronouncements startled her, Sophie said, and she almost laughed at Fanshawe for being so solemn about it. The whole scene was out of character for him, and she wondered if it didn't have something to do with the fact that she had just become pregnant. Perhaps the idea of fatherhood had sobered him into a new sense of responsibility; perhaps he was so determined to prove his good intentions that he had overstated the case. Whatever the reason, she found herself glad that he had changed his mind. As her pregnancy advanced, she even began to have secret dreams of Fanshawe's success, hoping that she would be able to quit her job and raise the child without any financial pressure. Everything had gone wrong, of course, and Fanshawe's work was soon forgotten, lost in the turmoil that followed his disappearance. Later, when the dust began to settle, she had resisted carrying out his instructions – for fear that it would jinx any chance she had of seeing him again. But eventually she gave in, knowing that Fanshawe's word had to be respected. That was why she had written to me. That was why I was sitting with her now.

For my part, I didn't know how to react. The proposition had caught me off guard, and for a minute or two I just sat there, wrestling with the enormous thing that had been thrust at me. As far as I could tell, there was no earthly reason for Fanshawe to have chosen me for this job. I had not seen him in more than ten years, and I was almost surprised to learn that he still remembered who I was. How could I be expected to take on such a responsibility – to stand in judgement of a man and say whether his life had been worth living? Sophie tried to explain. Fanshawe had not been in touch, she said, but he had often talked to her about me, and each time my name had been mentioned, I was described as his best friend in the world – the one true friend he had ever had. He had also managed to keep up with my work, always buying the magazines in which my articles appeared, and sometimes even reading the pieces aloud to her. He admired what I did, Sophie said; he was proud of me, and he felt that I had it in me to do something great.

All this praise embarrassed me. There was so much intensity in Sophie's voice, I somehow felt that Fanshawe was speaking through her, telling me these things with his own lips. I admit that I was flattered, and no doubt that was a natural feeling under the circumstances. I was having a hard time of it just then, and the fact was that I did not share this high opinion of myself. I had written a great many articles, it was true, but I did not see that as a cause for celebration, nor was I particularly proud of it. As far as I was concerned, it was just a little short of hack work. I had begun with great hopes, thinking that I would become a novelist, thinking that I would eventually be able to write something that would touch people and make a difference in their lives. But time went on, and little by little I realized that this was not going to happen. I did not have such a book inside me, and at a certain point I told myself to give up my dreams. It was simpler to go on writing articles in any case. By working hard, by moving steadily from one piece to the next, I could more or less earn a living – and, for whatever it was worth, I had the pleasure of seeing my name in print almost constantly. I understood that things could have been far more dismal than they were. I was not quite thirty, and already I had something of a reputation. I had begun with reviews of poetry and novels, and now I could write about nearly anything and do a creditable job. Movies, plays, art shows, concerts, books, even baseball games – they had only to ask, and I would do it. The world saw me as a bright young fellow, a new critic on the rise, but inside myself I felt old, already used up. What I had done so far amounted to a mere fraction of nothing at all. It was so much dust, and the slightest wind would blow it away.

Fanshawe's praise, therefore, left me with mixed feelings. On the one hand, I knew that he was wrong. On the other hand (and this is where it gets murky), I wanted to believe that he was right. I thought: is it possible that I've been too hard on myself? And once I began to think that, I was lost. But who wouldn't jump at the chance to redeem himself – what man is strong enough to reject the possibility of hope? The thought flickered through me that I could one day be resurrected in my own eyes, and I felt a sudden burst of friendship for Fanshawe across the years, across all the silence of the years that had kept us apart.

That was how it happened. I succumbed to the flattery of a man who wasn't there, and in that moment of weakness I said yes. I'll be glad to read the work, I said, and do whatever I can to help. Sophie smiled at this – whether from happiness or disappointment I could never tell – and then stood up from the sofa and carried the baby into the next room. She stopped in front of a tall oak cupboard, unlatched the door, and let it swing open on its hinges. There you are, she said. There were boxes and binders and folders and notebooks cramming the shelves – more things than I would have thought possible. I remember laughing with embarrassment and making some feeble joke. Then, all business, we discussed the best way for me to carry the manuscripts out of the apartment, eventually deciding on two large suitcases. It took the better part of an hour, but in the end we managed to squeeze everything in. Clearly, I said, it was going to take me some time to sift through all the material. Sophie told me not to worry, and then she apologized for burdening me with such a job. I said that I understood, that there was no way she could have refused to carry out Fanshawe's request. It was all very dramatic, and at the same time gruesome, almost comical. The beautiful Sophie delicately put the baby down on the floor, gave me a great hug of thanks, and then kissed me on the cheek. For a moment I thought she was going to cry, but the moment passed and there were no tears. Then I hauled the two suitcases slowly down the stairs and onto the street. Together, they were as heavy as a man.

2

The truth is far less simple than I would like it to be. That I loved Fanshawe, that he was my closest friend, that I knew him better than anyone else – these are facts, and nothing I say can ever diminish them. But that is only a beginning, and in my struggle to remember things as they really were, I see now that I also held back from Fanshawe, that a part of me always resisted him. Especially as we grew older, I do not think I was ever entirely comfortable in his presence. If envy is too strong a word for what I am trying to say, then I would call it a suspicion, a secret feeling that Fanshawe was somehow better than I was. All this was unknown to me at the time, and there was never anything specific that I could point to. Yet the feeling lingered that there was more innate goodness in him than in others, that some unquenchable fire was keeping him alive, that he was more truly himself than I could ever hope to be.

Early on, his influence was already quite pronounced. This extended even to very small things. If Fanshawe wore his belt buckle on the side of his pants, then I would move my belt into the same position. If Fanshawe came to the playground wearing black sneakers, then I would ask for black sneakers the next time my mother took me to the shoe store. If Fanshawe brought a copy of *Robinson Crusoe* with him to school, then I would begin reading *Robinson Crusoe* that same evening at home. I was not the only one who behaved like this, but I was perhaps the most devoted, the one who gave in most willingly to the power he held over us. Fanshawe himself was not aware of that power, and no doubt that was the reason he continued to hold it. He was indifferent to the attention he received, calmly going about his business, never using his influence to manipulate others. He did not play the pranks the rest of us did; he did not make mischief; he did not get into trouble with the teachers. But no one held this against him. Fanshawe stood apart from us, and yet he was the one who held us together, the one we approached to arbitrate our disputes, the one we could count on to be fair and to cut through our petty quarrels. There was something so attractive about him that you always wanted him beside you, as if you could live within his sphere and be touched by what he was. He was there for you, and yet at the same time he was inaccessible. You felt there was a secret core in him that could never be penetrated, a mysterious centre of hiddenness. To imitate him was somehow to participate in that mystery, but it was also to understand that you could never really know him.

I am talking about our very early childhood – as far back as five, six, seven years old. Much of it is buried now, and I know that even memories can be false. Still, I don't think I would be wrong in saying that I have kept the aura of those days inside me, and to the extent that I can feel what I felt then, I doubt those feelings can lie. Whatever it was that Fanshawe eventually became, my sense is that it started for him back then. He formed himself very quickly, was already a sharply defined presence by the time we started school. Fanshawe was visible, whereas the rest of us were creatures without shape, in the throes of constant tumult, floundering blindly from one moment to the next. I don't mean to say that he grew up fast – he never seemed older than he was – but that he was already himself before he grew up. For one reason or another, he never became subject to the same upheavals as the rest of us. His dramas were of a different order – more internal, no doubt more brutal – but with none of the abrupt changes that seemed to punctuate everyone else's life.

One incident is particularly vivid to me. It concerns a birthday party that Fanshawe and I were invited to in the first or second grade, which means that it falls at the very beginning of the period I am able to talk about with any precision. It was a Saturday afternoon in spring, and we walked to the party with another boy, a friend of ours named Dennis Walden. Dennis had a much harder life than either of us did: an alcoholic mother, an overworked father, innumerable brothers and sisters. I had been to his house two or three times – a great, dark ruin of a place – and I can remember being frightened by his mother, who made me think of a fairy-tale witch. She would spend the whole day behind the closed door of her room, always in her bathrobe, her pale face a nightmare of wrinkles, poking her head out every now and then to scream something at the children. On the day of the party, Fanshawe and I had been duly equipped with presents to give the birthday boy, all wrapped in coloured paper and tied with ribbons. Dennis, however, had nothing, and he felt bad about it. I can remember trying to console him with some empty phrase or other: it didn't matter, no one really cared, in all the confusion it wouldn't be noticed. But Dennis did care, and that was what Fanshawe immediately understood. Without any explanation, he turned to Dennis and handed him his present. Here, he said, take this one – I'll tell them I left mine at home. My first reaction was to think that Dennis would resent the gesture, that he would feel insulted by Fanshawe's pity. But I was wrong. He hesitated for a moment, trying to absorb this sudden change of fortune, and then nodded his head, as if acknowledging the wisdom of what Fanshawe had done. It was not an act of charity so much as an act of justice, and for that reason Dennis was able to accept it without humiliating himself. The one thing had been turned into the other. It was a piece of magic, a combination of off-handedness and total conviction, and I doubt that anyone but Fanshawe would have pulled it off.

After the party, I went back with Fanshawe to his house. His mother was there, sitting in the kitchen, and she asked us about the party and whether the birthday boy had liked the present she had bought for him. Before Fanshawe had a chance to say anything, I blurted out the story of what he had done. I had no intention of getting him into trouble, but it was impossible for me to keep it to myself. Fanshawe's gesture had opened up a whole new world for me: the way someone could enter the feelings of another and take them on so completely that his own were no longer important. It was the first truly moral act I had witnessed, and nothing else seemed worth talking about. Fanshawe's mother was not so enthusiastic, however. Yes, she said, that was a kind and generous thing to do, but it was also wrong. The present had cost her money, and by giving it away Fanshawe had in some sense stolen that money from her. On top of that, Fanshawe had acted impolitely by showing up without a present – which reflected badly on her, since she was the one responsible for his actions. Fanshawe listened carefully to his mother and did not say a word. After she was finished, he still did not speak, and she asked him if he understood. Yes, he said, he understood. It probably would have ended there, but then, after a short pause, Fanshawe went on to say that he still thought he was right. It didn't matter to him how she felt: he would do the same thing again the next time. A scene followed this little exchange. Mrs Fanshawe became angry at his impertinence, but Fanshawe stuck to his guns, refusing to budge under the barrage of her reprimands. Eventually, he was ordered to his room and I was told to leave the house. I was appalled by his mother's unfairness, but when I tried to speak up in his defence, Fanshawe waved me off. Rather than protest any more, he took his punishment silently and disappeared into his room.

The whole episode was pure Fanshawe: the spontaneous act of goodness, the unswerving belief in what he had done, and the mute, almost passive giving in to its consequences. No matter how remarkable his behaviour was, you always felt that he was detached from it. More than anything else, it was this quality that sometimes scared me away from him. I would get so close to Fanshawe, would admire him so intensely, would want so desperately to measure up to him – and then, suddenly, a moment would come when I realized that he was alien to me, that the way he lived inside himself could never correspond to the way I needed to live. I wanted too much of things, I had too many desires, I lived too fully in the grip of the immediate ever to attain such indifference. It mattered to me that I do well, that I impress people with the empty signs of my ambition: good grades, varsity letters, awards for whatever it was they were judging us on that week. Fanshawe remained aloof from all that, quietly standing in his corner, paying no attention. If he did well, it was always in spite of himself, with no struggle, no effort, no stake in the thing he had done. This posture could be unnerving, and it took me a long time to learn that what was good for Fanshawe was not necessarily good for me.

I do not want to exaggerate, however. If Fanshawe and I eventually had our differences, what I remember most about our childhood is the passion of our friendship. We lived next door to each other, and our fenceless backyards merged into an unbroken stretch of lawn, gravel, and dirt, as though we belonged to the same household. Our mothers were close friends, our fathers were tennis partners, neither one of us had a brother: ideal conditions therefore, with nothing to stand between us. We were born less than a week apart and spent our babyhoods in the backyard together, exploring the grass on all fours, tearing apart the flowers, standing up and taking our first steps on the same day. (There are photographs to document this.) Later, we learned baseball and football in the backyard together. We built our forts, played our games, invented our worlds in the backyard, and still later, there were our rambles through the town, the long afternoons on our bicycles, the endless conversations. It would be impossible, I think, for me to know anyone as well as I knew Fanshawe then. My mother recalls that we were so attached to each other that once, when we were six, we asked her if it was possible for men to get married. We wanted to live together when we grew up, and who else but married people did that? Fanshawe was going to be an astronomer, and I was going to be a vet. We were thinking of a big house in the country – a place where the sky would be dark enough at night to see all the stars and where there would be no shortage of animals to take care of.

In retrospect, I find it natural that Fanshawe should have

become a writer. The severity of his inwardness almost seemed to demand it. Even in grammar school he was composing little stories, and I doubt there was ever a time after the age of ten or eleven when he did not think of himself as a writer. In the beginning, of course, it didn't seem to mean much. Poe and Stevenson were his models, and what came out of it was the usual boyish claptrap. 'One night, in the year of our Lord seventeen hundred and fifty-one, I was walking through a murderous blizzard toward the house of my ancestors, when I chanced upon a spectre-like figure in the snow.' That kind of thing, filled with overblown phrases and extravagant turns of plot. In the sixth grade, I remember, Fanshawe wrote a short detective novel of about fifty pages, which the teacher let him read to the class in ten-minute installments each day at the end of school. We were all proud of Fanshawe and surprised by the dramatic way he read, acting out the parts of each of the characters. The story escapes me now, but I recall that it was infinitely complex, with the outcome hinging on something like the confused identities of two sets of twins.

Fanshawe was not a bookish child, however. He was too good at games for that, too central a figure among us to retreat into himself. All through those early years, one had the impression there was nothing he did not do well, nothing he did not do better than everyone else. He was the best baseball player, the best student, the best looking of all the boys. Any one of these things would have been enough to give him special status – but together they made him seem heroic, a child who had been touched by the gods. Extraordinary as he was, however, he remained one of us. Fanshawe was not a boy-genius or a prodigy; he did not have any miraculous gift that would have set him apart from the children his own age. He was a perfectly normal child – but more so, if that is possible, more in harmony with himself, more ideally a normal child than any of the rest of us.

At heart, the Fanshawe I knew was not a bold person. Nevertheless, there were times when he shocked me by his willingness to jump into dangerous situations. Behind all the surface composure, there seemed to be a great darkness: an urge to test himself, to take risks, to haunt the edges of things. As a boy, he had a passion for playing around construction sites, clambering up ladders and scaffolds, balancing on planks over an abyss of machinery, sandbags, and mud. I would hover in the background as Fanshawe performed these stunts, silently imploring him to stop, but never saying anything – wanting to go, but afraid to lest he should fall. As time went on, these impulses became more articulate. Fanshawe would talk to me about the importance of 'tasting life'. Making things hard for yourself, he said, searching out the unknown – this was what he wanted, and more and more as he got older. Once, when we were about fifteen, he persuaded me to spend the weekend with him in New York – roaming the streets, sleeping on a bench in the old Penn Station, talking to bums, seeing how long we could last without eating. I remember getting drunk at seven o'clock on Sunday morning in Central Park and puking all over the grass. For Fanshawe this was essential business – another step toward proving oneself – but for me it was only sordid, a miserable lapse into something I was not. Still, I continued to go along with him, a befuddled witness, sharing in the quest but not quite part of it, an adolescent Sancho astride my donkey, watching my friend do battle with himself.

A month or two after our weekend on the bum, Fanshawe took me to a brothel in New York (a friend of his arranged the visit), and it was there that we lost our virginity. I remember a small brownstone apartment on the Upper West Side near the river – a kitchenette and one dark bedroom with a flimsy curtain hanging between them. There were two black women in the place, one fat and old, the other young and pretty. Since neither one of us wanted the older woman, we had to decide who would go first. If memory serves, we actually went into the hall and flipped a coin. Fanshawe won, of course, and two minutes later I found myself sitting in the little kitchen with the fat madam. She called me sugar, reminding me every so often that

she was still available, in case I had a change of heart. I was too
nervous to do anything but shake my head, and then I just sat
there, listening to Fanshawe's intense and rapid breathing on
the other side of the curtain. I could only think about one thing:
that my dick was about to go into the same place that Fanshawe's was now. Then it was my turn, and to this day I have
no idea what the girl's name was. She was the first naked
woman I had seen in the flesh, and she was so casual and
friendly about her nakedness that things might have gone well
for me if I hadn't been distracted by Fanshawe's shoes – visible
in the gap between the curtain and the floor, shining in the light
of the kitchen, as if detached from his body. The girl was sweet
and did her best to help me, but it was a long struggle, and even
at the end I felt no real pleasure. Afterward, when Fanshawe
and I walked out into the twilight, I didn't have much to say for
myself. Fanshawe, however, seemed rather content, as if the
experience had somehow confirmed his theory about tasting
life. I realized then that Fanshawe was much hungrier than I
could ever be.

We led a sheltered life out there in the suburbs. New York
was only twenty miles away, but it could have been China for all
it had to do with our little world of lawns and wooden houses.
By the time he was thirteen or fourteen, Fanshawe became a
kind of internal exile, going through the motions of dutiful
behaviour, but cut off from his surroundings, contemptuous of
the life he was forced to live. He did not make himself difficult
or outwardly rebellious, he simply withdrew. After command-
ing so much attention as a child, always standing at the exact
centre of things, Fanshawe almost disappeared by the time we
reached high school, shunning the spotlight for a stubborn
marginality. I knew that he was writing seriously by then
(although by the age of sixteen he had stopped showing his
work to anyone), but I take that more as a symptom than as a
cause. In our sophomore year, for example, Fanshawe was the
only member of our class to make the varsity baseball team. He
played extremely well for several weeks, and then, for no

apparent reason, quit the team. I remember listening to him describe the incident to me the day after it happened: walking into the coach's office after practice and turning in his uniform. The coach had just taken his shower, and when Fanshawe entered the room he was standing by his desk stark naked, a cigar in his mouth and his baseball cap on his head. Fanshawe took pleasure in the description, dwelling on the absurdity of the scene, embellishing it with details about the coach's squat, pudgy body, the light in the room, the puddle of water on the grey concrete floor – but that was all it was, a description, a string of words divorced from anything that might have concerned Fanshawe himself. I was disappointed that he had quit, but Fanshawe never really explained what he had done, except to say that he found baseball boring.

As with many gifted people, a moment came when Fanshawe was no longer satisfied with doing what came easily to him. Having mastered all that was demanded of him at an early age, it was probably natural that he should begin to look for challenges elsewhere. Given the limitations of his life as a high school student in a small town, the fact that he found that elsewhere inside himself is neither surprising nor unusual. But there was more to it than that, I believe. Things happened around that time in Fanshawe's family that no doubt made a difference, and it would be wrong not to mention them. Whether they made an essential difference is another story, but I tend to think that everything counts. In the end, each life is no more than the sum of contingent facts, a chronicle of chance intersections, of flukes, of random events that divulge nothing but their own lack of purpose.

When Fanshawe was sixteen, it was discovered that his father had cancer. For a year and a half he watched his father die, and during that time the family slowly unravelled. Fanshawe's mother was perhaps hardest hit. Stoically keeping up appearances, attending to the business of medical consultations, financial arrangements, and trying to maintain the household, she swung fitfully between great optimism over the chances of

217

recovery and a kind of paralytic despair. According to Fanshawe, she was never able to accept the one inevitable fact that kept staring her in the face. She knew what was going to happen, but she did not have the strength to admit that she knew, and as time went on she began to live as though she were holding her breath. Her behaviour became more and more eccentric: all-night binges of manic house-cleaning, a fear of being in the house alone (combined with sudden, unexplained absences from the house), and a whole range of imagined ailments (allergies, high blood pressure, dizzy spells). Toward the end, she started taking an interest in various crackpot theories – astrology, psychic phenomena, vague spiritualist notions about the soul – until it became impossible to talk to her without being worn down to silence as she lectured on the corruption of the human body.

Relations between Fanshawe and his mother became tense. She clung to him for support, acting as though the family's pain belonged only to her. Fanshawe had to be the solid one in the house; not only did he have to take care of himself, he had to assume responsibility for his sister, who was just twelve at the time. But this brought with it another set of problems – for Ellen was a troubled, unstable child, and in the parental void that ensued from the illness she began to look to Fanshawe for everything. He became her father, her mother, her bastion of wisdom and comfort. Fanshawe understood how unhealthy her dependence on him was, but there was little he could do about it short of hurting her in some irreparable way. I remember how my own mother would talk about 'poor Jane' (Mrs Fanshawe) and how terrible the whole thing was for the 'baby'. But I knew that in some sense it was Fanshawe who suffered the most. It was just that he never got a chance to show it.

As for Fanshawe's father, there is little I can say with any certainty. He was a cipher to me, a silent man of abstracted benevolence, and I never got to know him well. Whereas my father tended to be around a lot, especially on the weekends, Fanshawe's father was rarely to be seen. He was a lawyer of some prominence, and at one time he had had political ambitions – but these had ended in a series of disappointments. He usually worked until late, pulling into the driveway at eight or nine o'clock, and often spent Saturday and part of Sunday at his office. I doubt that he ever knew quite what to make of his son, for he seemed to be a man with little feeling for children, someone who had lost all memory of having been a child himself. Mr Fanshawe was so thoroughly adult, so completely immersed in serious, grown-up matters, that I imagine it was hard for him not to think of us as creatures from another world.

He was not yet fifty when he died. For the last six months of his life, after the doctors had given up hope of saving him, he lay in the spare bedroom of the Fanshawe house, watching the yard through the window, reading an occasional book, taking his pain-killers, dozing. Fanshawe spent most of his free time with him then, and though I can only speculate on what happened, I assume that things changed between them. At the very least, I know how hard he worked at it, often staying home from school to be with him, trying to make himself indispensable, nursing him with unflinching attentiveness. It was a grim thing for Fanshawe to go through, too much for him perhaps, and though he seemed to take it well, summoning up the bravery that is possible only in the very young, I sometimes wonder if he ever managed to get over it.

There is only one more thing I want to mention here. At the end of this period – the very end, when no one expected Fanshawe's father to last more than a few days – Fanshawe and I went for a drive after school. It was February, and a few minutes after we started, a light snow began to fall. We drove aimlessly, looping through some of the neighbouring towns, paying little attention to where we were. Ten or fifteen miles from home, we came upon a cemetery; the gate happened to be open, and for no particular reason we decided to drive in. After a while, we stopped the car and began to wander around on foot. We read the inscriptions on the stones, speculated on what each of those lives might have been, fell silent, walked some more, talked, fell

219

silent again. By now the snow was coming down heavily, and the ground was turning white. Somewhere in the middle of the cemetery there was a freshly dug grave, and Fanshawe and I stopped at the edge and looked down into it. I can remember how quiet it was, how far away the world seemed to be from us. For a long time neither one of us spoke, and then Fanshawe said that he wanted to see what it was like at the bottom. I gave him my hand and held on tightly as he lowered himself into the grave. When his feet touched the ground he looked back up at me with a half-smile, and then lay down on his back, as though pretending to be dead. It is still completely vivid to me: looking down at Fanshawe as he looked up at the sky, his eyes blinking furiously as the snow fell onto his face.

By some obscure train of thought, it made me think back to when we were very small – no more than four or five years old. Fanshawe's parents had bought some new appliance, a television perhaps, and for several months Fanshawe kept the cardboard box in his room. He had always been generous in sharing his toys, but this box was off limits to me, and he never let me go in it. It was his secret place, he told me, and when he sat inside and closed it up around him, he could go wherever he wanted to go, could be wherever he wanted to be. But if another person ever entered his box, then its magic would be lost for good. I believed this story and did not press him for a turn, although it nearly broke my heart. We would be playing in his room, quietly setting up soldiers or drawing pictures, and then, out of the blue, Fanshawe would announce that he was going into his box. I would try to go on with what I had been doing, but it was never any use. Nothing interested me so much as what was happening to Fanshawe inside the box, and I would spend those minutes desperately trying to imagine the adventures he was having. But I never learned what they were, since it was also against the rules for Fanshawe to talk about them after he climbed out.

Something similar was happening now in that open grave in the snow. Fanshawe was alone down there, thinking his thoughts, living through those moments by himself, and though I was present, the event was sealed off from me, as though I was not really there at all. I understood that this was Fanshawe's way of imagining his father's death. Again, it was a matter of pure chance: the open grave was there, and Fanshawe had felt it calling out to him. Stories happen only to those who are able to tell them, someone once said. In the same way, perhaps, experiences present themselves only to those who are able to have them. But this is a difficult point, and I can't be sure of any of it. I stood there waiting for Fanshawe to come up, trying to imagine what he was thinking, for a brief moment trying to see what he was seeing. Then I turned my head up to the darkening winter sky – and everything was a chaos of snow, rushing down on top of me.

By the time we started walking back to the car, the sun had set. We stumbled our way through the cemetery, not saying anything to each other. Several inches of snow had fallen, and it kept coming down, more and more heavily, as though it would never stop. We reached the car, climbed in, and then, against all our expectations, couldn't get moving. The back tyres were stuck in a shallow ditch, and nothing we did made any difference. We pushed, we jostled, and still the tyres spun with that horrible, futile noise. Half an hour went by, and then we gave up, reluctantly deciding to abandon the car. We hitch-hiked home in the storm, and another two hours went by before we finally made it back. It was only then that we learned that Fanshawe's father had died during the afternoon.

Several days went by before I found the courage to open the suitcases. I finished the article I was working on, I went to the movies, I accepted invitations I normally would have turned down. These tactics did not fool me, however. Too much depended on my response, and the possibility of being disappointed was something I did not want to face. There was no difference in my mind between giving the order to destroy Fanshawe's work and killing him with my own hands. I had been given the power to obliterate, to steal a body from its grave and tear it to pieces. It was an intolerable position to be in, and I wanted no part of it. As long as I left the suitcases untouched, my conscience would be spared. On the other hand, I had made a promise, and I knew that I could not delay forever. It was just at this point (gearing myself up, getting ready to do it) that a new dread took hold of me. If I did not want Fanshawe's work to be bad, I discovered, I also did not want it to be good. This is a difficult feeling for me to explain. Old rivalries no doubt had something to do with it, a desire not to be humbled by Fanshawe's brilliance – but there was also a feeling of being trapped. I had given my word. Once I opened the suitcases, I would become Fanshawe's spokesman – and I would go on speaking for him, whether I liked it or not. Both possibilities frighened me. To issue a death sentence was bad enough, but working for a dead man hardly seemed better. For several days I moved back and forth between these fears, unable to decide which one was worse. In the end, of course, I did open the suitcases. But by then it probably had less to do with Fanshawe than it did with Sophie. I wanted to see her again, and the sooner I got to work, the sooner I would have a reason to call her.

I am not planning to go into any details here. By now, everyone knows what Fanshawe's work is like. It has been read and discussed, there have been articles and studies, it has become public property. If there is anything to be said, it is only that it took me no more than an hour or two to understand that my feelings were quite beside the point. To care about words, to have a stake in what is written, to believe in the power of books – this overwhelms the rest, and beside it one's life becomes very small. I do not say this in order to congratulate myself or to put my actions in a better light. I was the first, but beyond that I see nothing to set me apart from anyone else. If Fanshawe's work had been any less than it was, my role would have been different – more important, perhaps, more crucial to the outcome of the story. But as it was, I was no more than an invisible instrument. Something had happened, and short of denying it, short of pretending I had not opened the suitcases, it would go on happening, knocking down whatever was in front of it, moving with a momentum of its own.

It took me about a week to digest and organize the material, to divide finished work from drafts, to gather the manuscripts into some semblance of chronological order. The earliest piece was a poem, dating from 1963 (when Fanshawe was sixteen), and the last was from 1976 (just one month before he disappeared). In all there were over a hundred poems, three novels (two short and one long), and five one-act plays – as well as thirteen notebooks, which contained a number of aborted pieces, sketches, jottings, remarks on the books Fanshawe was reading, and ideas for future projects. There were no letters, no diaries, no glimpses into Fanshawe's private life. But that was something I had expected. A man does not spend his time hiding from the world without making sure to cover his tracks. Still, I had thought that somewhere among all the papers there might be some mention of me – if only a letter of instruction or a notebook entry naming me his literary executor. But there was nothing. Fanshawe had left me entirely on my own.

I telephoned Sophie and arranged to have dinner with her the following night. Because I suggested a fashionable French

restaurant (way beyond what I could afford), I think she was able
to guess my response to Fanshawe's work. But beyond this hint
of a celebration, I said as little as I could. I wanted everything to
advance at its own pace – no abrupt moves, no premature
gestures. I was already certain about Fanshawe's work, but I was
afraid to rush into things with Sophie. Too much hinged on how I
acted, too much could be destroyed by blundering at the start.
Sophie and I were linked now, whether she knew it or not – if
only to the extent that we would be partners in promoting
Fanshawe's work. But I wanted more than that, and I wanted
Sophie to want it as well. Struggling against my eagerness, I
urged caution on myself, told myself to think ahead.

She wore a black silk dress, tiny silver earrings, and had swept
back her hair to show the line of her neck. As she walked into the
restaurant and saw me sitting at the bar, she gave me a warm,
complicitous smile, as though telling me she knew how beautiful
she was, but at the same time commenting on the weirdness of
the occasion – savouring it somehow, clearly alert to the outlandish implications of the moment. I told her that she was stun-
ning, and she answered almost whimsically that this was her first
night out since Ben had been born – and that she had wanted to
'look different'. After that, I stuck to business, trying to hang back
within myself. When we were led to our table and given our seats
(white tablecloth, heavy silverware, a red tulip in a slender vase
between us), I responded to her second smile by talking about
Fanshawe.

She did not seem surprised by anything I said. It was old news
for her, a fact that she had already come to terms with, and what I
was telling her merely confirmed what she had known all along.
Strangely enough, it did not seem to excite her. There was a
wariness in her attitude that confused me, and for several
minutes I was lost. Then, slowly, I began to understand that her
feelings were not very different from my own. Fanshawe had
disappeared from her life, and I saw that she might have good
reason to resent the burden that had been imposed on her. By
publishing Fanshawe's work, by devoting herself to a man who

was no longer there, she would be forced to live in the past, and whatever future she might want to build for herself would be tainted by the role she had to play: the official widow, the dead writer's muse, the beautiful heroine in a tragic story. No one wants to be part of a fiction, and even less so if that fiction is real. Sophie was just twenty-six years old. She was too young to live through someone else, too intelligent not to want a life that was completely her own. The fact that she had loved Fanshawe was not the point. Fanshawe was dead, and it was time for her to leave him behind.

None of this was said in so many words. But the feeling was there, and it would have been senseless to ignore it. Given my own reservations, it was odd that I should have been the one to carry the torch, but I saw that if I didn't take hold of the thing and get it started, the job would never get done.

'You don't really have to get involved,' I said. 'We'll have to consult, of course, but that shouldn't take up much of your time. If you're willing to leave the decisions to me, I don't think it will be very bad at all.'

'Of course I'll leave them to you,' she said. 'I don't know the first thing about any of this. If I tried to do it myself, I'd get lost within five minutes.'

'The important thing is to know that we're on the same side,' I said. 'In the end, I suppose it boils down to whether or not you can trust me.'

'I trust you,' she said.

'I haven't given you any reason to,' I said. 'Not yet, in any case.'

'I know that. But I trust you anyway.'

'Just like that?'

'Yes. Just like that.'

She smiled at me again, and for the rest of the dinner we said nothing more about Fanshawe's work. I had been planning to discuss it in detail – how best to begin, what publishers might be interested, what people to contact, and so on – but this no longer seemed important. Sophie was quite content not to think about it, and now that I had reassured her that she didn't have to, her playfulness gradually returned. After so many difficult months, she finally had a chance to forget some of it for a while, and I could see how determined she was to lose herself in the very simple pleasures of this moment: the restaurant, the food, the laughter of the people around us, the fact that she was here and not anywhere else. She wanted to be indulged in all this, and who was I not to go along with her?'

I was in good form that night. Sophie inspired me, and it didn't take long for me to get warmed up. I cracked jokes, told stories, performed little tricks with the silverware. The woman was so beautiful that I had trouble keeping my eyes off her. I wanted to see her laugh, to see how her face would respond to what I said, to watch her eyes, to study her gestures. God knows what absurdities I came out with, but I did my best to detach myself, to bury my real motives under this onslaught of charm. That was the hard part. I knew that Sophie was lonely, that she wanted the comfort of a warm body beside her – but a quick roll in the hay was not what I was after, and if I moved too fast that was probably all it would turn out to be. At this early stage, Fanshawe was still there with us, the unspoken link, the invisible force that had brought us together. It would take some time before he disappeared, and until that happened, I found myself willing to wait.

All this created an exquisite tension. As the evening progressed, the most casual remarks became tinged with erotic overtones. Words were no longer simply words, but a curious code of silences, a way of speaking that continually moved around the thing that was being said. As long as we avoided the real subject, the spell would not be broken. We both slipped naturally into this kind of banter, and it became all the more powerful because neither one of us abandoned the charade. We knew what we were doing, but at the same time we pretended not to. Thus my courtship of Sophie began – slowly, decorously, building by the smallest of increments.

After dinner we walked for twenty minutes or so in the late

November darkness, then finished up the evening with drinks in a bar downtown. I smoked one cigarette after another, but that was the only clue to my tumult. Sophie talked for a while about her family in Minnesota, her three younger sisters, her arrival in New York eight years ago, her music, her teaching, her plan to go back to it next fall – but we were so firmly entrenched in our jocular mode by then that each remark became an excuse for additional laughter. It would have gone on, but there was the babysitter to think about, and so we finally cut it short at around midnight. I took her to the door of her apartment and made my last great effort of the evening.

'Thank you, doctor,' Sophie said. 'The operation was a success.'

'My patients always survive,' I said. 'It's the laughing gas. I just turn on the valve, and little by little they get better.'

'That gas might be habit-forming.'

'That's the point. The patients keep coming back for more – sometimes two or three operations a week. How do you think I paid for my Park Avenue apartment and the summer place in France?'

'So there's a hidden motive.'

'Absolutely. I'm driven by greed.'

'Your practice must be booming.'

'It was. But I'm more or less retired now. I'm down to one patient these days – and I'm not sure if she'll be coming back.'

'She'll be back,' Sophie said, with the coyest, most radiant smile I had ever seen. 'You can count on it.'

'That's good to hear,' I said. 'I'll have my secretary call her to schedule the next appointment.'

'The sooner the better. With these long-term treatments, you can't waste a moment.'

'Excellent advice. I'll remember to order a new supply of laughing gas.'

'You do that, doctor. I really think I need it.'

We smiled at each other again, and then I wrapped her up in a big bear hug, gave her a brief kiss on the lips, and got down the stairs as fast as I could.

227

I went straight home, realized that bed was out of the question, and then spent two hours in front of the television, watching a movie about Marco Polo. I finally conked out at around four, in the middle of the *Twilight Zone* rerun.

My first move was to contact Stuart Green, an editor at one of the larger publishing houses. I didn't know him very well, but we had grown up in the same town, and his younger brother, Roger, had gone through school with me and Fanshawe. I guessed that Stuart would remember who Fanshawe was, and that seemed like a good way to get started. I had run into Stuart at various gatherings over the years, perhaps three or four times, and he had always been friendly, talking about the good old days (as he called them) and always promising to send my greetings to Roger the next he saw him. I had no idea what to expect from Stuart, but he sounded happy enough to hear from me when I called. We arranged to meet at his office one afternoon that week.

It took him a few moments to place Fanshawe's name. It was familiar to him, he said, but he didn't know from where. I prodded his memory a bit, mentioned Roger and his friends, and then it suddenly came back to him. 'Yes, yes, of course,' he said. 'Fanshawe. That extraordinary little boy. Roger used to insist that he would grow up to be President.' That's the one, I said, and then I told him the story.

Stuart was a rather prissy fellow, a Harvard type who wore bow ties and tweed jackets, and though at bottom he was little more than a company man, in the publishing world he was what passed for an intellectual. He had done well for himself so far – a senior editor in his early thirties, a solid and responsible young worker – and there was no question that he was on the rise. I say all this only to prove that he was not someone who would be automatically susceptible to the kind of story I was telling. There was very little romance in him, very little that was not cautious and business-like – but I could feel that he was interested, and as I went on talking, he even seemed to become excited.

He had nothing to lose, of course. If Fanshawe's work didn't appeal to him, it would be simple enough for him to turn it down. Rejections were the heart of his job, and he wouldn't have to think twice about it. On the other hand, if Fanshawe was the writer I said he was, then publishing him could only help Stuart's reputation. He would share in the glory of having discovered an unknown American genius, and he would be able to live off this coup for years.

I handed him the manuscript of Fanshawe's big novel. In the end, I said, it would have to be all or nothing – the poems, the plays, the other two novels – but this was Fanshawe's major work, and it was logical that it should come first. I was referring to *Neverland*, of course. Stuart said that he liked the title, but when he asked me to describe the book, I said that I'd rather not, that I thought it would be better if he found out for himself. He raised an eyebrow in response (a trick he had probably learned during his year at Oxford), as if to imply that I shouldn't play games with him. I wasn't, as far as I could tell. It was just that I didn't want to coerce him. The book could do the work itself, and I saw no reason to deny him the pleasure of entering it cold: with no map, no compass, no one to lead him by the hand.

It took three weeks for him to get back to me. The news was neither good nor bad, but it seemed hopeful. There was probably enough support among the editors to get the book through, Stuart said, but before they made the final decision they wanted to have a look at the other material. I had been expecting that – a certain prudence, playing it close to the vest – and told Stuart that I would come around to drop off the manuscripts the following afternoon.

'It's a strange book,' he said, pointing to the copy of *Neverland* on his desk. 'Not at all your typical novel, you know. Not your typical anything. It's still not clear that we're going ahead with it, but if we do, publishing it will be something of a risk.'

'I know that,' I said. 'But that's what makes it interesting.'

'The real pity is that Fanshawe isn't around. I'd love to be able to work with him. There are things in the book that should be changed, I think, certain passages that should be cut. It would make the book even stronger.'

'That's just editor's pride,' I said. 'It's hard for you to see a manuscript and not want to attack it with a red pencil. The fact is, I think the parts you object to now will eventually make sense to you, and you'll be glad you weren't able to touch them.'

'Time will tell,' said Stuart, not ready to concede the point. 'But there's no question,' he went on, 'no question that the man could write. I read the book more than two weeks ago, and it's been with me ever since. I can't get it out of my head. It keeps coming back to me, and always at the strangest moments. Stepping out of the shower, walking down the street, crawling into bed at night – whenever I'm not consciously thinking about anything. That doesn't happen very often, you know. You read so many books in this job that they all tend to blur together. But Fanshawe's book stands out. There's something powerful about it, and the oddest thing is that I don't even know what it is.'

'That's probably the real test,' I said. 'The same thing happened to me. The book gets stuck somewhere in the brain, and you can't get rid of it.'

'And what about the other stuff?'

'Same thing,' I said. 'You can't stop thinking about it.'

Stuart shook his head, and for the first time I saw that he was honestly impressed. It lasted no more than a moment, but in that moment his arrogance and posturing suddenly disappeared, and I almost found myself wanting to like him.

'I think we might be on to something,' he said. 'If what you say is true, then I really think we might be on to something.'

We were, and as things turned out, perhaps even more than Stuart had imagined. *Neverland* was accepted later that month, with an option on the other books as well. My quarter of the advance was enough to buy me some time, and I used it to work on an edition of the poems. I also went to a number of directors to see if there was any interest in doing the plays. Eventually, this came off, too, and a production of three one-acts was planned for a small downtown theatre – to open about six weeks after *Neverland* was published. In the meantime, I persuaded the editor of one of the bigger magazines I occasionally wrote for to let me do an article on Fanshawe. It turned out to be a long, rather exotic piece, and at the time I felt it was one of the best things I had ever written. The article was scheduled to appear two months before the publication of *Neverland* – and suddenly it seemed as though everything was happening at once.

I admit that I got caught up in it all. One thing kept leading to another, and before I knew it a small industry had been set in motion. It was a kind of delirium, I think. I felt like an engineer, pushing buttons and pulling levers, scrambling from valve chambers to circuit boxes, adjusting a part here, devising an improvement there, listening to the contraption hum and chug and purr, oblivious to everything but the din of my brainchild. I was the mad scientist who had invented the great hocus-pocus machine, and the more smoke that poured from it, the more noise it produced, the happier I was.

Perhaps that was inevitable; perhaps I needed to be a little mad in order to get started. Given the strain of reconciling myself to the project, it was probably necessary for me to equate Fanshawe's success with my own. I had stumbled onto a cause, a thing that justified me and made me feel important, and the more fully I disappeared into my ambitions for Fanshawe, the more sharply I came into focus for myself. This is not an excuse; it is merely a description of what happened. Hindsight tells me that I was looking for trouble, but at the time I knew nothing about it. More important, even if I had known, I doubt that it would have made a difference.

Underneath it all was the desire to stay in touch with Sophie. As time went on, it became perfectly natural for me to call her three or four times a week, to see her for lunch, to stop by for an afternoon stroll through the neighbourhood with Ben. I introduced her to Stuart Green, invited her along to meet the theatre director, found her a lawyer to handle contracts and other legal matters. Sophie took all this in her stride, treating these encounters more as social occasions than as business talks, making it clear to the people we saw that I was the one in charge. I sensed that she was determined not to feel indebted to Fanshawe, that whatever happened or did not happen, she would continue to keep her distance from it. The money made her happy, of course, but she never really connected it to Fanshawe's work. It was an unlikely gift, a winning lottery ticket that had dropped from the sky, and that was all. Sophie saw through the whirlwind from the very start. She understood the fundamental absurdity of the situation, and because there was no greed in her, no impulse to press her own advantage, she did not lose her head.

I worked hard at courting her. No doubt my motives were transparent, but perhaps that was to the good. Sophie knew that I had fallen in love with her, and the fact that I did not pounce on her, that I did not force her to declare her feelings for me, probably did more to convince her of my seriousness than anything else. Still, I could not wait forever. Discretion has its role, but too much of it can be fatal. A moment came when I could feel that we were no longer jousting with each other, that things between us had already been settled. In thinking about this moment now, I am tempted to use the traditional language of love. I want to talk in metaphors of heat, of burning, of barriers melting down in the face of irresistible passions. I am aware of how overblown these terms might sound, but in the end I believe they are accurate. Everything had changed for me, and words that I had never understood before suddenly began to make sense. This came as a revelation, and when I finally had time to absorb it, I wondered how I had managed to live so long without learning this simple thing. I am not talking about desire so much as knowledge, the discovery that two people, through desire, can create a thing more powerful than either of them can create alone. This knowledge changed me, I think, and actually made me feel more human. By belonging to Sophie, I began to feel as though I belonged to everyone else as well. My true place in the world, it turned out, was somewhere beyond myself, and if that place was inside me, it was also unlocatable. This was the tiny hole between self and not-self, and for the first time in my life I saw this nowhere as the exact centre of the world.

It happened to be my thirtieth birthday. I had known Sophie

for about three months by then, and she insisted on making an evening of it. I was reluctant at first, never having paid much attention to birthdays, but Sophie's sense of occasion finally won me over. She bought me an expensive, illustrated edition of *Moby Dick*, took me to dinner in a good restaurant, and then ushered me along to a performance of *Boris Godunov* at the Met. For once, I let myself go with it, not trying to second-guess my happiness, not trying to stay ahead of myself or outmanoeuvre my feelings. Perhaps I was beginning to sense a new boldness in Sophie; perhaps she was making it known to me that she had decided things for herself, that it was too late now for either one of us to back off. Whatever it was, that was the night when everything changed, when there was no longer any question of what we were going to do. We returned to her apartment at eleven-thirty, Sophie paid the drowsy babysitter, and then we tiptoed into Ben's room and stood there for a while watching him as he slept in his crib. I remember distinctly that neither one of us said anything, that the only sound I could hear was the faint gurgling of Ben's breath. We leaned over the bars and studied the shape of his little body – lying on his stomach, legs tucked under him, ass in the air, two or three fingers stuck in his mouth. It seemed to go on for a long time, but I doubt it was more than a minute or two. Then, without any warning, we both straightened up, turned towards each other, and began to kiss. After that, it is difficult for me to speak of what happened. Such things have little to do with words, so little, in fact, that it seems almost pointless to try to express them. If anything, I would say that we were falling into each other, that we were falling so fast and so far that nothing could catch us. Again, I lapse into metaphor. But that is probably beside the point. For whether or not I can talk about it does not change the truth of what happened. The fact is, there never was such a kiss, and in all my life I doubt there can ever be such a kiss again.

I spent that night in Sophie's bed, and from then on it became impossible to leave it. I would go back to my own apartment during the day to work, but every evening I would return to Sophie. I became a part of the household – shopping for dinner, changing Ben's diapers, taking out the garbage – living more intimately with another person than I had ever lived before. Months went by, and to my constant bewilderment, I discovered that I had a talent for this kind of life. I had been born to be with Sophie, and little by little I could feel myself becoming stronger, could feel her making me better than I had been. It was strange how Fanshawe had brought us together. If not for his disappearance, none of this would have happened. I owed him a debt, but other than doing what I could for his work, I had no chance to pay it back.

My article was published, and it seemed to have the desired effect. Stuart Green called to say that it was a 'great boost' – which I gathered to mean that he felt more secure now in having accepted the book. With all the interest the article had generated, Fanshawe no longer seemed like such a long shot. Then *Neverland* came out, and the reviews were uniformly good, some of them extraordinary. It was all that one could have hoped for. This was the fairy tale that every writer dreams about, and I admit that even I was a little shocked. Such things are not supposed to happen in the real world. Only a few weeks after publication, sales were greater than had been expected for the whole edition. A second printing eventually went to press, there were ads placed in newspapers and magazines, and then the book was sold to a paperback company for republication the following year. I don't mean to imply that the book was a bestseller by commercial standards or that Sophie was on her way to becoming a millionaire, but given the seriousness and difficulty of Fanshawe's work, and given the public's tendency to stay away from such work, it was a success beyond anything we had imagined possible.

In some sense, this is where the story should end. The young genius is dead, but his work will live on, his name will be remembered for years to come. His childhood friend has rescued the beautiful young widow, and the two of them will live happily ever after. That would seem to wrap it up, with nothing left but a final curtain call. But it turns out that this is only the beginning. What I have written so far is no more than a prelude, a quick synopsis of everything that comes before the story I have to tell. If there were no more to it than this, there would be nothing at all – for nothing would have compelled me to begin. Only darkness has the power to make a man open his heart to the world, and darkness is what surrounds me whenever I think of what happened. If courage is needed to write about it, I also know that writing about it is the one chance I have to escape. But I doubt this will happen, not even if I manage to tell the truth. Stories without endings can do nothing but go on forever, and to be caught in one means that you must die before your part in it is played out. My only hope is that there is an end to what I am about to say, that somewhere I will find a break in the darkness. This hope is what I define as courage, but whether there is reason to hope is another question entirely.

It was about three weeks after the plays had opened. I spent the night at Sophie's apartment as usual, and in the morning I went uptown to my place to do some work. I remember that I was supposed to be finishing a piece on four or five books of poetry – one of those frustrating, hodge-podge reviews – and I was having trouble concentrating. My mind kept wandering away from the books on my desk, and every five minutes or so I would pop up from my chair and pace about the room. A strange story had been reported to me by Stuart Green the day before, and it was hard for me to stop thinking about it.

According to Stuart, people were beginning to say that there was no such person as Fanshawe. The rumour was that I had invented him to perpetrate a hoax and had actually written the books myself. My first response was to laugh, and I made some crack about how Shakespeare hadn't written any plays either. But now that I had given some thought to it, I didn't know whether to feel insulted or flattered by this talk. Did people not trust me to tell the truth? Why would I go to the trouble of creating an entire body of work and then not want to take credit for it? And yet – did people really think I was capable of writing a book as good as *Neverland*? I realized that once all of Fanshawe's manuscripts had been published, it would be perfectly possible for me to write another book or two under his name – to do the work myself and yet pass it off as his. I was not planning to do this, of course, but the mere thought of it opened up certain bizarre and intriguing notions to me: what it means when a writer puts his name on a book, why some writers choose to hide behind a pseudonym, whether or not a writer has a real life anyway. It struck me that writing under another name might be something I would enjoy – to invent a secret identity for myself – and I wondered why I found this idea so attractive. One thought kept leading me to another, and by the time the subject was exhausted, I discovered that I had squandered most of the morning.

Eleven-thirty rolled around – the hour of the mail – and I made my ritual excursion down the elevator to see if there was anything in my box. This was always a crucial moment of the day for me, and I found it impossible to approach it calmly. There was always the hope that good news would be sitting there – an unexpected cheque, an offer of work, a letter that would somehow change my life – and by now the habit of anticipation was so much a part of me that I could scarcely look at my mailbox without getting a rush. This was my hiding place, the one spot in the world that was purely my own. And yet it linked me to the rest of the world, and in its magic darkness there was the power to make things happen.

There was only one letter for me that day. It came in a plain white envelope with a New York postmark and had no return address. The handwriting was unfamiliar to me (my name and address were printed out in block letters), and I couldn't even begin to guess who it was from. I opened the envelope in the elevator – and it was then, standing there on my way to the ninth floor, that the world fell on top of me.

'Don't be angry with me for writing to you,' the letter began. 'At the risk of causing you heart failure, I wanted to send you one last word – to thank you for what you have done. I knew that you were the person to ask, but things have turned out even better than I thought they would. You have gone beyond the possible, and I am in your debt. Sophie and the child will be taken care of, and because of that I can live with a clear conscience.

'I'm not going to explain myself here. In spite of this letter, I want you to go on thinking of me as dead. Nothing is more important that that, and you must not tell anyone that you've heard from me. I am not going to be found, and to speak of it would only lead to more trouble than it's worth. Above all, say nothing to Sophie. Make her divorce me, and then marry her as soon as you can. I trust you to do that – and I give you my blessings. The child needs a father, and you're the only one I can count on.

'I want you to understand that I haven't lost my mind. I made certain decisions that were necessary, and though people have suffered, leaving was the best and kindest thing I have ever done.

'Seven years from the day of my disappearance will be the day of my death. I have passed judgement on myself, and no appeals will be heard.

'I beg you not to look for me. I have no desire to be found, and it seems to me that I have the right to live the rest of my life as I see fit. Threats are repugnant to me – but I have no choice but to give you this warning: if by some miracle you manage to track me down, I will kill you.

'I'm pleased that so much interest has been taken in my writing. I never had the slightest inkling that anything like this could happen. But it all seems so far away from me now. Writing books belongs to another life, and to think about it now leaves me cold. I will never try to claim any of the money – and I gladly give it to you and Sophie. Writing was an illness that plagued me for a long time, but now I have recovered from it.

'Rest assured that I won't be in touch again. You are free of me now, and I wish you a long and happy life. How much better that everything should come to this. You are my friend, and my one hope is that you will always be who you are. With me it's another story. Wish me luck.'

There was no signature at the bottom of the letter, and for the next hour or two I tried to persuade myself that it was a prank. If Fanshawe had written it, why would he have neglected to sign his name? I clung to this as evidence of a trick, desperately looking for an excuse to deny what had happened. But this optimism did not last very long, and little by little I forced myself to face the facts. There could be any number of reasons for the name to be left out, and the more I thought about it, the more clearly I saw that this was precisely why the letter should be considered genuine. A prankster would make a special point of including the name, but the real person would not think twice about it: only someone not out to deceive would have the self-assurance to make such an apparent mistake. And then there were the final sentences of the letter: '. . . remain who you are. With me it's another story.' Did this mean that Fanshawe had become someone else? Unquestionably he was living under another name – but how was he living – and where? The New York postmark was something of a clue, perhaps, but it just as easily could have been a blind, a bit of false information to throw me off his track. Fanshawe had been extremely careful: I read the letter over and over, trying to pull it apart, looking for an opening, a way to read between the lines – but nothing came of it. The letter was opaque, a block of darkness that thwarted every attempt to get inside it. In the end I gave up, put the letter in a drawer of my desk, and admitted that I was lost, that nothing would ever be the same for me again.

What bothered me most, I think, was my own stupidity. Looking back on it now, I saw that all the facts had been given to me at the start – as early as my first meeting with Sophie. For years Fanshawe publishes nothing, then he tells his wife what to do if anything should happen to him (contact me, get his work published), and then he vanishes. It was all so obvious. The man wanted to leave, and he left. He simply got up one day and walked out on his pregnant wife, and because she trusted him, because it was inconceivable to her that he would do such a thing, she had no choice but to think he was dead. Sophie had deluded herself, but given the situation, it was hard to see how she could have done otherwise. I had no such excuse. Not once from the very beginning had I thought things through for myself. I had jumped right in with her, had rejoiced in accepting her misreading of the facts, and then had stopped thinking altogether. People have been shot for smaller crimes than that.

The days went by. All my instincts told me to confide in Sophie, to share the letter with her, and yet I couldn't bring myself to do it. I was too afraid, too uncertain as to how she would react. In my stronger moods, I argued to myself that keeping silent was the only way to protect her. What possible good would it do for her to know that Fanshawe had walked out on her? She would blame herself for what had happened, and I didn't want her to be hurt. Underneath this noble silence, however, there was a second silence of panic and fear. Fanshawe was alive – and if I let Sophie know it, what would this knowledge do to us? The thought that Sophie might want him back was too much for me, and I did not have the courage to risk finding out. This was perhaps my greatest failure of all. If I had believed enough in Sophie's love for me, I would have been willing to risk anything. But at the time there seemed to be no other choice, and so I did what Fanshawe had asked me to do – not for him, but for myself. I locked up the secret inside me and learned to hold my tongue.

A few more days went by, and then I proposed marriage to Sophie. We had talked about it before, but this time I took it out of the realm of talk, making it clear to her that I meant business. I realized that I was acting out of character (humourless, inflexible), but I couldn't help myself. The uncertainty of the situation was impossible to live with, and I felt that I had to resolve things right then and there. Sophie noticed this change in me, of course, but since she didn't know the reason for it, she interpreted it as an excess of passion – the behaviour of a nervous, overly ardent male, panting after the thing he wanted most (which was also true). Yes, she said, she would marry me. Did I ever really think she would turn me down?

'And I want to adopt Ben, too,' I said. 'I want him to have my name. It's important that he grow up thinking of me as his father.'

Sophie answered that she wouldn't have it any other way. It was the only thing that made sense – for all three of us.

'And I want it to happen soon,' I went on, 'as soon as possible. In New York, you couldn't get a divorce for a year – and that's too long, I couldn't stand waiting that long. But there are other places, Alabama, Nevada, Mexico, God knows where. We could go off on a vacation, and by the time we got back, you'd be free to marry me.'

Sophie said that she liked the way that sounded – 'free to marry me'. If it meant going somewhere for a while, she would go, she said, she would go anywhere I wanted.

'After all,' I said, 'he's been gone for more than a year now, almost a year and a half. It takes seven years before a dead person can be declared officially dead. Things happen, life moves on. Just think: we've known each other for almost a year.'

'To be precise,' Sophie answered, 'you walked through that door for the first time on November twenty-fifth, nineteen-seventy-six. In eight more days it will be exactly a year.'

'You remember.'

'Of course I remember. It was the most important day of my life.'

240

We took a plane to Birmingham, Alabama on November twenty-seventh and were back in New York by the first week of December. On the eleventh we were married in City Hall, and afterward we went to a drunken dinner with about twenty of our friends. We spent that night at the Plaza, ordered a room service breakfast in the morning, and later that day flew to Minnesota with Ben. On the eighteenth, Sophie's parents gave us a wedding party at their house, and on the night of the twenty-fourth we celebrated Norwegian Christmas. Two days later, Sophie and I left the snow and went to Bermuda for a week and a half, then returned to Minnesota to fetch Ben. Our plan was to start looking for a new apartment as soon as we got back to New York. Somewhere over western Pennsylvania, about an hour into the flight, Ben peed through his diapers onto my lap. When I showed him the large dark spot on my pants, he laughed, clapped his hands together, and then, looking straight into my eyes, called me Da for the first time.

I dug into the present. Several months passed, and little by little it began to seem possible that I would survive. This was life in a foxhole, but Sophie and Ben were down there with me, and that was all I really wanted. As long as I remembered not to look up, the danger could not touch us.

We moved to an apartment on Riverside Drive in February. Settling in carried us through to mid-spring, and I had little chance to dwell on Fanshawe. If the letter did not vanish from my thoughts altogether, it no longer posed the same threat. I was secure with Sophie now, and I felt that nothing could break us apart – not even Fanshawe, not even Fanshawe in the flesh. Or so it appeared to me then, whenever I happened to think of it. I understand now how badly I was deceiving myself, but I did not find that out until much later. By definition, a thought is something you are aware of. The fact that I did not once stop thinking about Fanshawe, that he was inside me day and night for all those months, was unknown to me at the time. And if you are not aware of having a thought, is it legitimate to say that you are thinking? I was haunted, perhaps, I was even possessed – but there were no signs of it, no clues to tell me what was happening.

Daily life was full for me now. I hardly noticed that I was doing less work than I had in years. I had no job to go off to in the morning, and since Sophie and Ben were in the apartment with me, it was not very difficult to find excuses for avoiding my desk. My work schedule grew slack. Instead of beginning at nine sharp every day, I sometimes didn't make it to my little room until eleven or eleven-thirty. On top of that, Sophie's presence in the house was a constant temptation. Ben still took one or two naps a day, and in those quiet hours while he slept, it was hard for me not to think about her body. More often than not, we wound up making love. Sophie was just as hungry for it as I was, and as the weeks passed, the house was slowly eroticized, transformed into a domain of sexual possibilities. The nether world rose up to the surface. Each room acquired its own memory, each spot evoked a different moment, so that even in the calm of practical life, a particular patch of carpet, say, or the threshold of a particular door, was no longer strictly a thing but a sensation, an echo of our erotic life. We had entered the paradox of desire. Our need for each other was inexhaustible, and the more it was fulfilled, the more it seemed to grow.

Every now and then, Sophie talked of looking for a job, but neither one of us felt any urgency about it. Our money was holding up well, and we even managed to put away quite a bit. Fanshawe's next book, *Miracles*, was in the works, and the advance from the contract had been heftier than the one from *Neverland*. According to the schedule that Stuart and I had charted out, the poems would come six months after *Miracles*, then Fanshawe's earliest novel, *Blackouts*, and last of all the plays. Royalties from *Neverland* started coming in that March, and with cheques suddenly arriving for one thing and another, all money problems evaporated. Like everything else that seemed to be happening, this was a new experience for me. For the past eight or nine years, my life had been a constant scrambling act, a frantic lunge from one paltry article to the next, and I had considered myself lucky whenever I could see ahead for more than a month or two. Care was embedded inside me; it was part of my blood, my corpuscles, and I hardly knew what it was to breathe without wondering if I could afford to pay the gas bill. Now, for the first time since I had gone out on my own, I realized that I didn't have to think about these things anymore. One morning, as I sat at my desk struggling over the final sentence of an article, groping for a phrase that was not there, it gradually dawned on me that I had been given a second chance. I could give this up and start again. I no longer had to write articles. I could move on to other things, begin to do the work I had always wanted to do. This was my chance to save myself, and I decided I'd be a fool not to take it.

More weeks passed. I went into my room every morning, but nothing happened. Theoretically, I felt inspired, and whenever I was not working, my head was filled with ideas. But each time I sat down to put something on paper, my thoughts seemed to vanish. Words died the moment I lifted my pen. I started a number of projects, but nothing really took hold, and one by one I dropped them. I looked for excuses to explain why I couldn't get going. That was no problem, and before long I had come up with a whole litany: the adjustment to married life, the responsibilities of fatherhood, my new workroom (which seemed too cramped), the old habit of writing for a deadline, Sophie's body, the sudden windfall – everything. For several days, I even toyed with the idea of writing a detective novel, but then I got stuck with the plot and couldn't fit all the pieces together. I let my mind drift without purpose, hoping to persuade myself that idleness was proof of gathering strength, a sign that something was about to happen. For more than a month, the only thing I did was copy out passages from books. One of them, from Spinoza, I tacked onto my wall: 'And when he dreams he does not want to write, he does not have the power to dream he wants to write; and when he dreams he wants to write, he does not have the power to dream he does not want to write.'

It's possible that I would have worked my way out of this slump. Whether it was a permanent condition or a passing phase is still unclear to me. My gut feeling is that for a time I was truly lost, floundering desperately inside myself, but I do not think this means my case was hopeless. Things were happening to me. I was living through great changes, and it was still too early to tell where they were going to lead. Then, unexpectedly, a solution presented itself. If that is too favourable a word, I will call it a compromise. Whatever it was, I put up very little resistance to it. It came at a vulnerable time for me, and my judgement was not all it should have been. This was my second crucial mistake, and it followed directly from the first.

I was having lunch with Stuart one day near his office on the Upper East Side. Midway through the meal, he brought up the Fanshawe rumours again, and for the first time it occurred to me that he was actually beginning to have doubts. The subject was so fascinating to him that he couldn't stay away from it. His manner was arch, mockingly conspiratorial, but underneath the pose I began to suspect that he was trying to trap me into a confession. I played along with him for a while, and then, growing tired of the game, said that the one foolproof method of settling the question was to commission a biography. I made this remark in all innocence (as a logical point, not as a suggestion), but it seemed to strike Stuart as a splendid idea. He began to gush: of course, of course, the Fanshawe myth explained, perfectly obvious, of course, the true story at last. In a matter of minutes he had the whole thing figured out. I would write the book. It would appear after all of Fanshawe's work had been published, and I could have as much time as I wanted – two years, three years, whatever. It would have to be an extraordinary book, Stuart added, a book equal to Fanshawe himself, but he had great confidence in me, and he knew I could do the job. The proposal caught me off guard, and I treated it as a joke. But Stuart was serious; he wouldn't let me turn him down. Give it some thought, he said, and then tell me how you feel. I remained sceptical, but to be polite I told him I would think about it. We agreed that I would give him a final answer by the end of the month.

I discussed it with Sophie that night, but since I couldn't talk to her honestly, the conversation was not much help to me.

'It's up to you,' she said. 'If you want to do it, I think you should go ahead.'

'It doesn't bother you?'

'No. At least I don't think so. It's already occurred to me that sooner or later there would be a book about him. If it had to happen, then better it should be by you than by someone else.'

'I'd have to write about you and Fanshawe. It might be strange.'

'A few pages will be enough. As long as you're the one who's writing them, I'm not really worried.'

'Maybe,' I said, not knowing how to continue. 'The toughest question, I suppose, is whether I want to get so involved in thinking about Fanshawe. Maybe it's time to let him fade away.'

'It's your decision. But the fact is, you could do this book better than anyone else. And it doesn't have to be a straight biography, you know. You could do something more interesting.'

'Like what?'

'I don't know, something more personal, more gripping. The story of your friendship. It could be as much about you as about him.'

'Maybe. At least it's an idea. The thing that puzzles me is how you can be so calm about it.'

'Because I'm married to you and I love you, that's how. If you decide it's something you want to do, then I'm for it. I'm not blind, after all. I know you've been having trouble with your work, and I sometimes feel that I'm to blame for it. Maybe this is the kind of project you need to get started again.'

I had secretly been counting on Sophie to make the decision for me, assuming she would object, assuming we would talk about it once and that would be the end of it. But just the opposite had happened. I had backed myself into a corner, and my courage suddenly failed me. I let a couple of days go by, and then I called Stuart and told him I would do the book. This got me another free lunch, and after that I was on my own.

There was never any question of telling the truth. Fanshawe had to be dead, or else the book would make no sense. Not only would I have to leave the letter out, but I would have to pretend that it had never been written. I make no bones about what I was planning to do. It was clear to me from the beginning, and I plunged into it with deceit in my heart. The book was a work of fiction. Even though it was based on facts, it could tell nothing but lies. I signed the contract, and afterwards I felt like a man who had signed away his soul.

I wandered in my mind for several weeks, looking for a way to begin. Every life is inexplicable, I kept telling myself. No matter how many facts are told, no matter how many details are given, the essential thing resists telling. To say that so and so was born here and went there, that he did this and did that, that he married this woman and had these children, that he lived, that he died, that he left behind these books or this battle or that bridge – none of that tells us very much. We all want to be told stories, and we listen to them in the same way we did when we were young. We imagine the real story inside the words, and to do this we substitute ourselves for the person in the story, pretending that we can understand him because we understand ourselves. This is a deception. We exist for ourselves, perhaps, and at times we even have a glimmer of who we are, but in the end we can never be sure, and as our lives go on, we become more and more opaque to ourselves, more and more aware of our own incoherence. No one can cross the boundary into another – for the simple reason that no one can gain access to himself.

I thought back to something that had happened to me eight years earlier, in June of 1970. Short of money, and with no immediate prospects for the summer, I took a temporary job as a census-taker in Harlem. There were about twenty of us in the group, a commando corps of field workers hired to track down people who had not responded to the questionnaires sent out in the mail. We trained for several days in a dusty second-floor loft across from the Apollo Theatre, and then, having mastered the intricacies of the forms and the basic rules of census-taker etiquette, dispersed into the neighbourhood with our red, white, and blue shoulder bags to knock on doors, ask questions, and return with the facts. The first place I went to turned out to be the headquarters of a numbers operation. The door opened a sliver, a head poked out (behind it I could see a dozen men in a bare room writing on long picnic tables), and I was politely told that they weren't interested. That seemed to set the tone. In one apartment I talked with a half-blind woman whose parents had been slaves. Twenty minutes into the interview, it finally dawned on her that I wasn't black, and she started cackling with laughter. She had suspected it all long, she said, since my voice was funny, but she had trouble believing it. I was the first white person who had ever been inside her house. In another apartment, I came upon a household of eleven people, none of them older than twenty-two. But for the most part no one was there. And when they were, they wouldn't talk to me or let me in. Summer came, and the streets grew hot and humid, intolerable in the way that only New York can be. I would begin my rounds early, blundering stupidly from house to house, feeling more and more like a man from the moon. I finally spoke to the supervisor (a fast-talking black man who wore silk ascots and a sapphire ring) and explained my problem to him. It was then that I learned what was really expected of me. This man was paid a certain amount for each form a member of his crew turned in. The better our results, the more money would go into his pocket. 'I'm not telling you what to do,' he said, 'but it seems to me that if you've given it an honest shot, then you shouldn't feel too bad.'

'Just give up?' I asked.

'On the other hand,' he continued philosophically, 'the government wants completed forms. The more forms they get, the better they're going to feel. Now I know you're an intelligent boy, and I know you don't get five when you put two and two together. Just because a door doesn't open when you knock on it doesn't mean that nobody's there. You've got to use your imagination, my friend. After all, we don't want the government to be unhappy, do we?'

The job became considerably easier after that, but it was no longer the same job. My field work had turned into desk work, and instead of an investigator I was now an inventor. Every day or two, I stopped by the office to pick up a new batch of forms and turn in the ones I had finished, but other than that I didn't have to leave my apartment. I don't know how many people I invented – but there must have been hundreds of them, perhaps thousands. I would sit in my room with the fan blowing in my face and a cold towel wrapped around my neck, filling out questionnaires as fast as my hand could write. I went in for big households – six, eight, ten children – and took special pride in concocting odd and complicated networks of relationships, drawing on all the possible combinations: parents, children, cousins, uncles, aunts, grandparents, common law spouses, stepchildren, half-brothers, half-sisters, and friends. Most of all, there was the pleasure of making up names. At times I had to curb my impulse towards the outlandish – the fiercely comical, the pun, the dirty word – but for the most part I was content to stay within the bounds of realism. When my imagination flagged, there were certain mechanical devices to fall back on: the colours (Brown, White, Black, Green, Grey, Blue), the Presidents (Washington, Adams, Jefferson, Fillmore, Pierce), fictional characters (Finn, Starbuck, Dimmsdale, Budd). I liked names associated with the sky (Orville Wright, Amelia Earhart), with silent humour (Keaton, Langdon, Lloyd), with long homeruns (Killebrew, Mantle, Mays), and with music (Schubert, Ives, Armstrong). Occasionally, I would dredge up the names of distant relatives or old school friends, and once I even used an anagram of my own.

It was a childish thing to be doing, but I had no qualms. Nor was it hard to justify. The supervisor would not object; the people who actually lived at the addresses on the forms would not object (they did not want to be bothered, especially not by a white boy snooping into their personal business); and the government would not object, since what it did not know could not hurt it, and certainly no more than it was already hurting itself. I even went so far as to defend my preference for large families on political grounds: the greater the poor population, the more obligated the government would feel to spend money on it. This was the dead souls scam with an American twist, and my conscience was clear.

That was on one level. At the heart of it was the simple fact that I was enjoying myself. It gave me pleasure to pluck names out of thin air, to invent lives that had never existed, that never would exist. It was not precisely like making up characters in a story, but something grander, something far more unsettling. Everyone knows that stories are imaginary. Whatever effect they might have on us, we know they are not true, even when they tell us truths more important than the ones we can find elsewhere. As opposed to the story writer, I was offering my creations directly to the real world, and therefore it seemed possible to me that they could affect this real world in a real way, that they could eventually become a part of the real itself. No writer could ask for more than that.

All this came back to me when I sat down to write about Fanshawe. Once, I had given birth to a thousand imaginary souls. Now, eight years later, I was going to take a living man and put him in his grave. I was the chief mourner and officiating clergyman at this mock funeral, and my job was to speak the right words, to say the thing that everyone wanted to hear. The two actions were opposite and identical, mirror images of one another. But this hardly consoled me. The first fraud had been a joke, no more than a youthful adventure, whereas the second fraud was serious, a dark and frightening thing. I was digging a grave, after all, and there were times when I began to wonder if I was not digging my own.

Lives make no sense, I argued. A man lives and then he dies, and what happens in between makes no sense. I thought of the story of La Chère, a soldier who took part in one of the earliest French expeditions to America. In 1562, Jean Ribaut left behind a number of men at Port Royal (near Hilton Head, South Carolina) under the command of Albert de Pierra, a madman who ruled through terror and violence. 'He hanged with his own hands a drummer who had fallen under his displeasure,' Francis Parkman writes, 'and banished a soldier, named La Chère, to a solitary island, three leagues from the fort, where he left him to starve.' Albert was eventually murdered in an uprising by his men, and the half-dead La Chère was rescued from the island. One would think that La Chère was now safe, that having lived through his terrible punishment he would be exempt from further catastrophe. But nothing is that simple. There are no odds to beat, no rules to set a limit on bad luck, and at each moment we begin again, as ripe for a low blow as we were the moment before. Things collapsed at the settlement. The men had no talent for coping with the wilderness, and famine and homesickness took over. Using a few makeshift tools, they spent all their energies on building a ship 'worthy of Robinson Crusoe' to get them back to France. On the Atlantic, another catastrophe: there was no wind, their food and water ran out. The men began to eat their shoes and leather jerkins, some drank sea water in desperation, and several died. Then came the inevitable descent into cannibalism. 'The lot was cast,' Parkman notes, 'and it fell on La Chère, the same wretched man whom Albert had doomed to starvation on a lonely island. They killed him, and with ravenous avidity portioned out his flesh. The hideous repast sustained them till land rose in sight, when, it is said, in a delirium of joy, they could no longer steer their vessel, but let her drift at the will of tide. A small English bark bore down upon them, took them all on board, and, after landing the feeblest, carried the rest prisoners to Queen Elizabeth.'

I use La Chère only as an example. As destinies go, his is by no means strange – perhaps it is even blander than most. At least he travelled along a straight line, and that in itself is rare, almost a blessing. In general, lives seem to veer abruptly from one thing to another, to jostle and bump, to squirm. A person heads in one direction, turns sharply in mid-course, stalls, drifts, starts up again. Nothing is ever known, and inevitably we come to a place quite different from the one we set out for. In my first year as a student at Columbia, I walked by a bust of Lorenzo Da Ponte every day on my way to class. I knew him vaguely as Mozart's librettist, but then I learned that he had also been the first Italian professor at Columbia. The one thing seemed incompatible with the other, and so I decided to look into it, curious to know how one man could wind up living two such different lives. As it turned out, Da Ponte lived five or six. He was born Emmanuele Conegliano in 1749, the son of a Jewish leather merchant. After the death of his mother, his father made a second marriage to a Catholic and decided that he and his children should be baptized. The young Emmanuele showed promise as a scholar, and by the time he was fourteen, the Bishop of Cenada (Monsignore Da Ponte) took the boy under his wing and paid all the costs of his education for the priesthood. As was the custom of the time, the disciple was given his benefactor's name. Da Ponte was ordained in 1773 and became a seminary teacher, with a special interest in Latin, Italian, and French literature. In addition to becoming a follower of the Enlightenment, he involved himself in a number of complicated love affairs, took up with a Venetian noblewoman, and secretly fathered a child. In 1776, he sponsored a public debate at the seminary in Treviso which posed the question whether civilization had succeeded in making mankind any happier. For this affront to Church principles, he was forced to take flight – first to Venice, then to Gorizia, and finally to Dresden, where he began his new career as a librettist. In 1782, he went to Vienna with a letter of introduction to Salieri and was eventually hired as 'poeta dei teatri imperiali', a position he held for almost ten years. It was during this period that he met Mozart and collaborated on the three operas that have preserved his name from oblivion. In 1790, however, when Leopold II curbed musical activities in Vienna because of the Turkish war, Da Ponte found himself out of a job. He went to Trieste and fell in love with an English woman named Nancy Grahl or Krahl (the name is still disputed). From there the two of them went to Paris, and then on to London, where they remained for thirteen years. Da Ponte's musical work was restricted to writing a few libretti for undistinguished composers. In 1805, he and Nancy emigrated to America, where he lived out the last thirty-three years of his life, for a time working as a shopkeeper in New Jersey and Pennsylvania, and dying at the age of eighty-nine – one of the first Italians to be buried in the New World. Little by little, everything had changed for him. From the dapper, unctuous ladies' man of his youth, an opportunist steeped in the political intrigues of both Church and court, he became a perfectly ordinary citizen of New York, which in 1805 must have looked like the end of the world to him. From all that to this: a hard-working professor, a dutiful husband, the father of four. When one of his children died, it is said, he was so distraught with grief that he refused to leave his house for almost a year. The point being that, in the end, each life is irreducible to anything other than itself. Which is as much as to say: lives make no sense.

I don't mean to harp on any of this. But the circumstances under which lives shift course are so various that it would seem impossible to say anything about a man until he is dead. Not only is death the one true arbiter of happiness (Solon's remark), it is the only measurement by which we can judge life itself. I once knew a bum who spoke like a Shakespearean actor, a battered, middle-aged alcoholic with scabs on his face and rags for clothes, who slept on the street and begged money from me constantly. Yet he had once been the owner of an art gallery on Madison Avenue. There was another man I knew who had once been considered the most promising young novelist in America. At the time I met him, he had just inherited fifteen thousand dollars from his father and was standing on a New York street corner passing out hundred dollar bills to strangers. It was all part of a plan to destroy the economic system of the United States, he explained to me. Think of what happens. Think of how lives burst apart. Goffe and Whalley, for example, two of the judges who condemned Charles I to death, came to Connecticut after the Restoration and spent the rest of their lives in a cave. Or Mrs Winchester, the widow of the rifle manufacturer, who feared that the ghosts of the people killed by her husband's rifles were coming to take her soul – and therefore continually added rooms onto her house, creating a monstrous labyrinth of corridors and hideouts, so that she could sleep in a different room every night and thereby elude the ghosts, the irony being that during the San Francisco earthquake of 1906 she was trapped in one of those rooms and nearly starved to death because she couldn't be found by the servants. There is also M. M. Bakhtin, the Russian critic and literary philosopher. During the German invasion of Russia in World War II, he smoked the only copy of one of his manuscripts, a book-length study of German fiction that had taken him years to write. One by one, he took the pages of his manuscript and used the paper to roll his cigarettes, each day smoking a little more of the book until it was gone. These are true stories. They are also parables, perhaps, but they mean what they mean only because they are true.

In his work, Fanshawe shows a particular fondness for stories of this kind. Especially in the notebooks, there is a constant retelling of little anecdotes, and because they are so frequent – and more so toward the end – one begins to suspect that Fanshawe felt they could somehow help him to understand himself. One of the very last (from February 1976, just two months before he disappeared) strikes me as significant.

'In a book I once read by Peter Freuchen,' Fanshawe writes, 'the famous Arctic explorer describes being trapped by a blizzard in northern Greenland. Alone, his supplies dwindling, he decided to build an igloo and wait out the storm. Many days passed. Afraid, above all, that he would be attacked by wolves – for he heard them prowling hungrily on the roof of his igloo – he would periodically step outside and sing at the top of his lungs in order to frighten them away. But the wind was blowing fiercely, and no matter how hard he sang, the only thing he could hear was the wind. If this was a serious problem, however, the problem of the igloo itself was much greater. For Freuchen began to notice that the walls of his little shelter were gradually closing in on him. Because of the particular weather conditions outside, his breath was literally freezing to the walls, and with each breath the walls became that much thicker, the igloo became that much smaller, until eventually there was almost no room left for his body. It is surely a frightening thing, to imagine breathing yourself into a coffin of ice, and to my mind considerably more compelling than, say, *The Pit and the Pendulum* by Poe. For in this case it is the man himself who is the agent of his own destruction, and further, the instrument of that destruction is the very thing he needs to keep himself alive. For surely a man cannot live if he does not breathe. But at the same time, he will not live if he does breathe. Curiously, I do not remember how Freuchen managed to escape his predicament. But needless to say, he did escape. The title of the book, if I recall, is *Arctic Adventure*. It has been out of print for many years.'

In June of that year (1978), Sophie, Ben, and I went out to New Jersey to see Fanshawe's mother. My parents no longer lived next door (they had retired to Florida), and I had not been back in years. As Ben's grandmother, Mrs Fanshawe had stayed in touch with us, but relations were somewhat difficult. There seemed to be an undercurrent of hostility in her toward Sophie, as though she secretly blamed her for Fanshawe's disappearance, and this resentment would surface every now and then in some offhand remark. Sophie and I invited her to dinner at reasonable intervals, but she accepted only rarely, and then, when she did come, she would sit there fidgeting and smiling, rattling on in that brittle way of hers, pretending to admire the baby, paying Sophie inappropriate compliments and saying what a lucky girl she was, and then leave early, always getting up in the middle of a conversation and blurting out that she had forgotten an appointment somewhere else. Still, it was hard to hold it against her. Nothing had gone very well in her life, and by now she had more or less stopped hoping it would. Her husband was dead; her daughter had gone through a long series of mental breakdowns and was now living on tranquillizers in a halfway house; her son had vanished. Still beautiful at fifty (as a boy, I thought she was the most ravishing woman I had ever seen), she kept herself going with a number of intricate love affairs (the roster of men was always in flux), shopping sprees in New York, and a passion for golf. Fanshawe's literary success had taken her by surprise, but now that she had adjusted to it, she was perfectly willing to assume responsibility for having given birth to a genius. When I called to tell her about the biography, she sounded eager to help. She had letters and photographs and documents, she said, and would show me whatever I wanted to see.

We got there by mid-morning, and after an awkward start, followed by a cup of coffee in the kitchen and a long talk about the weather, we were taken upstairs to Fanshawe's old room. Mrs Fanshawe had prepared quite thoroughly for me, and all the materials were laid out in neat piles on what had been Fanshawe's desk. I was stunned by the accumulation. Not knowing what to say, I thanked her for being so helpful – but in fact I was frightened, overwhelmed by the sheer bulk of what was there. A few minutes later, Mrs Fanshawe went downstairs and out into the backyard with Sophie and Ben (it was a warm, sunny day), and I was left there alone. I remember looking out the window and catching a glimpse of Ben as he waddled across the grass in his diaper-padded overalls, shrieking and pointing as a robin skimmed overhead. I tapped on the window, and when Sophie turned around and looked up, I waved to her. She smiled, blew me a kiss, and then walked off to inspect a flower bed with Mrs Fanshawe.

I settled down behind the desk. It was a terrible thing to be sitting in that room, and I didn't know how long I would be able to take it. Fanshawe's baseball glove lay on a shelf with a scuffed-up baseball inside it; on the shelves above it and below it were the books he had read as a child; directly behind me was the bed, with the same blue-and-white checkered quilt I remembered from years before. This was the tangible evidence, the remains of a dead world. I had stepped into the museum of my own past, and what I found there nearly crushed me.

In one pile: Fanshawe's birth certificate, Fanshawe's report cards from school, Fanshawe's Cub Scout badges, Fanshawe's high school diploma. In another pile: photographs. An album of Fanshawe as a baby; an album of Fanshawe and his sister; an album of the family (Fanshawe as a two-year-old smiling in his father's arms, Fanshawe and Ellen hugging their mother on the backyard swing, Fanshawe surrounded by his cousins). And then the loose pictures – in folders, in envelopes, in little boxes: dozens of Fanshawe and me together (swimming, playing catch, riding bikes, mugging in the yard; my father with the two

257

of us on his back; the short haircuts, the baggy jeans, the ancient cars behind us: a Packard, a DeSoto, a wood-pannelled Ford station wagon). Class pictures, team pictures, camp pictures. Pictures of races, of games. Sitting in a canoe, pulling on a rope in a tug-of-war. And then, toward the bottom, a few from later years: Fanshawe as I had never seen him. Fanshawe standing in Harvard Yard; Fanshawe on the deck of an Esso oil tanker; Fanshawe in Paris, in front of a stone fountain. Last of all, a single picture of Fanshawe and Sophie – Fanshawe looking older, grimmer; and Sophie so terribly young, so beautiful, and yet somehow distracted, as though unable to concentrate. I took a deep breath and then started to cry, all of a sudden, not aware until the last moment that I had those tears inside me – sobbing hard, shuddering with my face in my hands.

A box to the right of the pictures was filled with letters, at least a hundred of them, beginning at the age of eight (the clumsy writing of a child, smudged pencil marks and erasures) and continuing on through the early seventies. There were letters from college, letters from the ship, letters from France. Most of them were addressed to Ellen, and many were quite long. I knew immediately that they were valuable, no doubt more valuable than anything else in the room – but I didn't have the heart to read them there. I waited ten or fifteen minutes, then went downstairs to join the others.

Mrs Fanshawe did not want the originals to leave the house, but she had no objection to having the letters photocopied. She even offered to do it herself, but I told her not to bother: I would come out again another day and take care of it.

We had a picnic lunch in the yard. Ben dominated the scene by dashing to the flowers and back again between each bite of his sandwich, and by two o'clock we were ready to go home. Mrs Fanshawe drove us to the bus station and kissed all three of us goodbye, showing more emotion than at any other time during the visit. Five minutes after the bus started up, Ben fell asleep in my lap, and Sophie took hold of my hand.

'Not such a happy day, was it?' she said.

'One of the worst,' I said.

'Imagine having to make conversation with that woman for four hours. I ran out of things to say the moment we got there.'

'She probably doesn't like us very much.'

'No, I wouldn't think so.'

'But that's the least of it.'

'It was hard being up there alone, wasn't it?'

'Very hard.'

'Any second thoughts?'

'I'm afraid so.'

'I don't blame you. The whole thing is getting pretty spooky.'

'I'll have to think it through again. Right now, I'm beginning to feel I've made a big mistake.'

Four days later, Mrs Fanshawe telephoned to say that she was going to Europe for a month and that perhaps it would be a good idea for us to take care of our business now (her words). I had been planning to let the matter slide, but before I could think of a decent excuse for not going out there, I heard myself agreeing to make the trip the following Monday. Sophie backed off from accompanying me, and I didn't press her to change her mind. We both felt that one family visit had been enough.

Jane Fanshawe met me at the bus station, all smiles and affectionate hellos. From the moment I climbed into her car, I sensed that things were going to be different this time. She had made an effort with her appearance (white pants, a red silk blouse, her tanned, unwrinkled neck exposed), and it was hard not to feel that she was enticing me to look at her, to acknowledge the fact that she was still beautiful. But there was more to it than that: a vaguely insinuating tone to her voice, an assumption that we were somehow old friends, on an intimate footing because of the past, and wasn't it lucky that I had come by myself, since now we were free to talk openly with each other. I found it all rather distasteful and said no more than I had to.

'That's quite a little family you have there, my boy,' she said, turning to me as we stopped for a red light.

'Yes,' I said. 'Quite a little family.'

'The baby is adorable, of course. A regular heart-throb. But a bit on the wild side, wouldn't you say?'

'He's only two. Most children tend to be high-spirited at that age.'

'Of course. But I do think that Sophie dotes on him. She seems so amused all the time, if you know what I mean. I'm not arguing against laughter, but a little discipline wouldn't hurt either.'

'Sophie acts that way with everyone,' I said. 'A lively woman is bound to be a lively mother. As far as I can tell, Ben has no complaints.'

A slight pause, and then, as we started up again, cruising along a broad commercial avenue, Jane Fanshawe added: 'She's a lucky girl, that Sophie. Lucky to have landed on her feet. Lucky to have found a man like you.'

'I usually think of it the other way around,' I said.

'You shouldn't be so modest.'

'I'm not. It's just that I know what I'm talking about. So far, all the luck has been on my side.'

She smiled at this briefly, enigmatically, as though judging me a dunce, and yet somehow conceding the point, aware that I wasn't going to give her an opening. By the time we reached her house a few minutes later, she seemed to have dropped her initial tactics. Sophie and Ben were no longer mentioned, and she became a model of solicitude, telling me how glad she was that I was writing the book about Fanshawe, acting as though her encouragement made a real difference – an ultimate sort of approval, not only of the book but of who I was. Then, handing me the keys to her car, she told me how to get to the nearest photocopy store. Lunch, she said, would be waiting for me when I got back.

It took more than two hours to copy the letters, which made it nearly one o'clock by the time I returned to the house. Lunch was indeed there, and it was an impressive spread: asparagus, cold salmon, cheese, white wine, the works. It was all set out on the dining table, accompanied by flowers and what were clearly the best dishes. The surprise must have shown on my face.

'I wanted to make it festive,' Mrs Fanshawe said. 'You have no idea how good it makes me feel to have you here. All the memories that come back. It's as though the bad things never happened.'

I suspected that she had already started drinking while I was gone. Still in control, still steady in her movements, there was a certain thickening that had crept into her voice, a wavering, effusive quality that had not been there before. As we sat down to the table, I told myself to watch it. The wine was poured in liberal doses, and when I saw her paying more attention to her glass than to her plate, merely picking at her food and eventually ignoring it altogether, I began to expect the worst. After some idle talk about my parents and my two younger sisters, the conversation lapsed into a monologue.

'It's strange,' she said, 'strange how things in life turn out. From one moment to the next, you never know what's going to happen. Here you are, the little boy who lived next door. You're the same person who used to run through this house with mud on his shoes – all grown up now, a man. You're the father of my grandson, do you realize that? You're married to my son's wife. If someone had told me ten years ago that this was the future, I would have laughed. That's what you finally learn from life: how strange it is. You can't keep up with what happens. You can't even imagine it.

'You even look like him, you know. You always did, the two of you – like brothers, almost like twins. I remember how when you were both small I would sometimes confuse you from a distance. I couldn't even tell which one of you was mine.

'I know how much you loved him, how you looked up to him. But let me tell you something, my dear. He wasn't half the boy you were. He was cold inside. He was all dead in there, and I don't think he ever loved anyone – not once, not ever in his life. I'd sometimes watch you and your mother across the yard – the way you would run to her and throw your arms around her neck, the way you would let her kiss you – and right there, smack in front of me, I could see everything I didn't have with my own son. He wouldn't let me touch him, you know. After the age of four or five, he'd cringe every time I got near him. How do you think that makes a woman feel – to have her own son despise her? I was so damned young back then. I wasn't even twenty when he was born. Imagine what it does to you to be rejected like that.

'I'm not saying that he was bad. He was a separate being, a child without parents. Nothing I said ever had an effect on him. The same with his father. He refused to learn anything from us. Robert tried and tried, but he could never get through to the boy. But you can't punish someone for a lack of affection, can you? You can't force a child to love you just because he's your child.

'There was Ellen, of course. Poor, tortured Ellen. He was good to her, we both know that. But too good somehow, and in the end it wasn't good for her at all. He brainwashed her. He made her so dependent on him that she began to think twice before turning to us. He was the one who understood her, the one who gave her advice, the one who could solve her problems. Robert and I were no more than figureheads. As far as the children were concerned, we hardly existed. Ellen trusted her brother so much that she finally gave up her soul to him. I'm not saying that he knew what he was doing, but I still have to live with the results. The girl is twenty-seven years old, but she acts as though she were fourteen – and that's when she's doing well. She's so confused, so panicked inside herself. One day she thinks I'm out to destroy her, the next day she calls me thirty times on the telephone. Thirty times. You can't even begin to imagine what it's like.

'Ellen's the reason why he never published any of his work, you know. She's why he quit Harvard after his second year. He was writing poetry back then, and every few weeks he would send her a batch of manuscripts. You know what those poems are like. They're almost impossible to understand. Very passionate, of course, filled with all that ranting and exhortation, but so obscure you'd think they were written in code. Ellen would spend hours puzzling over them, acting as if her life depended on it, treating the poems as secret messages, oracles written directly to her. I don't think he had any idea what was happening. Her brother was gone, you see, and these poems were all she had left of him. The poor baby. She was only fifteen at the time, and already falling to pieces anyway. She would pore over those pages until they were all crumpled and dirty, lugging them around with her wherever she went. When she got really bad, she would go up to perfect strangers on the bus and force them into their hands. "Read these poems," she'd say. "They'll save your life."

'Eventually, of course, she had that first breakdown. She wandered off from me in the supermarket one day, and before I knew it she was taking those big jugs of apple juice off the shelves and smashing them on the floor. One after another, like someone in a trance, standing in all that broken glass, her ankles bleeding, the juice running everywhere. It was horrible. She got so wild, it took three men to restrain her and carry her off.

'I'm not saying that her brother was responsible. But those damned poems certainly didn't help, and rightly or wrongly he blamed himself. From then on, he never tried to publish anything. He came to visit Ellen in the hospital, and I think it was too much for him, seeing her like that, totally beside herself, totally crazy – screaming at him and accusing him of hating her. It was a real schizoid break, you know, and he wasn't able to deal with it. That's when he took the vow not to publish. It was a kind of penance, I think, and he stuck to it for the rest of his life, didn't he, he stuck to it in that stubborn, brutal way of his, right to the end.

'About two months later, I got a letter from him informing me that he had quit college. He wasn't asking my advice, mind you, he was telling me what he'd done. Dear mother, and so on and so forth, all very noble and impressive. I'm dropping out of school to relieve you of the financial burden of supporting me. What with Ellen's condition, the huge medical costs, the blankety x and y and z, and so on and so forth.

'I was furious. A boy like that throwing his education away for nothing. It was an act of sabotage, but there wasn't anything I could do about it. He was already gone. A friend of his at Harvard had a father who had some connection with shipping – I think he represented the seamen's union or something – and he managed to get his papers through that man. By the time the letter reached me, he was in Texas somewhere, and that was that. I didn't see him again for more than five years.

'Every month or so a letter or postcard would come for Ellen, but there was never any return address. Paris, the south of France, God knows where, but he made sure that we didn't have any way of getting in touch with him. I found this behaviour despicable. Cowardly and despicable. Don't ask me why I saved the letters. I'm sorry I didn't burn them. That's what I should have done. Burned the whole lot of them.'

She went on like this for more than an hour, her words gradually mounting in bitterness, at some point reaching a moment of sustained clarity, and then, following the next glass of wine, gradually losing coherence. Her voice was hypnotic. As long as she went on speaking, I felt that nothing could touch me anymore. There was a sense of being immune, of being protected by the words that came from her mouth. I scarcely bothered to listen. I was floating inside that voice, I was surrounded by it, buoyed up by its persistence, going with the flow of syllables, the rise and fall, the waves. As the afternoon light came streaming through the windows onto the table, sparkling in the sauces, the melting butter, the green wine bottles, everything in the room became so radiant and still that I began to find it unreal that I should be sitting there in my own body. I'm melting, I said to myself, watching the butter soften in its dish, and once or twice I even thought that I mustn't let this go on, that I mustn't allow the moment to slip away from me, but in the end I did nothing about it, feeling somehow that I couldn't.

I make no excuses for what happened. Drunkenness is never more than a symptom, not an absolute cause, and I realize that it would be wrong for me to try to defend myself. Nevertheless, there is at least the possibility of an explanation. I am fairly certain now that the things that followed had as much to do with the past as with the present, and I find it odd, now that I have some distance from it, to see how a number of ancient feelings finally caught up with me that afternoon. As I sat there listening to Mrs Fanshawe, it was hard not to remember how I had seen her as a boy, and once this began to happen, I found myself stumbling onto images that had not been visible to me in years. There was one in particular that struck me with great force: an afternoon in August when I was thirteen or fourteen, looking through my bedroom window into the yard next door and seeing Mrs Fanshawe walk out in a red two-piece bathing suit, casually unhook the top half, and lie down on a lawn chair with her back to the sun. All this happened by chance. I had been sitting by my window day-dreaming, and then, unexpectedly, a beautiful woman comes sauntering into my field of vision, almost naked, unaware of my presence, as though I had conjured her myself. This image stayed with me for a long time, and I returned to it often during my adolescence: a little boy's lust, the quick of late-night fantasies. Now that this woman was apparently in the act of seducing me, I hardly knew what to think. On the one hand, I found the scene grotesque. On the other hand, there was something natural about it, even logical, and I sensed that if I didn't use all my strength to fight it, I was going to allow it to happen.

There's no question that she made me pity her. Her version of Fanshawe was so anguished, so fraught with the signs of genuine unhappiness, that I gradually weakened to her, fell into her trap. What I still don't understand, however, is to what extent she was conscious of what she was doing. Had she planned it in advance, or did the thing just happen by itself? Was her rambling speech a ploy to wear down my resistance, or was it a spontaneous burst of true feeling? I suspect that she was telling the truth about Fanshawe, her own truth at any rate, but that is not enough to convince me – for even a child knows that the truth can be used for devious ends. More importantly, there is the question of motive. Close to six years after the fact, I still haven't come up with an answer. To say that she found me irresistible would be far-fetched, and I am not willing to delude myself about that. It was much deeper, much more sinister. Recently, I've begun to wonder if she didn't somehow sense a hatred in me for Fanshawe that was just as strong as her own. Perhaps she felt this unspoken bond between us, perhaps it was the kind of bond that could be proved only through some perverse, extravagant act. Fucking me would be like fucking Fanshawe – like fucking her own son – and in the darkness of this sin, she would have him again – but only in order to destroy him. A terrible revenge. If this is true, then I do not have the luxury of calling myself her victim. If anything, I was her accomplice.

It began not long after she started to cry – when she finally exhausted herself and the words broke apart, crumbling into tears. Drunk, filled with emotion, I stood up, walked over to where she was sitting, and put my arms around her in a gesture of comfort. This carried us across the threshold. Mere contact was enough to trigger a sexual response, a blind memory of other bodies, of other embraces, and a moment later we were kissing, and then, not many moments after that, lying naked on her bed upstairs.

Although I was drunk, I was not so far gone that I didn't know what I was doing. But not even guilt was enough to stop me. This moment will end, I said to myself, and no one will be hurt. It has nothing to do with my life, nothing to do with Sophie. But then, even as it was happening, I discovered there was more to it than that. For the fact was that I liked fucking Fanshawe's mother – but in a way that had nothing to do with pleasure. I was consumed, and for the first time in my life I found no tenderness inside me. I was fucking out of hatred, and I turned it into an act of violence, grinding away at this woman as though I wanted to pulverize her. I had entered my own darkness, and it was there that I learned the one thing that is more terrible than anything else: that sexual desire can also be the desire to kill, that a moment comes when it is possible for a man to choose death over life. This woman wanted me to hurt her, and I did, and I found myself revelling in my cruelty. But even then I knew that I was only halfway home, that she was no more than a shadow, and that I was using her to attack Fanshawe himself. As I came into her the second time – the two of us covered with sweat, groaning like creatures in a nightmare – I finally understood this. I wanted to kill Fanshawe. I wanted Fanshawe to be dead, and I was going to do it. I was going to track him down and kill him.

I left her in the bed asleep, crept out of the room, and called for a taxi from the phone downstairs. Half an hour later I was on the bus back to New York. At the Port Authority Terminal, I went into the men's room and washed my hands and face, then took the subway uptown. I got home just as Sophie was setting the table for dinner.

The worst of it began then. There were so many things to hide from Sophie, I could barely show myself to her at all. I turned edgy, remote, shut myself up in my little work-room, craved only solitude. For a long time Sophie bore with me, acting with a patience I had no right to expect, but in the end even she began to wear out, and by the middle of the summer we had started quarrelling, picking at each other, squabbling over things that meant nothing. One day I walked into the house and found her crying on the bed, and I knew then that I was on the verge of smashing my life.

For Sophie, the problem was the book. If only I would stop working on it, then things would return to normal. I had been too hasty, she said. The project was a mistake, and I should not be stubborn about admitting it. She was right, of course, but I kept arguing the other side to her: I had committed myself to the book, I had signed a contract for it, and it would be cowardly to back out. What I didn't tell her was that I no longer had any intention of writing it. The book existed for me now only in so far as it could lead me to Fanshawe, and beyond that there was no book at all. It had become a private matter for me, something no longer connected to writing. All the research for the biography, all the facts I would uncover as I dug into his past, all the work that seemed to belong to the book – these were the very things I would use to find out where he was. Poor Sophie. She never had the slightest notion of what I was up to – for what I claimed to be doing was in fact no different from what I actually did. I was piecing together the story of a man's life. I was gathering information, collecting names, places, dates, establishing a chronology of events. Why I persisted like this still baffles me. Everything had been reduced to a single impulse: to find Fanshawe, to speak to Fanshawe, to confront Fanshawe one last time. But I could never take it farther than that, could never pin down an image of what I was hoping to achieve by such an encounter. Fanshawe had written that he would kill me, but that threat did not scare me off. I knew that I had to find him – that nothing would be settled until I did. This was the given, the first principle, the mystery of faith: I acknowledged it, but I did not bother to question it.

In the end, I don't think that I really intended to kill him. The murderous vision that had come to me with Mrs Fanshawe did not last, at least not on any conscious level. There were times when little scenes would flash through my head – of strangling Fanshawe, of stabbing him, of shooting him in the heart – but others had died similar deaths inside me over the years, and I did not pay much attention to them. The strange thing was not that I might have wanted to kill Fanshawe, but that I sometimes imagined he *wanted* me to kill him. This happened only once or twice – at moments of extreme lucidity – and I became convinced that this was the true meaning of the letter he had written. Fanshawe was waiting for me. He had chosen me as his executioner, and he knew that he could trust me to carry out the job. But that was precisely why I wasn't going to do it. Fanshawe's power had to be broken, not submitted to. The point was to prove to him that I no longer cared – that was the crux of it: to treat him as a dead man, even though he was alive. But before I proved this to Fanshawe, I had to prove it to myself, and the fact that I needed to prove it was proof that I still cared too much. It was not enough for me to let things take their course. I had to shake them up, bring them to a head. Because I still doubted myself, I needed to run risks, to test myself before the greatest possible danger. Killing Fanshawe would mean nothing. The point was to find him alive – and then to walk away from him alive.

The letters to Ellen were useful. Unlike the notebooks, which tended to be speculative and devoid of detail, the letters were highly specific. I sensed that Fanshawe was making an effort to entertain his sister, to cheer her up with amusing stories, and consequently the references were more personal than elsewhere. Names, for example, were often mentioned – of college friends, of shipmates, of people he knew in France. And if there were no return addresses on the envelopes, there were nevertheless many places discussed: Baytown, Corpus Christi, Charleston, Baton Rouge, Tampa, different neighbourhoods in Paris, a village in southern France. These things were enough to get me started, and for several weeks I sat in my room making lists, correlating people with places, places with times, times with people, drawing maps and calendars, looking up addresses, writing letters. I was hunting for leads, and anything that held even the slightest promise I tried to pursue. My assumption was that somewhere along the line Fanshawe had made a mistake – that someone knew where he was, that someone from the past had seen him. This was by no means sure, but it seemed like the only plausible way to begin.

The college letters are rather plodding and sincere – accounts of books read, discussions with friends, descriptions of dormitory life – but these come from the period before Ellen's breakdown, and they have an intimate, confidential tone that the future letters abandon. On the ship, for example, Fanshawe rarely says anything about himself – except as it might pertain to an anecdote he has chosen to tell. We see him trying to fit into his new surroundings, playing cards in the dayroom with an oiler from Louisiana (and winning), playing pool in various low-life bars ashore (and winning), and then explaining his success as a fluke: 'I'm so geared up not to fall on my face, I've somehow gone beyond myself. A surge of adrenalin, I think.' Descriptions of working overtime in the engine room, 'a hundred and forty degrees, if you can believe it – my sneakers filled up with so much sweat, they squished as though I'd been walking in puddles'; of having a wisdom tooth pulled by a drunken dentist in Baytown, Texas, 'blood all over the place, and little bits of tooth cluttering the hole in my gums for a week.' As a newcomer with no seniority, Fanshawe was moved from job to job. At each port there were crew members who left the ship to go home and others who came aboard to take their places, and if one of these fresh arrivals preferred Fanshawe's job to the one that was open, the Kid (as he was called) would be bumped to something else. Fanshawe therefore worked variously as an ordinary seaman (scraping and painting the deck), as a utility man (mopping floors, making beds, cleaning toilets), and as a messman (serving food and washing dishes). This last job was the hardest, but it was also the most interesting, since ship life chiefly revolves around the subject of food: the great appetites nurtured by boredom, the men literally living from one meal to the next, the surprising delicacy of some of them (fat, coarse men judging dishes with the haughtiness and disdain of eighteenth-century French dukes). But Fanshawe was given good advice by an old-timer the day he started the job: 'Don't take no shit from no one,' the man said. 'If a guy complains about the food, tell him to button it. If he keeps it up, act like he's not there and serve him last. If that don't do the trick, tell him you'll put ice water in his soup the next time. Even better, tell him you'll piss in it. You gotta let them know who's boss.'

We see Fanshawe carrying the captain his breakfast one morning after a night of violent storms off Cape Hatteras: Fanshawe putting the grapefruit, the scrambled eggs, and the toast on a tray, wrapping the tray in tinfoil, then further wrapping it in towels, hoping the plates will not blow off into the water when he reaches the bridge (since the wind is holding at seventy miles per hour); Fanshawe then climbing up the ladder, taking his first steps on the bridge, and then, suddenly, as the wind hits him, doing a wild pirouette – the ferocious air shooting under the tray and pulling his arms up over his head, as though he were holding on to a primitive flying machine, about to launch himself over the water; Fanshawe, summoning all his strength to pull down the tray, finally wrestling it to a position flat against his chest, the plates miraculously not slipping, and then, step by struggling step, walking the length of the bridge, a tiny figure dwarfed by the havoc of the air around him; Fanshawe, after how many minutes, making it to the other end, entering the forecastle, finding the plump captain behind the wheel, saying, 'Your breakfast, captain', and the helmsman turning, giving him the briefest glance of recognition and replying, in a distracted voice, 'Thanks, kid. Just put it on the table over there.'

Not everything was so amusing to Fanshawe, however. There is mention of a fight (no details given) that seems to have disturbed him, along with several ugly scenes he witnessed ashore. An instance of nigger-baiting in a Tampa bar, for example: a crowd of drunks ganging up on an old black man who had wandered in with a large American flag – wanting to sell it – and the first drunk opening the flag and saying there weren't enough stars on it – 'this flag's a fake' – and the old man denying it, almost grovelling for mercy, as the other drunks start grumbling in support of the first – the whole thing ending when the old man is pushed out the door, landing flat on the sidewalk, and the drunks nodding approval, dismissing the matter with a few comments about making the world safe for democracy. 'I felt humiliated,' Fanshawe wrote, 'ashamed of myself for being there.'

Still, the letters are basically jocular in tone ('Call me Redburn', one of them begins), and by the end one senses that Fanshawe has managed to prove something to himself. The ship is no more than an excuse, an arbitrary otherness, a way to test himself against the unknown. As with any initiation, survival itself is the triumph. What begin as possible liabilities – his Harvard education, his middle-class background – he eventually turns to his advantage, and by the end of his stint he is the acknowledged intellectual of the crew, no longer just the 'Kid' but at times also the 'Professor', brought in to arbitrate disputes (who was the twenty-third President, what is the population of Florida, who played left field for the 1947 Giants) and consulted regularly as a source of obscure information. Crew members ask

272

his help in filling out bureaucratic forms (tax schedules, insurance questionnaires, accident reports), and some even ask him to write letters for them (in one case, seventeen love letters for Otis Smart to his girlfriend Sue-Ann in Dido, Louisiana). The point is not that Fanshawe becomes the centre of attention, but that he manages to fit in, to find a place for himself. The true test, after all, is to be like everyone else. Once that happens, he no longer has to question his singularity. He is free – not only of others, but of himself. The ultimate proof of this, I think, is that when he leaves the ship, he says goodbye to no one. He signs off one night in Charleston, collects his pay from the captain, and then just disappears. Two weeks later he arrives in Paris.

No word for two months. And then, for the next three months, nothing but postcards. Brief, elliptical messages scrawled on the back of commonplace tourist shots: Sacré Coeur, the Eiffel Tower, the Conciergerie. When the letters do begin to come, they arrive fitfully, and say nothing of any great importance. We know that by now Fanshawe is deep into his work (numerous early poems, a first draft of *Blackouts*), but the letters give no real sense of the life he is leading. One feels that he is in conflict, unsure of himself in regard to Ellen, not wanting to lose touch with her and yet unable to decide how much or how little to tell her. (And the fact is that most of these letters are not even read by Ellen. Addressed to the house in New Jersey, they are of course opened by Mrs Fanshawe, who screens them before showing them to her daughter – and more often than not, Ellen does not see them. Fanshawe, I think, must have known this would happen, at least would have suspected it. Which further complicates the matter – since in some way these letters are not written to Ellen at all. Ellen, finally, is no more than a literary device, the medium through which Fanshawe communicates with his mother. Hence her anger. For even as he speaks to her, he can pretend to ignore her.)

For about a year the letters dwell almost exclusively on objects (buildings, streets, descriptions of Paris), hashing out meticulous catalogues of things seen and heard, but Fanshawe himself is barely present. Then, gradually, we begin to see some of his acquaintances, to sense a slow gravitation towards the anecdote – but still, the stories are divorced from any context, which gives them a floating, disembodied quality. We see, for example, an old Russian composer by the name of Ivan Wyshnegradsky, now nearly eighty years old – impoverished, a widower, living alone in a shabby apartment on the rue Mademoiselle. 'I see this man more than anyone else,' Fanshawe declares. Then not a word about their friendship, not a glimmer of what they say to each other. Instead, there is a lengthy description of the quarter-tone piano in the apartment, with its enormous bulk and multiple keyboards (built for Wyshnegradsky in Prague almost fifty years before, and one of only three quarter-tone pianos in Europe), and then, making no further allusions to the composer's career, the story of how Fanshawe gives the old man a refrigerator. 'I was moving to another apartment last month,' Fanshawe writes. 'Since the place was furnished with a new refrigerator, I decided to give the old one to Ivan as a present. Like many people in Paris, he has never had a refrigerator – storing his food for all these years in a little box in the wall of his kitchen. He seemed quite pleased by the offer, and I made all the arrangements to have it delivered to his house – carrying it upstairs with the help of the man who drove the truck. Ivan greeted the arrival of this machine as an important event in his life – bubbling over like a small child – and yet he was wary, I could see that, even a bit daunted, not quite sure what to make of this alien object. "It's so big," he kept saying, as we worked it into place, and then, when we plugged it in and the motor started up – "Such a lot of noise." I assured him that he would get used to it, pointing out all the advantages of this modern convenience, all the ways in which his life would be improved. I felt like a missionary: big Father Know-It-All, redeeming the life of this stone-age man by showing him the true religion. A week or so went by, and Ivan called me nearly every day to tell me how happy he was with the refrigerator, describing all the new foods he was able to buy and keep in his house. Then disaster.

"I think it's broken," he said to me one day, sounding very contrite. The little freezer section on top had apparently filled up with frost, and not knowing how to get rid of it, he had used a hammer, banging away not only at the ice but at the coils below it. "My dear friend," he said, "I'm very sorry." I told him not to fret – I would find a repair man to fix it. A long pause on the other end. "Well," he said at last, "I think maybe it's better this way. The noise, you know. It makes it very hard to concentrate. I've lived so long with my little box in the wall, I feel rather attached to it. My dear friend, don't be angry. I'm afraid there's nothing to be done with an old man like me. You get to a certain point in life, and then it's too late to change." '

Further letters continue this trend, with various names mentioned, various jobs alluded to. I gather that the money Fanshawe earned on the ship lasted for about a year and that afterwards he scrambled as best he could. For a time it seems that he translated a series of art books; at another time there is evidence that he worked as an English tutor for several lycée students; still again, it seems that he worked the graveyard shift one summer at the *New York Times* Paris office as a switchboard operator (which, if nothing else, indicates that he had become fluent in French); and then there is a rather curious period during which he worked off and on for a movie producer – revising treatments, translating, preparing script synopses. Although there are few autobiographical allusions in any of Fanshawe's works, I believe that certain incidents in *Neverland* can be traced back to this last experience (Montag's house in chapter seven; Flood's dream in chapter thirty). 'The strange thing about this man,' Fanshawe writes (referring to the movie producer in one of his letters), 'is that while his financial dealings with the rich border on the criminal (cutthroat tactics, outright lying), he is quite gentle with those down on their luck. People who owe him money are rarely sued or taken to court – but are given a chance to work off their debts by rendering him services. His chauffeur, for example, is a destitute marquis who drives around in a white Mercedes. There is an old baron who does nothing but xerox papers. Every time I visit the apartment to turn in my work, there is some new lackey standing in the corner, some decrepit nobleman hiding behind the curtains, some elegant financier who turns out to be the messenger boy. Nor does anything go to waste. When the ex-director who had been living in the maid's room on the sixth floor committed suicide last month, I inherited his overcoat – and have been wearing it ever since. A long black affair that comes down almost to my ankles. It makes me look like a spy.'

As for Fanshawe's private life, there are only the vaguest hints. A dinner party is referred to, a painter's studio is described, the name Anne sneaks out once or twice – but the nature of these connections is obscure. This was the kind of thing I needed, however. By doing the necessary legwork, by going out and asking enough questions, I figured I would eventually be able to track some of these people down.

Besides a three-week trip to Ireland (Dublin, Cork, Limerick, Sligo), Fanshawe seems to have remained more or less fixed. The final draft of *Blackouts* was completed at some point during his second year in Paris; *Miracles* was written during the third, along with forty or fifty short poems. All this is rather easy to determine – since it was around this time that Fanshawe developed the habit of dating his work. Still unclear is the precise moment when he left Paris for the country, but I believe it falls somewhere between June and September of 1971. The letters become sparse just then, and even the notebooks give no more than a list of the books he was reading (Raleigh's *History of the World* and *The Journeys* of Cabeza de Vaca). But once he is ensconced in the country house, he gives a fairly elaborate account of how he wound up there. The details are unimportant in themselves, but one crucial thing emerges: while living in France Fanshawe did not hide the fact that he was a writer. His friends knew about his work, and if there was ever any secret, it was only meant for his family. This is a definite slip on his part – the only time in any of the letters he gives himself away. 'The Dedmons, an American couple I know in Paris,' he writes, 'are unable to visit their country house for the next year (they're going to Japan). Since the place has been broken into once or twice, they're reluctant to leave it empty – and have offered me the job of caretaker. Not only do I get it rent-free, but I'm also given the use of a car and a small salary (enough to get by on if I'm very careful). This is a lucky break. They said they would much rather pay me to sit in the house and write for a year than rent it out to strangers.' A small point, perhaps, but when I came across it in the letter, I was heartened. Fanshawe had momentarily let down his guard – and if it happened once, there was no reason to assume it could not happen again.

As examples of writing, the letters from the country surpass all the others. By now, Fanshawe's eye has become incredibly sharp, and one senses a new availability of words inside him, as though the distance between seeing and writing had been narrowed, the two acts now almost identical, part of a single, unbroken gesture. Fanshawe is preoccupied by the landscape, and he keeps returning to it, endlessly watching it, endlessly recording its changes. His patience before these things is never less than remarkable, and there are passages of nature writing in both the letters and notebooks as luminous as any I have read. The stone house he lives in (walls two feet thick) was built during the Revolution: on one side is a small vineyard, on the other side is a meadow where sheep graze; there is a forest behind (magpies, rooks, wild boar), and in front, across the road, are the cliffs that lead up to the village (population forty). On these same cliffs, hidden in a tangle of bushes and trees, are the ruins of a chapel that once belonged to the Knights Templar. Broom, thyme, scrub oak, red soil, white clay, the Mistral – Fanshawe lives amidst these things for more than a year, and little by little they seem to alter him, to ground him more deeply in himself. I hesitate to talk about a religious or mystical experience (these terms mean nothing to me), but from all the evidence it seems that Fanshawe was alone for the whole time, barely seeing anyone, barely even opening his mouth. The stringency of this life disciplined him. Solitude became a passageway into the self, an instrument of discovery. Although he was still quite young at the time, I believe this period marked the beginning of his maturity as a writer. From now on, the work is no longer promising – it is fulfilled, accomplished, unmistakably his own. Starting with the long sequence of poems written in the country (*Ground Work*), and then on through the plays and *Neverland* (all written in New York), Fanshawe is in full flower. One looks for traces of madness, for signs of the thinking that eventually turned him against himself – but the work reveals nothing of the sort. Fanshawe is no doubt an unusual person, but to all appearances he is sane, and when he returns to America in the fall of 1972, he seems totally in command of himself.

My first answers came from the people Fanshawe had known at Harvard. The word *biography* seemed to open doors for me, and I had no trouble getting appointments to see most of them. I saw his freshman roommate; I saw several of his friends; I saw two or three of the Radcliffe girls he had dated. Nothing much came of it, however. Of all the people I met, only one said anything of interest. This was Paul Schiff, whose father had made the arrangements for Fanshawe's job on the oil tanker. Schiff was now a paediatrician in Westchester County, and we spoke in his office one evening until quite late. There was an earnestness about him that I liked (a small, intense man, his hair already thinning, with steady eyes and a soft, resonant voice), and he talked openly, without any prodding. Fanshawe had been an important person in his life, and he remembered their friendship well. 'I was a diligent boy,' Schiff said. 'Hard-working, obedient, without much imagination. Fanshawe wasn't intimidated by Harvard the way the rest of us were, and I think I was in awe of that. He had read more than anyone else – more poets, more philosophers, more novelists – but the business of school seemed to bore him. He didn't care about grades, cut class a lot, just seemed to go his own way. In freshman year, we lived down the hall from each other, and for some reason he picked me out to be his friend. After that, I sort of tagged along after him. Fanshawe had so many ideas about everything, I think I learned more from him than from any of my classes. It was a bad case of hero-worship, I suppose – but Fanshawe helped me, and I haven't forgotten it. He was the one who taught me to think for myself, to make my own choices. If it hadn't been for him, I never would have become a doctor. I switched to pre-med because he convinced me to do what I wanted to do, and I'm still grateful to him for it.

'Midway through our second year, Fanshawe told me that he was going to quit school. It didn't really surprise me. Cambridge wasn't the right place for Fanshawe, and I knew that he was restless, itching to get away. I talked to my father, who represented the seamen's union, and he worked out that job for Fanshawe on the ship. It was arranged very neatly. Fanshawe was whisked through all the paperwork, and a few weeks later he was off. I heard from him several times – postcards from here and there. Hi, how are you, that kind of thing. It didn't bother me though, and I was glad that I'd been able to do something for him. But then, all those good feelings eventually blew up in my face. I was in the city one day about four years ago, walking along Fifth Avenue, and I ran into Fanshawe, right there on the street. I was delighted to see him, really surprised and happy, but he hardly even talked to me. It was as though he'd forgotten who I was. Very stiff, almost rude. I had to force my address and phone number into his hand. He promised to call, but of course he never did. It hurt a lot, I can tell you. The son-of-a-bitch, I thought to myself, who does he think he is? He wouldn't even tell me what he was doing – just evaded my questions and sauntered off. So much for college days, I thought. So much for friendship. It left an ugly taste in my mouth. Last year, my wife bought one of his books and gave it to me as a birthday present. I know it's childish, but I haven't had the heart to open it. It just sits there on the shelf collecting dust. It's very strange, isn't it? Everyone says it's a masterpiece, but I don't think I can ever bring myself to read it.'

This was the most lucid commentary I got from anyone. Some of the oil tanker shipmates had things to say, but nothing that really served my purpose. Otis Smart, for example, remembered the love letters Fanshawe had written for him. When I reached him by telephone in Baton Rouge, he went on about them at great length, even quoting some of the phrases Fanshawe had made up ('my darling twinkle-toes', 'my pumpkin squash woman', 'my wallow-dream wickedness', and so on), laughing as he spoke. The damndest thing was, he said, that the whole time he was sending those letters to Sue-Ann, she was fooling around with someone else, and the day he got home she announced to him that she was getting married. 'It's just as well,' Smart added. 'I ran into Sue-Ann back home last year, and she's up to about three hundred pounds now. She looks like a cartoon fat lady – strutting down the street in orange stretch pants with a mess of brats bawling around her. It made me laugh, it did – remembering the letters. That Fanshawe really cracked me up. He'd get going with some of those lines of his, and I'd start rolling on the floor like a monkey. It's too bad about what happened. You hate to hear about a guy punching his ticket so young.'

Jeffrey Brown, now a chef in a Houston restaurant, had been the assistant cook on the ship. He remembered Fanshawe as the one white crew member who had been friendly to him. 'It wasn't easy,' Brown said. 'The crew was mostly a bunch of rednecks, and they'd just as soon spit at me as say hello. But Fanshawe stuck by me, didn't care what anyone thought. When we got into Baytown and places like that, we'd go ashore together for drinks, for girls, whatever. I knew those towns better than Fanshawe did, and I told him that if he wanted to stick with me, we couldn't go into the regular sailors' bar. I knew what my ass would be worth in places like that, and I didn't want trouble. No problem, Fanshawe said, and off we'd go to the black sections, no problem at all. Most of the time, things were pretty calm on the ship – nothing I couldn't handle. But then this rough customer came on for a few weeks. A guy named Cutbirth, if you can believe it, Roy Cutbirth. He was a stupid honky oiler who finally got thrown off the ship when the Chief Engineer figured out he didn't know squat about engines. He'd cheated on his oiler's test to get the job – just the man to have down there if you want to blow up the ship. This Cutbirth was dumb, mean and dumb. He had those tattoos on his knuckles – a letter on each finger: L-O-V-E on the right hand, H-A-T-E on the left. When you see that kind of crazy shit, you just want to keep away. This guy once bragged to Fanshawe about how he used to spend his Saturday nights back home in Alabama – sitting on a hill over the interstate and shooting at cars. A charming fellow, no matter how you put it. And then there was this sick eye he had, all bloodshot and messed up. But he liked to brag about that, too. Seems he got it one day when a piece of glass flew into it. That was in Selma, he said, throwing bottles at Martin Luther King. I don't have to tell you that this Cutbirth wasn't my bosom buddy. He used to give me a lot of stares, muttering under his breath and nodding to himself, but I paid no attention. Things went on like that for a while. Then he tried it with Fanshawe around, and the way it came out, it was just a little too loud for Fanshawe to ignore. He stops, turns to Cutbirth, and says, "What did you say?" And Cutbirth, all tough and cocky, says something like "I was just wondering when you and the jungle bunny are getting married, sweetheart." Well, Fanshawe was always peaceable and friendly, a real gentleman, if you know what I mean, and so I wasn't expecting what happened. It was like watching that hulk on the TV, the man who turns into a beast. All of a sudden he got angry, I mean raging, damned near *beside* himself with anger. He grabbed Cutbirth by the shirt and just threw him against the wall, just pinned him there and held on, breathing right into his face. "Don't ever say that again," Fanshawe says, his eyes all on fire. "Don't ever say that again, or I'll kill you." And damned if you didn't believe him when he said it. The guy was ready to kill, and Cutbirth knew it. "Just joking," he says. 'Just making a little joke." And that was the end of it – real fast. The whole thing didn't take more than half a blink. About two days later, Cutbirth got fired. A lucky thing, too. If he'd stayed around any longer, there's no telling what might have happened.'

I got dozens of statements like this one – from letters, from phone conversations, from interviews. It went on for months, and each day the material expanded, grew in geometric surges, accumulating more and more associations, a chain of contacts that eventually took on a life of its own. It was an infinitely hungry organism, and in the end I saw that there was nothing to prevent it from becoming as large as the world itself. A life touches one life, which in turn touches another life, and very quickly the links are innumerable, beyond calculation. I knew about a fat woman in a small Louisiana town; I knew about a demented racist with tattoos on his fingers and a name that defied understanding. I knew about dozens of people I had never heard of before, and each one had been a part of Fanshawe's life. All well and good, perhaps, and one might say that this surplus of knowledge was the very thing that proved I was getting somewhere. I was a detective, after all, and my job was to hunt for clues. Faced with a million bits of random information, led down a million paths of false inquiry, I had to find the one path that would take me where I wanted to go. So far, the essential fact was that I hadn't found it. None of these people had seen or heard from Fanshawe in years, and short of doubting everything they told me, short of beginning an investigation into each one of them, I had to assume they were telling the truth.

What it boiled down to, I think, was a question of method. In some sense, I already knew everything there was to know about Fanshawe. The things I learned did not teach me anything important, did not go against any of the things I already knew. Or, to put it another way: the Fanshawe I had known was not the same Fanshawe I was looking for. There had been a break somewhere, a sudden, incomprehensible break – and the things I was told by the various people I questioned did not account for it. In the end, their statements only confirmed that what happened could not possibly have happened. That Fanshawe was kind, that Fanshawe was cruel – this was an old story, and I already knew it by heart. What I was looking for was something different, something I could not even imagine: a purely ir-rational act, a thing totally out of character, a contradiction of everything Fanshawe had been up to the moment he vanished. I kept trying to leap into the unknown, but each time I landed, I found myself on home ground, surrounded by what was most familiar to me.

The farther I went, the more the possibilities narrowed. Per-haps that was a good thing, I don't know. If nothing else, I knew that each time I failed, there would be one less place to look. Months went by, more months than I would like to admit. In February and March I spent most of my time looking for Quinn, the private detective who had worked for Sophie. Strangely enough, I couldn't find a trace of him. It seemed that he was no longer in business – not in New York, not anywhere. For a while I investigated reports of unclaimed bodies, ques-tioned people who worked at the city morgue, tried to track down his family – but nothing came of it. As a last resort, I considered hiring another private detective to look for him, but then decided not to. One missing man was enough, I felt, and then, little by little, I used up the possibilities that were left. By mid-April, I was down to the last one. I held out for a few more days, hoping I would get lucky, but nothing developed. On the morning of the twenty-first, I finally walked into a travel agency and booked a flight to Paris.

I was supposed to leave on a Friday. On Tuesday, Sophie and I went shopping for a record player. One of her younger sisters was about to move to New York, and we were planning to give her our old record player as a present. The idea of replacing it had been in the air for several months, and this finally gave us an excuse to go looking for a new one. So we went downtown that Tuesday, bought the thing, and then lugged it home in a cab. We hooked it up in the same spot where the old one had been and then packed away the old one in the new box. A clever solution, we thought. Karen was due to arrive in May, and in the mean time we wanted to keep it somewhere out of sight. That was when we ran into a problem.

Storage space was limited, as it is in most New York apartments, and it seemed that we didn't have any left. The one closet that offered any hope was in the bedroom, but the floor was already crammed with boxes – three deep, two high, four across and there wasn't enough room on the shelf above. These were the cartons that held Fanshawe's things (clothes, books, odds and ends), and they had been there since the day we moved in. Neither Sophie nor I had known what to do with them when she cleaned out her old place. We didn't want to be surrounded by memories of Fanshawe in our new life, but at the same time it seemed wrong just to throw the things away. The boxes had been a compromise, and eventually we no longer seemed to notice them. They became a part of the domestic landscape – like the broken floorboard under the living room rug, like the crack in the wall above our bed – invisible in the flux of daily life. Now, as Sophie opened the door of the closet and looked inside, her mood suddenly changed.

'Enough of this,' she said, squatting down in the closet. She pushed away the clothes that were draped over the boxes, clicking hangers against each other, parting the jumble in frustration. It was an abrupt anger, and it seemed to be directed more at herself than at me.

'Enough of what?' I was standing on the other side of the bed, watching her back.

'All of it,' she said, still flinging the clothes back and forth. 'Enough of Fanshawe and his boxes.'

'What do you want to do with them?' I sat down on the bed and waited for an answer, but she didn't say anything. 'What do you want to do with them, Sophie?' I asked again.

She turned around and faced me, and I could see that she was on the point of tears. 'What good is a closet if you can't even use it?' she said. Her voice was trembling, losing control. 'I mean

he's dead, isn't he? And if he's dead, why do we need all this
. . . all this' – gesturing, groping for the word – 'garbage. It's like
living with a corpse.'

'If you want, we can call the Salvation Army today,' I said.

'Call them now. Before we say another word.'

'I will. But first we'll have to open the boxes and sort through
them.'

'No. I want it to be everything, all at once.'

'It's fine for clothes,' I said. 'But I wanted to hold on to the
books for a while. I've been meaning to make a list, and I
wanted to check for any notes in the margins. I could finish in
half an hour.'

Sophie looked at me in disbelief. 'You don't understand anything, do you?' she said. And then, as she stood up, the tears
finally came out of her eyes – child's tears, tears that held
nothing back, falling down her cheeks as if she didn't know they
were there. 'I can't get through to you anymore. You just don't
hear what I'm saying.'

'I'm doing my best, Sophie.'

'No, you're not. You think you are, but you're not. Don't you
see what's happening? Your bringing him back to life.'

'I'm writing a book. That's all – just a book. But if I don't take
it seriously, how can I hope to get it done?'

'There's more to it than that. I know it, I can feel it. If the two
of us are going to last, he's got to be dead. Don't you understand that? Even if he's alive, he's got to be dead.'

'What are you talking about? Of course he's dead.'

'Not for much longer. Not if you keep it up.'

'But you were the one who got me started. You wanted me to
do the book.'

'That was a hundred years ago, my darling. I'm so afraid I'm
going to lose you. I couldn't take it if that happened.'

'It's almost finished, I promise. This trip is the last step.'

'And then what?'

'We'll see. I can't know what I'm getting into until I'm in it.'

'That's what I'm afraid of.'

285

'You could go with me.'

'To Paris?'

'To Paris. The three of us could go together.'

'I don't think so. Not the way things are now. You go alone. At least then, if you come back, it will be because you want to.'

'What do you mean "if"?'

'Just that. "If". As in, "if you come back." '

'You can't believe that.'

'But I do. If things go on like this, I'm going to lose you.'

'Don't talk like that, Sophie.'

'I can't help it. You're so close to being gone already. I sometimes think I can see you vanishing before my eyes.'

'That's nonsense.'

'You're wrong. We're coming to the end, my darling, and you don't even know it. You're going to vanish, and I'll never see you again.'

Things felt oddly bigger to me in Paris. The sky was more present than in New York, its whims more fragile. I found myself drawn to it, and for the first day or two I watched it constantly – sitting in my hotel room and studying the clouds, waiting for something to happen. These were northern clouds, the dream clouds that are always changing, massing up into huge grey mountains, discharging brief showers, dissipating, gathering again, rolling across the sun, refracting the light in ways that always seem different. The Paris sky has its own laws, and they function independently of the city below. If the buildings appear solid, anchored in the earth, indestructible, the sky is vast and amorphous, subject to constant turmoil. For the first week, I felt as though I had been turned upside-down. This was an old-world city, and it had nothing to do with New York – with its slow skies and chaotic streets, its bland clouds and aggressive buildings. I had been displaced, and it made me suddenly unsure of myself. I felt my grip loosening, and at least once an hour I had to remind myself why I was there.

My French was neither good nor bad. I had enough to understand what people said to me, but speaking was difficult, and there were times when no words came to my lips, when I struggled to say even the simplest things. There was a certain pleasure in this, I believe – to experience language as a collection of sounds, to be forced to the surface of words where meanings vanish – but it was also quite wearing, and it had the effect of shutting me up in my thoughts. In order to understand what people were saying, I had to translate everything silently into English, which meant that even when I understood, I was understanding at one remove – doing twice the work and getting half the result. Nuances, subliminal associations, undercurrents – all these things were lost on me. In the end, it would probably not be wrong to say that everything was lost on me.

Still, I pushed ahead. It took me a few days to get the investigation started, but once I made my first contact, others followed. There were a number of disappointments, however. Wyshnegradsky was dead; I was unable to locate any of the people Fanshawe had tutored in English; the woman who had hired Fanshawe at the *New York Times* was gone, had not worked there in years. Such things were to be expected, but I took them hard, knowing that even the smallest gap could be fatal. These were empty spaces for me, blanks in the picture, and no matter how successful I was in filling the other areas, doubts would remain, which meant that the work could never be truly finished.

I spoke to the Dedmons, I spoke to the art book publishers Fanshawe had worked for, I spoke to the woman named Anne (a girlfriend, it turned out), I spoke to the movie producer. 'Odd jobs,' he said to me, in Russian-accented English, 'that's what he did. Translations, script summaries, a little ghost-writing for my wife. He was a smart boy, but too stiff. Very literary, if you know what I'm saying. I wanted to give him a chance to act – even offered to give him fencing and riding lessons for a picture we were going to do. I liked his looks, thought we could make something of him. But he wasn't interested. I've got other eggs to fry, he said. Something like that. It didn't matter. The picture made millions, and what do I care if the boy wants to act or not?'

There was something to be pursued here, but as I sat with this man in his monumental apartment on the Avenue Henri Martin, waiting for each sentence of his story between phone calls, I suddenly realized that I didn't need to hear any more. There was only one question that mattered, and this man couldn't answer it for me. If I stayed and listened to him, I would be given more details, more irrelevancies, yet another pile of useless notes. I had been pretending to write a book for too long now, and little by little I had forgotten my purpose. Enough, I said to myself, consciously echoing Sophie, enough of this, and then I stood up and left.

The point was that no one was watching me anymore. I no longer had to put up a front as I had at home, no longer had to delude Sophie by creating endless busy-work for myself. The charade was over. I could discard my non-existent book at last. For about ten minutes, walking back to my hotel across the river, I felt happier than I had in months. Things had been simplified, reduced to the clarity of a single problem. But then, the moment I absorbed this thought, I understood how bad the situation really was. I was coming to the end now, and I still hadn't found him. The mistake I was looking for had never surfaced. There were no leads, no clues, no tracks to follow. Fanshawe was buried somewhere, and his whole life was buried with him. Unless he wanted to be found, I didn't have a ghost of a chance.

Still, I pushed ahead, trying to come to the end, to the very end, burrowing blindly through the last interviews, not willing to give up until I had seen everyone. I wanted to call Sophie. One day, I even went so far as to walk to the post office and wait in line for the foreign operator, but I didn't go through with it. Words were failing me constantly now, and I panicked at the thought of losing my nerve on the phone. What was I supposed to say, after all? Instead, I sent her a postcard with a photograph of Laurel and Hardy on it. On the back I wrote: 'True marriages never make sense. Look at the couple on the other side. Proof that anything is possible, no? Perhaps we should start wearing derbies. At the very least, remember to clean out the closet before I return. Hugs to Ben.'

I saw Anne Michaux the following afternoon, and she gave a little start when I entered the café where we had arranged to meet (Le Rouquet, Boulevard Saint Germain). What she told me about Fanshawe is not important: who kissed who, what happened where, who said what, and so on. It comes down to more of the same. What I will mention, however, is that her initial double take was caused by the fact that she mistook me for

Fanshawe. Just the briefest flicker, as she put it, and then it was gone. The resemblance had been noticed before, of course, but never so viscerally, with such immediate impact. I must have shown my reaction, for she quickly apologized (as if she had done something wrong) and returned to the point several times during the two or three hours we spent together – once even going out of her way to contradict herself: 'I don't know what I was thinking. You don't look at all like him. It must have been the American in both of you.'

Nevertheless, I found it disturbing, could not help feeling appalled. Something monstrous was happening, and I had no control over it anymore. The sky was growing dark inside – that much was certain; the ground was trembling. I found it hard to sit still, and I found it hard to move. From one moment to the next, I seemed to be in a different place, to forget where I was. Thoughts stop where the world begins, I kept telling myself. But the self is also in the world, I answered, and likewise the thoughts that come from it. The problem was that I could no longer make the right distinctions. This can never be that. Apples are not oranges, peaches are not plums. You feel the difference on your tongue, and then you know, as if inside yourself. But everything was beginning to have the same taste to me. I no longer felt hungry, I could no longer bring myself to eat.

As for the Dedmons, there is perhaps even less to say. Fanshawe could not have chosen more fitting benefactors, and of all the people I saw in Paris, they were the kindest, the most gracious. Invited to their apartment for drinks, I stayed on for dinner, and then, by the time we reached the second course, they were urging me to visit their house in the Var – the same house where Fanshawe had lived, and it needn't be a short visit, they said, since they were not planning to go there themselves until August. It had been an important place for Fanshawe and his work, Mr Dedmon said, and no doubt my book would be enhanced if I saw it myself. I couldn't disagree with him, and no sooner were these words out of my mouth than Mrs Dedmon was on the phone making arrangements for me in her precise and elegant French.

There was nothing to hold me in Paris anymore, and so I took the train the following afternoon. This was the end of the line for me, my southward trek to oblivion. Whatever hope I might have had (the faint possibility that Fanshawe had returned to France, the illogical thought that he had found refuge in the same place twice) evaporated by the time I got there. The house was empty; there was no sign of anyone. On the second day, examining the rooms on the upper floor, I came across a short poem Fanshawe had written on the wall – but I knew that poem already, and under it there was a date: 25 August 1972. He had never come back. I felt foolish now even for thinking it.

For want of anything better to do, I spent several days talking to people in the area: the nearby farmers, the villagers, the people of surrounding towns. I introduced myself by showing them a photograph of Fanshawe, pretending to be his brother, but feeling more like a down-and-out private eye, a buffoon clutching at straws. Some people remembered him, others didn't, still others weren't sure. It made no difference. I found the southern accent impenetrable (with its rolling 'r's and nasalized endings) and barely understood a word that was said to me. Of all the people I saw, only one had heard from Fanshawe since his departure. This was his closest neighbour – a tenant farmer who lived about a mile down the road. He was a peculiar little man of about forty, dirtier than anyone I had ever met. His house was a dank, crumbling seventeenth-century structure, and he seemed to live there by himself, with no companions but his truffle dog and hunting rifle. He was clearly proud of having been Fanshawe's friend, and to prove how close they had been he showed me a white cowboy hat that Fanshawe had sent to him after returning to America. There was no reason not to believe his story. The hat was still in its original box and apparently had never been worn. He explained that he was saving it for the right moment, and then launched into a political harangue that I had trouble following. The revolution was coming, he said, and when it did, he was going to buy a white horse and a machine gun, put on his hat, and ride down the main street in town, plugging all the shopkeepers who had collaborated with the Germans during the War. Just like in America, he added. When I asked him what he meant, he delivered a rambling, hallucinatory lecture about cowboys and Indians. But that was a long time ago, I said, trying to cut him short. No, no, he insisted, it still goes on today. Didn't I know about the shootouts on Fifth Avenue? Hadn't I heard of the Apaches? It was pointless to argue. In defence of my ignorance, I told him that I lived in another neighbourhood.

I stayed on in the house for a few more days. My plan was to do nothing for as long as I could, to rest up. I was exhausted, and I needed a chance to regroup before going back to Paris. A day or two went by. I walked through the fields, visited the woods, sat out in the sun reading French translations of American detective novels. It should have been the perfect cure: holing up in the middle of nowhere, letting my mind float free. But none of it really helped. The house wouldn't make room for me, and by the third day I sensed that I was no longer alone, that I could never be alone in that place. Fanshawe was there, and no matter how hard I tried not to think about him, I couldn't escape. This was unexpected, galling. Now that I had stopped looking for him, he was more present to me than ever before. The whole process had been reversed. After all these months of trying to find him, I felt as though I was the one who had been found. Instead of looking for Fanshawe, I had actually been running away from him. The work I had contrived for myself – the false book, the endless detours – had been no more than an attempt to ward him off, a ruse to keep him as far away from me as possible. For if I could convince myself that I was looking for him, then it necessarily followed that he was somewhere else – somewhere beyond me, beyond the limits of my life. But I had been wrong. Fanshawe was exactly where I was, and he had been there since the beginning. From the moment his letter arrived, I had been struggling to imagine him, to see him as he might have been – but my mind had always conjured a blank. At best, there was one impoverished image: the door of a locked room. That was the extent of it: Fanshawe alone in that room, condemned to a mythical solitude – living perhaps, breathing perhaps, dreaming God knows what. This room, I now discovered, was located inside my skull.

Strange things happened to me after that. I returned to Paris, but once there I found myself with nothing to do. I didn't want to look up any of the people I had seen before, and I didn't have the courage to go back to New York. I became inert, a thing that could not move, and little by little I lost track of myself. If I am able to say anything about this period at all, it is only because I have certain documentary evidence to help me. The visa stamps in my passport, for example; my airplane ticket, my hotel bill, and so on. These things prove to me that I remained in Paris for more than a month. But that is very different from remembering, and in spite of what I know, I still find it impossible. I see things that happened, I encounter images of myself in various places, but only at a distance, as though I were watching someone else. None of it feels like memory, which is always anchored within; it's out there beyond what I can feel or touch, beyond anything that has to do with me. I have lost a month from my life, and even now it is a difficult thing for me to confess, a thing that fills me with shame.

A month is a long time, more than enough time for a man to come apart. Those days come back to me in fragments when they come at all, bits and pieces that refuse to add up. I see myself falling down drunk on the street one night, standing up, staggering towards a lamppost, and then vomiting all over my shoes. I see myself sitting in a movie theatre with the lights on and watching a crowd of people file out around me, unable to remember the film I had just seen. I see myself prowling the rue Saint-Denis at night, picking out prostitutes to sleep with, my head burning with the thought of bodies, an endless jumble of naked breasts, naked thighs, naked buttocks. I see my cock being sucked, I see myself on a bed with two girls kissing each other, I see an enormous black woman spreading her legs on a bidet and washing her cunt. I will not try to say that these things are not real, that they did not happen. It's just that I can't account for them. I was fucking the brains out of my head, drinking myself into another world. But if the point was to obliterate Fanshawe, then my binge was a success. He was gone – and I was gone along with him.

The end, however, is clear to me. I have not forgotten it, and I feel lucky to have kept that much. The entire story comes down to what happened at the end, and without that end inside me now, I could not have started this book. The same holds for the two books that come before it, *City of Glass* and *Ghosts*. These three stories are finally the same story, but each one represents a different stage in my awareness of what it is about. I don't claim to have solved any problems. I am merely suggesting that a moment came when it no longer frightened me to look at what had happened. If words followed, it was only because I had no choice but to accept them, to take them upon myself and go where they wanted me to go. But that does not necessarily make the words important. I have been struggling to say goodbye to something for a long time now, and this struggle is all that really matters. The story is not in the words; it's in the struggle.

One night, I found myself in a bar near the Place Pigalle. *Found* is the term I wish to use, for I have no idea of how I got there, no memory of entering the place at all. It was one of those clip joints that are common in the neighbourhood: six or eight girls at the bar, the chance to sit at a table with one of them and buy an exorbitantly priced bottle of champagne, and then, if one is so inclined, the possibility of coming to a certain financial agreement and retiring to the privacy of a room in the hotel next door. The scene begins for me as I'm sitting at one of the tables with a girl, just having received the bucket of champagne. The girl was Tahitian, I remember, and she was beautiful: no more than nineteen or twenty, very small, and wearing a dress of white netting with nothing underneath, a crisscross of cables over her smooth brown skin. The effect was superbly erotic. I remember her round breasts visible in the diamond-shaped openings, the overwhelming softness of her neck when I leaned over and kissed it. She told me her name, but I insisted on calling her Fayaway, telling her that she was an exile from Typee and that I was Herman Melville, an American sailor who had come all the way from New York to rescue her. She hadn't the vaguest idea of what I was talking about, but she continued to smile, no doubt thinking me crazy as I rambled on in my sputtering French, unperturbed, laughing when I laughed, allowing me to kiss her wherever I liked.

We were sitting in an alcove in the corner, and from my seat I was able to take in the rest of the room. Men came and went, some popping their heads through the door and leaving, some staying for a drink at the bar, one or two going to a table as I had done. After about fifteen minutes, a young man came in who was obviously American. He seemed nervous to me, as if he had never been in such a place before, but his French was surprisingly good, and as he fluently ordered a whiskey at the bar and started talking to one of the girls, I saw that he meant to stay for a while. I studied him from my little nook, continuing to run my hand along Fayaway's leg and to nuzzle her with my face, but the longer he stood there, the more distracted I became. He was tall, athletically built, with sandy hair and an open, somewhat boyish manner. I guessed his age at twenty-six or twenty-seven – a graduate student, perhaps, or else a young lawyer working for an American firm in Paris. I had never seen this man before, and yet there was something familiar about him, something that stopped me from turning away: a brief scald, a weird synapse of recognition. I tried out various names on him, shunted him through the past, unravelled the spool of associations – but nothing happened. He's no one, I said to myself, finally giving up. And then, out of the blue, by some muddled chain of reasoning, I finished the thought by adding: and if he's no one, then he must be Fanshawe. I laughed out loud at my joke. Ever on the alert, Fayaway laughed with me. I knew that nothing could be more absurd, but I said it again: Fanshawe. And then again: Fanshawe. And the more I said it, the more it pleased me to say it. Each time the word came out of my mouth, another burst of laughter followed. I was intoxicated by the sound of it; it drove me to a pitch of raucousness, and little by little Fayaway seemed to grow confused. She had probably thought I was referring to some sexual practice, making some joke she couldn't understand, but my repetitions had gradually robbed the word of its meaning, and she began to hear it as a threat. I looked at the man across the room and spoke the word again. My happiness was immeasurable. I exulted in the sheer falsity of my assertion, celebrating the new power I had just bestowed upon myself. I was the sublime alchemist who could change the world at will. This man was Fanshawe because I said he was Fanshawe, and that was all there was to it. Nothing could stop me anymore. Without even pausing to think, I whispered into Fayaways's ear that I would be right back, disengaged myself from her wonderful arms, and sauntered over to the pseudo-Fanshawe at the bar. In my best imitation of an Oxford accent, I said:

'Well, old man, fancy that. We meet again.'

He turned around and looked at me carefully. The smile that had been forming on his face slowly diminished into a frown. 'Do I know you?' he finally asked.

'Of course you do,' I said, all bluster and good humour. 'The name's Melville. Herman Melville. Perhaps you've read some of my books.'

He didn't know whether to treat me as a jovial drunk or a dangerous psychopath, and the confusion showed on his face. It was a splendid confusion, and I enjoyed it thoroughly.

'Well,' he said at last, forcing out a little smile, 'I might have read one or two.'

'The one about the whale, no doubt.'

'Yes. The one about the whale.'

'I'm glad to hear it,' I said, nodding pleasantly, and then put my arm around his shoulder. 'And so, Fanshawe,' I said, 'what brings you to Paris this time of year?'

The confusion returned to his face. 'Sorry,' he said, 'I didn't catch that name.'

'Fanshawe.'

'Fanshawe?'

'Fanshawe. F-A-N-S-H-A-W-E.'

'Well,' he said, relaxing into a broad grin, suddenly sure of himself again, 'that's the problem right there. You've mixed me up with someone else. My name isn't Fanshawe. It's Stillman. Peter Stillman.'

'No problem,' I answered, giving him a little squeeze. 'If you want to call yourself Stillman, that's fine with me. Names aren't important, after all. What matters is that I know who you really are. You're Fanshawe. I knew it the moment you walked in. "There's the old devil himself," I said. "I wonder what he's doing in a place like this?"'

He was beginning to lose patience with me now. He removed my arm from his shoulder and backed off. 'That's enough,' he said. 'You've made a mistake, and let's leave it at that. I don't want to talk to you anymore.'

'Too late,' I said. 'Your secret's out, my friend. There's no way to hide from me now.'

'Leave me alone,' he said, showing anger for the first time. 'I don't talk to lunatics. Leave me alone, or there'll be trouble.'

The other people in the bar couldn't understand what we were saying, but the tension had become obvious, and I could feel myself being watched, could feel the mood shift around me. Stillman suddenly seemed to panic. He shot a glance at the woman behind the bar, looked apprehensively at the girl beside him, and then made an impulsive decision to leave. He pushed me out of his way and started for the door. I could have let it go at that, but I didn't. I was just getting warmed up, and I didn't want my inspiration to be wasted. I went back to where Fayaway was sitting and put a few hundred francs on the table. She feigned a pout in response. 'C'est mon frère,' I said. 'Il est fou. Je dois le poursuivre.' And then, as she reached for the money, I blew her a kiss, turned around, and left.

Stillman was twenty or thirty yards ahead of me, walking quickly down the street. I kept pace with him, hanging back to avoid being noticed, but not letting him move out of sight. Every now and then he looked back over his shoulder, as though expecting me to be there, but I don't think he saw me until we were well out of the neighbourhood, away from the crowds and commotion, slicing through the quiet, darkened core of the Right Bank. The encounter had spooked him, and he behaved like a man running for his life. But that was not difficult to understand. I was the thing we all fear most: the belligerent stranger who steps out from the shadows, the knife that stabs us in the back, the speeding car that crushes us to death. He was right to be running, but his fear only egged me on, goaded me to pursue him, made me rabid with determination. I had no plan, no idea of what I was going to do, but I followed him without the slightest doubt, knowing that my whole life hinged on it. It is important to stress that by now I was completely lucid – no wobbling, no drunkenness, utterly clear in my head. I realized that I was acting outrageously. Stillman was not Fanshawe – I knew that. He was an arbitrary choice, totally innocent and blank. But that was the thing that thrilled me – the randomness of it, the vertigo of pure chance. It made no sense, and because of that, it made all the sense in the world.

A moment came when the only sounds in the street were our footsteps. Stillman looked back again and finally saw me. He began moving faster, breaking into a trot. I called after him: 'Fanshawe.' I called after him again: 'It's too late. I know who you are, Fanshawe.' And then, on the next street: 'It's all over, Fanshawe. You'll never get away.' Stillman said nothing in response, did not even bother to turn around. I wanted to keep talking to him, but by now he was running, and if I tried to talk, it would only have slowed me down. I abandoned my taunts and went after him. I have no idea how long we ran, but it seemed to go on for hours. He was younger than I was, younger and stronger, and I almost lost him, almost didn't make it. I pushed myself down the dark street, passing the point of exhaustion, of sickness, frantically hurtling toward him, not allowing my self to stop. Long before I reached him, long before I even knew I was going to reach him, I felt as though I was no longer inside myself. I can think of no other way to express it. I couldn't feel myself anymore. The sensation of life had dribbled out of me, and in its place there was a miraculous euphoria, a sweet poison rushing through my blood, the undeniable odour of nothingness. This is the moment of my death, I said to myself, this is when I die. A second later, I caught up to Stillman and tackled him from behind. We went crashing to the pavement, the two of us grunting on impact. I had used up all my strength, and by now I was too short of breath to defend myself, too drained to struggle. Not a word was said. For several seconds we grappled on the sidewalk, but then he managed to break free of my grip, and after that there was nothing I could do. He started pounding me with his fists, kicking me with the points of his shoes, pummelling me all over. I remember trying to protect my face with my hands; I remember the pain and how it stunned me, how much it hurt and how desperately I wanted not to feel it anymore. But it couldn't have lasted very long, for nothing else comes back to me. Stillman tore me apart, and by the time he was finished, I was out cold. I can remember waking up on the sidewalk and being surprised that it was still night, but that's the extent of it. Everything else is gone.

For the next three days I didn't move from my hotel room. The shock was not so much that I was in pain, but that it would not be strong enough to kill me. I realized this by the second or third day. At a certain moment, lying there on the bed and looking at the slats of the closed shutters, I understood that I had lived through it. It felt strange to be alive, almost incomprehensible. One of my fingers was broken; both temples were gashed; it ached even to breathe. But that was somehow beside the point. I was alive, and the more I thought about it, the less I understood. It did not seem possible that I had been spared.

Later that same night, I wired Sophie that I was coming home.

I am nearly at the end now. There is one thing left, but that did not happen until later, until three more years had passed. In the mean time, there were many difficulties, many dramas, but I do not think they belong to the story I am trying to tell. After my return to New York, Sophie and I lived apart for almost a year. She had given up on me, and there were months of confusion before I finally won her back. From the vantage point of this moment (May 1984), that is the only thing that matters. Beside it, the facts of my life are purely incidental.

On 23 February 1981, Ben's baby brother was born. We named him Paul, in memory of Sophie's grandfather. Several months later (in July) we moved across the river, renting the top two floors of a brownstone house in Brooklyn. In September, Ben started kindergarten. We all went to Minnesota for Christmas, and by the time we got back, Paul was walking on his own. Ben, who had gradually taken him under his wing, claimed full credit for the development.

As for Fanshawe, Sophie and I never talked about him. This was our silent pact, and the longer we said nothing, the more we proved our loyalty to each other. After I returned the advance money to Stuart Green and officially stopped writing the biography, we mentioned him only once. That came on the day we decided to live together again, and it was couched in strictly practical terms. Fanshawe's books and plays had continued to produce a good income. If we were going to stay married, Sophie said, then using the money for ourselves was out of the question. I agreed with her. We found other ways to earn what we had to and placed the royalty money in trust for Ben – and subsequently for Paul as well. As a final step, we hired a literary agent to manage the business of Fanshawe's work: requests to perform plays, reprint negotiations, contracts, whatever needed to be done. To the extent that we were able to act, we did. If Fanshawe still had the power to destroy us, it would only be because we wanted him to, because we wanted to destroy ourselves. That was why I never bothered to tell Sophie the truth – not because it frightened me, but because the truth was no longer important. Our strength was in our silence, and I had no intention of breaking it.

Still, I knew that the story wasn't over. My last month in Paris had taught me that, and little by little I learned to accept it. It was only a matter of time before the next thing happened. This seemed inevitable to me, and rather than deny it anymore, rather than delude myself with the thought that I could ever get rid of Fanshawe, I tried to prepare myself for it, tried to make myself ready for anything. It is the power of this *anything*, I believe, that has made the story so difficult to tell. For when anything can happen – that is the precise moment when words begin to fail. To the degree that Fanshawe became inevitable, that was the degree to which he was no longer there. I learned to accept this. I learned to live with him in the same way I lived with the thought of my own death. Fanshawe himself was not death – but he was like death, and he functioned as a trope for death inside me. If not for my breakdown in Paris, I never would have understood this. I did not die there, but I came close, and there was a moment, perhaps there were several moments, when I tasted death, when I saw myself dead. There is no cure for such an encounter. Once it happens, it goes on happening; you live with it for the rest of your life.

The letter came early in the spring of 1982. This time the postmark was from Boston, and the message was terse, more urgent than before. 'Impossible to hold out any longer,' it said. 'Must talk to you. 9 Columbus Square, Boston; April 1st. This is where it ends, I promise.'

I had less than a week to invent an excuse for going to Boston. This turned out to be more difficult than it should have been. Although I persisted in not wanting Sophie to know anything (feeling that it was the least I could do for her), I somehow balked at telling another lie, even though it had to be done. Two or three days slipped by without any progress, and in the end I concocted some lame story about having to consult papers in the Harvard Library. I can't even remember what papers they were supposed to be. Something to do with an article I was going to write, I think, but that could be wrong. The important thing was that Sophie did not raise any objections. Fine, she said, go right ahead, and so on. My gut feeling is that she suspected something was up, but that is only a feeling, and it would be pointless to speculate about it here. Where Sophie is concerned, I tend to believe that nothing is hidden.

I booked a seat for April first on the early train. On the morning of my departure, Paul woke up a little before five and climbed into bed with us. I roused myself an hour later and crept out of the room, pausing briefly at the door to watch Sophie and the baby in the dim grey light – sprawled out, impervious, the bodies I belonged to. Ben was in the kitchen upstairs, already dressed, eating a banana and drawing pictures. I scrambled some eggs for the two of us and told him that I was about to take a train to Boston. He wanted to know where Boston was.

'About two hundred miles from here,' I said.

'Is that as far away as space?'

'If you went straight up, you'd be getting close.'

'I think you should go to the moon. A rocket ship is better than a train.'

'I'll do that on the way back. They have regular flights from Boston to the moon on Fridays. I'll reserve a seat the moment I get there.'

'Good. Then you can tell me what it's like.'

'If I find a moon rock, I'll bring one back for you.'

'What about Paul?'

'I'll get one for him, too.'

'No thanks.'

'What does that mean?'

'I don't want a moon rock. Paul would put his in his mouth and choke.'

'What would you like instead?'

'An elephant.'

'There aren't any elephants in space.'

'I know that. But you aren't going to space.'

'True.'

'And I bet there are elephants in Boston.'

'You're probably right. Do you want a pink elephant or a white elephant?'

'A grey elephant. A big fat one with lots of wrinkles.'

'No problem. Those are the easiest ones to find. Would you like it wrapped up in a box, or should I bring it home on a leash?'

'I think you should ride it home. Sitting on top with a crown on your head. Just like an emperor.'

'The emperor of what?'

'The emperor of little boys.'

'Do I get to have an empress?'

'Of course. Mommy is the empress. She'd like that. Maybe we should wake her up and tell her.'

'Let's not. I'd rather surprise her with it when I get home.'

'Good idea. She won't believe it until she sees it anyway.'

'Exactly. And we don't want her to be disappointed. In case I can't find the elephant.'

'Oh, you'll find it, Dad. Don't worry about that.'

'How can you be so sure?'

'Because you're the emperor. An emperor can get anything he wants.'

It rained the whole way up, the sky even threatening snow by the time we reached Providence. In Boston, I bought myself an umbrella and covered the last two or three miles on foot. The streets were gloomy in the piss-grey air, and as I walked to the South End, I saw almost no one: a drunk, a group of teenagers, a telephone man, two or three stray mutts. Columbus Square

303

consisted of ten or twelve houses in a row, fronting on a cobbled island that cut it off from the main thoroughfare. Number nine was the most dilapidated of the lot – four stories like the others, but sagging, with boards propping up the entranceway and the brick façade in need of mending. Still, there was an impressive solidity to it, a nineteenth-century elegance that continued to show through the cracks. I imagined large rooms with high ceilings, comfortable ledges by the bay window, moulded ornaments in the plaster. But I did not get to see any of these things. As it turned out, I never got beyond the front hall.

There was a rusted metal clapper in the door, a half-sphere with a handle in the centre, and when I twisted the handle, it made the sound of someone retching – a muffled, gagging sound that did not carry very far. I waited, but nothing happened. I twisted the bell again, but no one came. Then, testing the door with my hand, I saw that it wasn't locked – pushed it open, paused, and went in. The front hall was empty. To my right was the staircase, with its mahogany banister and bare wooden steps: to my left were closed double doors, blocking off what was no doubt the parlour; straight ahead there was another door, also closed, that probably led to the kitchen. I hesitated for a moment, decided on the stairs, and was about to go up when I heard something from behind the double doors – a faint tapping, followed by a voice I couldn't understand. I turned from the staircase and looked at the door, listening for the voice again. Nothing happened.

A long silence. Then, almost in a whisper, the voice spoke again. 'In here,' it said.

I went to the doors and pressed my ear against the crack between them. 'Is that you, Fanshawe?'

'Don't use that name,' the voice said, more distinctly this time. 'I won't allow you to use that name.' The mouth of the person inside was lined up directly with my ear. Only the door was between us, and we were so close that I felt as if the words were being poured into my head. It was like listening to a man's heart beating in his chest, like searching a body for a pulse. He

304

stopped talking, and I could feel his breath slithering through the crack.

'Let me in,' I said. 'Open the door and let me in.'

'I can't do that,' the voice answered. 'We'll have to talk like this.'

I grabbed hold of the door knob and shook the doors in frustration. 'Open up,' I said. 'Open up, or I'll break the door down.'

'No,' said the voice. 'The door stays closed.' By now I was convinced that it was Fanshawe in there. I wanted it to be an impostor, but I recognized too much in that voice to pretend it was anyone else. 'I'm standing here with a gun,' he said, 'and it's pointed right at you. If you come through the door, I'll shoot.'

'I don't believe you.'

'Listen to this,' he said, and then I heard him turn away from the door. A second later a gun went off, followed by the sound of plaster falling to the floor. I tried to peer through the crack in the mean time, hoping to catch a glimpse of the room, but the space was too narrow. I could see no more than a thread of light, a single grey filament. Then the mouth returned, and I could no longer see even that.

'All right,' I said, 'you have a gun. But if you don't let me see you, how will I know you are who you say you are?'

'I haven't said who I am.'

'Let me put it another way. How can I know I'm talking to the right person?'

'You'll have to trust me.'

'At this late date, trust is about the last thing you should expect.'

'I'm telling you that I'm the right person. That should be enough. You've come to the right place, and I'm the right person.'

'I thought you wanted to see me. That's what you said in your letter.'

'I said that I wanted to talk to you. There's a difference.'

'Let's not split hairs.'

'I'm just reminding you of what I wrote.'

'Don't push me too far, Fanshawe. There's nothing to stop me from walking out.'

I heard a sudden intake of breath, and then a hand slapped violently against the door. 'Not Fanshawe!' he shouted. 'Not Fanshawe – ever again!'

I let a few moments pass, not wanting to provoke another outburst. The mouth withdrew from the crack, and I imagined that I heard groans from somewhere in the middle of the room – groans or sobs, I couldn't tell which. I stood there waiting, not knowing what to say next. Eventually, the mouth returned, and after another long pause Fanshawe said, 'Are you still there?'

'Yes.'

'Forgive me. I didn't want it to begin like this.'

'Just remember,' I said, 'I'm only here because you asked me to come.'

'I know that. And I'm grateful to you for it.'

'It might help if you explained why you invited me.'

'Later. I don't want to talk about that yet.'

'Then what?'

'Other things. The things that have happened.'

'I'm listening.'

'Because I don't want you to hate me. Can you understand that?'

'I don't hate you. There was a time when I did, but I'm over that now.'

'Today is my last day, you see. And I had to make sure.'

'Is this where you've been all along?'

'I came here about two years ago, I think.'

'And before that?'

'Here and there. That man was after me, and I had to keep moving. It gave me a feeling for travel, a real taste for it. Not at all what I had expected. My plan had always been to sit still and let the time run out.'

'You're talking about Quinn?'

306

'Yes. The private detective.'

'Did he find you?'

'Twice. Once in New York. The next time down South.'

'Why did he lie about it?'

'Because I scared him to death. He knew what would happen to him if anyone found out.'

'He disappeared, you know. I couldn't find a trace of him.'

'He's somewhere. It's not important.'

'How did you manage to get rid of him?'

'I turned everything around. He thought he was following me, but in fact I was following him. He found me in New York, of course, but I got away – wriggled right through his arms. After that, it was like playing a game. I led him along, leaving clues for him everywhere, making it impossible for him not to find me. But I was watching him the whole time, and when the moment came, I set him up, and he walked straight into my trap.'

'Very clever.'

'No. It was stupid. But I didn't have any choice. It was either that or get hauled back – which would have meant being treated like a crazy man. I hated myself for it. He was only doing his job, after all, and it made me feel sorry for him. Pity disgusts me, especially when I find it in myself.'

'And then?'

'I couldn't be sure if my trick had really worked. I thought Quinn might come after me again. And so I kept on moving, even when I didn't have to. I lost about a year like that.'

'Where did you go?'

'The South, the Southwest. I wanted to stay where it was warm. I travelled on foot, you see, slept outside, tried to go where there weren't many people. It's an enormous country, you know. Absolutely bewildering. At one point, I stayed in the desert for about two months. Later, I lived in a shack at the edge of a Hopi reservation in Arizona. The Indians had a tribal council before giving me permission to stay there.'

'You're making this up.'

'I'm not asking you to believe me. I'm telling you the story, that's all. You can think anything you want.'

'And then?'

'I was somewhere in New Mexico. I went into a diner along the road one day to get a bite to eat, and someone had left a nespaper on the counter. So I picked it up and read it. That's when I found out that a book of mine had been published.'

'Were you surprised?'

'That's not quite the word I would use.'

'What, then?'

'I don't know. Angry, I think. Upset.'

'I don't understand.'

'I was angry because the book was garbage.'

'Writers never know how to judge their work.'

'No, the book was garbage, believe me. Everything I did was garbage.'

'Then why didn't you destroy it?'

'I was too attached to it. But that doesn't make it good. A baby is attached to his caca, but no one fusses about it. It's strictly his own business.'

'Then why did you make Sophie promise to show me the work?'

'To appease her. But you know that already. You figured that out a long time ago. That was my excuse. My real reason was to find a new husband for her.'

'It worked.'

'It had to work. I didn't pick just anyone, you know.'

'And the manuscripts?'

'I thought you would throw them away. It never occurred to me that anyone would take the work seriously.'

'What did you do after you read that the book had been published?'

'I went back to New York. It was an absurd thing to do, but I was a little beside myself, not thinking clearly anymore. The book trapped me into what I had done, you see, and I had to wrestle with it all over again. Once the book was published, I couldn't turn back.

'I thought you were dead.'

'That's what you were supposed to think. If nothing else, it proved to me that Quinn was no longer a problem. But this new problem was much worse. That's when I wrote you the letter.'

'That was a vicious thing to do.'

'I was angry at you. I wanted you to suffer, to live with the same things I had to live with. The instant after I dropped it in the mailbox, I regretted it.'

'Too late.'

'Yes. Too late.'

'How long did you stay in New York?'

'I don't know. Six or eight months, I think.'

'How did you live? How did you earn the money to live?'

'I stole things.'

'Why don't you tell the truth?'

'I'm doing my best. I'm telling you everything I'm able to tell.'

'What else did you do in New York?'

'I watched you. I watched you and Sophie and the baby. There was even a time when I camped outside your apartment building. For two or three weeks, maybe a month. I followed you everywhere you went. Once or twice, I even bumped into you on the street, looked you straight in the eye. But you never noticed. It was fantastic the way you didn't see me.'

'You're making all this up.'

'I must not look the same anymore.'

'No one can change that much.'

'I think I'm unrecognizable. But that was a lucky thing for you. If anything had happened, I probably would have killed you. That whole time in New York, I was filled with murderous thoughts. Bad stuff. I came close to a kind of horror there.'

'What stopped you?'

'I found the courage to leave.'

'That was noble of you.'

'I'm not trying to defend myself. I'm just giving you the story.'

'Then what?'

'I shipped out again. I still had my merchant seaman's card, and I signed on with a Greek freighter. It was disgusting, truly repulsive from beginning to end. But I deserved it; it was exactly what I wanted. The ship went everywhere – India, Japan, all over the world. I didn't get off once. Every time we came to a port, I would go down to my cabin and lock myself in. I spent two years like that, seeing nothing, doing nothing, living like a dead man.'

'While I was trying to write the story of your life.'

'Is that what you were doing?'

'So it would seem.'

'A big mistake.'

'You don't have to tell me. I found that out for myself.'

'The ship pulled into Boston one day, and I decided to get off. I had saved a tremendous amount of money, more than enough to buy this house. I've been here ever since.'

'What name have you been using?'

'Henry Dark. But no one knows who I am. I never go out. There's a woman who comes twice a week and brings me what I need, but I never see her. I leave her a note at the foot of the stairs, along with the money I owe her. It's a simple and effective arrangement. You're the first person I've spoken to in two years.'

'Do you ever think that you're out of your mind?'

'I know it looks like that to you – but I'm not, believe me. I don't even want to waste my breath talking about it. What I need for myself is very different from what other people need.'

'Isn't this house a bit big for one person?'

'Much too big. I haven't been above the ground floor since the day I moved in.'

'Then why did you buy it?'

'It cost almost nothing. And I liked the name of the street. It appealed to me.'

'Columbus Square?'

'Yes.'

'I don't follow.'

'It seemed like a good omen. Coming back to America – and then finding a house on a street named after Columbus. There was a certain logic to it.'

'And this is where you're planning to die.'

'Exactly.'

'Your first letter said seven years. You still have a year to go.'

'I've proved the point to myself. There's no need to go on with it. I'm tired. I've had enough.'

'Did you ask me to come here because you thought I would stop you?'

'No. Not at all. I'm not expecting anything from you.'

'Then what do you want?'

'I have some things to give you. At a certain point, I realized that I owed you an explanation for what I did. At least an attempt. I've spent the past six months trying to get it down on paper.'

'I thought you gave up writing for good.'

'This is different. It has no connection with what I used to do.'

'Where is it?'

'Behind you. On the floor of the closet under the stairs. A red notebook.'

I turned around, opened the closet door, and picked up the notebook. It was a standard spiral affair with two hundred ruled pages. I gave a quick glance at the contents and saw that all the pages had been filled: the same familiar writing, the same black ink, the same small letters. I stood up and returned to the crack between the doors.

'What now?' I asked.

'Take it home with you. Read it.'

'What if I can't?'

'Then save it for the boy. He might want to see it when he grows up.'

'I don't think you have any right to ask that.'

'He's my son.'

'No, he's not. He's mine.'

'I won't insist. Read it yourself, then. It was written for you anyway.'

'And Sophie?'

'No. You mustn't tell her.'

'That's the one thing I'll never understand.'

'Sophie?'

'How you could walk out on her like that. What did she ever do to you?'

'Nothing. It wasn't her fault. You must know that by now. It's just that I wasn't meant to live like other people.'

'How were you meant to live?'

'It's all in the notebook. Whatever I managed to say now would only distort the truth.'

'Is there anything else?'

'No, I don't think so. We've probably come to the end.'

'I don't believe you have the nerve to shoot me. If I broke down the door now, you wouldn't do a thing.'

'Don't risk it. You'd die for nothing.'

'I'd pull the gun out of your hand. I'd knock you senseless.'

'There's no point to that. I'm already dead. I took poison hours ago.'

'I don't believe you.'

'You can't possibly know what's true or not true. You'll never know.'

'I'll call the police. They'll chop down the door and drag you off to the hospital.'

'One sound at the door – and a bullet goes through my head. There's no way you can win.'

'Is death so tempting?'

'I've lived with it for so long now, it's the only thing I have left.'

I no longer knew what to say. Fanshawe had used me up, and as I heard him breathing on the other side of the door, I felt as if the life were being sucked out of me. 'You're a fool,' I said, unable to think of anything else. 'You're a fool, and you deserve to die.' Then, overwhelmed by my own weakness and stupidity, I started pounding the door like a child, shaking and sputtering, on the point of tears.

'You'd better go now,' Franshawe said. 'There's no reason to drag this out.'

'I don't want to go,' I said. 'We still have things to talk about.'

'No, we don't. It's finished. Take the notebook and go back to New York. That's all I ask of you.'

I was so exhausted that for a moment I thought I was going to fall down. I clung to the doorknob for support, my head going black inside, struggling not to pass out. After that, I have no memory of what happened. I found myself outside, in front of the house, the umbrella in one hand and the red notebook in the other. The rain had stopped, but the air was still raw, and I could feel the dankness in my lungs. I watched a large truck clatter by in the traffic, following its red tail-light until I couldn't see it anymore. When I looked up, I saw that it was almost night. I started walking away from the house, mechanically putting one foot in front of the other, unable to concentrate on where I was going. I think I fell down once or twice. At one point, I remember waiting on a corner and trying to get a cab, but no one stopped for me. A few minutes after that, the umbrella slipped from my hand and fell into a puddle. I didn't bother to pick it up.

It was just after seven o'clock when I arrived at South Station. A train for New York had left fifteen minutes earlier, and the next one wasn't scheduled until eight-thirty. I sat down on one of the wooden benches with the red notebook on my lap. A few late commuters straggled in; a janitor slowly moved across the marble floor with a mop; I listened in as two men talked about the Red Sox behind me. After ten minutes of fighting off the impulse, I at last opened the notebook. I read steadily for almost an hour, flipping back and forth among the pages, trying to get a sense of what Fanshawe had written. If I say nothing about what I found there, it is because I understood very little. All the words were familiar to me, and yet they seemed to have been put together strangely, as though their final purpose was to

313

cancel each other out. I can think of no other way to express it. Each sentence erased the sentence before it, each paragraph made the next paragraph impossible. It is odd, then, that the feeling that survives from this notebook is one of great lucidity. It is as if Fanshawe knew his final work had to subvert every expectation I had for it. These were not the words of a man who regretted anything. He had answered the question by asking another question, and therefore everything remained open, unfinished, to be started again. I lost my way after the first word, and from then on I could only grope ahead, faltering in the darkness, blinded by the book that had been written for me. And yet, underneath this confusion, I felt there was something too willed, something too perfect, as though in the end the only thing he had really wanted was to fail – even to the point of failing himself. I could be wrong, however. I was hardly in a condition to be reading anything at that moment, and my judgement is possibly askew. I was there, I read those words with my own eyes, and yet I find it hard to trust in what I am saying.

I wandered out to the tracks several minutes in advance. It was raining again, and I could see my breath in the air before me, leaving my mouth in little bursts of fog. One by one, I tore the pages from the notebook, crumpled them in my hand, and dropped them into a trash bin on the platform. I came to the last page just as the train was pulling out.